PENGUIN BOOKS

ACCIDENTAL WARRIOR

Geoffrey Picot was born and educated in Jersey and spent eighteen years in provincial and national journalism, mainly on the staff of the *Gloucestershire Echo* and the *Daily Mail.* He gave up this occupation to enter the field of investment advice and management, subsequently editing *The Investor* newsletter, managing personal investment portfolios at Hambros Bank and becoming a personal financial consultant with Hill Samuel. Married with two grown-up sons, he lives in Beckenham, Kent.

Mr Picot served in the army from 1940–46.

Recent acclaim for *Accidental Warrior*:

'It gets the atmosphere of battle very well indeed' – David Warren, DSO, OBE, MC

'A completely authentic account of what happened and of the feelings of those who were there' – Horace Wright, MC and bar

ACCIDENTAL WARRIOR

Geoffrey Picot

PENGUIN BOOKS

PENGUIN BOOKS

Published by the Penguin Group
Penguin Books Ltd, 27 Wrights Lane, London W8 5TZ, England
Penguin Books USA Inc., 375 Hudson Street, New York, New York 10014, USA
Penguin Books Australia Ltd, Ringwood, Victoria, Australia
Penguin Books Canada Ltd, 10 Alcorn Avenue, Toronto, Ontario, Canada M4V 3B2
Penguin Books (NZ) Ltd, 182–190 Wairau Road, Auckland 10, New Zealand

Penguin Books Ltd, Registered Offices: Harmondsworth, Middlesex, England

First published by The Book Guild, 1993
Published in Penguin Books 1994
1 3 5 7 9 10 8 6 4 2

Filmset by Datix International Limited, Bungay, Suffolk
Printed in England by Clays Ltd, St Ives plc
Set in 11/13 pt Monophoto Ehrhardt

Dedicated to
JOAN
who is glad she did not know
what was going on

The awful unfolding of history imposed on two million of my generation the terrible duty of close-quarter fighting against a brave and fanatical enemy.

At least some of us who survived and emerged with morale intact have found an uncovenanted benefit that has lifted our lives: the knowledge that, though we thought it hardly possible, we were capable of even that duty.

Contents

List of Illustrations and Maps   ix
Army Organization   xii
A Battalion Organization (1944–5)   xiii
Foreword   1

1. *Whence These Victors*   7

2. *Pay Corps and Artillery: A Long
   Apprenticeship*   14
   Not Such a Mighty Pen   14
   What Kind of a Gunner?   21

3. *1st Hampshires: Getting Ready for D-Day*   28
   Brief Expectations   28
   Joining the Goliaths   30

4. *Battle of Normandy: The Slogging Match*   41
   Monty's Plan   41
   They Fought Magnificently   43
   Speed is the Essence   50
   My First Pitched Battle   59
   Go Forward, Always Forward   66
   First Hottot Clash   72
   Aggressive Defence   76
   Was Second Hottot Really a Defeat?   88
   Some Rest at Last   102
   A Long Right Hook   108

5. *Battle of Normandy: The Breakthrough*   115
   Our Best Attack Since D-Day   115

CONTENTS

The New General 131
Hitler's Worst Day 137

6. *The Race to Brussels* 157
New Type of Warfare 157
Evil Pictures 161
A Tumultuous Reception 172
Even More Rapture 181
'The War Is Over' 191
To Antwerp 201

7. *The Arnhem Disaster* 212
Hold at All Costs 212
Definitely Not a Bridge Too Far 217
Protecting the Flank 231
Where It All Went Wrong 239

8. *First Battalion's Last Battle* 244
A Superb Observation Post 244
Expensive Victory 250
Back to England 256

9. *Across the Rhine* 264
Out of the Battle Line 264
Joining the 7th Hampshires 268
A Textbook Attack 270
Berlin or Bust 278
Fix Bayonets! 279
Emotion Stifled Many a Voice 287

10. *Thank God for the Bomb* 294

11. *Questions I Am Asked* 299
Index 309

List of Illustrations
and Maps

ILLUSTRATIONS

1. A painting by Leslie Wilcox, RISMA, of the 1st Hampshires storming Le Hamel on D-Day. (Reproduced by kind permission of Brigadier R. G. Long, CBE, MC, DL, Colonel of the Royal Hampshire Regiment (1992) and by courtesy of Brigadier D. J. Warren, DSO, OBE, MC, DL)
2. Beach scene after landing, 6 June 1944. (Imperial War Museum)
3. Troops wading through the surf from landing craft to the beaches, 7 June 1944. (Imperial War Museum)
4. Soldiers of the Hampshires occupying German weapons pit, Arromanches, 6 June 1944. (Rupert Curtis Collection, Musée du Débarquement, Arromanches)
5. Soldiers of the Hampshires in Arromanches, 6 June 1944. (Rupert Curtis Collection, Musée du Débarquement, Arromanches)
6. Tanks moving inland, 7 June 1944. (Imperial War Museum)
7. Tank and troops in a village, 12 June 1944. (Imperial War Museum)
8. Engineers sweeping for mines, Tilly. (Imperial War Museum)
9. A medical orderly attending to a wounded enemy. (Imperial War Museum)
10. The author, 1944.
11. The author, 1990.
12. The author with his brother, Bernard, 1941.

13. Gordon Layton aged nineteen.
14. Gordon Layton, 1992.
15. Malcolm Bradley, 1940.
16. Malcolm Bradley, 1992.
17. Infantry poised to attack over open country. (Imperial War Museum)
18. Normandy *bocage*. (*The Times*)
19. A three-inch mortar crew, well dug in and about to fire. (Imperial War Museum)
20. British infantry ready to open fire. (Imperial War Museum)
21. Frank Waters, MC, 1940s.
22. Frank Waters, MC, 1992
23. E. G. (Horace) Wright, MC and bar, 1940s.
24. E. G. (Horace) Wright, MC and bar, 1992.
25. The village of Vernon in ruins. (Imperial War Museum)
26. The River Seine a few miles from Vernon. (Imperial War Museum)
27. Burning German vehicles on road to Brussels. (Imperial War Museum)
28. The Hampshires and other units receiving an ecstatic welcome in Brussels. (Imperial War Museum)
29. The Hampshires crossing the Escaut bridge. (Imperial War Museum)
30. Infantry in Asten, ten miles east of Eindhoven. (Imperial War Museum)
31. Soldiers of the 7th Hampshires, Cloppenberg. (Imperial War Museum)
32. The author and Francis Morgan.
33. German troops, after their surrender, on Lüneburg Plain, 5 May 1945. (Imperial War Museum)
34. The author with members of his platoon, June 1945.
35. A memorial at Le Hamel 'to our glorious liberators'.
36. Eight Hampshire veterans and two French officials at the Le Hamel memorial in 1984.

LIST OF ILLUSTRATIONS AND MAPS

MAPS

Normandy battlefield   xiv
The dash to Brussels   xv
Attack on Arnhem   xvi
Final advance   xvii

Army Organization

Three battalions (usually) were grouped as a *brigade* (commanded by brigadier).

Three brigades (or occasionally a different number) with a full range of supporting weapons and services were grouped as a *division* (commanded by major-general).

Several divisions were grouped as a *corps*.

Several corps made an *army*.

Two or more armies made an *army group*.

The British 21st army group was commanded by *General (later Field Marshal) Montgomery, Commander-in-Chief.*

The 21st army group and eventually three US army groups plus all air and naval forces were commanded by *General Eisenhower, Supreme Commander.*

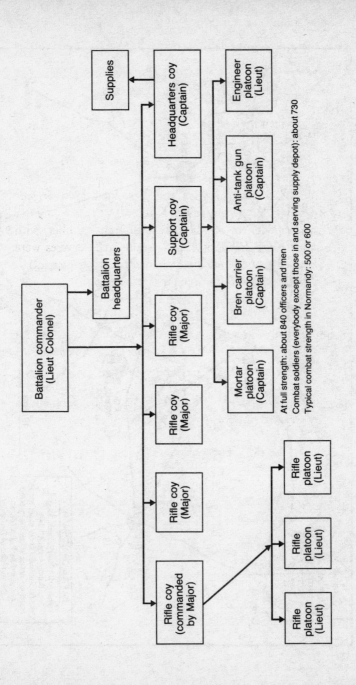

At full strength: about 840 officers and men

Combat soldiers (everybody except those in and serving supply depot): about 730

Typical combat strength in Normandy: 500 or 600

Battalion commander
(Lieut Colonel)

Battalion headquarters

Rifle coy
(commanded by Major)

Rifle coy
(Major)

Rifle coy
(Major)

Rifle coy
(Major)

Support coy
(Captain)

Headquarters coy
(Captain)

Supplies

Rifle platoon
(Lieut)

Rifle platoon
(Lieut)

Rifle platoon
(Lieut)

Mortar platoon
(Captain)

Bren carrier platoon
(Captain)

Anti-tank gun platoon
(Captain)

Engineer platoon
(Lieut)

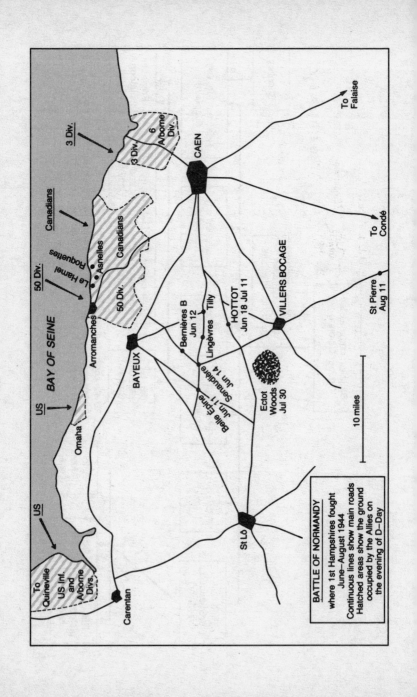

BATTLE OF NORMANDY
where 1st Hampshires fought
June–August 1944
Continuous lines show main roads
Hatched areas show the ground
occupied by the Allies on
the evening of D–Day

10 miles

BAY OF SEINE

US

US

US

Omaha

Arromanches

Le Hamel
Asnelles
Roquettes

Canadians

3 Div.

50 Div.

Canadians

3 Div.

6
A'borne
Div.

CAEN

To Falaise

To Condé

To
Quineville

US Inf.
and
A'borne Divs.

Carentan

St Lô

BAYEUX

Belle Épine
Jun 11

Senaudière
Jun 14

Bernières B
Jun 12

Lingèvres

Tilly

HOTTOT
Jun 18 Jul 11

Ectot
Woods
Jul 30

VILLERS BOCAGE

St Pierre
Aug 11

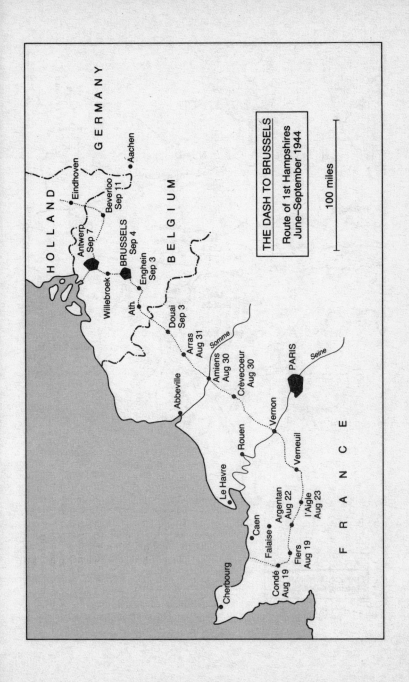

THE DASH TO BRUSSELS

Route of 1st Hampshires
June–September 1944

100 miles

HOLLAND

GERMANY

Eindhoven

Beverloo
Sep 11

Aachen

Antwerp
Sep 7

BELGIUM

BRUSSELS
Sep 4

Willebroek

Enghein
Sep 3

Ath

Doual
Sep 3

Arras
Aug 31

Somme

Abbeville

Amiens
Aug 30

Crèvecoeur
Aug 30

PARIS

Seine

Vernon

Rouen

Verneuil

Le Havre

Caen

Argentan
Aug 22

l'Aigle
Aug 23

Falaise

Flers
Aug 19

Cherbourg

Condé
Aug 19

FRANCE

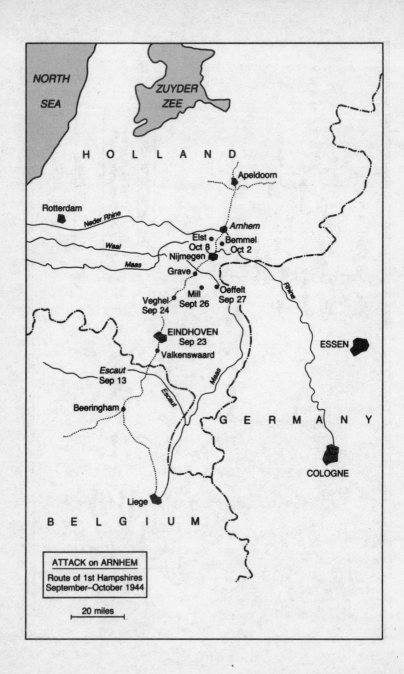

NORTH SEA

ZUYDER ZEE

H O L L A N D

Apeldoorn

Rotterdam

Neder Rhine

Arnhem

Elst
Oct 8 • • Bemmel
Oct 2

Waal

Nijmegen

Maas

Grave

Oeffelt
Sep 27

Veghel • Mill
Sep 24 Sept 26

EINDHOVEN
Sep 23

Rhine

ESSEN

Valkenswaard

Escaut
Sep 13

Escaut

Maas

Beeringham •

G E R M A N Y

COLOGNE

Liege

B E L G I U M

ATTACK on ARNHEM

Route of 1st Hampshires
September–October 1944

20 miles

NORTH SEA

HOLLAND

Wilhelmshaven •

• Bremerhaven

Gnarrenburg
May 4

Bremen •

Cloppenburg
April 13

• Bawinkel

GERMANY

• Hengelo

■ Osnabruck

• Munster

• Rees
March 25

Rhine

FINAL ADVANCE

Route of 7th Hampshires
March–May 1945

20 miles

Foreword

by

Sir Philip Goodhart, MP 1957–92

Former Under-Secretary of State, Ministry of Defence

In May 1940, Geoffrey Picot, a nineteen-year-old recruit from Jersey, joined a Royal Army Pay Corps unit in Bournemouth. As he recalls: 'I must have been in nearly the safest position of any soldier. Moreover I was not even submitted to any squarebashing. No sergeant-major shouted or swore at me. I was simply fitted out with a uniform. Then my new comrades and I would march every morning the short distance from our billet in a peace-time guest house to our office in one of the town's best hotels.'

Two years later, the Army changed their medical classifications. Those who wore glasses were to be judged on what they could see when wearing them. Geoffrey Picot, who had been medically classified as a C3, became an A1.

As he recalls: 'This changed everything for me ... I did not like being a clerk. It was simple, boring work and a very small contribution to the war effort ... Ambition awoke. While not welcoming danger, it would be nice if I could find a more physically active, mentally challenging role, where I could make a contribution the memory of which I could happily live with for the rest of my life.'

Young Geoffrey Picot was commissioned in the Royal Artillery, where he served in a mixed anti-aircraft unit outside Portsmouth and then, when the War Office decided that they had a surplus of young gunnery officers, and a shortage of potential infantry platoon commanders, Geoffrey Picot was re-trained and joined the 1st Battalion of the Hampshire Regiment. This battalion had already fought in

North Africa, in Sicily and Italy. Now, as part of the 50th Division the Hampshires were to be in the first wave of the assault on Normandy. On D-Day they captured Arromanches, which was to be the site of the artificial harbours that were to be towed over from England. In that first assault, the Hampshires lost 64 soldiers killed and 118 wounded – nearly half the losses incurred by the Army during the whole Falklands campaign. At the end of D-Day, nearly half the battalion's officers were casualties. Lieutenant Picot took command of the battalion's mortar platoon a few days later. Two months after D-Day, the 1st Hampshires were poised to take part in the great break-out from Normandy. By then Geoffrey Picot was the second oldest survivor among the nine battalion mortar officers in the 50th Division.

Between 6 June and 17 November, the 1st Hampshires, whose fighting strength was usually between 500 and 600, lost 231 killed – which was nearly twice what most battalions fighting in France suffered, and about 1,050 wounded. Total casualties therefore were about 1,250. In other words, with each casualty being swiftly replaced by a reinforcement, the battalion was effectively wiped out twice. And, as Geoffrey Picot notes: 'At the end of that it was still a superbly efficient fighting machine.'

For the final Spring offensive into Germany, Geoffrey Picot had become a platoon commander with the 7th Hampshires. In the closing stages of the war he led his platoon in a charge:

To help us on our way we are to have a rolling barrage of artillery fire, moving forward at a pre-determined speed, about 100 yards every minute. The barrage will make the enemy cower at the bottom of their slit trenches or in the cellars of their buildings. If we arrive at these positions the instant the barrage lifts we can kill or capture them all. But if the enemy spring to their firing positions before we can get there they will be able to mow us down mercilessly.

All depends on our keeping up with the shell-fire. 'Lean on the barrage', we have been taught in training. 'It is better to risk casualties from the occasional shell from your own side falling short than to allow the enemy a few seconds to recover.'

I place a section of ten men in front, in line abreast. I follow immediately behind, with the other twenty-five members of my platoon strung out behind me. The barrage starts and we move with it. For ten minutes I do not stop shouting.

'Keep up the pace. Don't slacken. Keep up the pace. Keep up. Don't stop. Keep up.'

A soldier complains. 'But there's a Spandau firing at us from over there on the right. I had better take it on.'

'No,' I yell. 'Don't stop for anything. Fire the Bren back at him from the hip if you like, but keep moving. Throw a smoke grenade if you like, but keep up, keep moving, keep up, don't stop.'

Another soldier reports: 'Two wounded enemy here, sir, we can't leave them.'

I reply: 'Yes, we can. Leave them. Leave everything. Just keep up with the barrage, that's all we've got to do. Keep up. Keep up. Don't lose the barrage.'

'It might be dangerous to leave them,' the soldier persists.

'Shut up,' I bellow. 'Don't stop. Keep up. Keep up.' There's plenty of shells landing everywhere. I'm not surprised there's some wounded.

One of my men reports: 'There's movement on our left, sir.'

'Fire as you go with anything you've got,' I reply.

'But don't stop. Keep up. Keep up. Faster, faster, keep up.'

I see a salvo of shells fall around our objective. A few seconds later Corporal Daley, a regular soldier who is commanding my leading section, enters through the front door of the house and I go through the side door. We have got there without being seriously impeded at any stage of our 1,000-yard advance.

Daley stands at the top of a flight of stairs leading to a cellar or basement. In his hand is a grenade. He is wondering whether to throw it into the cellar in case there are any Germans there. He decides not to. But in case there is anybody he orders in his best pigeon-German: 'Kommen-ze oop.'

There is a pause of a couple of seconds; then up comes a German soldier holding a machine-gun in front of him and surrendering. Daley passes him along to me. I take his gun from him and push him into a room.

Daley tries his luck again. 'Kommen-ze oop,' he shouts.

And up comes a second enemy soldier, also armed, also surrendering. He hands his weapon to me and moves into the room indicated.

'Kommen-ze oop,' orders Daley again.

A third German comes up, then a fourth, and a fifth, and a sixth . . . until there are thirteen of them.

If we had not leaned on the barrage, if we had given them time to recover their nerve and man their posts, they could have decimated my platoon as we crossed the open ground. Instead we have thirteen prisoners and there are a number of enemy wounded and possibly dead in the surrounding fields; and we have suffered no casualties.

It is ironic that Geoffrey Picot, who was given a clerk's

job because of his eyesight, should have written one of the most perceptive and clear-eyed accounts of infantry combat to emerge from the Second World War.

He never particularly wanted to join the Hampshire Regiment but he has given us a superb record of a glorious chapter in the history of a regiment which has lost its separate identity in the re-organization of the Army following the end of the Cold War.

'Was it worth it?' Geoffrey Picot asks, and gives the answer. 'Yes. In 1940 Churchill had warned that the world "might sink into the abyss of a new dark age made more sinister and perhaps more protracted by the lights of perverted science". To avoid that we had to defeat "a maniac of ferocious genius, the repository and expression of the most virulent hatreds that ever corroded the human breast – Corporal Hitler". To have played a part in that task is the greatest service that anybody of my age can have rendered to our fellow men.'

Fortunately he has given us a brilliant account of the proper role that he played in that honourable task.

SIR PHILIP GOODHART
March, 1992

[1]

Whence These Victors

I know now, in 1993, exactly what it was like to be a front-line soldier in the last decisive battle of history: Normandy.

On 8 June 1944, D-Day plus 2, I waded ashore and immediately took my place as a junior infantry officer in a ferocious campaign that stretched over four countries, lasted 334 days, put Britain on a unique pedestal of honour, liberated seven nations, released the German people from their own tyranny and settled the quality of life in half of Europe for fifty years, if not indefinitely.

I know now exactly what it was like because as soon as the guns stopped firing, while the details and the atmosphere of the fighting were still burning in my memory, I wrote it all down: what I had done, said, felt, seen, heard.

Events had so scorched themselves on my mind that I could recall nearly every particular on a day-to-day basis. There was the move from that slit trench in one field to the other trench in a different field, this advance, that check, this tactical move sideways, clambering from an observation post on a hillock to another post in an attic, the shelling and mortaring we suffered, our response, casualties among comrades, replacement by strangers, my fear, everybody's fear, keeping two fingers crossed in hope, then weary sadness, the tiredness of it all, sleeping rough, the lack of sleep, what the commanding officer ordered me to do, the orders I gave to men under me, the sun-bathing when we were not in the front line, the rain when we were, the quality, character, feel, atmosphere of it all. Everything was crystal clear.

Thus I have recorded here exactly what it was like to serve under a commanding officer whose ambition was to die for his King and Country, who constantly urged me and everyone else to 'keep going forward, always forward' though who sometimes neglected to give me orders that I needed. I have described the surprise I felt at finding myself less frightened in battle than I had expected, though four weeks after telling this to a friend I was asking the earth to open up and swallow me for safety as RAF Typhoon aircraft fired rockets into my area by mistake.

I have reported the fact that, because of heavy casualties, the maintenance of morale became a problem. I was ordered to take another officer into close arrest because he had failed to move his headquarters sufficiently close to the enemy.

In one attack a group of soldiers got under cover and stayed there. When my sergeant told them to go forward one man replied: 'I've got a wife and kids to think about. I'm not moving.' 'I'm married, too, but this is not the time to think of your wife,' the sergeant answered.

Marriage! What visions that arouses! I married during the campaign and when I rejoined the battle I found that I was no longer in the quite-exposed-enough job of mortar platoon commander but now in war's most dangerous position of all: rifle platoon commander. It was then March 1945. We still had to cross the Rhine, the widest and most easily defended river in Europe. What was my chance of seeing another summer, I wondered. Would I ever play another game of cricket? Was my marriage just a step to nowhere, a few days' bliss before oblivion? Shortly after that I was leading a bayonet charge, the only time I did.

Fifty years on one can regard Normandy as a victory comfortably won by the British and American forces, but it did not seem like that at the time.

We soldiers knew that our country's fate hinged on the

result. If the Allies failed to win Normandy; if we were held in a 1914–18 type of stalemate; worse still, if we were driven back into the sea, there would probably have had to be a negotiated peace which would have left Hitler, the Nazis and the Gestapo in power. Britain would not have had the resources, nor indeed the morale, to launch another invasion.

Nor was the victory easily or quickly gained. For several weeks the British public could not understand why its army was making so little progress. Nor could the soldiers. In July I agreed with my friend in a neighbouring battalion that Montgomery was stuck and needed to be replaced. And General Eisenhower, supreme commander, wanted to sack him.

It was Churchill who saved Montgomery. The pair had a tête-à-tête in the general's caravan on 21 July, forty-five long and seemingly disappointing days after the landings, and the prime minister emerged convinced that Montgomery was on the edge of a great victory.

A little over three weeks later triumph came suddenly, stunningly, totally. When Hitler heard the details on 15 August he wailed: 'This is the worst moment of my life.'

Who won the battle? Hundreds of thousands of ordinary chaps like me, a segment of the conscripted youth of the nation, butchers, bakers, candlestick makers, civilians at heart who had never imagined we had military qualities. We had been drilled and trained, some of us trying to do the best we could, others not trying too hard, and then we were ordered into battle. So well had we been transformed into warriors that, with the outstanding aid of a handful of regular soldiers who had survived earlier battles, we trounced the most disciplined and ferocious nation in the world.

Before the war I considered myself to be unargumentative, unoffending, unquarrelsome, unaggressive, unbrave. I was a lowly-paid newspaper reporter in Jersey, teaching in a Methodist Sunday school each week.

Midway through the war this modest assessment of myself was confirmed when I was told I was too weak, dreamy, soft and slow to be commissioned in the field artillery.

On 13 June 1944, seven days after D-Day, as mortar platoon commander in the 1st Battalion of the Hampshire Regiment, I found myself in the direst situation of my life. We were advancing comfortably, having been notified by intelligence sources that the way ahead was clear. The commanding officer had placed a vanguard company of 100 men in front. I was in the orders group that followed behind them, this being a group of about a dozen officers to whom the commander would give any orders that became necessary.

Suddenly our confidence is shattered. Enemy mortar bombs drop among us. Then comes the wicked crack of the German Spandau machine-guns. Caught on the road, we are helpless. We rush to the banks and hedges. Something has gone drastically wrong. The enemy are attacking us, and not we them.

I lie on the ground and hug the bank for dear life. Mortar bombs drop close and bullets clip the trees above. The bullets are getting lower, the enemy must be in the trees. What has happened to the vanguard company?

Somebody shouts: 'They are firing as they come.' I look at my pistol. It is a small weapon with which to defend myself.

'Stick your head above the bank and spot them,' yells one of the officers in my group. 'Don't let them do all the firing. Give the buggers some of it back.' He practises what he preaches, and, looking over the bank, he fires burst after burst with his Sten light machine-gun.

This is obviously the way to fight the battle. If you hug the ground and do nothing you just let the enemy advance and kill you. If you rise up and fight you stand a chance. For some minutes the exchanges are fierce.

The colonel appears on the scene, seemingly fearless. Standing up, with only a thin tree to protect him, he waves his revolver and roars at us: 'That's right. Give it back to them. We're just the boys to stop them. We're just the boys to drive them back.

'They won't gain another inch. I'm going to send somebody around to get at their flanks. That will stop them.' And he strides across the road to find somebody to attack the enemy flanks, on the way encouraging everyone he sees and shouting: 'We're just the boys to drive them back.'

But why doesn't he give me some orders? There are six mortars some way down the road. Doesn't he want them to fire at the enemy? Why doesn't he tell me where the enemy are?

As I get no orders I must use my initiative. I leave my embattled group and run back along the road at top speed, using every vehicle I can as cover from the machine-gunning and mortaring that is sweeping the road. After half a mile I locate my mortars and hurriedly order them to be set up for action in a farmyard.

'Line them up parallel to the road,' I shout. That should aim them in the general direction of the enemy. Now what range do we want? Say I have run 800 yards, the vanguard company would be 200 yards ahead of the orders group, the enemy main force perhaps another 200 yards away, allow another 300 yards for safety. 'Range 1,500 yards . . . rapid fire.'

The crews hurl bombs down the mortar barrels every few seconds. Then: 'Right two degrees . . . rapid fire.' I must spray these bombs everywhere. So: 'Left four degrees . . . rapid fire.' Then: 'Up 200 yards . . . rapid fire.'

We will soon run out of ammunition, so a sergeant drives back to the supply vehicle at the end of the column for more. We keep on firing as fast as we can, spraying the bombs over a wide area. The sergeant goes back again for still more ammunition. We continue to hurl our bombs in the rough direction of the enemy, more and more of them, over an expanding target area.

In less than half an hour we fire something like a thousand bombs. The German attack fades. We cease firing. A strange quiet descends on the battlefield.

Somebody suggests we must search the fields and woods to our right and left for signs of the enemy. With my pistol poised I examine a copse. And I make a decision. In spite of what I have been taught, never again will I go into battle armed with just a silly little pistol. I'll carry a Sten gun in future and plenty of ammunition.

There is no sign of the foes. They have left the battlefield. So we re-group.

Alarming rumours had spread around the rear areas. 'The battalion has been wiped out.' When the confusion is sorted out we find we have not suffered as badly as that, but out of about 500 of us nineteen are dead and nearly sixty wounded.

It was not always like that.

Individual reactions to battle varied widely. Many are described in this narrative. I should make my own clear. At the prospect of fighting I was horrified. Machine-gun bullets, shells and casualties are terrible companions. And as the weeks rolled by an insidious fear began to gnaw at me. When I looked around at my companions I saw that very few had been in battle longer than I had. Most of those who landed on D-Day were soon wounded or killed. How much longer could I defy the law of averages?

It was then that a subtle military factor rescued my morale. I could see that most men were absorbing the strain reasonably well, so I decided I had better try to look as if I was. Only later did I learn that all were frightened and most took pains to conceal their fear. Nearly all of us played this concealment game. Thus, a man pretending to be brave gave bravery to his comrades; as they, with their pretence, likewise gave bravery to him.

But first we all had to be moulded into warriors. It is worth describing this mysterious process.

[2]

Pay Corps and Artillery:
A Long Apprenticeship

NOT SUCH A MIGHTY PEN

I was nineteen years of age when, on 3 September 1939, I heard the prime minister, Neville Chamberlain, say in his thin, unhappy voice that we were at war with Germany. Though not unexpected, the news was terrifying.

The general belief was that, as in 1914–18, huge armies would clash in almost continuous combat along the border of France and Germany and this time there would be the additional horror of the aerial bombing of towns and cities.

But nothing like that happened. The armies on the Western Front did little more than stare at one another. No towns were bombed. Life in Jersey was hardly changed. At dances the band would play 'Run, Rabbit, Run', a skit on a lone German bomber having frightened a rabbit in the Scottish countryside, and 'We'll Hang out our Washing on the Siegfried Line'. The wonderful defensive Maginot Line that ran along part of the French border was evidently much better than their Siegfried Line. But what was afoot?

Conscription had been introduced in Britain during the summer of 1939. Some people in Jersey volunteered for their favourite branch of one of the services. Others waited to be called up. The Jersey States were expected to enact an identical conscription law, but for some reason unknown to me they did not do so. But there were enlistment arrangements in the island. I was medically examined and classified as C3 because, being short-sighted, I could not see anything without my glasses. Accordingly, I volunteered for the

Royal Army Pay Corps and was given a simple test which consisted of elementary mathematics, essay writing and the taking down of dictation. I became an army Class 3 clerk and in May 1940 joined a unit at Bournemouth.

I must have been in nearly the safest position of any soldier. Moreover I was not even submitted to any square-bashing. No sergeant-major shouted or swore at me. I was simply fitted out with a uniform. Then my new comrades and I would march every morning the short distance from our billet in a peace-time guest house to our office in one of the town's best hotels. At midday we were marched back again. Then in the afternoon we were again marched to and fro. The actual work of entering soldiers' pay slips in ledgers was not very militaristic and there was no restriction on our movements when not at work. Soon we were tasting the delights of Bournemouth's dance halls, cinemas and pubs. We were simply civilians in uniform.

On 10 May the land war started in earnest, with the Germans attacking France, Belgium and Holland. Most people then assumed that the pattern of the Great War would be followed: that the Germans would have initial success but if they broke through the Maginot Line they would be held on the Somme, or if not there on the Marne, or if not there somewhere else, and eventually, when the full British army was deployed, would be thrown back and defeated.

This easy confidence was smashed in a few weeks when the German army annihilated the forces opposing them and occupied all those parts of Europe they wanted, including the Channel Islands, where my parents and sister remained, effectively prisoners with 50,000 others. Just before this occupation started my father wrote to say: 'I have not lost confidence in our final victory and still believe that Hitler will bite off more than he can chew and in that way bring about his own failure.' (A year later by quite unnecessarily invading Russia Hitler was to do just that.) Two of my brothers escaped from Jersey before the Germans got there; a third brother had been on the high seas with the navy since 4 September 1939.

It is difficult now to recall the full severity of the shock the British nation suffered by the defeat of France and the occupation of this small group of British Channel Islands. The German victory was so total and so quickly achieved! It was earned by the tactically novel use of tanks and by deliberately employing parachutists, which at that time seemed to be almost something from science fiction. Nothing like this had happened before. And now the German army was threatening to invade England. It was a terrible outlook. We had only a small army. Hitler was all-powerful. And his Gestapo were torturers.

The only rational thing for Britain to have done was to make peace on the best terms we could get. When the war had been a matter of Germany versus France plus Britain, Germany had been able to destroy France with one brisk stroke. Now Italy had entered the war on Germany's side and Germany controlled the productive resources of most of continental Europe. So it was now Germany plus Italy plus Europe's productive capacity versus only Britain.

Yet against all logical reasoning almost everyone in the country seemed to decide that we should fight on and that we were bound to win in the end. Neither the military chiefs nor Winston Churchill, the new prime minister, had any idea how we would be able to win. At a meeting of the Cabinet Defence Committee Churchill commented: 'The question might be asked, "How are we to win the war?" This question was frequently posed in the years 1914 to 1918 but not even those at the centre of things could have possibly given a reply as late as August 1918.' So on that ground he did not answer his own question.

In later years much has been made rightly of the fact that

for a year, June 1940 to June 1941, Britain stood alone and thereby saved the world from Nazi-ism. It is interesting to recall that to stand alone was scarcely a decision of either government or people. It was simply an expression of the national character.

Churchill fanned the flames of ardour with some of the most inspiring speeches ever delivered. In the words a generation later of President Jack Kennedy of the United States: 'He mobilized the English language and sent it into battle.'

The main duty station of Pay Corps clerks ceased to be our desks and became the coastal promenade between Bournemouth and Boscombe. This we patrolled in pairs at night, each armed with a rifle and five rounds of ammunition. None of us had as much as fired a single practice round; ammunition was too scarce for that. Through the darkness I used to peer out at the sea wondering what I should do if I were to observe the outline of an invasion fleet approaching with hundreds of tanks on board.

Churchill's admonition to troops and civilians alike had been: 'Let us brace ourselves to our duty and so bear ourselves that if the British Empire and its Commonwealth lasts for a thousand years men will still say "This was their finest hour".'

Rumours abounded among the Pay Corps soldiers. One was that the Germans had landed at Dymchurch (near Folkestone) and had been thrown back; another was that we had used secret under-sea flame-throwers to destroy the invasion. Both of course were rubbish.

In August and September the Battle of Britain was fought, a little of it in our sight in the sky above Bournemouth but most of it over south-east England. Every evening the wireless would report how many planes the RAF had shot down and what losses they had suffered. The score might be 54–16 in our favour, or 73–21, or 175–62. It was almost like hearing the latest score of a cricket Test match. Both the RAF and the German air force greatly exaggerated the number of planes they shot down because when one plane fell from the sky many pilots would claim that they alone had shot it.

Churchill told the House of Commons: 'Never in the field of human conflict was so much owed by so many to so few.' It was a sentence that has gone into our language and into our history. The air battle reached a peak in September when Goering, the German air commander, signalled his defeat by calling off the daylight attacks and switching his bombing forces to night-time raids on London. Britain would not now be invaded. We had avoided defeat. The RAF's Fighter Command had lost 915 aircraft and had shot down 1,733 German planes. I learnt that two of my school friends had been killed; others had been shot down and rescued.

With the invasion threat thus scotched, Pay Corps clerks now worried less about defending our coast and concentrated more on our ledgers.

Most of us were young chaps, twenty or twenty-one years of age. In certain matters some of us were losing our ignorance and innocence. (I dare say in the 1980s and 1990s this would be lost much earlier.) One day, when I happened to be confined to my bed with a high temperature, the unit was marched to a cinema to see a film warning soldiers against catching venereal disease. I was told that when the film showed how the disease was treated – in those days apparently by inserting a syringe along the central canal of the penis to administer an injection – one particularly brawny soldier fainted and collapsed in the aisle.

Many of us were curious to learn the mysteries of sexual intercourse. 'I'm going to find out all about it when I get my leave,' announced one of the lads in my section.

'We shall want a full report when you return,' we told him.

When he came back from leave he was crestfallen. He had been to the red light district in Soho and availed himself of the services of a prostitute. 'It was all over in five minutes,' he complained bitterly to us, 'and when I got out into the street and realized I had paid her £1 (nearly three times a soldier's weekly pocket money) I thought of all the other things I could have done with the money. I could have bought sixty half-pints of beer, or forty bars of cream chocolate, and either of those things would have lasted much longer than five minutes!'

There were a number of ATS women (soldiers of the Auxiliary Territorial Service) in the Pay Corps. One evening when I was strolling quietly along a road, minding my own business, I was approached by one such young woman soldier, who said to me: 'I want to get out of the army. I can only get my release if I am pregnant.' I looked at her, turned tail and ran for my life.

The news now mainly concerned the bombing blitz on London and then other cities and towns. Hundreds of people were killed, many more injured, innumerable homes, offices, factories destroyed. Soldiers began to worry more and more about their families than themselves. Folk were helpless. Nothing could be done about it. Those who suffered and survived got on with their war effort as best they could. People generally did not seek sympathy. Anyone who complained or whined would have lost his friends.

Elsewhere in 1941 and early 1942 the war continued to run badly for us. In North Africa our army advanced 500 miles westward, only to be driven back 400 miles. It then recaptured those 400 miles of territory, only to be driven back beyond its first starting point. It seemed we could not get the better of the brilliant German General Rommel.

In the Far East a comparatively small Japanese army flung us out of Malaya, Singapore and Burma and threatened India. At Singapore the fixed heavy guns were facing the wrong way. Attack had been expected from the sea. Instead it came from the opposite direction, the land. Lieutenant-General A.E. Percival had to go forward with a huge white flag surrendering 130,000 British troops.

But nationally spirits had been brightened by two sensational events in 1941, the invasion of Russia by Germany on 22 June and the Japanese attack on America's Pearl Harbor on 7 December. This made Russia and the United States our allies and most people now felt we were bound to win in the end. As Churchill had said to his colleagues a year earlier, it was not necessary then to know how.

Meanwhile strange events had been stirring at Bournemouth. Some time in 1941 or 1942 the military authorities changed their medical classifications. Henceforward those who wore glasses were to be judged on what they could see wearing them, not on what they could see without. At a stroke of the pen I became A1.

This changed everything for me. It was by no means certain that I, and others similarly affected, would be allowed to remain in the Pay Corps even if we wanted to. We could easily be transferred to any other arm of the service, including the most dangerous ones, and sent into battle anywhere, including the most horrible places. Or nothing at all might happen. We might just stay where we were indefinitely.

It did not take me long to decide on my course of action. I did not like being a clerk. It was simple, boring work and a very small contribution to the war effort. I could be more useful than that, I was sure. Promotion to lance-corporal had hardly thrilled me. Various of my school friends were commissioned in different branches and services and rising up the promotion ladder. If they could do that, so could I. Ambition awoke. While not welcoming danger, it would be nice if I could find a more physically active, mentally challenging, role, where I could make a contribution the memory of which I could happily live with for the rest of my life.

The answer was to apply for a commission. But in what? As I had a mathematical bent the artillery was my first thought. But what about the tanks? At this stage of the war they were winning all the headline glamour.

One evening I walked with a girlfriend along the cliff top of Bournemouth explaining to her the rival attractions of the Royal Artillery and Royal Armoured Corps. It seemed a very evenly balanced issue. I thought I couldn't make up my mind. It must have been the most boring walk this poor girl had ever had. Next evening I told her I had decided. It was to be the artillery. 'I know that,' she observed patiently, 'that was obvious to me from everything you said last night. I could have told you that when you said goodbye.'

So I applied through the proper channels of my Pay Corps unit to be considered for a commission in the artillery. For a long time nothing happened. Then a fellow lance-corporal who was in the unit headquarter office whispered in my ear that my application had been lost and he did not know whether that was on purpose or not. I applied again and shortly after that I was sent to a neighbouring artillery battery for a month for their senior officer to report on my suitability. My duties there were not exacting and evidently the officer made a favourable report.

WHAT KIND OF A GUNNER?

With about thirty others I attended a three-day War Office selection board at Winchester. We were tested physically, mentally, psychologically. We had to go over an obstacle course and run a cross-country race, before the start of which we were given a complicated message which had to be delivered correctly at the end. (This was to show whether we could think even when exhausted.) In small teams we had, for example, to get across a river in a set time without getting our feet wet. We each had a presence of mind test, such as: 'A man who has had a bit too much to drink tells you he has seen a parachute slowly descending on to the nearby cricket field; what do you do? Do it! Now!' Later, equipped with mythical machine-gun and mortar, we had to organize an attack on an isolated outpost.

A debate was staged, in which we all had to take part. Then, presumably to test whether we could think logically, we each had to present a recommendation from a committee to a superior officer. I had to present to Hitler the German General Staff's recommendation that he should attack Spain from the south of France and go through to capture Gibraltar.

Psychology was just becoming popular and the selection board attached much importance to some peculiar tests. In one a board member would shout out a series of words at four-second intervals and in that time you had to write down what came immediately to your mind. Most of the words seemed to concern either war (Nelson, hero, death, etc.) or sex (girlfriend, love, mother, etc.). In another test we were shown a picture and were required to describe it. Mine was of the side of a house with a ladder leading from an upstairs window to the ground and a man half-way along the ladder. In my description I made great play of the fact that the man was half way UP the ladder as I thought that would show optimism, whereas to see him as half-way DOWN would show pessimism. However, perhaps that was wrong. Perhaps climbing down would have shown that he had successfully accomplished whatever he went up for!

How useful was this psychology? One fellow told me he had been asked time and time again whether he had had a happy home life. Yes, he replied, and in whatever form the question was asked he always gave the same answer.

'What's strange about that?' I inquired.

'Well, to tell you the truth,' he said, 'my parents were divorced when I was a young boy, but I was careful not to tell them that. Do you think they sensed something was wrong from some of my answers?'

We took our meals with the selection board members and throughout the three days they continually chatted informally with us. I do not think they worried what school one had been to, or whether one ate one's peas with a knife. I assume they chose as best they could according to their lights. At the end each applicant went before the full board for a final interview. The senior officer told me I was quite unfitted for the field artillery! I was too slow, too sleepy, too weak, too soft, too dreamy and so forth. However, I would be good enough for the anti-aircraft artillery! Would I accept that?

At this I said in a flash: 'What a good idea, sir! I'd like that very much.'

Months later, in 1945, when I was leading infantry charges against the enemy and holding the view that artillery officers were so far behind the real fighting line as to be practically base wallahs, I ruefully reflected that either the senior officer had made a misjudgement or the nation had indeed had to scrape the bottom of the barrel. And I held these views even more ruefully when in July 1945 I learned I was to be an infantry mortar officer in an airborne division.

In February 1943 I was posted to the Officer Cadet Training Unit of the Anti-Aircraft Artillery at Llandrindod Wells. I was about to become a proper soldier; better than that, a proper officer. One of the first things that happened to cadets there was to be sent on a week's battle course in Snowdonia. Being February when I went, it was cold and often raining. We marched and marched, ran and ran, uphill and down, charged with bayonets again and again always uphill, waded along streams, had thunderflashes thrown at our heels, crawled flat on our stomachs for long distances along mud and slush while live machine-gun bullets were fired a foot or so above our backsides. (That teaches you to keep flat.) We had little food until evening. Then we had to light a fire, dry our clothes, cook our supper, find somewhere not too cold to sleep with the aid of a blanket or two; and prepare for similar exertions next day.

One cadet failed to complete the ordeal in good spirit. He was struggling through the mud for the umpteenth time that day. He was exhausted. He was carrying a rifle and much else. An instructor, standing in the dry and apparently fresh, was yelling at him. 'Hurry up, Cadet Snooks. (I invent the name). What have you stopped for? Where have you been all day?' etc., etc.

Snooks could stand no more. He stood up straight, took a firm grip of his rifle, loaded it, pointed it at the instructor and said: 'Fuck off.'

As soon as the battle course was over Snooks was returned to his unit in his existing NCO rank. He was not officer material. Those of us who survived this training in good trim thought we had become indestructible. (Later on, in my eight months of frontline fighting, I was never once as severely physically tested as on that battle course.)

Back at Llandrindod Wells we were taught thoroughly. First, aircraft recognition. Second, how to operate radar sets. These could locate an object in the sky; then you would have to keep the object in your radar sights. This transmitted a blob of light on to a huge map, enabling you to trace the aircraft's path. Third, you had to operate the predictor, which would nowadays be called a computer. The predictor followed the course of the aircraft and predicted where it would be in twenty seconds' time, or twenty-five seconds or thirty seconds. This was necessary because if the aircraft was flying high it would take that kind of time for a shell to reach it. Predictions could only be made on the assumption the aircraft kept a steady course and height. If you aimed accurately and the aircraft changed course you were bound to miss. Pilots knew this and consequently heavy anti-aircraft guns scored few hits. (This was changed by the later invention of proximity fuses and heat-seeking fuses.) The fourth skill we had to learn was the loading, aiming and firing of guns.

There were also strenuous exercises which involved us crawling along streams and under low bridges in the town itself. Civilians would see some of this and mutter sympathetically: 'Poor boys, fancy having to do that!' I cannot imagine what they would have thought if they had seen what we had to do on the battle course.

Towards the end of our training I was called before the battery commander. This was ominous, I thought. What was he dissatisfied with? Not aircraft recognition surely, I had got full marks for that. Not gun drill, I knew I was good at that. Surely not the radar or the predictor, I could work those well. Not general conduct, there had been no complaint.

But yes. 'There is one aspect of your work that is very poor,' he began, 'and unless it improves I shall not be able to pass you.' I listened horrified. 'It's your stick drill.'

My what! But I overcame my astonishment and said: 'Yes, sir.' Officers sometimes carried a short stick as part of the uniform. It could either be carried under the left armpit or 'at the trail', that is in the right hand and held horizontal to the ground. The manner in which I transferred the stick from one position to the other left something to be desired.

'Yes, sir.' I promised to improve. I had previously thought that senior officers spent much time thinking how to defeat the enemy in battle. I was learning that perhaps they did not.

Our passing out parade was held a few days later, in July (1943). We were minutely inspected by a senior officer who

25

made sure that our new officer uniforms, carefully fitted by the best Llandrindod Wells tailor, were perfect in every respect. Such is my sense of the absurd that, standing immaculately to attention and not blinking an eyelid while I was scrutinized from top to toe, I could hardly prevent myself bursting into laughter. When we marched off the parade ground, second lieutenants now, while the band played 'Colonel Bogey' I was among those who thought: 'And the same to you!'

I joined a mixed (men and women) heavy anti-aircraft battery outside Portsmouth. The war had moved on. The RAF were now making massive bombing raids. Each day casualties seemed small but they mounted inexorably. One of my cricketing friends was killed when, returning from a raid, his damaged bomber crashed into the North Sea.

The United States navy had won the decisive battle of Midway in the Pacific in June 1942. Australia and India were no longer threatened. The supremely confident General Montgomery, always sure he knew better than everybody else, had won the battle of Alamein in October 1942. Not the beginning of the end, but perhaps the end of the beginning, commented Churchill. The Germans had been cleared out of North Africa. Another of my close friends, in command of some anti-tank guns, had played his part there.

At my artillery battery we had plenty of practice. I soon showed that I was adept at plotting the course of approaching aircraft and giving the appropriate orders to the gun crews. I had just come from the top training unit and in addition my assessment of angles and distances, and of seconds, was quite good. It seemed I was at least as skilful as the women officers who were evidently better than the men. The major in command of the battery was overjoyed. For months he had writhed in discomfort at the superior performance of his women officers. Now I had shown that men could be just as good, and therefore men were better!

We went into action against enemy planes a few times but I do not think we ever hit any.

Life was good. The officers' mess was comfortable, food was excellent (much better than civilians got), my companions were friendly, our practices were interesting, our engagements with the enemy were exciting, there was very little danger, and it was pleasant and satisfactory to be an officer even if at that stage of the war the anti–aircraft artillery was no longer a glamorous arm of the service. As far as civilians were concerned and for the courtesies of life in general an officer was an officer and probably a gentleman.

I did not know that a metaphorical bomb was about to fall on my head.

[3]

1st Hampshires:
Getting Ready for D-Day

BRIEF EXPECTATIONS

'You've been posted to the Isle of Man to attend an infantry course,' the officer commanding the battery told me.

'What!'

'I don't want to lose you, but there's nothing I can do about it. The orders are quite specific. Apparently all anti-aircraft officers under a certain age and below a particular rank will be going eventually.

'The fact is that the German air force does not seem much of a threat any more and a lot of extra infantry officers are going to be wanted for the second front.'

'Second Front Now' was the great propagandist cry. Our arms were beginning to prosper. We had taken Sicily; Italy had changed sides and was now our ally; American army divisions were flooding into Britain; Russia, after suffering enormous casualties, had held the line at Moscow, Leningrad and Stalingrad and her troops were now pushing the once-so-confident Germans back. Second Front Now was needed to give them more help than they got from the Italian campaign. It was needed for our victory: total, absolute, final victory.

Of course anti-aircraft gunners would not be needed in large numbers, but I wondered why nobody had thought of that before. Would I have done better to have stayed in the Pay Corps? Impossible to say. Would I have been better in the field artillery? Definitely. How strange that the selection board's decision to downgrade me to the anti-aircraft artillery had resulted in a swift upgrading in danger and that, sleepy, weak and useless as they thought I was, I was now to be thrust into the most arduous, demanding and terrifying of all military roles.

There were more than a hundred of us on this Isle of Man course. Training was tough and thorough. In case we were not physically fit there was a great deal of running to do, usually wearing a heavy pack and steel helmet and carrying a rifle, and over difficult ground. We were taught about infantry weapons: rifle, bayonet, machine-guns, hand grenades, mortars. We were taught tactics and went on strenuous exercises by day and night.

We knew there was no escape from our grim future. What did they say was the average length of an infantry lieutenant's life in battle? Never mind, it might be different now. And we were all in this together. (It is curious how this simple thought gives immense strength.)

We countered the atmosphere of foreboding by living exuberantly: by drinking large quantities of beer, by dancing away the night at the local *palais de danse*, and by organizing parties for the raucous, half-drunken singing of soldier choruses of pithy wit and extreme vulgarity. The officer instructors would join in with us and often after heavy drinking parties we would find the next morning's training to be particularly energetic. It did not seem to matter how much beer you drank as long as you could sweat it out next morning. And if the instructors let their hair down with us at night, training next day was disciplined and strict. Fun was fun and we were all pals together. Training was serious: we were given orders and we obeyed them.

Most of the instructors expected to be posted to front line battalions before the invasion was launched. 'I do not imagine for one moment that I shall survive the war,' one of them said to me, 'so let's have another drink.'

And then: 'Let's have another.'

'And another.'

'One more.'

Some behaved differently. One morning a colleague confided to me with a triumphant smile: 'Well, even if death is to be my fate at least I shall have lived.'

'Oh?' I asked.

'I did it last night. And she said I could come back again if I wanted.'

A few days after that conversation we were on the way to our battalions.

JOINING THE GOLIATHS

With four colleagues in January 1944 I joined the 1st Hampshires at Long Melford, Suffolk. John Lloyd, who had been in searchlights since the start of the war, regarded this as a major personal catastrophe. 'Me, in the second front! It's unbelievable,' he used to say. Harry Wise recalled the advice his father gave him in 1939: 'Don't go into the infantry, my son.' But he accepted his plight philosophically; what would come would come, and he was ready for it. Ken Edwards thought a lot about his wife and child and brooded anxiously. Chris Needham accepted his position with good grace. He knew he was in a sticky corner but many other people were too and he was quietly determined to give a good account of himself. I was gloomy. I thought fate had played a scurvy trick on me, and the task ahead seemed altogether beyond me.

I have no knowledge or record of what happened to John. Harry, I know, fought for months as a rifle platoon commander in cool and stalwart style until he was mortally wounded a few miles south of Arnhem. Ken, as commander of a platoon of Bren gun carriers, stuck resolutely to his nerve-racking task throughout the battle of Normandy and the advance to Nijmegen. Chris was killed twelve days after he landed in Normandy when he was leading a charge against an enemy machine-gun post. My experiences are described in the pages that follow. If at the time of joining the battalion we had known our fate we would have grieved at our suffering but would have been astonished at our accomplishment.

The 1st Hampshires had already been at the sharp point of a number of battles. In 1939 they had been in Palestine where, under the command of the then little-known Major-General Montgomery, they were fighting Arabs. In 1940, having been trained in desert warfare, they were among the 30,000 men in North Africa who, under General Wavell, drove the Italians out of Egypt. Then, when the Germans built up their forces in Sicily and threatened Malta, the battalion was sent to Malta.

There they were under prolonged heavy bombardment, for standing up to which the island was awarded the George Cross. Supplies were scarce and food was severely rationed. In 1943 they played a major role in the assault on the Sicilian coast. After that they had again been one of the battalions leading the attack on the Italian coast. Now they were back in England. I could scarcely have joined a battalion that was more battle-hardened or whose record showed greater success. How on earth would I fit in with these Goliaths?

With some of my Isle of Man pals I quickly became friends with Gordon Layton and Malcolm Bradley. At nineteen Gordon was the youngest officer I had met and probably the keenest. On leaving school he had enlisted in the Home Guard. At eighteen he had volunteered for the army and, after serving in a young soldiers' battalion, was accepted for officer training. He passed, and was commissioned into the Hampshire Regiment. Little did he dream how brief would be his fighting career.

Malcolm Bradley was different. He had fought with the battalion in Sicily, where he was wounded. A tall, splendidly strong-looking athlete, he wore his experiences lightly. When we chatted in the village pub in the evenings it was clear that hard campaigning had not interfered with his love of beer.

One day an extremely young-looking commanding officer, still in his twenties, announced: 'We are going to be an assault battalion in the invasion of Europe.' To my surprise nobody cheered. As a number of the officers and sergeants who had foregathered to hear this announcement had already been decorated for bravery I thought they would be happy at the chance to win more glory. Not a bit of it! They were as solemn, nervous and sad as I was. So these were not a special breed! They were rather like me. It was ordinary men who were going to have to win the war. We did not have any other kind. Or so it seemed.

I was told to join the mortar platoon as understudy to their commander. I noticed at once the immense respect they had for their previous commander in battle, Frank Waters, who was now adjutant (or battalion chief secretary). They admired his coolness in action, his quickness and insight. And I soon came to regard Sergeant Wetherick as the most efficient NCO I had ever met. Without any bullying or commotion he had the forty-five-man platoon completely under control.

'When I landed in Sicily I didn't get hurt,' he told me, 'but when I landed in Italy I was wounded, so at that rate when I land in France I'll get killed.' But his cheerful tone showed he did not believe his own forecast. (He was right not to believe it.)

I got to know the members of my platoon as quickly as possible and as thoroughly as I could. Many of them accepted the fact from their previous experience that the strain of battle could prove too much for some people. I was learning fast. These were indeed ordinary men.

General Montgomery, who was to command the invasion land forces, came to see us. His reputation was sky-high. The general public's view was that with him in command every battle would be won; without him most would be lost. That was based on the fact that with other generals in command we had lost many battles: in France and Belgium (1940), in the North African desert (1940–42), in Malaya and Singapore (1941–2). With Monty in command we had won: Alamein and other desert battles, Sicily, the Italian invasion.

The making of this extraordinary reputation had begun in the desert outside Cairo in August 1942 when he took command of an Eighth Army that had lost belief in itself. It had advanced hundreds of miles, and it had retreated hundreds of miles, time and again. There had been changes of commanders, alterations of tactics, indecisive issuing of orders, much argument. Morale at army headquarters was dangerously low. Into this situation strode Monty to announce: 'Here we will stand and fight. There will be no further withdrawal . . . If we cannot stay here alive, then let us stay here dead.'

The effect was electrifying. Here was a commander who knew his own mind, who could give orders and would have them obeyed. And, having flung his personality at the headquarters staff, he went around his forward troops spreading confidence everywhere. His story was simple. Now that he was in command everything would be all right. Everybody was to do exactly what he ordered and in that way every battle would be won.

He spoke in homely direct language spiced with sporting metaphors and quotations from the Bible. 'Let us hit Rommel (the German commander) for six right out of Africa,' and 'The Lord mighty in battle will give us the victory.' His self-confidence and audacity proved inspiring. Having enthused his El Alamein army, he waited till reinforcements arrived to give him overwhelming strength. Churchill thought there was not time to wait and ordered him to attack in September (1942). No, Monty would not do that. An attack in September would fail; an attack in October would bring victory.

So Churchill had to wait. Monty continued to build up his forces; then on 23 October he attacked, won the decisive Battle of El Alamein, which in many ways was the pivot on which the war turned; he went on to knock Rommel for six out of Africa; with the Lord mighty in battle he conquered Sicily and launched the attack on Italy. Not surprisingly he was highly regarded by the troops and ecstatically worshipped by the general population. When he came home to England crowds cheered wherever they caught sight of him.

But he was ruthless in replacing senior officers who did not fit in with his wishes and soon a collection of critics arose. He was a showman, they said, a self-publicist of genius, a lucky general because he came to the fore when the Allies began to have superior equipment after his predecessors had had to campaign without adequate guns and tanks.

But Monty was more than a magical morale raiser. For thirty years he had studied the military art with fanatical devotion. With his sharp, perceptive brain he had thought problems through and carefully tried out practice solutions. He had trained himself to perfection. After taking command he made it his business to know better than most generals what the capacity was of each of his formations; he assessed a little better than others what the strength was of the enemy in front of them; he gauged better than some the enemy's next move; he was more skilful than others in bringing to bear all his fire power on one area; and intuitively successful in choosing that area. He controlled his battles. He kept his forces balanced. He unbalanced the enemy and made the enemy dance to his tune. He was quite simply the best general on either side.

Field Marshal Harding, who served under him in North Africa and later became Chief of the Imperial General Staff, said of Montgomery: 'As a commander in battle he ranks with Marlborough and Wellington; as a leader he had the inspiration of Nelson.'

Like other great men Monty had curious idiosyncrasies. He never smoked or drank and invariably went to bed around 9.30 p.m., even on the eve or during the midst of battle. He read the Bible assiduously but was not against his troops indulging in what he called 'horizontal refreshment' with free-wheeling females. He was totally devoid of tact, believing he knew everything and that anybody who disagreed with him was useless (his favourite description), and, unpleasantly, he never allowed anyone to share the slightest sliver of his glory.

He visited all his troops before the invasion, to enthuse them and create confidence in himself. At Long Melford the 1st Hampshires, 1st Dorsets and 2nd Devons, each about 850 strong, were drawn up on three sides of a square. Monty mounted the bonnet of a jeep and declared: 'The second front has already started. The softening-up process is being carried out by Bomber Command and the American air force.' He told us he had specially chosen the famous 50th Division, of which these battalions were a part, to lead the invasion assault because of their experience and prowess.

At one such gathering, however, he was not well received. Some of those troops were not too keen to be told that as a reward for their past bravery they were now going to be allowed to undertake special risks. There were rumblings of discontent. Next morning two commanding officers were sacked. Rumbling in the ranks, said Monty, indicated low morale, and low morale was the fault of commanding officers, so they must go.

Around that time the King visited the Hampshire

battalion. A number of officers and men were presented to him and he spent several hours watching assault landing exercises.

Every morning of that spring I saw hundreds of white vapour trails stretching across the clear East Anglian sky, and at the front of each vapour trail, apparently pulling it and making it ever longer, was a Flying Fortress, America's super heavy bomber specially built for daylight raiding. All those trails led to Germany. I took off my hat to those aircrews who kept up a terrific offensive day after day. As I watched the planes fly over I thought of the damage they would do and the number of lives indirectly they would save. I wished them luck. I hoped they would save mine.

One day we were taken to see the 'funny' tanks at Southwold on the Suffolk coast which were going to help us in the invasion. These had been produced by a division under the command of Major-General Percy Hobart and they were a marvellous example of Heath Robinson magic. Hobart, an awkward cuss like his brother-in-law General Montgomery, had been prematurely retired from the army in 1940. So he joined the Home Guard and became a corporal. Churchill rescued him from obscurity and in 1943 he was asked to create the various tank-based devices that would be needed to support an infantry attack on a defended coast. Some work on the problem had already been done.

First, the infantry wanted tanks that could swim ashore so that they could lead the way. So engineers strapped huge canvas sheets, perhaps ten feet high, all the way around a tank and fitted two propellers to the back. Sure enough, the tank swam. Somebody must then have told Hobart that was not good enough. When tanks got to soft sand they would get bogged down. So long strips of criss-crossing wire were bundled up and attached to the front of a tank. A way was found to lay out the bundle by using an activating lever in the tank and the tank crew could thereby lay their own firm surface in front of them.

Ah, but tanks could be blown up by mines.

So on another tank the engineers rigged up a flail. This was a number of chains attached to a rotating barrel carried between horse-and-cart shafts about five yards in front of the tank proper. With these chains the tank crew flailed the ground some distance in front of them, thus exploding mines harmlessly. But suppose tanks were held up by a deep ditch or ravine? For that the engineers built a long bridge which could be carried on the nose of a tank and lowered when necessary. But how could tanks cope with a heavily protected pillbox from which a powerful gun could fire? Ah, for this the tanks would need to carry a big bomb and a method of hurling it the required distance.

Each tank could carry only one of these devices, so half a dozen may be needed to cover all eventualities. It was marvellous to think one or other could be whistled up as required. As we went around this extraordinary exhibition our eyes widened and our imaginations soared. When General Montgomery first saw the contraptions he said: 'They are the key which will unlock the German defences and let us in.'

After that we carried out landing exercises at Studland Bay near Bournemouth. For us soldiers they were easy enough. Running ashore and finding a suitable place to set up the mortars so as to be ready to fire was not difficult, but I believe the chief purpose of the exercises was to check that the staff work was correct.

In April I had a week's leave and on returning from this I found the battalion had moved to the New Forest; it was now in a camp surrounded by barbed wire. Shortly I was included in a small group that was posted to a reinforcement holding unit at Aldershot. Because of the heavy casualties that were expected in the initial assault the battalion had been given more than its normal complement of thirty-eight officers. So those of us who were surplus, as I clearly was since the mortar platoon needed only one officer, were sent to this reinforcement unit to await events. Nobody there seemed to have any information. There was nothing to do. We just waited. Spring ended, summer started. There were long sunny days. The strains of 'Lily Marlene', whistled or hummed, kept floating on the air. The weeks went on. Whatever was happening about the invasion? I was frequently able to spend evenings in London with my girlfriend Joan. I spent Sunday 4 June with her and promised to see her again next evening. But on the fifth we were confined to camp, and before dawn on 6 June (D-Day) I was in a large party on our way to Southampton. As we got near to the port civilians cheered us. They had heard the news.

This had been given out on the wireless. 'Under the command of General Eisenhower, Allied naval forces, supported by strong air forces, began landing Allied armies this morning on the northern coast of France.'

In the afternoon Churchill told the House of Commons: 'The first of a series of landings in force upon the European continent has taken place . . . An immense armada of upwards of 4,000 ships . . . crossed the Channel. Massed airborne landings have been successfully effected behind the enemy lines (loud cheers) and landings on the beaches are proceeding . . . The Anglo–American Allies are sustained by about 11,000 first-line aircraft . . . So far the commanders engaged report that everything is proceeding according to plan.

'And what a plan! This vast operation is undoubtedly the most complicated and difficult that has ever occurred. It involves tides, winds, waves, visibility both from the air and sea standpoint, and the combined employment of land, air and sea forces in the highest degree of intimacy and in contact with conditions which could not and cannot be fully foreseen. There are already hopes that actual tactical surprise has been attained, and we hope to furnish the enemy with a succession of surprises during the course of the fighting (cheers).

'The ardour and the spirit of the troops, as I saw myself, embarking in these last few days was splendid to witness. Nothing that equipment, science and forethought could do has been neglected, and the whole process of opening this great new front will be pursued with the utmost resolution both by the commanders and by the United States and British governments whom they serve' (loud cheers).

Mr Arthur Greenwood, for the Labour Party, rose to say: 'We are living through momentous hours . . . There is nothing much that we can do, except perhaps to pledge ourselves, and to pledge our physical and spiritual resources to the unstinted aid of the men and women who are serving overseas (cheers), to let them know the pride we shall feel in their victories and the sadness that we shall feel about their losses.'

During that evening Churchill made a further speech in the House. 'I can state that this operation is proceeding in a thoroughly satisfactory manner,' he declared to loud cheers. 'Many dangers and difficulties which at this time last night appeared extremely formidable are behind us (cheers). The passage of the sea has been made with far less loss than we apprehended. The resistance of the shore batteries has been greatly weakened by the bombing of the air force, and the superior bombardment of our ships quickly reduced their fire to dimensions which did not affect the problem (cheers).

'The landings of the troops on a broad front . . . have been very effective, and troops have penetrated in some cases several miles inland (prolonged cheers) . . . The outstanding feature has been the landings of the airborne troops which were of course on a scale far larger than anything that has been seen so far in the world.

'These landings took place with extremely little loss and

with great accuracy (cheers) ... The airborne troops are well established and the landings and the follow-ups are all proceeding with much less loss, very much less, than we expected (cheers) ... We have captured various bridges which were of importance and which were not blown up. There is even fighting in the town of Caen inland.

'But all this, although a very valuable first step, a vital and essential first step, gives no indication of what may be the course of the battle in the next days and weeks, because the enemy will now probably endeavour to concentrate on this area, and in that event heavy fighting will soon begin and will continue without end, as we can push troops in and he can bring other troops up.

'It is therefore a most serious time that we enter upon. Thank God that we enter upon it with our great allies all in good heart and all in good friendship! (loud and prolonged cheers)'.

Later that evening the King called the nation to prayer. In a wireless broadcast he said: 'At this historic moment surely no one of us is too busy, too young or too old to play a part in a nation-wide, perchance a world-wide, vigil of prayer as the great crusade sets forth.'

[4]

Battle of Normandy:
The Slogging Match

MONTY'S PLAN

While Churchill was speaking in the House I was on a slow train from Aldershot to Southampton. Before I describe my arrival in the Normandy battle zone it will be useful to recall, first, the main features of this momentous two-months encounter, and then to tell how the 1st Hampshires fared in one of the crucial D-Day clashes.

General Montgomery's plan was to land five infantry assault divisions, each of about 18,000 men, in the Bay of the Seine, roughly from Caen in the east to Quineville in the west, a front of about fifty miles. Two of these divisions were British, two American and one Canadian. In addition the eastern flank was to be protected by one British airborne division and the western flank by two American airborne divisions. On the first day the seaborne divisions were meant to advance at least ten miles inland to take Caen and Bayeux and armoured columns were to thrust twenty miles south to take Villers Bocage. Once a substantial bridgehead was established, massive Allied forces would be brought in. The British would make strong attacks south-east from Caen in order to draw most of the German armour on to that sector. When this was achieved the Americans would break out near St Lô in the west and drive south and east towards Paris, thereby encircling the German army and pinning them back to the Seine. It was hoped a good victory would be scored and Montgomery reckoned the war could end that year (1944).

The initial technical problems facing the planners and commanders were immense, as Churchill said. Nobody knew how to make a full-scale landing on a strongly defended coast. It had never been done before. And however thorough the planning had been during the previous two years and however skilful the commanders were, the battle was bound to create the most dire risks for every individual soldier, for the Germans had planned their defence thoroughly, their experienced commanders were skilful too, and their soldiers would fight both with the courage natural to them and with the desperate frenzy of men defending the best line of defence they could possibly have.

Yet it was of vital historical importance that the landing should be successfully made. If the invasion forces had been thrown back into the sea it was difficult to see then how the war could have been won. Presumably it would have meandered into a stalemate.

The prowess of the 150,000 men who won the D-Day battle attracts a special aura. They ensured that the second front could be opened and that the German army would eventually be defeated.

In fact the initial assault achieved about 75 per cent of what was desired. The daunting coastal defences were smashed. Allied forces got ashore in great strength, though the lodgement area was less than ten miles deep. Caen was threatened but not taken, while Villers Bocage unfortunately was not approached.

Now the build-up could proceed. This remarkable initial success was scored at a cost of 11,000 casualties, which was many fewer than had been feared. After all, in 1916 on the first day of the Battle of the Somme the British army had suffered 60,000 casualties without gaining anything of importance.

But as the build-up went on the first great controversy between General Eisenhower of America, who was supreme commander, and General Montgomery, who was land forces commander, started. Eisenhower became critical of Montgomery's slow progress. His deputy, the British airman Air Marshal Tedder, was furiously anti-Montgomery; so were other air marshals because Montgomery had failed to capture the landing fields they wanted; so were other British and American generals at Eisenhower's headquarters. Montgomery, who could create personal enemies at record-breaking speed, was in grave danger of being sacked. Fortunately Field Marshal Sir Alan Brooke, Chief of the Imperial General Staff, supported him and skilfully arranged for Churchill to visit him at his forward headquarters.

On 21 July the two talked in Montgomery's caravan. By then the British had drawn 645 enemy tanks and 92 infantry battalions on to their front. The Americans, now with a bigger army than the British, were faced by only 190 enemy tanks and 85 infantry battalions. If the exact numbers were not known at that time the general picture would have been established by aerial reconnaissance and other means. Churchill emerged from the caravan beaming. Monty's position was safe. His critics could pipe down.

Four days later the Americans broke through at St Lô, then, using mainly recently landed troops, stormed south and east to carry out a vast encircling movement that threatened to capture the entire German army in that theatre of war. Monty had won his battle. The dour tenacity of the British and the unstoppable dash of the Americans had made it a victory of stunning proportions.

THEY FOUGHT MAGNIFICENTLY

6 June

In the first few hours of D-Day nearly everything went wrong for the Hampshires. To begin with, the anti-seasick tablets were issued only shortly before the soldiers boarded their assault landing craft. Many had already been seasick and they certainly had not properly recovered by the time they reached the beach. Secondly, several of the craft grounded on a false sea bottom fifty yards out. The exit doors were opened and, thinking they were on the beach, the leading men jumped out. This lightened the craft and caused them to surge forward, hitting the men and sending them with their heavy equipment to the bottom.

Thirdly, the coastal defences in front of them, which were supposed to have been knocked out by bombardment, were still intact. Thousands of naval shells and rockets and more than 1,000 bombs from Flying Fortress aircraft had all missed their targets, and the troops immediately came under murderous artillery, mortar and machine-gun fire from a number of strongpoints.

Fourthly, at the moment of landing there was no armoured support, nor were there gaps in the minefields which were to have been created by flail tanks. The rough sea had prevented these tanks from swimming ashore and they had had to land slightly behind schedule in the orthodox manner from their landing craft.

Fortunately the battalion had been thoroughly trained on one issue in particular. 'On D-Day the beach you land on will be the most unhealthy place in the world. As soon as you get on the beach, get off the beach – inland. Get on the beach, get off the beach! Get on the beach, get off the beach!' And that is just what the troops did. Once on the beach they ran inland. Directly in front of them the strongpoint of Le Hamel, which had survived the bombardment, was firing energetically, so the planned frontal assault was abandoned and the riflemen swung left and raced inland to seize first Les Roquettes, then Asnelles. There were many casualties in that dash off the beach.

From Asnelles the battalion attacked Le Hamel from the rear, now getting splendid assistance from the tanks, particularly the bomb-hurling funnies. There was also a remarkable effort by one tank gunner who, from 300 yards, succeeded in firing a shell through the narrow embrasure of an enemy pillbox. The battalion took Le Hamel, but only after suffering further heavy casualties.

There was yet more to do. The soldiers advanced three miles along the coast, helped by a barrage from a destroyer and other vessels, and took Arromanches, their main objective, which was urgently wanted as the site for the artificial harbours which were to be towed over from England. By then half the officers and one third of the men were casualties. There were 64 dead and 118 wounded.

The severity of this can be shown by a comparison with the Falklands war. In that campaign the army (excluding Royal Marines) suffered: killed 123, wounded 200, injured not directly by the enemy 97, sick 38. Thus in one day this one Hampshire battalion sustained about half the dead and wounded a 5,000-strong army suffered in sixteen days of Falklands fighting.

In *The Path of the 50th*, the authoritative history of that division (by Ewart W. Clay, published by Gale and Polden in 1950) the Hampshires' performance is described as 'a very fine operation carried out in the face of the most determined resistance'. Major David Warren, who took command at a crucial stage when the commanding officer was wounded and others killed, was awarded the DSO.

By nightfall most of the other battalions in the division were on or near their objectives, their casualties mercifully having been lighter than the Hampshires'. The crust of the German defences was broken and the important market town and communication centre of Bayeux was ready to fall comfortably into British hands next morning.

'The whole of the famous 50th Division has fought magnificently,' a spokesman at General Montgomery's head-quarters exultantly told the newspapers. Montgomery's decision to use these high-quality veteran troops in the assault had been justified. Perhaps he need not have been so concerned that day back in England when he told them what their formidable task would be and some had sounded bolshie. The best soldiers sometimes are bolshie.

Elsewhere that day the situation was generally, but not uniformly, satisfactory. Several miles to the left of the 50th Division the Canadians had landed. They were held up near the beach for some time, but after that made fast progress. They too broke through the defensive crust and established themselves ashore.

Farther to their left, the British 3rd Division landed in good order and made for Caen. But their advance was slow and they failed to take that vital objective. They were later to be much criticized for this failure and one of their brigadiers was relieved of his command. The failure was to have a significant effect on the entire campaign.

To the left of them the 6th Airborne Division, which had dropped during the early hours of D-Day, captured all their objectives, thus securing the Allied flank. Greatly daring, gliders had crash-landed on one important bridge. But airborne troops carry only light equipment, so they were vulnerable to counter-attack. They dug themselves in and waited anxiously for relief by seaborne soldiers with heavier weapons.

Two men in an outpost were looking and listening for this relief. Gradually a harsh and weird noise came to their ears. As it grew louder they recognized it as the sound of bagpipes. Brigadier Lord Lovat was urging his commandos forward and he had ordered his personal piper Bill Millin to play 'Blue Bonnets over the Border'.

Ten miles to the right of the Hampshires the greatest drama and disaster was occurring. One American division landing on the beach code-named Omaha found themselves, like the Hampshires, under heavy shell fire and machine-gun fire. Unlike the Hampshires, they could not look forward to help from General Hobart's funnies, for although Montgomery had offered the American army half of everything Hobart had, the Americans were untypically unenthusiastic about the gadgets which to them represented British under-confidence and over-insurance. Nor apparently had anybody drilled into these troops: 'Get on the beach, get off the beach!' They got on the beach and in the face of this heavy fire stayed at the water's edge. It was not a sensible thing to do, for they remained under fire and sustained casualties but had no means of hitting back.

For several hours there was bloody chaos. The American land forces commander, General Omar Bradley, later said: 'After six hours we held ten yards of beach.' He seriously considered withdrawing that attack and reinforcing other beaches. But early in the afternoon Colonel George Taylor moved among the troops and said: 'There are two kinds of people on this beach, those that are dead and those that are gonna be dead, so let's get to hell off it.'

With that exhortation the soldiers dashed through the murderous fire to the protection of the sea wall and went on to make a remarkable advance inland. But why did they not make the dash six hours earlier? Why did they accept six hours of unnecessary suffering? The answer, I think, lies in human nature. Faced with the prospect of running into heavy fire, all one's instinct urges one to stop. Sometimes this can overpower a simple intelligent assessment. Usually in these circumstances troops will go forward. The Hampshires certainly did. I would guess that the reasons why some men advance and others do not lie in: one, the quality of training of a battalion; two, the on-the-spot leadership particularly of lieutenants and sergeants in those first crucial seconds; three, the degree to which men have fire in their belly (do they want to win the war or are they not overmuch concerned?); and four, the individual character of each man.

Since these American soldiers later fought extremely well I suspect the fault lay in their inadequate assault training.

Several miles to the right of Omaha beach another American division had been landed by the US navy in the wrong place but where there was little opposition. Their commander, Brigadier-General Roosevelt (son of President Teddy Roosevelt), had to decide whether to advance from there or to move to the correct landing place where supplies and reinforcements would be arriving. He thought for a moment, then, neatly forgetting five years of history, said: 'I guess we'll start the war from here.' Facing little opposition, his troops quickly established a large bridgehead. (Later in the campaign Brigadier-General Roosevelt died of a heart attack while asleep in bed.)

Two American airborne divisions had been dropped inland to secure the right flank of the invasion area. Owing to faulty air navigation they were scattered over a vast space instead of being concentrated in certain centres. Some men were thirty miles from where they were supposed to be but did not know it. This blunder turned out to be quite useful. When the Germans found parachutists in many distant places they could not make head or tail of what the Allies were planning.

The greatest drama of D-Day concerned what did not happen. The Germans hoped we would not be able to effect a good landing. If we did they wanted to drive us back into the sea at once. They had Panzer (armoured) forces ready for this near Caen. As soon as their commanders knew about the landings they alerted this force and decided it should make for the coast between the Canadian and British divisions, which early in the morning certainly did not have enough armour ashore to fight a major tank encounter. But the commanders refrained from ordering their Panzers into battle. They had been instructed not to deploy them without the permission of Hitler. And in the early hours of 6 June neither the German general staff nor Hitler believed that the Normandy landing represented the Allies' main effort. They thought it was a feint. By the time Hitler could be persuaded to agree to the deployment of the Panzers the British had sufficient tanks ashore to counter the threat.

But what would have happened if those Panzers had made an early attack? At one stage there was little to stop them reaching the landing areas. What chaos and bloodshed would have followed! And how would it have turned out?

As D-Day wore on, the German defensive system was broken time and time again and very satisfactory lodgement areas were established ashore. The extraordinary degree of our success can be indicated by the fact that when I stepped on to the beach on D + 2 all was peace and quiet. Of the 11,000 casualties sustained on D-Day by eight seaborne and airborne divisions, 3,000 were suffered by the one division on Omaha beach.

In Britain news of the landings occupied most of the newspaper front pages. 'So Far All Goes to Plan' headlined the *Evening Standard*, while the *Daily Mirror* said: 'Invaders thrusting inland', which was followed by a correspondent's story: 'I saw them leap to beach.' Hitler is taking personal command of the battle, underground sources were quoted as saying, and, intriguingly, German radio was reported to have announced that further Allied landings had been made at Calais and Boulogne. This was untrue, but the Allied High Command had made serious attempts to make the Germans believe that the main invasion would come later in that area, so perhaps the German radio had made the announcement in the hope of drawing out an incautious comment from London.

SPEED IS THE ESSENCE
7–11 June

When I left Southampton on D + 1 my naval brother Bernard was already at anchor off one of the Normandy beaches. He had navigated HMS *Hilary* across the Channel and when he dropped anchor a mile offshore at 6 a.m. on D-Day he thought: 'I hope the noise of the anchor going down doesn't wake the enemy ashore.'

I did not know he was there. He did not know I was on my way. It was years before we found out.

Bernard had been involved in the 1940 Norway campaign and fought in the Battle of Oran, where French warships were sunk to prevent them falling under German control. He had served on Atlantic patrols and in the 1942 North African events. And he had helped to put the army ashore at Sicily and at Salerno. And now Normandy.

At Southampton everything was more leisurely than I had expected and there was much waiting. 'Speed is of the essence of the contract,' I had been told many times as I waited at the reinforcement camp. What visions that conjured up! I imagined we would all rush to a ship, move quickly aboard in an orderly manner till we were tidily packed like sardines; then the ship would sail at full speed for France, where we would jump off and hurry inland at forced-march pace till we joined our battalions at battle station. Not a bit of it!

A ship came into Southampton but my party of reinforcements was kept waiting for three hours before we were allowed on board. Eventually the ship sailed, and approached the coast of Normandy where we waited for half a day. An army going into a fight needs to be extremely carefully organized. Not only must soldiers be moved to the required place at the correct time, but a huge quantity of varied and complicated equipment (not just all types of

50

ammunition and food) must be there as well. Marshalling an army can be a slow and ponderous exercise.

When we were at last ordered to go ashore, each man was told to make his own way inland to a transit centre. We were all seriously overloaded with heavy packs on our backs and other military equipment. This was supposed to be limited to 60 lb a man but everybody seemed to have much more.

'Get off the beach. It doesn't matter how or where. Just get off the beach,' had been our overriding instruction at the reinforcement camp. But now, D + 2, the beach seemed peaceful and quiet. There were a few wrecked vehicles, a handful of soldiers going unconcernedly about their business, mine-free lanes marked by white tape. Nobody was worrying about us. Rather automatically we formed ourselves into a column and began to trek inland. I walked with my pal Chris Needham, and the loads we were carrying were so heavy that we were obliged to put them down and rest every few hundred yards. Then we came across a wheelbarrow just strong enough to bear the weight of our two kits. Taking turns to push the barrow, we progressed rather faster. We met military policemen who warned us to beware of snipers. That shook me. A heavy kitbag and an unloaded pistol were not likely to be much use against a sniper. After a time we were shepherded into a field where we ate the rations we had been carrying and brewed a cup of tea. Shortly a convoy of trucks arrived to take us to a reinforcement centre, which proved to be just a field, where we were to stay the night. I lay down on the grass to sleep but it began to rain so Chris and I found a sheet of corrugated iron and, supporting it by four pegs, established a roof over our heads. So tired were we that we both slept soundly and were surprised to be told next morning that German planes had bombed the beach and machine-gunned the roads and had been answered with anti-aircraft gunfire. Rumours were flying around. 'Marseilles is in our hands.' 'We've landed in Norway.' Alas, not true.

Chris and I moved up to join the Hampshire battalion. They now had a new commanding officer, their third in the campaign still only three days old. Lieutenant-Colonel C.R. Howie, seemingly in his late thirties, was probably older than most infantry commanders. He would quickly get to know everyone. He welcomed Chris and me in a fatherly manner. Would I be able to take over the three-inch mortar platoon because their officer had been wounded? Yes. Chris went to command a rifle platoon. I was not to see him again.

At full strength a mortar platoon would have six mortars capable of firing up to about 3,000 yards. The general tactic would be to set them up some way behind the main fighting line and to establish an observation post as close to the fighting line as possible; to use either hastily laid field telephone or (less reliably) wireless for communication; and for the man in the observation post to direct the firing. The mortars could be regarded as the battalion's own instant artillery, going everywhere with it, always in its area, always available.

But, unlike artillery, mortars were not an accurate weapon. Their bombs would fall anywhere within an oval of about 100 yards long and 50 yards wide. Thus ranging was always difficult and they needed to be employed against a large target, such as some woods, and not a small target, like a house. Each mortar with its crew, ammunition, wireless and telephone sets could be loaded on to a carrier, that is an open-topped, tracked vehicle which could move over rough ground and had some protective armour. A mortar carrier was in fact a Bren machine-gun carrier used for another purpose.

There would normally be about forty-five men including

several sergeants in the platoon. But in the landing this group had lost one of its sergeants, three vehicles and most of its wireless equipment. They had suffered much less than the rest of the battalion and were in good spirits. I think they knew that in making such a successful invasion they had accomplished a minor miracle.

I learned that one of my friends, Gordon Layton, had been wounded in the landing. He was leading his platoon against an enemy gun position near Arromanches. Some Germans waved a white flag and surrendered, but others later opened fire and Gordon was hit in the leg and chest. The crew of the ambulance that took him away found that they could not open a gate leading to the beach, so they had to make a detour. Later the gate was found to have been booby-trapped.

I spent the first half hour with my platoon sitting on the grass censoring their letters. This was not a difficult task. Soldiers could write what they liked as long as there was nothing which, if the letter fell into the hands of the enemy, could help the enemy. Broadly speaking, that meant that no mention must be made of particular battalions or divisions or other formations, that there must be no reference to places such as Bayeux or Arromanches, and that there should be no discussion of weapons.

Not wishing to linger on personal remarks and knowing that my soldiers knew perfectly well what to write about, I was racing through these letters quickly when another officer approached me and, evidently thinking (surprisingly) that I might know more than he did, asked me: 'Do you think I ought to pass this letter? This chap is telling his girlfriend that he performed enormous heroics on the beach and with the aid of only a handful of pals stormed through enemy defences, killing and capturing them in great numbers.'

'So what?' I asked.

'Well, he didn't do anything of the sort. In fact he was always lagging behind.'

'So what?' I repeated. 'He's not giving any military information away. What he tells his girlfriend is not our business – nor how many girlfriends he tells it to.'

Horace Wright, an experienced campaigner, agreed, and gave me this advice: 'Never use the scissors. If there is something you cannot pass, take it back to the soldier, explain why, and ask him to write the letter again.'

Soon I was called to attend my first orders group of the campaign. Colonel Howie told his company commanders, support platoon commanders (including me) and commanders of various supporting weapons that we were about to go forward to take over positions from another battalion at present in contact with the enemy. I was to be in the reconnaissance party that went ahead of the main body. I now had to call my own order group, made up of sergeants who commanded the three sections of my platoon and one or two other key people, and tell them how we were to carry out the orders I had received. In this case it was quite simple.

My normal method of travelling would have been in a carrier but on this occasion I had to make do with the pillion seat on a motor bike ridden by a skilful and battle-hardened soldier. The rest of the platoon with all their vehicles would take their appointed place in the battalion's column of march.

The way to the front line was through Bayeux, and as our reconnaissance party sped into the town it was exhilarating to think what had been accomplished in only a few days. I kept my eye on David Hammond, who was commanding the Bren machine-gun carrier platoon, in some respects a companion organization to the mortar platoon. He had fought in Sicily and Italy. He was obviously sensible and confident. I judged him a good fellow to keep next to. I was going to try to follow his example.

'St Lô 35 kilomètres,' read the sign at Bayeux. 'I expect that's the next place we're making for, sir,' said my rider.

On reaching the battalion we were relieving I was shown over the mortar positions. They were all in one field, grouped in three sections of two, each facing a different way to give the battalion all-round protection, and each section connected by telephone to an observation post manned by a senior NCO. A main road ran through the position of one of the rifle companies, and there were reports that an enemy reconnaissance car frequently approached a bend in this road, fired off a few quick shots, then got to hell out of it as fast as possible. One section of mortars was aimed at this bend and if the NCO manning one of the observation posts saw the car approach all he had to do was lift the telephone and order: 'Fire!' A shower of mortar bombs would then fall around the car (if our limited accuracy allowed such a result).

My platoon arrived about an hour after I had seen these positions. We took them over smoothly, the other unit departed; and I reported to Colonel Howie that everything was in order and that I was giving the battalion all-round protection. He warned me that there was particular danger of our being attacked from the rear. The German car did not materialize and soon people began to say the story had been invented to keep us alert.

I was now in contact with the enemy, notionally at any rate. It was a very gentle introduction to fighting, for we were defending some fields that nobody wanted to take from us. We were organized for battle. Everybody had a duty. There was a slit trench for every man to sleep in at night. The platoon sergeant organized guard duties, issued blankets, handed out the rations and arranged for the digging of deep latrines. I had to keep in close touch with the commanding officer.

We lived on compo rations. These were in a tin which

you put in boiling water for a few minutes. On opening the tin you had a complete hot meal. It could be sausages and beans for breakfast, which could be followed by biscuits and jam; or it could be stewed meat with carrots and potatoes for dinner, followed by rice or duff. Tea would consist of biscuits, butter and jam. We had plenty of sweets and chocolate and ample tea to drink. (After some weeks most of us yearned for bread – good, clean, white bread – instead of everlasting biscuits. It was a long time before field bakeries were able to supply us with bread.)

During our second night in that position, while I was sleeping soundly, I was awakened to be summoned to another orders group where Colonel Howie announced plans for an advance that would start shortly after dawn. The battalion had been ordered to move forward 2,000 or 3,000 yards, going through several woods and clearing them of enemy, and then to occupy some high ground dominating the village of La Belle Épine. This looked likely to create severe fighting. Two rifle companies were to lead, then somewhere near the middle of the column would be Colonel Howie and his orders group, which included me.

When our attack started the orders group waited for the rifle companies to make a reasonable advance, then moved forward in bounds. Howie was seldom with us. He would race ahead to reconnoitre, scour the flanks and contact junior commanders to impart some of his limitless enthusiasm to them. Soon I could hear continuous automatic fire and judged that the leading troops were becoming engaged in battle. Not so, said the experienced Sergeant Wetherick. 'That's all Bren gun fire. Our chaps like to put a few bursts of it into a wood before they enter. The German Spandau machine-guns fire much faster. You'll soon learn to tell the difference.' I did.

We reached our objective without the mortar platoon being called into action and I was sent off with a reconnaissance party to establish my mortar positions. I went by motor bike, again riding pillion. We took a wrong turning and went into the village by mistake. Here we were stopped by civilians crowding around us. Although we hardly knew it, we were liberating them. They gave us hard-boiled eggs, which we ate there and then. They shook our hands, slapped us on the back, and then the oldest inhabitants with the toughest beards kissed us.

I decided to site the mortars in an orchard at the back of a farm. I entered the farmhouse to pick out an observation post and as I walked through the building I noticed a large picture of a French general whom I could not recognize. Had it been Marshal Foch of 1918 fame or General de Gaulle I would have saluted it. Had it been Marshal Pétain I would have been most annoyed. The occupiers offered me wine and all was friendly until I told them we were going to site the mortars in their orchard. '*Non, non!*' they said, holding up their hands in horror. '*Oui,*' I said, and we set up the mortars.

Soon after I had got my platoon in position I was called to battalion headquarters where there was consternation. Our area was going to be shelled by the enemy during the night apparently. (I do not know how they knew but I accepted the information unquestioningly.) Colonel Howie was telling everyone to dig in deeply and to remain in their positions. I returned to my platoon and found they were being sniped at. In fact it was not easy to get to them. I had to dash from building to hedge, and from hedge to bank, and some of our own troops nearly had a shot at me when I suddenly appeared at their back. I ordered my platoon to take up emergency positions along a hedge and we prepared to deal with the sniper, but none of us found out where he was. However, after some time the sniping stopped, so someone must have found out.

Then soldiers from another battalion began walking back

through our positions, with frightful tales that their unit had been counter-attacked by dozens of tanks and they were the only survivors left. It seemed to me that there were a lot of only survivors. I realized then that our La Belle Épine position had originally been a reserve one; only now were we in the front line. The other battalion had been heavily attacked and it had had to adjust some of its positions. The battle was very near to us. This was going to be my first taste. I was afraid an attack might come that night. I told my chaps in a rather bellicose manner that we were going to stay there till morning, come what may, that no amount of shelling would shift us from our slit trenches, and that we would return any fire more liberally than we got it. At night all was quiet, so I dozed off, though fully expecting to be roused at some time. But I woke up in the morning to realize that the night had been untroubled. Here was one lesson of war. The enemy is not always in good shape. When you are unhappy and fearing an attack, so perhaps is he.

I recalled the advice a senior officer had given me. 'If at nightfall the situation is chaotic and desperate, just sit tight and wait for daybreak and you will find everything will be all right.' Maybe there was more sense than foolishness in that.

We were on the extreme right flank of the British army. The next unit to us was on the extreme left flank of the American army. The juncture between two allied armies always tends to be the weakest point of the line. It was necessary for the Hampshire battalion frequently to send a patrol to the right to check that the Americans were where we thought they were, and they had to do likewise. All went well.

But once an American lieutenant told a group of our soldiers: 'I was coming along a sunken road with my buddy. As we turned around a bend I saw two soldiers approaching from around another bend, and my first thought was that it was some of you guys. Then I realized they were wearing Jerry helmets, so I fired my carbine.

'There was a terrible silence. Just as I knew the weapon had not fired I saw these two Jerries raise their arms in surrender. Now what do yer think of that?'

MY FIRST PITCHED BATTLE

12 June

That morning we moved on again, pushing inland as fast as we could, so as to make the beachhead as large as possible. We had secured a footing on a lateral road at La Belle Épine, and, instead of attacking along that road, we doubled back on our tracks intending to strike the road a thousand or so yards eastward at La Senaudière. But long before we reached it our leading elements contacted opposition. I was some way down the column and the first I knew was that everybody had stopped. We were approaching Bernières Bocage. I was called to an orders group and received instructions. So far I had had experience of uncontested defence, then of uncontested advance; now, four years 284 days after Chamberlain declared war and four years 33 days after I joined the army, I was to fight my first pitched battle.

The enemy was entrenched in some woods in a valley – I expect he held the high ground on either side too – and he was also in a village beyond the woods. Men from two rifle companies were going to attack, and I had to get the mortars in position and be ready to fire to support the advance as it went in. There was quiet before the storm. Nobody was firing yet. I detailed sergeants to act as fire observers with each of the companies, and arranged for a wireless link between them and me. We ranged the mortars on some prominent object near the enemy; I saw our men go forward to start the attack; and then the fog of war came down on me like a blanket. I could not get my observers on the wireless so although I heard a lot of small arms fire I had no real knowledge of what was happening. I had thirty men and six mortars, but because of wireless failure (which later came to be a depressingly frequent feature) we were of little use.

I sent a dispatch rider to battalion headquarters but they had moved and nobody knew where. So we put the mortars back on their carriers and trucks and drove along the road to find the headquarters. We were now under continuous shelling by German 88mm guns. Part of the road was under enemy observation, so drivers had to hurl their vehicles along at maximum speed. The 88mm guns gave a sharp whizz, an angry bang and created an ugly black cloud of dust hopefully not too close to you. About half a mile down the road we found the headquarters consolidating around a crossroads in the village of Bernières Bocage. It was uncomfortable there. Shells were bursting everywhere. People were ducking and milling around to find out where everybody else was. Most of the houses were shattered.

I was told the story of the attack. It had been a limited success only. Enemy Spandaus and mortars had held it up. One company commander was killed when he led a charge, with a few brave men behind him, straight at a Spandau nest. This officer may not have shouted a hip-hip-hurrah when, back at Long Melford, he had been told this battalion was going to be one of those leading the assault on the coast but, clearly, when the chips were down, no danger was going to deflect him from his fateful duty. My fire observers told me: 'It was hell there, sir. We could not get you on the wireless, though we could hear one another.'

The battalion attack was still continuing. Two companies had been held up but a third was now working its way across the fields on the right of the original line of advance.

Four or five hundred yards away, they were still making progress. They wanted fire support. There was no artillery officer with us and in any case it seemed we were not scheduled to receive any artillery support. Nor were there any tanks to give us fire power. There was only my mortar platoon to help the advancing company and I did not have a wireless set powerful or reliable enough to link the mortars with a fire observer among this company. The only way a link could be achieved would be by using a telephone cable. So I grabbed the one large drum of cable we had and set out to lay a line to the forward troops.

I took with me a very capable sergeant who had joined us as a reinforcement only twenty-four hours before but had already shown that he was made of stern stuff. Together, we hurried through woods and across fields laying out this telephone cable from this unwieldy drum as fast as we could. It was frightening. We two were on our own, hastening to the unknown, with no knowledge of what was happening on our flanks, hoping we would soon catch sight of our troops. After about a mile we found them, walking across an open field while fire was coming from their right flank.

'Go on, put some of that back,' shouted Major John Littlejohns, and several Bren gunners returned the fire.

Over one hedge I peeped and saw my first dead Germans. Two lads of about nineteen had been killed by a grenade. I looked at them and shuddered. A limb was twisted the wrong way round, a stomach was ripped open, a face looked ghastly in death. Not long before they would have been goose-stepping their jackbooted way around Nuremberg and other cities to the frenzied applause of the crowds. Hitler would have been boasting of their valour and people in the democracies would have been trembling. My last thought at the sight was that I hoped it would not happen to me.

We had now used all our cable and were clearly not going to be any use to Major Littlejohns and his company. He told us to go back. We did, but going back was even more difficult than coming out, for we had to re-coil the cable as we went – after all, it was the only cable we had – and this was not easy. It got caught on every awkward tree, hedge and twist in the route. We saved all we could. Some we cut and left. Half-way back some retreating soldiers overtook us.

'Why are you going back?' I asked.

'We've been counter-attacked by tanks and the major told us to get back as best we could,' was their answer.

I pressed them, and they insisted the major had ordered them back. After that we left rather more of the cable and saved rather less. I kept looking down the road to see whether tanks were coming. What a panic-creating phrase that is: 'Tanks are coming!' How quickly the word spreads! What fear it causes! And how seldom it is true!

This time it was partially true. The leading platoon had encountered tanks and the major had withdrawn it slightly, presumably in order to get the best position for his Piat. This was a small weapon which could destroy a tank, but its range was not much more than fifty yards and you had to score a bull's-eye first time. It could only be used effectively by an extremely bold man with an unerring eye.

Littlejohns was standing firm with his company although he was then more than a mile in front of the rest of the battalion. Either his company would have to come back or much of the battalion would have to go forward. Soon Colonel Howie ordered him back some distance. Then the battalion prepared to make another, and this time a stronger, attack. There was to be no rest. The bridgehead had to be enlarged.

Next morning we started confidently on another advance to La Senaudière and beyond. Intelligence sources said the way was open, so Colonel Howie arranged for one rifle company to lead, strung out in open formation across the fields, as vanguard. The orders group followed closely behind, on foot, on the road. Behind us were the rest of the battalion, perhaps 500 men, now well organized, with scores of vehicles. My six mortars in six carriers with a lot of ammunition were in the column.

There followed the encounter I have described in the first chapter. We were caught on the road when the Germans made a swift surprise attack. Just as Sergeant Wetherick had told me at Long Melford, Frank Waters had been cool and composed in battle, leading his group's retaliatory fire. And, as I was now beginning to understand, the colonel had remarkable energy and courage but his leadership was not very methodical.

We re-grouped after that setback, and that night more reinforcements came to us, among them my friend Ken Edwards who had joined the battalion with me on completion of the Isle of Man course. He took command of the carrier platoon, for David Hammond, whom I had earlier thought of modelling myself on, had been killed. Hammond had been sent out with a foot patrol to attack an enemy mortar detachment. As the mortars were not likely to be in an exposed position the patrol would have had to make a very deep and silent penetration of the enemy area. Not surprisingly, Hammond and four others were killed. Although I had been in action less than a week I now regarded myself as experienced and I told Ken that fighting was not as bad as one had expected; and in fact I had been less frightened than I had thought I would be.

Jimmy James, a rotund, red-faced, jovial Welsh lawyer, who was a captain and an experienced mortar officer, also joined us that night and was given command of support company, which gave him oversight over me. He may well have known more about mortars than I did, but he never once attempted to interfere with me and he always gave me every backing he could. Thanks, Jimmy. The battalion was very short of senior officers and one rifle company was commanded by a lieutenant, two ranks below what was normally required, and he was apparently an inefficient lieutenant at that. Howie had asked Jimmy whether he would take over that company and Jimmy had replied that he did not have any qualification for that job but if that was the commanding officer's decision he would do his best. Howie decided not to press the point.

Some mail arrived that night and was quickly distributed. I sat down to write my first letter to England. My only paper was a sheet from a field message pad, measuring four and a half inches by six and a half inches. 'My darling Joan,' I wrote to the girl I had stood up on 5 June when I had to stay in camp preparatory to travelling to Southampton to sail to Normandy:

> Just to let you know that I am OK and in the best of health. And that I love you. A few days ago I was the first to enter a small hamlet and was greeted with flowers, eggs, wine, whisky, slaps on the back and kisses from old men badly in need of a shave.
>
> It has not all been so pleasant, but so far all is well. I shall write a long letter when I get the chance. Will you please let Don [one of my brothers] know I am OK. I haven't time to write to him as well as you . . .
>
> We get a bar of chocolate and a packet of sweets every day. I like that but I love you more . . . Kisses, hugs and love,
>
> GEOFFREY

(It will be observed that we were more than just good friends.)

Not having an envelope, I folded the paper in half, and

then into three, tucking in one section. The surface that carried the address (Miss J. Bradley, 68 Lugard Rd, Peckham, London SE15) and which was therefore the front of the 'envelope' measured three inches by two inches. It was safely delivered by the Post Office and has been preserved to this day.

If I had hoped to have a good night's sleep I was disappointed, for I was awakened by a runner, conveying an urgent order from the commanding officer for me to fire on to a road running along the left of an orchard, for tanks were attacking us from that direction, and where there were tanks there were always infantry. Although mortars could not knock out tanks they could knock out infantry and if the infantry could be made to leave, the tanks would not stay there alone. That orchard, I knew, was rather close to our forward positions, and if any bombs fell slightly short they would damage our own troops. But this was not the time to question an order. The colonel was running the battle, not I; so we fired away at the target. The gunners joined in with their twenty-five pounders.

Nothing more was heard or seen of the enemy, so the fire was called off and we all settled down to a few more hours valuable sleep, until I was called to orders group early next morning. There was some annoyance at the night's artillery and mortar fire, for two casualties had been reported among our own troops, and many officers did not believe that enemy tanks had been anywhere near our own positions. Who had reported the presence of these tanks to the commanding officer? The inefficient lieutenant who was commanding a company. Had he actually heard the tanks? No, but his forward section commander had. What was his name? Corporal X. Was he a reliable NCO? As far as the lieutenant knew, yes. There the matter was left.

GO FORWARD, ALWAYS FORWARD
14–18 June

We were going to attack again before midday, with the same objective: La Senaudière. It seemed that our division was making a concentrated effort to capture the La Senaudière–Lingèvres–Tilly road, and it was rumoured that when we had secured that area we would be ordered to take Villers Bocage and that after that we would be pulled out of the line for a rest.

For this first attack we would have RAF support. Light and medium bombers were going to be used on enemy forward positions, and heavy bombers on targets some way back. In order to prevent casualties to our own troops we had to withdraw about 500 yards and dig ourselves well in. This would allow a fairly large safety area in case there was any mistake.

As it turned out, the air support looked to me puny. I saw a few fighters in the distance, that was all, the heavier machines must have been farther on. My orders were to carry out a fire programme against certain targets for a fixed period of time; then, ten minutes after the attack proper had started, to move my mortars over the start line and, following up closely, wait for further orders. I established my observation post in the attic of a house, which gave me a fairly good view of woods and buildings we thought the enemy was occupying. The mortars were positioned in a farmyard not more than thirty yards from the observation post. In order to get a decent view I had to peep through a small window which I could only reach by standing on a small ladder which threatened to collapse at any moment.

Jimmy, who the night before had been made company commander, was in the attic with me to help. Our system of fire control was this: I observed through the window, and gave an order to him. He leaned out of a lower window and bellowed the order down to a man standing outside the back door, who shouted the order to Sergeant Wetherick standing near the mortars, who gave the order to the mortar crews. Fortunately the exactness of the orders was correctly maintained throughout this relay.

We ranged and got on to our targets and bombed them severely. But after I had been leaning out of the window for some time, bullets began to whizz uncomfortably close to me, and I thought that either I had been spotted or someone had guessed we would be using this window for observation. So I stood away from the window and gave my orders, for example 'six rounds, fire', listened to the bombs being fired, counted twenty-five to estimate the time they were in the air, then popped my head up just in time to see them land and explode. Then I ducked down again, and worked out the necessary correction, gave the new order and did not look out of the window until the next bombs were about to land.

The softening-up process finished, it was time for the riflemen to go forward. We quickly loaded mortars on to their carriers and at H + 10 (ten minutes after zero hour) moved to the battalion start line. But instead of finding riflemen all over the place in follow-up formation the entire area was deserted. We heard the occasional whine of the sniper's bullet. I was not sure whether I was late at the start line or early; whether the attack had gone in and left us behind, or whether it had not begun yet and we were out there alone. According to my watch it was H + 10 and the place should have been a hive of activity. I sent a carrier to the old position of battalion headquarters for the crew to find out whether anybody was still there, and on the way back they attracted small arms fire. Then they told me the attack had not started yet, that we were virtually in no man's land and must withdraw.

What had happened was that as our troops pulled back to give the RAF a satisfactory safety area the enemy moved forward and took over our positions. This had naturally held up the first wave of our attack, but it soon got going and before long the soldiers were advancing with great dash.

Colonel Howie in his carrier was encouraging and urging on everyone he saw. 'I am going forward' were the words most frequently on his lips. He kept pushing me forward. 'Get into position there!' 'Move up there!' 'Go forward!' We hardly had time to get the mortars off the carriers and into a firing position before he would tell us to move up again. He placed great value on maintaining the impetus of the attack, and I found it an exhilarating experience to be always going forward in a noisy vehicle. There was a feeling of triumph in the air.

Howie brought me up to La Senaudière village, then indicated a target to me on the map. It was a copse, about 200 yards ahead. The minimum satisfactory range of a three-inch mortar was 500 yards, so I said to him: 'We're too close for that, sir, I shall have to go back a couple of hundred yards and fire from there.'

'No, no, no, don't go back, fire from here,' he said. 'I'll give you another target.' And he picked one out farther ahead. I thought it was strange that it did not seem to matter to him what we fired *at*, only where we fired *from*. Presumably he thought the sight of anybody going back would be bad for the morale of others. 'Nobody is to go back,' was his constant theme.

So we stayed where we were, set up the mortars behind some houses, and started firing. There was an explosion about twenty yards in front of us, and I did not know, nor unduly worry, what had caused it. It was just one of those noises of battle. Then I heard another explosion which appeared to come from a burning building only a few yards to the right.

'Look out, there's a tank shelling us,' somebody cried. A three-inch mortar, or even six of them, is not the weapon with which to fight a tank. It did not take me long to say: 'Put the mortars on the carriers and get back across the field into the wood.' My company commander Jimmy agreed, and so did Howie, though he remained where he was. I clung on to the back of the carrier while it raced for the cover of the woods, never so thankful as when we were there. Our firing position had been too exposed and too forward. One of my sergeants suggested sardonically we should try to get bayonets fixed on to the barrels of the mortars if we were going to be required as far forward as that again.

Under cover of the woods we got the mortars ready for action and waited. Shortly the adjutant approached, looking for Colonel Howie who was wanted back at his headquarters to speak to the brigade commander. 'He's forward with the leading company,' I said, so the adjutant told me to find him and give him the message. This was easier said than done, for there was now a very large field separating us and a Spandau had started to fire in our direction from our left flank. (Those who get their picture of a battle from films where seemingly hundreds of rival soldiers are packed into a few hundred square yards may have difficulty in imagining a real battlefield. You and a couple of pals can be hundreds of yards away from anybody else; you may not have much idea where friend or foe are. You fire from a concealed position to a hidden target. And how on earth do you find out what is going on?) I located another officer and together we made our way across this awful exposed space, each taking it in turn to run while the other was ready to give any necessary retaliatory fire.

I found Howie but he was busy organizing the forward troops into defensive positions and showing everybody he was there, implying that everything was under control. He told me to return to his headquarters and let the brigadier know he would speak to him as soon as he could.

The battle was beginning to die away now, as battles do. There is no referee to blow a whistle when time is up; the firing just gets less and less until all is quiet.

We had been without proper sleep for nearly a week and the strain was beginning to tell on most of us. Throughout most days we had been fighting. At night soldiers had patrolled, stood sentry or kept observation. Officers had attended orders groups, then called their own orders groups to brief their juniors. Once the excitement and haste of battle had ceased I realized how weary I was.

I smoked cigarettes just to stay awake (I did not smoke them normally). I splashed water into my eyes. I dare not sit down on the roadside or in the hedge, much though I wanted to, because I knew if I did I would fall asleep, and if I fell asleep the whole platoon would follow suit. Some were already dozing on the road, others kept awake with difficulty.

Our attack had been stopped. The riflemen just were not capable of going forward any more. But we had won the crossroads of La Senaudière. To the left the road ran to Lingèvres and Tilly, most of which was captured that day by other battalions and the rest the following day. But Villers Bocage was far, far away.

That night, just in case the enemy should think of attacking us while we were worn out, our artillery put down a very heavy barrage. German big guns were in action too, but I slept through all the noise. I don't suppose for a moment the Germans were in a fit condition to attack anybody that night. They may have been more tired than we were. With the RAF constantly pounding their communications they must have found it difficult to bring up reinforcements.

Supreme Headquarters told the Press that night: 'The

Villers Bocage zone has seen fighting without cease and on balance it has been even. We have not consolidated our hold on the village and at one time were out of it. Now we may be back.'

They did not seem to know very much.

We stayed at La Senaudière in defensive positions for four days.

Most of the first two days were spent sleeping. On the third day Colonel Howie, who was absolutely indefatigable, called together all the NCOs, and later all the officers, and gave us a pep talk. A Spandau is not such a good weapon as a Bren, he insisted. We could easily have manufactured thousands of Spandaus if we had wanted them, but Brens were better. He emphasized a Piat would knock out a German tank and urged us to have confidence in it. General Montgomery thought the war would be over in six months, but Howie thought three months would finish it, if we all did our duty.

A number of writers since the war have established that what Howie said then, though he doubtless believed it, was quite wrong. Much of the German equipment was better than ours. Their tanks had a more penetrating gun and heavier protective armour and therefore were better weapons for this slogging match. Their 88mm guns were better than our twenty-five pounders. Their Spandaus fired faster than our Brens. They had a better collection of mortars and a better anti-tank projectile than our Piat.

But we also had advantages. Firstly, overwhelming air support. Secondly, an abundance of all weapons and ammunition which enabled our artillery barrages to be much heavier than theirs, severe though theirs were. Thirdly, manoeuvrability. We had apparently limitless petrol and could deploy wherever we chose. They were far less mobile.

The fourth day of our defensive duty was a Sunday and many of us, each carrying his own rifle or Sten gun, attended a religious service followed by holy communion in an orchard less than a mile from the enemy. We were going to make another attack next day.

Supreme Headquarters announced: 'The Allies are fighting well within themselves and our prospects are improving every hour.' I wonder what that first phrase meant.

FIRST HOTTOT CLASH

19 June

We were now to make a frontal attack on Hottot, an elongated village along an important lateral road on high ground. The battalion's orders were to advance through the village and occupy a ridge between there and Villers Bocage, our final objective being two and a half miles from the start line. We were getting into the thick *bocage* country, which meant woods and orchards by the dozen and every hedgerow lined with tall trees.

Our visibility was simply the length of a small field, you never saw more than that. To control our firing from an observation post was practically out of the question so we had to do all our firing off the map, from map reference to map reference. Fortunately I had a special aptitude for this and several times in later weeks when we advanced after firing a barrage with the use of map references only we found we had been acceptably accurate.

Colonel Howie's orders to me were to split the mortar platoon into three sections, one to back up whatever rifle company was leading the attack, the second to leap-frog through as the advance progressed, and the third to be under his personal command in a flying column that he might want to send anywhere. I was not happy about this forthcoming encounter because there was clear evidence that the fighting was getting stiffer. We had always made progress but never seemed to have reached our final objective. I think I was also beginning to get the old soldier's feeling that our battalion was the only unit fighting the battle. Where was everybody else? (No doubt they all thought the same.) Moreover as I looked around and saw how many people had joined the campaign after I had I realized how severe our casualties had been and wondered how long I could defy the law of averages by remaining unscathed.

The moment our artillery barrage began the Germans answered in like manner, bringing down their fire on our start line, which considerably upset us. Jimmy was called there for last-minute orders and he told me how he stood behind a carrier with Howie, listening to what the latter had to say and ducking down every few seconds as he heard a shell whistling over. And while he was going up and down like a jack-in-the-box and saying 'Yes, sir' and 'That will be all right, sir', Howie remained standing up and paid not the slightest attention to the shells. Every now and again he would pause in his orders and gaze thoughtfully up at the clouds as if enchanted by their beauty. Jimmy was given command of a flying column of supporting arms and sent off with a company on the left flank where he spent a couple of unhappy days.

We started to move forward and the first firing position of the mortars was behind a garden wall about 100 yards off the road, but the medical officer asked me whether we could move as his first aid post was nearby and the sound of our firing would not help his wounded patients. He accepted that the interest of the battle had to come first but if we could perform our task equally well somewhere else would we please do so? We did.

We moved up slowly behind the main advance. Shells were bursting everywhere, some hitting the tops of trees and exploding there to create a wide fall-out. But I was surprised to notice how near you could be to a ground explosion without necessarily being hurt. However, a signaller, sheltering beside me in a ditch, was killed by an air burst. A large piece of shrapnel entered his back. I felt helpless, and for a moment I did not know what to do, but it did not matter, for nothing anybody could have done would have saved him. In a few minutes he was dead. Other shells bursting near my mortars wounded two men, one of whom died later that day.

As we moved forward I found it very unnerving to see the bodies of those who had died while leading the first wave of the attack; bodies that remained in strange postures, presumably where the blast had left them.

We had been told to get off the road as much as possible, firstly because it was a likely place for the enemy to bring down his shell fire and secondly to avoid congestion. But as we took our mortars forward to keep up with the attack we found many people keeping to the road. It had this advantage: if there were troops in front of you you knew the road had been cleared. If you went off the road to a flank you were not quite sure how much of the flank we held.

There were still snipers firing across the roadway from the woods. We answered by spraying the treetops with automatic fire, but the sniping continued. So Bill Hand, who was commanding the anti-tank platoon, went off on his own with a Bren gun to stalk the sniper. Half an hour later he was carried back with a bullet through both legs. He had been wounded once before, in Sicily or Italy; and he was to be wounded again later, in Holland. Colonel Howie shook hands with him. 'Hard luck, Bill,' he said. Britain owes its thanks to men like Bill who sought out the Germans and fought them. He could easily have stayed with the rest of us and left the job to somebody else, or nobody.

Our leading company got into Hottot only to be forced to withdraw when counter-attacked by tanks. On our left the

2nd Devons also got into the village but they were ordered to make a similar withdrawal for the same reason. Thus when we all dug in for the night we were several hundred yards short of Hottot. We had been held up not only by tanks but by dogged and fierce infantry, by heavy defensive artillery fire brought down where we least liked it, and by mines and booby traps left in the gaps of hedges and in all manner of places where a soldier would unsuspectingly go. That evening two majors walking through a gap in a hedge near battalion headquarters exploded a mine and both were wounded. On that Howie issued an order that troops would never go through an obvious gap in a hedge, but would push their way through the thickest part of it.

I slept that night in a ditch and at first light began a search with one of my sergeants for the best possible position for the mortars. He spotted a deserted two-roomed cottage with thick walls. We called the platoon over. Slit trenches were dug behind the cottage for each man; then we dug in the mortars. I visited the section that was with Jimmy and found they had had a hard time. They supported their company valiantly, firing continuously from the same position for an hour and a half. But that was their undoing. They were in the same place too long, giving the Germans time to take a series of compass bearings on the sound of their firing and then to shell them heavily. They had casualties, including one killed, and that had shaken the rest. They altered their position, and when I visited them they were well dug in.

It was during this day that my friend Chris Needham, who had landed at my shoulder on 8 June, was killed. He was struck down when leading a charge on a machine-gun post. Like most of my friends, he was a gentle man. How often gentleness and courage go together!

The wounding of the two majors, both of whom had landed on D-Day and had been stalwart commanders ever since, highlighted a problem and indeed a growing crisis. If a battalion suffers light casualties it is easy to absorb their replacements. Morale, cohesion and team spirit can be maintained. But when there are heavy casualties particularly among the senior officers, it is much more difficult to maintain these qualities.

The private soldiers naturally do not respond so well to the command of strangers. By now of the ten key men in a fighting outfit, battalion and rifle company commanders and their seconds in command, I think only one was still with us. It is surprising therefore that the battalion continued to fight so well, though I doubt whether it ever again performed as superbly as it obviously had done on D-Day.

The official communiqué after our battle said: 'Our positions in Tilly area firm. Very heavy fighting continued near Hottot.'

AGGRESSIVE DEFENCE
20 June–8 July

For a fortnight we had been battling our way inland, the opposition getting stiffer with every encounter. Now we occupied a defensive position. We were not required to make any more attacks for the time being, though we were to defend aggressively.

Elsewhere too the front was stabilizing. The initial rush of General Montgomery's army had created a beachhead that, though considerable in size, was smaller than what was expected and wanted. All troops found themselves in a grim static battle. There was a continuous fifty-mile front line looping south and bounded at both ends by the sea. Along this line stood battalions practically shoulder to shoulder. Field Marshal Rommel, the German commander, had succeeded in hemming us in, temporarily at least. There were no open flanks so little scope for manoeuvre. It was one of those few times in the Second World War when the fighting resembled what was normal in the Great War. Unknown to us, General Montgomery was about to start the next phase of his campaign. This would be to draw the main strength of the enemy, particularly armour, to the Caen front and thus enable the Americans to break through against weakened defences on the distant right flank.

Colonel Howie was superb at aggression. This took the form of sending out frequent fighting patrols to harry the enemy wherever they could be found and ordering the firing of many mortar and artillery barrages at suspected enemy positions. Fighting patrols went out nearly every day or night. My mortar platoon would often have to fire in support as a patrol made its last dash; or sometimes, if this was not required, we would have to be ready to support a patrol if it encountered trouble.

One night I established a forward observation post and covered a patrol that went out to destroy a tank and beat up an enemy post. I put down a heavy barrage for a few minutes, then lifted the range as the fighting patrol ran in. We waited anxiously for the success signal but it never came. The battalion second-in-command, Major Geoffrey Drewitt, said to me: 'They are in trouble. Keep on firing.' Every few seconds he added: 'Are the mortars firing? Put down some rapid fire.'

Eventually the patrol came back, all well. They had completed their task, although they had taken a little longer than planned, and they had omitted to fire the success signal. Their leader, a young eager lieutenant, wanted to go back again and knock out another tank, but Major Drewitt would not let him as he thought the Germans would not be caught napping again. The lieutenant, who led many good patrols, was later awarded the MC.

But not all these fighting patrols went off well. There

was one in daylight which had the whole Bren carrier and mortar platoons supporting it, but which ended in disaster. The patrol commander's orders were to go to two positions and beat up either or both if he found any enemy there. He found no opposition at the first post, and none at the second, so he proceeded to a third post, where he met trouble and suffered casualties. One man was killed and the patrol commander and two others wounded.

Under cover of a smokescreen another officer went out with a patrol to rescue the wounded. The second officer was also wounded and unable to do any good. Finally stretcher bearers were able to get to the casualties and bring them in. But the patrol commander should never have gone farther than he was ordered.

One day Colonel Howie said to me: 'I want you to take a telephone and a drum of cable and go into the farm a few hundred yards in front of our forward company. The farm is unoccupied; we sent a patrol there this morning. From there you should be able to see a tank in a nearby orchard. Mortar the tank with phosphorous smoke. The crew won't like that. They'll lose their visibility and, fearing attack from an infantry Piat, will pull back. Take a few men with you for your protection.'

I took Danny, a staunch cockney corporal, with me to operate the telephone while I spotted. When I explained the purpose of the patrol to him he said resignedly: 'The colonel's barmy.' I also had a section of eight riflemen and a Bren gunner for my protection.

When you walk out in front of the front line your imagination can play tricks with you. Is that a face peering through that cluster of leaves? No, it is just more leaves. Is that a machine-gun over there? No, it is just a protruding bough. You have to keep going carefully and steadily.

We reached the farm without adventure. We connected the telephone, and I looked cautiously into the orchard to

1. A painting by Leslie Wilcox, RISMA, of the 1st Hampshires storming Le Hamel on D-Day. The battalion met some of the fiercest resistance encountered by any British soldiers that day because a number of enemy strong points facing them had miraculously survived intense naval and air bombardment. The Hampshire casualties totalled 182, representing about one third of the men and one half of the officers. By the evening all objectives had been taken.

2. It is the afternoon of D-Day, 6 June 1944. The assault troops are already a few miles inland. Others, shown here, are clearing obstacles and stacking stores. Soon more follow-up troops will be landing, to widen the assault area.

3. Soldiers wading ashore on D + 1 to reinforce the assault battalions. The scene was similar when the author landed the next day.

4. Soldiers of the Hampshires, having taken Arromanches, occupy a German weapons pit overlooking the town on the evening of D-Day.

5. Elsewhere in Arromanches that evening, Hampshire soldiers and French children are all smiles.

6. General view of a landing area on D + 1 as tanks move inland along a firm road surface towards the front beyond Arromanches. There are already barrage balloons protecting ships and beach workers.

7. Tanks and troops move inland through a French village near the coast on 12 June. The arrival of men and material is continuous.

8. While the Hampshires attacked La Senaudière, other battalions of the 50th Division attacked Lingèvres and Tilly. Tilly looked like this the day after it was captured and resembled many villages in Normandy at the time. Engineers are sweeping the main square for mines.

9. A medical orderly of the 50th Division attends to a wounded enemy during the early days of the Normandy battle, while other captured Germans look on.

10/11/12. The author: *above left*, as an Infantry Captain, 1944; *above right*, enjoying his pension, 1990; and *left*, with his brother Bernard, 1941.

13/14. Gordon Layton was nineteen when he led his platoon in a cliff-top attack near Arromanches. *Right*, Gordon Layton in 1992.

15/16. Malcolm Bradley in 1940 and *right*, in 1992. In July 1944 he was one of the many platoon commanders to be wounded in Normandy.

17. An attack over open country in the early days of the battle, before the *bocage* country was reached. Here a section of infantrymen kneel as they wait for the order to advance.

18. Normandy *bocage*, showing the limited visibility. As a result of this, there were very few good observation posts. Most roads were under fairly continual bombardment, so engineers blew gaps in hedges and constructed tracks. Here infantry, well spaced out, are moving along such a track to forward positions.

try and see this tank. It was not there. So we carried out a target-ranging programme on the area, so as to know the range should the tank ever return, and we mortared the rear of the orchard in case there was anybody there. I think there must have been, for the Germans responded with heavy artillery fire on our general battalion area and also Spandau'd the farm buildings, possibly guessing we were using them as an observation post. We made a quick getaway.

My mortars were in action several times every day. Frequently Howie would require me to fire harassing shots on suspected enemy positions. And whenever our forward troops detected the slightest sign of movement in front of them we would bring down a heavy barrage. Sounds were often heard coming from this orchard, and the telephone order 'Barrage on the orchard now' became a commonplace. We used our bombs lavishly.

One evening the BBC's main news bulletin was led by a report from their war correspondent Frank Gillard, who said: 'The chief incident occurring yesterday was in front of Hottot where an almost continuous programme of harassing fire was carried out by our mortars. After one particularly heavy spell of firing on a wood four figures appeared from the wood carrying a white flag. They stated that during the day they had been subjected to murderous fire from British artillery and mortars. They lost two company commanders in succession and by the evening there were only thirty left in their unit out of eighty. It was then they decided to surrender.

'Immediately we sent out a strong patrol to mop up the enemy position. They fired into woods and hedges, killing a number of Germans. This is typical of the domination our infantry are rapidly securing over the enemy.'

If we were defending our position aggressively, the Germans were holding theirs fiercely. Our entire battalion area was subjected to continuous shell fire. There were heavy barrages at night, occasional barrages by day, a few mortar bombs at any time. Forward positions, reserve positions and rear positions were all shelled. Battalion Headquarters was bombarded so regularly that Howie began to think the enemy must have picked up his position from his wireless. Roads were a frequent target. So were prominent buildings and valleys, the latter presumably because the enemy thought our mortars would be sited there. There was no escape from the bombardment. You simply had to ensure you were as well protected as possible.

There had been no rain for some days and the ground was very dry, so any vehicular movement tended to raise dust which would attract immediate heavy fire. So vehicles had to restrict their speed to walking pace or slower. Large notices were put up saying: 'No dust, no shells,' or 'Your dust turns us to ashes.'

One morning the noise of a carrier bringing up the rations to a forward company caused a number of casualties. The Germans, only 200 yards or so away, heard the noise and fired one shell in that direction. It landed in the middle of a company area, killing some soldiers and wounding others. Among those hurt was my ever-cheerful friend Malcolm Bradley, who had been injured once before, in Sicily.

All this time my mortars had been sited behind the two-roomed cottage the sergeant and I had found when the Hottot battle had died away. The walls were stout and would probably keep out everything except a large-calibre shell. By sleeping on the floor you would be below the level of the window and thus safe from shrapnel and the bullets that whistled through the trees at night. The only risk seemed to be from a direct hit on the roof from a mortar bomb. We crammed into the building as many of the platoon as we could. The rest had to dig a trench outside and sleep there. They were probably in the safest place of all.

The only alternative would have been to have dug a series of trenches in the centre of an open field. There, with a roof of twigs and sods, you would be safe against anything except a direct hit. But we thought our building was just as safe.

The enemy would obviously seek to find our position by taking compass bearings on the sound of our firing and, if they could, on the flash of our firing at night. In order to baffle them, whenever we had time we carried our mortars 300 or 400 yards away in various directions before firing. We only fired from our cottage when we had to do so instantly, without warning. In this way we hoped to avoid detection, and we did. Some soldiers thought the Germans were magicians at locating our mortars but I never thought they were. I always considered that the danger of our being counter-mortared was exaggerated. Certainly during these weeks we were not more shelled and mortared than other parts of the battalion area.

Colonel Howie did not like my platoon staying in one place for more than a few days. Time and again he urged me to move but always I insisted: 'I am sure we are in the safest possible position and we can carry out your orders from there as well as from anywhere else.'

Eventually he glowered at me: 'I will hold you personally responsible for any casualties in your platoon.'

Fortunately we had no casualties while we were there.

This difference of opinion did not stop Howie promoting me from lieutenant to captain, which, as I had been commissioned for less than a year, pleased me greatly. I had the feeling that when we were caught on the road before La Senaudière he liked the way I ran to get the mortars into action without waiting for orders.

My timetable on a typical day in this area was:

0530 hours	Roll reluctantly out of bed. Put jacket and boots over the clothes I had been sleeping in and supervise dawn stand-to.
0600	Take off boots, wrap a blanket around me, and sleep.
0730	Get up and wash.
0830	Breakfast of spam, beans, biscuits and margarine, with tea to drink.
0945	Organize a harassing shoot on to enemy positions for ten minutes.
1015	Polish boots (yes, I swear that's correct), pick up Sten gun, and report with map to commanding officer for conference. Nine times out of ten the Germans would mortar the area while the conference was taking place. We would all rush for the few available slit trenches. Howie would usually lose the race and be the last man under cover. While everybody else grabbed steel helmets Frank Waters, seemingly carefree, would content himself with placing a thin wooden mapboard over his head muttering: 'Bastards!'
1100	Visit all mortar crews and tell them any news I had learned at the conference. Have a cup of tea with them.
1200	Answer urgent call for fire, forward troops having seen movement in front of them. Enemy withdraws and fighting does not develop.
1245	Time for tiffin, a light meal of biscuits, margarine, cheese, jam and tea. Sometimes chocolates and sweets as well.
1300 onwards	Laze in the sun. Wash socks. Read letters. Write letters. Think. Argue.

1900	Supper, main meal of the day, Irish stew, peaches and tea, with any biscuits and jam left over from previous meals.
2100	Stand-to.
2130	Meditate and chat.
2330	Stand by to cover night patrol. Patrol is successful and mortar support is not required.
0030	Wrap blanket around me, lie down, say a prayer for a quiet night, and sleep.

For the private soldier this was a very trying period. Most of the day he spent sitting in a slit trench. He did his turn on guard, he ate his meals fairly regularly, slept when he could, disliked the prospect of being sent on a fighting patrol, and occasionally changed trenches with another soldier in a different field. He wrote quite a number of letters, and was greatly joyed when there was some mail for him. Those who have not fought abroad will never be able to understand what a letter from home means to a soldier's morale. All those devoted wives who daily wrote to their man did more good than they could have imagined.

But sitting in a trench, being shelled and having nothing to do except think of the next shell, played havoc with men's nerves. The strain was not so bad for officers, and in a lesser degree for NCOs, for they had various things to organize and that gave them something to think about. For the private soldier who had nothing to think about, it was a hard time. One example will suffice.

One evening one of my sergeants told me that a private – let us call him George – wanted to see me. I had noticed him in a slit trench many a time, meek, dumb and expressionless. He told me he could stand it no longer, and said he wanted to get back into a building and rest for a few nights. I had every sympathy with him, but had I sent him back and put him on a supply vehicle every other chap whose nerve was beginning to fail would say he too could stand it no longer and could he be sent back behind the line? And soon I would have no platoon left. Boredom, loss of nerve, bomb-happiness had to be fought and overcome. I spoke quietly to George and said he must stick it out. He said he couldn't. I said he had to, and that had to be that.

He went back to his position, and stayed there. He stuck it out. Months afterwards, when conditions were much happier, I was amazed at the change in him. The dumb, listless face now wore a small contented smile, his eyes had become alert, and he looked once more happy and confident.

We were under shell fire one day when a soldier from the Durham Light Infantry, who was bringing up rations for that unit, took shelter with me behind our cottage wall. 'Just fancy,' he said as a shell whistled over, 'if one of those hits you, you're gone.'

There was a lull in the firing, so he ran on his way. But the lull was only temporary. Something else whistled over, and exploded near him. He was gone. That was what life was like. Death could come quickly. 'They die forgotten, as a dream dies at the opening day.' That was just the end of you. This thought preyed on the minds of many soldiers all the way through the campaign.

At a later occasion, at a burial in an area just to our rear, the padre said: 'If the Christian religion means anything at all it means that this is not the end of this soldier. We believe in the Christian religion; if we did not we could not be giving him a burial such as this. And the Christian religion means that his soul and spirit live on; only his body stays in the earth. We cannot feel sorry for him, because he has gone to a better place than this. We can feel sorry for his family and the friends he has left behind, but for him, no.'

During this period Colonel Howie encouraged junior

commanders to do something to relieve the battle monotony being experienced by all troops. He allowed me to have a third of the men out of action at a time. They could be sent miles behind the line and spend the afternoon sunbathing in the nude – it was beautiful weather; or they could be given something to do, such as hunt around for cardboard and wood and make a draughts board. It mattered not what they did. The important thing was that they should have relief from the nervous strain of battle.

One unpleasant duty fell to me while we were in that position. With Ken Edwards, the carrier commander, who shared quarters with me in our cottage, I was called to battalion headquarters and told to take one of our officers into custody. The gentleman concerned had recently taken command of the anti-tank platoon and had his headquarters sited well in the rear. Howie took a dim view of that on principle, and on several occasions it took the lieutenant a long time to get to battalion headquarters for a conference, so Howie told him to move his platoon headquarters forward. The lieutenant did not do so; he was ordered again by the colonel and given a time limit to do it. The time had expired and he had not moved. So Ken and I had to go and tell him he was under arrest.

We found him sitting happily among some of his platoon, and Ken said to him: 'Will you come over here and have a word with us, old chap?' Having drawn him away from the men, we explained to him the situation and said we had been ordered to keep him with us in our cottage. He shrugged his shoulders philosophically and came with us. At the cottage we treated him as a guest and I do not think any of the men knew he was under a cloud. They probably thought he was paying a friendly call on us, or else that we were conferring. After a few hours Ken took him to higher authority some way behind the fighting and we never saw, nor heard of, him again.

There is going to be a big attack at Caen, we were told one day, by many new divisions which have just been landed. Our battalion would not be involved. During the evening we saw heavy bombers softening up the defences.

On 26 June the attack started. Three days later the *Daily Mail* headlined: 'Montgomery smashes through – Rommel's bridgehead ring shattered – Big tank battle now raging.' The report said British forces had broken through the German holding line and were engaging crack panzer troops in the greatest battle since D-Day. The British were driving forward on a broad front and the Germans had made nine counter-attacks in a desperate attempt to halt us.

German reports said Montgomery had used his air forces on an unprecedented scale. 'They swept like a hurricane ahead of the land troops.'

But in fact the great British attack failed, or half failed. We broke into the main German battle line, not through it. Later the word seeped through to us outside Hottot that a break through had never been intended. The Germans kept reinforcing that sector. Perhaps Montgomery smiled as he saw a little more of his plan maturing.

Meanwhile the newspaper maps annoyed us, by always showing Hottot in our hands, whereas we were still 500 yards or more from it. One newspaper correspondent visited the battalion and John, the intelligence officer, took him to the forward positions, and said: 'This is the front line. It is as far forward as I am taking you. But according to your paper Hottot is in our hands and that is another half mile farther on. If you'd like to go there and look you can, but I am not going with you.'

One incident had its amusing side. On the average one or two Germans walked in every day and gave themselves up, saying they could not stand our artillery and mortar fire any longer. And they all told us there were plenty more of their friends waiting for the opportunity to surrender.

Colonel Howie, quick to consider novel ideas, thought of fighting a psychological battle. He applied to his seniors for a loud hailer, and the request went up and up the chain of command to a very high level. Finally Howie got his loud hailer, with a Pole who could speak German to do the hailing.

The loudspeaker was set up, and the first sentence from the Pole told the enemy not to shell him while he was speaking. If they fired on him they were threatened with ten shells and ten mortar bombs for every one they put over. (I had drawn up a special stock of ammunition for this and all the platoon were standing by.) The Pole then read out the script to the Germans. Nothing happened. The performance was repeated, but still we got no prisoners. In fact we did not get another prisoner until the next battle was fought. Obviously the broadcast had put the German officers on their guard. They no doubt watched their troops very closely to see none had the chance to surrender.

But what was in the script? For some time nobody could get an English translation, but eventually the intelligence officer told me it was simply a news broadcast. Howie's idea had been to threaten the Germans with ten times the amount of artillery fire they were already receiving if they did not surrender within twenty-four hours. That might have worked. To give a news broadcast was useless.

After a fortnight in these positions some of our neighbouring troops were withdrawn and our battalion had to hold a larger area. In order not to let the Germans know we had thinned out, my platoon had to occupy two mortar sites that had been used by our neighbours and fire frequently from there, as well as from those we were already using.

Several reinforcements arrived. Among them was Ben, who became my driver. He handled a carrier very well, and although he frequently told me he was frightened and his knees were knocking together he always found enough courage to do his job.

Another was Monty, my extremely conscientious signaller. Not only did he keep in wireless communication with all required headquarters, but he could also receive BBC news on his set, and he passed on this news to everybody, adding his own forecast of future events.

WAS SECOND HOTTOT REALLY A DEFEAT?
9–11 July

In the early days of July the German wireless was warning their people about the strength of the Allied forces. 'Ships are bringing countless batteries to Normandy for an all-out assault of decisive importance,' ran one report. Staff officers were quoted as saying the big attack would begin as soon as the army group under the American General Patton, which was still in southern England, reached Normandy. Another German report said new Allied landings were expected at any moment.

Meanwhile it was General Montgomery's tactic to make strong attacks on different days all along the line with the object of drawing enemy armour to our front and of denying the Germans knowledge of where our main thrust would eventually come from.

On 9 July our battalion was moved back into reserve in order to prepare for a major assault on Hottot and beyond. We would be on the extreme right flank, with the Devons on our left and two other battalions following closely behind. Our rifle companies were going to have plenty of tank support, and for the best part of a day the infantrymen and tank crews practised the tactics they were going to use.

The country was typical *bocage* land: fairly level (although there was some high ground beyond Hottot) and small square fields always hedged by high trees. It was going to be a case of attacking field by field, the infantry advancing to one hedge under cover of the tanks' fire; then waiting there for the tanks to join them; then the infantry going forward under tank covering fire to the next hedge and waiting there for the tanks to join them; and so on. This was not tank country; we infantrymen had to accept that; but how we longed for the time when we would be fighting in tank country, when tanks could lead, or at least go forward abreast of our riflemen.

When demonstrated on a blackboard the plan looked simple, and undoubtedly it was the right one to use. But in practice it was never easy to carry out a blackboard-planned attack because of the terrific artillery fire the Germans put down among the attacking troops. It was easy enough in training to say: 'Your section stays here until the leading section reaches there'; but it is not so easy for one section to remain where it is and wait for a signal if it is being heavily shelled and there is no cover available. Alternatively those in the leading formation who are about to face small arms fire might want to stay where they are, while those behind may have a great desire to hurry up and get the job over. There can be an element of 'Those behind cried forward, and those in front cried back.' And control is more difficult when there are people who only want to find some good cover and stay there. Against determined opposition even the simplest of plans is difficult to execute.

My own problems were of a different nature. I was required to arrange for a mortar sergeant to be in the forefront of every rifle company and, equipped with a wireless set (which the enemy might easily spot), to control our fire.

My first objection to this was that no matter how far forward the sergeants went, nor to what danger they exposed themselves, they would never be able to find an observation post; the nature of the *bocage* terrain precluded that. My second objection was that even if by some miracle they were able to find an observation post they would not be able to communicate with the mortar positions over any distance longer than 1,000 yards. Their wireless sets were of poor quality and in this wooded country with more powerful tank and artillery wireless sets on the air that would be the limit of their effective range. As the attack would no doubt proceed at an uneven and irregular pace there would be great difficulty in keeping the mortars within that distance of the leading riflemen.

My suggestion was that as previously I should fire on to map references nominated by company or platoon commanders, these targets to be relayed to me through various company headquarters. Not being a slave to the training manual, my only thought was that mortar tactics should be governed by the nature of the ground we would be fighting over. But Howie instinctively stood by the book. He had been taught in England that mortar fire controllers had to be with the leading troops; and that was that. However, I insisted that an observer needed to be able to see at least 200 yards ahead to serve any purpose, and I asked Major Littlejohns, who would be leading one of the forward companies, what was the maximum visibility he expected to have. His reply was 40 to 100 yards. Thereupon Howie conceded my main point. He agreed that if the observers could not see any reasonable distance ahead they should move with the company commanders and support them as required.

The night before the attack Howie gave out his detailed orders to the largest group I had ever attended. Besides our own company and support platoon commanders, there were tank commanders, flame-throwing tank commanders, artillery representatives, heavy mortar and machine-gun commanders, one or two liaison officers, the medical officer and the padre. The size of the group was an indication of the amount of help we were going to get. Howie said that the orders he had received were that the battalion had to capture Hottot and exploit southwards from it, but he would only give us orders to take us as far as Hottot and when we got there and consolidated he would issue further orders over the air for the exploitation.

As we sat on the grass he strode up and down in front of us. 'This battalion *will* capture Hottot,' he shouted with great emphasis. 'We *will* capture Hottot and we *will* hold it at all costs. This is how we will attack.' And he went on to give specific orders to everyone.

For my part I had to fire first of all on a time programme; then I had to move up by bounds behind the assault, keeping within range of my fire observers' wirelesses, and be ready to engage all targets required by the assault troops. Sergeant Wetherick, who had brought up a large stock of ammunition and stacked it in a number of dumps, would need to be prepared to hasten back along the supply line if we looked like getting short.

Howie was fierce, storming and confident. But there were some of us who could not feel so confident. We had tried to capture Hottot once and had failed. We had sat outside the village for three weeks and given it the name Hot Spot. Were we now to be banging our heads against a brick wall?

Most of my men slept that night on the ground beside their carriers with large tarpaulins covering both the vehicles and themselves. About half a dozen, myself among them, got into a barn and slept on the straw. We were up before it was light and cooked a breakfast of sausages and beans on an open fire, the smoke of which we hoped would not be spotted by the Germans. (Petrol cookers which gave off less smoke had been supplied to us but had developed faults.)

11 July: At 6.30 a.m. we move up near the start line, put the mortars in pits we had previously dug and line up on our first target. I look at my watch and see the minute hand creep slowly towards seven o'clock. Everything is quiet. But how many officers, I wonder, are watching a hand move towards seven o'clock? How many men stand by with shells or mortar bombs in their hands? How many machine-gunners are lying down beside their guns? How many men with Sten gun in hand are waiting for someone to order 'Forward'? How many people are praying from the bottom of their heart: 'Protect me this day, Lord'? Back at various command posts commanders, liaison officers, intelligence officers are looking at their maps, lavishly marked with chinagraph pencil. Somebody is murmuring softly: 'In another minute they go in.'

0700 hours! A deafening roar from the heavy guns behind me, the wicked crackle of Vickers machine-gun fire! To add the noise of my six mortars to the awful din is like putting a small flame to a furnace. But every little helps. I have to shout at the top of my voice to be heard, and even then my voice carries only a few yards. I give orders by signals.

The Germans must know now that a big attack is coming in. On the start line Major Littlejohns will be saying: 'OK, away we go!' For a long time the roar of artillery does not stop. As terrific salvoes swish overhead we wish our riflemen luck. The bark of machine-guns is so continuous that it gets on one's nerves. We hear some shells bursting near us and occasionally one or two land very near, forcing us to duck into our trenches.

My signaller Monty is joined by a companion, Frank, so we have two wireless sets in case one breaks down. But something very much like a circus is taking place between them. Reception is perfect, they both insist, yet they are receiving different messages. One says our riflemen have reached code-line Orange and are running into heavy opposition on their way to code-line Apple. The other says the attack has not started yet.

What am I to do? I have to move up as soon as possible. This is for me to judge. But what on earth is the real situation?

Eventually the signallers report that the confusion has been straightened out. They tell me exactly how far the rifle companies have gone. They are vague about what the trouble between them was and I do not question them as there are other matters to worry about.

(But months later I learned that one of them had tuned in to a wrong wavelength and had been receiving messages from the Devons! Had he been the only signaller I had, the consequences flowing from that mistake do not bear thinking about. Suppose all my battalion had been asking me for help and I had not heard!)

For a time the attack goes well, and I move one of my sections about 1,000 yards forward. We do not move along the roads this time. We have learnt our lesson from the previous battle. The engineers have blown gaps in the hedges immediately behind the assault troops and every vehicle goes across country and through these gaps.

Travelling up in my carrier I find the enemy shellfire has been intense on our forward troops. We at the back escaped most of it. I am undecided whether to occupy a farmyard I had provisionally fixed on in my planning or not. The buildings would give excellent protection, but I feel they would also provide a likely target. Farther over to the left is a valley. There we would be concealed, but the valley also is a likely target because the enemy know we will be tempted to fire mortars from there.

So I choose the corner of a field midway between the farm and the valley. This site affords little protection, so we will have to dig slits behind the carriers for safety, but it is an unlikely place for the enemy to fire at. I get one section into action there, and the other two sections soon come up, so all six mortars are sited in an area about fifty yards square.

Many salvoes from enemy guns are landing near a hedge 200 or 300 yards behind us, and I am thankful they didn't land there when we were moving up. At the same time I hope the Germans won't drop their range because we are directly in their line of fire. They put down a heavy barrage on the farm buildings, and that makes me very pleased I decided against going there.

All the same, the shelling is uncomfortably close. The loud crack of explosions, the sight of a disintegrating hedge and the thick black smoke that hangs around, the reeking smell of burning cordite: all this gives me a sinking feeling. We dig in as fast as we can, and with shells bursting around us that is pretty fast.

One shell explodes near one of my carriers and the camouflage netting on the vehicle catches alight. I see the flames spreading, and, realizing there are phosphorous bombs on the carrier, I am fearful of what might happen. The driver runs to the vehicle very quickly and uses the fire extinguishers to put the flames out.

Our battalion's assault is held up but I do not know why. No one is calling for our support, so I fire off occasional harassing shots. During a lull the soldiers brew up some tea and produce a meal of biscuits, cheese and sardines.

Near the farmhouse on my right I see my friend the intelligence officer, so I ask him for the latest information. He does not know very much. We have not yet reached Hottot but he believes we are not far off. Colonel Howie has gone forward to see for himself.

The issue of the battle hangs in the balance and when we see RAF rocket-firing Typhoons coming to support us we are all thrilled. Rockets are usually decisive against enemy gun positions and it is probably artillery that is holding us up. With eager anticipation we watch the Typhoons fly in. They dive to attack. Surely they are diving early! Yes, they are. What on earth are they up to? And then, slap in the centre of the battalion area, they loose off their rockets. There is a swish and a shuddering explosion. As I crouch in a slit trench the earth trembles, but I tremble more.

I do not know whether to stay there or to get out of my trench and wave our identification flags. There is only one thing I really want at that moment and that is for the earth to open and swallow me up for safety. The planes circle around again, and I notice one lad wildly waving identification flags at them. Finally the Typhoons fly home.

At 1530 hours Colonel Howie calls me up on the wireless telling me to put down a heavy barrage at 1600 hours on certain targets. The artillery is going to fire an enormous barrage at that time, and the attack is to be resumed.

So at 1600 hours the performance that had taken place at 0700 hours is repeated. But our troops are not in such good condition now. Morale was in a fragile state even before the Typhoon pilots made their tragic mistake. I learn that two of the company commanders have been wounded and there have been heavy casualties.

Our second attack does not get very far. The enemy retaliates with artillery fire and a heavy salvo lands among my mortars. One of my men is wounded in the arm, and another goes bomb-happy as a result of four mortar bombs falling simultaneously a few yards from his trench, hugging the earth and crying like a child. With difficulty we persuade him to allow himself to be taken to the regimental aid post. He is suffering from headache and his sight has become blurred. (After a week or so he recovered completely.)

Two of my mortars are damaged but the men keep to their task and fire the other four resolutely. Sergeant Johnson is marvellously calm and his calmness spreads. We are determined to fire two bombs for every one that lands near us, or is it ten for every one?

We have been in that position too long. It is just possible the enemy have guessed where we are. I decide to move. It is unwise to go forward, for we are already close enough to the leading troops. I see no great safety in going to either flank. So I resolve to move back about 400 yards. It is time to take advantage of the mortar's long range. Two sections go back first, while the third remains where it is, ready to fire. Then, when the first two are in action, the third joins them.

I learn that Colonel Howie has been killed. Our attack fails to take Hottot. Major Drewitt, now acting commanding officer, reorganizes the front positions into a defensive posture. I go to meet him to be given defensive and SOS tasks. These I organize. Then we lick our wounds.

Of the four fire observers I had with rifle companies two came back to me that evening. The German shellfire, they said, had been deadly. One of the leading platoons had got to within fifty yards of the Hottot road but its strength had been so depleted by casualties that it could make no further advance.

The other two fire observers had been wounded but neither seriously. One returned to duty a fortnight later. (He told me then: 'Some of the troops were not very willing to go forward. One group got under cover and stayed there. When I told them to go forward with the rest one chap said to me: "I've got a wife and kids to think about. I'm not moving." I told him: "I'm married too, but this is not the time to think of your wife."')

As I was checking my area during the evening I came across a soldier lying on the ground. Wounded, I thought, or dead. Getting closer, I noticed the man was a stretcher bearer. He was lying face downwards and was sobbing. He was shaking, too, like a leaf, and could hardly speak. There was nothing physically the matter with him. He was bomb-happy. Slowly, he began to speak to me.

He had been called forward to attend to the wounded, he said, but on his way he had walked into a heavy barrage which had been more than he could stand. His nerves went and he lay on the ground, prostrate with fear. He had been there since early in the morning. It was now getting dark. I reminded him gently of those who had been leading the attack. They had had to stick all the shelling and they had had to contend with a lot of small arms fire as well. He realized he had let them down. I wanted to get him to the doctor, but he was so badly shaken that he could not lift himself off the ground, so I had to call two other soldiers to help him to his feet and lead him away.

When finally I prepared for sleep that night I felt all in. I took off my steel helmet and was astonished to find it had an indentation the size of a small egg. I must have been hit by a small piece of falling shrapnel or a nearly-spent bullet. In the haste, excitement, frenzy and fear of battle I had not noticed. Well, no point in worrying now. I snuggled into a trench, wrapped a dirty blanket around my muddy battle dress and boots, used the inside of my helmet as a pillow and went instantly to sleep.

Next morning we were relieved by the 1st Dorsets and went into reserve.

Battalion casualties in the attack have been given as 120 out of an effective force of fewer than 700. The total killed was 43, about two-thirds of the number who died on D-Day. But whereas on 6 June all objectives had been taken, albeit at heavy cost, on 11 July no objectives were taken, at heavy cost. But this may be true only in measurement of territory. It is impossible to say what casualties we inflicted on the Germans or what effect we had in drawing their forces, and particularly their armour, to our front so as to give our United States comrades the opportunity to make a decisive breakthrough. We may have accomplished more that we realized.

Colonel Howie was killed while directing the final assault of the two leading companies. He was an extraordinary commander. He fought the enemy with a furious passion. He encouraged, enthused, chivvied everyone into attack. 'Keep going forward. Always go forward.' When battle was joined it was his custom to site his headquarters well forward; and then himself to go forward of that. He spent more time within a stone's throw of the enemy than any-where else. And when things were quiet he was known to take the humble weapon of the Piat and go hunting German tanks. He told one of our officers it was his ambition to die for King and Country. He achieved this ambition without knowing he had been awarded the DSO.

And yet . . .

Did he have the tactical skill needed to command a battalion? Did he have the empathy necessary to command men? During our days around Hottot I was aware that some of our officers did not think it was his job to be so far forward so often. The farther forward he was the narrower became his scope of command. There was also criticism of his decision to send David Hammond and his companions on what seemed an impossible mission. And I doubted his skill after that occasion when he had shown himself not much interested in the target I should fire at, only interested that I should fire (at anything?) from a very forward position.

My thought at the time of his death was that if he had survived much longer he would have won the Victoria Cross, but what would his frenzied leadership have done to the battalion?

Our accumulating casualties were creating a serious problem. All the soldiers who landed on D-Day had been together in the battalion for months, many for years. And although the cost on that day was high the achievement was wonderful. But as the Normandy casualties mounted and reinforcements were brought in there was an obvious danger that the battalion could become, in part, a collection of hastily thrown together soldiers who had not had time to become the kind of team in which the courage of individuals becomes shared and enhanced in a group.

A second disconcerting factor was that we could not see we were making much progress. We may have been, but we could not see it, we did not know, nobody said.

And a third factor was that those who had fought in earlier campaigns and had been in Normandy since 6 June must have been running out of courage. Most men have a finite amount of this commodity and it can get used up. Very few have an inexhaustible supply.

Thus morale was bound to become a problem throughout the whole of the army. On the grapevine it was said that one battalion, the 6th Duke of Wellington's, had turned tail and fled. The truth was less horrendous than that, but it has since become known that the commanding officer of that battalion wrote a report saying that his men were inflicting wounds on themselves, many were suffering from hysteria, officers and NCOs were not wearing badges of rank, there was no *esprit de corps* and the battalion would not be fit to return to battle until it was reorganized and retrained. 'I have twice had to stand at the end of a track and draw my revolver on retreating men,' the commanding officer wrote.

General Montgomery's response was to sack the officer, disband the unit and feed the soldiers as reinforcements to other battalions.

This must be taken as the worst example of a battalion. However shaken people may be I cannot begin to comprehend a situation in which officers and NCOs do not wear badges of rank. I have no idea whether the 1st Hampshires were at the other end of the scale, the best; but far from being unfit for the campaign we were shortly to win a notable battle accolade.

The Germans had no such problems. Anybody deserting from their army was shot. Thus everybody stayed in their firing line.

It is easy to make yourself scarce in battle. All you do is find somewhere to hide, stay there till the shooting has stopped, then look for your unit and say you had lost your way. Such soldiers would be court martialled for desertion. One day one soldier in our battalion facing this charge asked for me to defend him. An accused could choose any officer he wanted for this purpose. I did not know this man at all. He must have picked my name out of a hat.

All I could say to the court was that he was a very young chap (nineteen); he had been a good soldier so far; his nerve had suddenly failed him; he very much regretted it and would try his hardest in future. He was sentenced to three years' penal servitude, as was every deserter because it had become known that longer sentences were always reduced to three years by the army commander.

It was after one of our Hottot battles that one of our battalion headquarter officers told me that he had encountered a soldier clearly running away. 'Turn round and go back to your platoon,' he ordered.

'No, I won't,' replied the soldier. 'I can't stand the danger. I'd rather spend three years in prison.' And he threw his rifle to the ground in a symbolic gesture.

'That's not the choice facing you,' retorted my friend, who then drew his revolver, pointed it at the soldier, released the safety catch and ordered: 'Go back to your platoon!'

The man picked up his rifle and made his way back to his battle station. I wonder how many times that scene was enacted in Normandy and how many times, if ever, the revolver was fired. The needs of battle override all other considerations.

Every time a soldier in my platoon was killed I would write a letter of condolence to his next-of-kin. Every officer did this. My headquarters may be in the cellar of a ruined house. There would be a table, a candle and an upturned box to serve as a chair. A few sheets of paper and a pen were available.

'Dear Mrs Snooks, You will already have been informed officially of the sad death in action of your son David. I write as his platoon commander to tell you ... and to assure you ... we shall all ... much missed ...'

The writing of these letters was accepted as a clear duty, but it did nothing for one's own morale.

101

SOME REST AT LAST

12–26 July

A couple of days after the Hottot battle I went with John, the intelligence officer, and others for three days' leave at an Arromanches rest camp, our party travelling there in three-ton lorries along dusty roads one hot afternoon. What a joy this was! A canvas bed instead of the hard earth; a tent over our heads instead of a groundsheet or nothing at all; water on tap nearby; and latrines with seats to sit on! For three days we were lifted out of the war into peace. The serenity of it all, the quiet and the cleanliness! My first act was to look where the trenches were in case of air attack, my second was to have a bath. I filled an enamel bowl with cold water, and, standing outside my tent, stripped and washed. That was it. Then I put on clean clothes and they felt delightful.

There was a film show at the rest camp, a library, facilities for riding horses and swimming. I spent most of my time resting, writing or wandering pleasantly along the cliffs and the beach. There were many minefields still uncleared, but they were all plainly marked. In the cool and tranquillity of evening I liked to walk along the cliffs and think about the Germans who had once defended them. I gazed with amazement at the enormous craters made by RAF bombs.

Those three days went far too quickly and it was with a heavy heart that I returned to the battalion expecting to find mud, dust, noise and danger. But the battalion had moved and we were now out of contact with the enemy, so life continued to be peaceful and sunny. My platoon was positioned in a valley, about fifty yards between each section. The sergeant in charge had sited my headquarters in a barn next to a farmyard which was used by various animals and consequently had a pungent smell. So I immediately moved to some trenches a fair distance away, where, with straw to lie on and a camouflage net to keep out the hot sun, I was extremely comfortable. The month's spirit ration had recently arrived, and I quietly sipped gin and orange.

Most of the soldiers liked the atmosphere of the farmyard; they were welcome to it! One of the senior sergeants who had recently reinforced us chatted to me. The war had given him two disappointments, he said. One was that, although promoted to sergeant in 1940, he had received no further promotion since (this, he reckoned, was because his superiors did not like his familiar attitude with the troops); the other was that the locusts had eaten five years of his life and now, aged thirty though he looked five years younger and was handsome, he was not yet married. He viewed his continuing bachelordom with alarm.

Our location was only semi-tactical and Major Drewitt wanted some activities or light training to be organized for the men to keep their minds active and to counter the dulling and deadening effect of their having sat so long in slit trenches. We did a little map reading and compass work, and for two or three hours every day we played rounders, which gave us enjoyment, exercise and a competitive interest.

Reinforcements were posted to us, and the mortar platoon was made up to full strength for the first time. Claude arrived and became my batman. He had been in the army only six months and had never had any leave. He was so timid that it seemed a shame he had been sent to war. He was a country lad brought up on a Norfolk farm and I do not think he could understand why I avoided the farmyard smell. At first the chaps used to pull his leg a lot but before many weeks had passed he became as good a leg-puller as any.

After a few days resting we had orders for another move, which was to take us over our old battlefields, into Hottot and beyond it. The enemy were believed to have pulled out, so this was not to be an attack; it was to be an advance, presumably unopposed. Drewitt's plan was to send forward two fighting patrols, each about a platoon strong, and for them to secure a small area on the objective; then for the rifle companies to move forward and build up on the patrols. Two of my sections were attached to these companies and moved with them. I was left with only one section and had to remain at the battalion command post, which was established in a great hole dug in the ground. The hole was so deep that once you were in it it was difficult to climb out. I had my batman and my driver with me and, wrapped inside my greatcoat, was a bottle of whisky and another of cordial, from which I sipped frequently.

The advance began during the evening and went on into the early hours of the morning. The night was very black and there was inevitably plenty of confusion. The men leading the patrols never knew when they might encounter booby traps or enemy soldiers. It was difficult for those behind to follow their path. Vehicles got bogged down and a lot of noise was made freeing them. But the patrols did their job well; their companies were able to build up on them and at daylight the rest of the battalion followed. Our advance was smoothly accomplished. The intelligence assessment had been right. The enemy had gone.

The village of Hottot, through which we passed, looked very unimposing, just a row of deserted and damaged houses on either side of a road which was covered with rubble. This, for which we had fought so hard, had now fallen into our hands like a ripe plum. There was no sign of the enemy anywhere, and we rode joyously over a crest into the valley below. I think we could be seen on this crest from some hills in the distance, for the Germans sent over a certain amount of artillery fire. So we quickly cut and blasted routes through hedges and woods, so that supplies could be taken to the front line without any movement being observed.

The layout of the battalion defensive position was reorganized, and I was given orders to leave one of my sections with a forward company and to re-site the other two in a central place. One sergeant had already found a sound position for the mortars and he had also established a useful observation post at the top of a slope from where he could see 500 or 600 yards over slightly rolling country. The artillery observation post was nearby and there was a platoon of our troops in a valley in front of him, so he was well protected.

The Germans soon began to shell us quite heavily. Their guns were active when the ration truck came up to my platoon in the evening, and the driver of the truck was mortally wounded by a piece of shrapnel entering his head. There was a touch of irony about the fact that the driver, who was up in the forward area for only a few moments, should be killed, and the rest of the platoon, who would have to lie there for some days, were unscathed throughout that time.

That night we all went to sleep in our trenches, only the guards remaining awake and alert. There was more shelling, and I was afraid someone might get hurt without anyone knowing about it. It was the guard's duty to watch for any shells falling in our area, and, as soon as possible after the shelling was over, to leave his slit trench and ascertain if everybody was all right. But often the guard would remain under cover long after the shelling had finished for fear that it would start again. So after any dangerous bout I used to shout out: 'Everybody OK?' and wait for favourable responses, then remind the guard of his duty. I always had a great fear myself of being left wounded without anyone knowing, and I did not mean to let that happen to anyone.

During the night a 75mm shell landed midway between

my trench and the next one, about five yards from both of us. I felt the breeze of the explosion and a lot of rubble was blown into my trench. My neighbours said they were smothered in rubble, but nothing more serious than that happened.

The next morning I set off to see my forward section, which was about half a mile away. I had nearly reached the rifle company they were with when I heard a swishing noise which I did not at first recognize. A moment later about ten mortar bombs fell thirty to fifty yards away. A sudden fear caught me, for I realized that if I had been hit nobody could have helped me and it might have been some hours before anyone would have come that way. I was only 150 yards from the company, so I ran the rest of the distance as fast as I could.

I found my section in quite a snug position behind a bank, and they had dug themselves well in, though they had not dug in the mortars, and I later got a rocket from the commanding officer because of this. Weapons always had to be dug in so that their crews could continue to operate them while under fire.

After a few days Major Drewitt ordered me to consolidate my whole platoon and move to yet another place. He wanted me completely away from the rest of the battalion, to get dug in, to dig alternate positions in some other place, and then answer the German mortaring with bomb for bomb, or better still, ten bombs for one bomb. I picked a position half way up the side of a hill, sufficiently below the crest to be concealed and sufficiently above the valley to be out of the way of any shells aimed there.

The ground, however, was very firm and digging was exceedingly hard work. All morning while we dug it rained, and in the afternoon while our wet clothes dried on us we dug again. We even used several grenades to blast a few holes, but even four grenades blew only a small pit. I was very annoyed when Drewitt rang me late in the afternoon and asked why we had not finished digging yet. In the end we never used the pits, nor did anybody else. Attacks had been put in on both our flanks and these had converged at a point in front of us, so that we had been pinched out of the battle. We were taken out of the line for a rest.

There had been rumours for many days that we were about to be relieved, but I did not believe these stories because I had heard them so many times before and they had always been wrong. It damaged the morale of the troops to be led to believe that they were being pulled out into reserve and then to find that that was not so, so I always advised my chaps not to believe these fairy tales and I tried to prevent people spreading them. But one old soldier in my platoon always had the news (so-called) and always knew it was true. He came to us with so many rumours that I suppose one had to be right in the end. On this occasion he got hold of the story that the entire 50th Division was being given a rest, and he persisted in telling everybody. I insisted that I knew nothing about it and wagered a bottle of whisky (my monthly spirit ration) that he was wrong. No sooner had I said that than I received the order to prepare to move; we were pulling out!

We packed all our kit on the carriers and at the appointed time drove away along narrow, muddy lanes to join the battalion convoy. In the fading light we drove to our rest zone. I felt we had earned our rest, for it was then 22 July and we had had little respite since the beginning of June.

It was while we were lazing that we heard that General Montgomery was directing a major attack at the extreme left of our sector in the general direction of Caen. As we were near the extreme right of the British sector the attack had not concerned us.

Montgomery's tactic, consistently pursued since he drew

up his plans in the early months of the year, was to draw as much of the German forces as he could, particularly their armour, on to the left flank to enable the Americans to break out on the right. On 18 July he had launched a strong armoured attack around Caen. He wanted the support of a massive air armada, including even heavy bombers. But most RAF chiefs did not approve of their bombers being withdrawn from their task of raiding German cities in order to help a land battle. To them that was a wrong order of priorities. So to persuade them to help Montgomery greatly exaggerated the importance of this thrust. This exaggeration secured the use of both medium and heavy bombers on a huge scale.

After the air bombardment very substantial British tank forces led the advance. That evening Montgomery announced that British and Canadian troops had broken through the enemy positions. 'And into the plain beyond,' exulted the newspapers. 'The big breakthrough,' headlined the *Daily Mail*, 'Armour now swarming into open country.' 'British army in full cry,' thundered *The Times*, 'Wide corridor through German front.'

Two days later Montgomery called off the attack. All the German reserves had now been drawn to his front. That was what he wanted. The way was now clear for the Americans to break through fifty miles away on the right.

A LONG RIGHT HOOK

This breakthrough had been several weeks in the making. First of all the US forces had to gain the important communication centre of St Lô, and they had found this nearly as difficult to achieve as the British had to take Caen. They writhed under the problems of fighting in the *bocage* country just as much as we did. They found, just as we had, that when a tank charged into one of these hedges at best its tracks merely carried it to the top of the barrier, exposing its vulnerable underside to enemy fire. At worst it just got stuck.

But from Sergeant Curtis C. Culin Jnr came a novel, simple and battle-winning idea. Why not fit some long steel prongs to the front of a tank near its base and drive it at speed at a hedge? Would it not get through? The idea was quickly tried. And at the first attempt the first tank went clean through the bank, removing a complete section of it, and continuing on its way without ever exposing its underside.

A demonstration was immediately laid on for General Bradley, the ground commander. He liked what he saw and at once ordered his tanks to be equipped as fast as possible with this rhinoceros-like hedge cutter. Thus armed, his men redoubled their efforts to take St Lô. From 11 to 17 July the battle raged. One battalion got to within 1,000 yards of the town, only to be partly surrounded by an enemy counter-attack.

Major Thomas D. Howie, who seems to have been as daring, charismatic and willing to sacrifice himself as his British namesake, led another battalion silently through an early morning mist, successfully to reinforce the nearly surrounded and by now somewhat shattered group. Asked then whether with only his one battalion he could continue to advance on St Lô, he replied, 'Will do', and set out to do so. He was killed by shellfire and his battalion made little further progress. As it turned out, they had done enough, for the Germans withdrew and on 18 July the Americans entered St Lô. The coffin carrying the body of Major Howie was covered with his country's flag and placed on the hood of one of the jeeps that led a US column into the town.

This was about the time that the Germans withdrew from Hottot, enabling the 1st Hampshires to walk fairly peacefully into it. It was also the day Montgomery started his heavy assault southwards from Caen to keep the enemy occupied and to suck in his reserves.

General Bradley's men now stood ready to break open the front. On 19 July the general flew to England to tell the Allied air forces what support he wanted. He pointed on his map to a prominent road running east to west. 'I want all bombing to be south of that road,' he said, 'and I want the pilots' bombing runs to be east to west or west to east. Then if any bombs fall short of the target they won't hurt my troops.'

'Sorry,' the air chiefs replied, 'the pilots must fly north to south; otherwise they would be much too exposed to heavy anti-aircraft fire.' The point was argued, and it is unclear where it was left.

'My soldiers will be at least 800 yards behind the bomb line,' was Bradley's next requirement.

'Better make that 3,000 yards,' answered the air chiefs.

On 24 July, when the battle was supposed to begin, Air Chief Marshal Sir Trafford Leigh-Mallory, the Briton who was commanding the Allied air forces, flew over the combat area and decided the weather was too bad for bombing. He ordered a postponement. But some pilots did not receive this order. They bombed, killing 25 US soldiers and wounding 131. Next day in better weather they bombed again, this time killing 111 more American troops, including a general, and wounding another 490.

Terrible as this was to the Americans, the bombing was very nearly an annihilating experience for the Germans. Their casualties were huge. Field Marshal von Kluge, their commander, had been lured away to the British front, where he sensed danger. But he took the curious precaution of sending a staff officer to the western flank to instruct battalions to hold their line, just south of St Lô, at all costs. Not a single man must leave his position.

One battalion commander who knew what the aerial bombardment had done to his troops flew into a rage. 'Out in front everyone is holding out,' he roared at the staff officer. 'Every one. My grenadiers, my engineers, my tank crews, they are all holding their ground. Not a single man is leaving his post. They are lying silent in their foxholes. They are dead. All dead.'

None the less the ground attack made very little progress, and by nightfall on the first day only a few hundred yards had been gained. Resistance had been furious, but one or two US divisional commanders suspected that behind the enemy's brave front line there were few, if any, reserves. So they took a chance and on the second day launched a full-scale tank attack. Their judgement was correct, and soon their tank columns were clean through the main enemy defences and advancing southwards at a speed not previously dreamed of in the battle.

Whereas in *bocage* country both British and American forces had often gained a few hundred yards a day, or a mile or two, now in only five days (in one of which there had been hardly any movement) General Bradley's men advanced forty miles to the south, reaching Avranches.

The decisive blow in the battle of Normandy had thus been struck. The German front was irretrievably broken and the American attack that had started with unmitigated disaster was now about to deliver a knock-out smack. This punch would come at the end of a huge, swift, 150-mile-long right hook which, hitting the enemy on the point of the jaw, would settle the issue and restore the pre-war map of western Europe.

From Avranches the Americans would turn east and, not seriously impeded, would race for Alençon, seventy miles away, then hasten north to Argentan, another twenty miles on, and if possible another fifteen miles to Falaise.

The Canadians, coming south from Caen, would also

make for Falaise, only twenty miles distant, and if possible tie up the Germans in a circle of Allied armour. Even if some enemy escaped before the knot was tied, their army would suffer severely and probably fatally and they would have to leave most of their equipment behind.

The job of the British, holding the centre of the battlefield, would be to make a series of independent strong thrusts to keep the Germans fully engaged and prevent them reinforcing the few battered units that stood in the way of the all-conquering US armour.

As these momentous events began to unfold, the 1st Hampshires, having been pulled out of the battle for the first time since 6 June, were innocently enjoying some rest.

Our new area was near some heavy guns, and my first reaction was: 'How lucky gunners are, to be able to live so far back!' Ernie Wetherick, the platoon sergeant, was there to greet us. He issued every man with a bivouac, and all the chaps had to do was to erect it, eat their supper and sleep. Most of them used their vehicle tarpaulins as well, and thus made a sizeable tent for half a dozen fellows. There were four bivouacs left over, so I used all of these as a canopy above my camp bed. I slept in pyjamas and felt very clean and civilized. The whole division had come back to this area for four days, and in order to give us undisturbed rest the artillery moved their gun positions.

During this period the lads were sent off in relays to take a shower at a nearby mobile bath unit.

We all met the new commanding officer, Lieutenant-Colonel Tony Turner, a large man who wore a pullover with badges of rank instead of a battledress like everybody else; he puffed contentedly at a pipe, seemed of a slightly retiring disposition and wore the ribbon of the MC.

The first ENSA entertainment party to land in Normandy had just arrived, and a large contingent from our battalion went by truck a couple of miles to see them perform. The concert was held in a barn, the seats being just bundles of brushwood. At the back of the barn stood a large number of French boys, who I dare say did not understand a word of what was said but showed considerable interest in the ladies' changing quarters, which were just the back of a vehicle with a few sheets of tentage put up to give them a little privacy.

During the concert most of my attention was given to a Devon officer who sat next to me and who wanted to discuss the difficulties of operating mortars without an observation post. He said his battalion had discussed this in great detail and the general opinion was that the mortar commander ought to go forward on patrol and register some targets before returning to his own lines.

I did not think this was much of a contribution to meeting the problem. It was true that Colonel Howie had once required me to do this outside Hottot but it was doubtful whether my patrol had served much purpose and surely the point was that you were not going to find decent observation posts lying about in no man's land waiting for someone to come and sit on them. Most fighting took place to gain observation posts. 'The only ground worth fighting for is high ground,' we had been taught at Long Melford. In any case the ploy did not answer the important and difficult problem, which was how to find a good observation post during an advance in the closely hedged *bocage* country.

After the show I took the six performers (three men and three women) to our battalion headquarters. As they walked through the bivouac area they were astonished at the miniature tents and huts the chaps had rigged up. They were surprised such cosy bivvies could be made with such little material. At headquarters we sat down to an agreeable dinner and had a few drinks. We sat on boxes, and our table was a board placed across four tall boxes. After six weeks of fighting in slit trenches it was certainly a change to have feminine company.

At nine o'clock the babble of our conversation ceased and we listened to the BBC news. Our guests were surprised that we, nearly in the front line, got our news from the wireless. They thought the wireless got its news from us. The truth was that a soldier normally knew very little of what was happening on other sectors and the wireless news was often more up to date than anything the unit's intelligence officer knew.

At nightfall the evening hate was turned on. Artillery on both sides opened up, as it always did at dark. We heard our own guns firing and German shells landing a long way away. The ENSA party inquired how far we were from the front line and when we told them about five or six miles they replied they would take great care to see they took the right road for Bayeux, where they were staying. The party broke up quite early, about half past ten.

We spent four days enjoying a mental rather than a physical rest. It was rest from battle, rest from the fear of death. We did some training to sharpen up our military skills, and we played a few games. Only the thought of the future marred our bliss. Too soon it would be time to go 'once more unto the breach, dear friends, once more'.

5

Battle of Normandy:
The Breakthrough

OUR BEST ATTACK SINCE D-DAY
27 July–4 August

Happily when we moved it was to take over a reserve position from the East Yorks, so we were not in contact with the enemy. I met their mortar platoon commander, and as he took me around his area I admired the amount of digging his chaps had done. There were twelve deep mortar pits – six battle positions and six alternatives. In addition they had dug in their seven carriers, and even dug alternative pits for those. 'The commanding officer likes a lot of digging,' this officer told me, 'because it keeps the men busy.'

He had registered some likely targets from a rather adventurous observation post very near the falling bombs, but as the battalion was in a reserve position their most likely role would be to counter-attack to regain ground lost by other battalions, in which case the targets he had registered would be of no use. My commanding officer did not require me to shoot and confirm the ranging.

Before the men of our battalion arrived I had a long talk with an East Yorks company commander. We both took an extremely gloomy view of the war. It had taken the invasion forces seven or eight weeks to gain a little strip of coast, perhaps about twenty miles deep. At the present rate of casualties we would not have an army left by the time we reached the battlefields of the First World War and even if we could find another army from somewhere it would take decades to reach Berlin. Montgomery was stuck. We had no doubt about that. Attacks were costly and gained only a few hundred yards. Montgomery's estimate of the fighting being over in six months was foolish.

'Now,' said this East Yorks officer, 'look at General Alexander in Italy. He's getting a move on. They'll have to bring him over here to make a success of this invasion.' We parted, thinking that the war, like the poor, would be with us for ever.

Members of my platoon held similar views. 'It wasn't like this in Sicily or Italy,' they repeatedly complained to me. 'There we fought a battle and the Germans pulled out. We got on the road and travelled ninety miles one day before we saw the enemy again. But here you fight a battle and nothing happens, except you fight another one later on, and nothing happens then either.'

We soldiers were not the only people who did not comprehend what was going on. On 29 July Alan Moorehead, perhaps the most famous of the war correspondents, wrote in the *Daily Express*:

I have a message from London this morning saying that people at home are puzzled by events in Normandy. They have the feeling that things are going slowly and that we are developing a battle of attrition along the lines of France in the last war. Can I explain . . .

The plan has not gone exactly according to plan because no plan ever does . . .

The Normandy situation is no worse or better than it was during those gruelling months when we fought along the Alamein line before the final battle of Alamein . . .

You put in an attack here and draw back there and do nothing in the other place and all the time you have to keep bluffing the enemy. He must never know whether or not a given blow is to be an all-out effort . . .

The battle for Germany is on. It is an immense business. It has very little to do with occupying stretches of country. It has everything to do with the stationary business of smashing up the German war machine . . .

Your armies are now engaged in the biggest life and death struggle of the whole war. The plan – our plan – provides that we shall break through. The subsequent pursuit will be twice as interesting and a quarter as important as this battle.

What my East Yorks pal and I did not know during our dismal conversation; what the members of my platoon could not guess as they forlornly thought of the easier campaigns of 1943; but what Alan Moorehead may just have sensed as he strove to put the best face he could on reports of unyielding events, was that at that exact time the American army, working to the plan of that battlefield master General Montgomery and buttressed by the British effort, were about to change the map of war-torn Europe; and they were to do this under the command of the war's most rumbustious leader, General Patton, and by exercising the most distinctive characteristic of their nation, the belief that nothing is beyond them.

We were in fact on the verge of several stiff, successful battles which would push the Germans into a vast, terrible slaughterhouse later to be known as the Falaise Gap and this, exceeding our wildest dreams, was going to lead to our incredible, hardly-hindered advance of 300 miles.

But the only future we were expecting as July came to an end was more dour battles and advances measured in yards rather than miles.

Shortly after we had taken over from the East Yorks the whole battalion 'stood to' while our new commanding officer came around to check that everything was to his liking. I did everything according to the book. I made sure every man in my platoon was wearing his equipment and steel helmet, and in addition to manning the six mortars I posted sentries and with a few spare men organized a little local protection. I was determined that on the colonel's first inspection of my platoon he would find everything correct. We waited a long time for him to come around. I think he must have gone to every other company before us and when he reached the mortar position he just took a quick glance at the weapons, asked me if everything was all right and told me we could stand down as soon as it was dark.

I later came to like Tony Turner very much. After giving me a job to do he would never worry how I did it, only that the job was done. He understood war-time officers better than some regular officers did and he always made it plain that his one ambition was if necessary to create, and certainly to command, a good battalion. He did not strangle himself with red tape, nor did he follow too strictly ancient regulations and old-time practices. He was an extremely practical man. The discipline he imposed and the standard of conduct he set were both for the benefit of the battalion. At times he feared for the safety of his men and it was widely felt that if he thought we were being maladroitly used by his superiors he would make his views firmly known to them.

I was glad when the day ended and I crawled into my trench to sleep because not only was moving up into battle positions unpleasant but there had been bickering among my men. A petty, stupid incident showed how taut our nerves had become. The positions we had taken over contained only thirty-five slit trenches and there were thirty-nine of us. So four men had the task of digging slits. But the group I asked to do the digging complained that it was always they who had to do the hard work and it was time somebody else took a turn. I remained firm and told their NCO that his group would have to dig. He adopted a rather aggressive and nearly disobedient attitude.

'We've always done the digging before. We're not doing it again. It's somebody else's turn.'

He was an extremely good man on the mortars but he was no good to me if he did not respect my authority. Quietly and firmly I repeated my order and asked him to cool off. He did. The digging was done and there was no further trouble. But surely we had more important things to worry about than this.

The night was quiet for us, though we heard next day that one of the rear headquarters had been disturbed by heavy shelling. For one day we enjoyed lovely July weather. I found a chair which someone had left behind and sat on it in the middle of a field for most of the day, writing letters and enjoying the sun and scenery. The chair was a marvellous luxury after sitting on the ground for two months. It made meals so much more enjoyable.

The battalion did not remain there long. We were briefed for an attack and I spent an afternoon reconnoitring positions for the mortars. Then I learned the attack was to be made from a different place. So another reconnaissance party set out, led by the commanding officer, to look at the new start line and to try and see some of the ground we would have to fight over. The tracks leading to the start line were very narrow and boggy. Jeeps and carriers travelled along them all right but I realized the fifteen-hundredweight trucks we used for bringing up our ammunition would have difficulty in getting through. After the reconnaissance we went back to the commanding officer's tent for his orders group. It was dark when he began to give out his orders and nearly midnight when he finished. We had to move at 4.30 a.m. and launch the attack soon after first light.

On our right in the St Lô sector, we were told, the Americans had achieved a breakthrough which had great possibilities; the 15th Scottish Division, containing nine battalions, had been switched to an important area near the junction of the British and American armies, and they were going to make a strong attack to support the American effort. Our job, with sixteen other battalions all working to a coherent plan, was to push forward in the general direction of Villers Bocage and beyond, and there were hopes that we would find it easier attacking there, through Ectot Woods, than we had done at Hottot.

While it was still dark on the morning of 30 July sentries went around to all the trenches, calling the occupants. We rolled up our blankets (covered with the eternal dust and ground), put them on the carriers, and made ready to move off in the battalion convoy to our firing position. As this was to be a major offensive the roads would be clogged with traffic for several hours before the start. So all unit moves had been planned and timed in advance. A battalion would be told to leave point A at time X and arrive at point B at time Y and it was not allowed to have any vehicles on the road except at those times and places. So in this case the commanding officer was moving his battalion in convoy at 5.30 a.m. and the mortar platoon had to fall in behind battalion headquarters.

Some people do not like getting up at five o'clock, and it took some shouting and bullying on my part to get the carriers marshalled in time. At the last moment I counted only six carriers – one missing! Two of the chaps had slept on in their trench, and the driver was waiting for them. We raked these fellows out and half pushed, half threw, them and their equipment and blankets on the last carrier. I loathed the thought of being out of place in a convoy because that would show sheer inefficiency. However, we occupied our correct position and, as daylight was beginning to break through, moved to the area of the start line.

I set up the six mortars behind some farm buildings which offered good protection. I had arranged for Sergeant Wetherick to bring up an extra supply of ammunition, but when zero hour came his fifteen-hundredweight truck had not arrived. We had an ambitious fire programme to carry out in support of the attacking riflemen, so we started at once and kept going strongly. Soon Sergeant Wetherick arrived, having been delayed by the narrow tracks and traffic jams. I was not surprised.

We had a good weight of artillery support and, although the Germans retaliated, life in our immediate area remained fairly comfortable. During a quiet spell the chaps brewed up some tea and prepared breakfast of bacon and biscuits, but they were fearful lest in the middle of their preparations I should need to order 'Move forward now'. Their luck held, for although the attacking infantry made progress, they did so slowly, and we were able to stay in our initial position for some hours. This new colonel, I discovered, was not like Howie; he did not want the mortars close to the front. As long as I could reach 500 or 600 yards in front of our troops he was content for me to be in what I judged the best firing position. We had good communication with the commanders of the leading formations and we energetically fulfilled their requirements.

This time the air support worked correctly. About 9.30 a.m. little black dots appeared in the sky behind us; they came nearer; we recognized them as aircraft; flight after flight of aircraft. They were Lancaster and Halifax heavy bombers flying in loose formation and, with a magnificent and impressive disregard of German fighter and anti-aircraft artillery defences, were only about 500 feet above the ground. Scores of bombers came overhead; the scores grew into hundreds; and we had to stop our firing so as not to endanger them. Their targets were not far away, for we felt the earth rumble as their bombs exploded. This air support gave our morale a great boost and it must also have had a substantial material effect. For half an hour the attack continued and I did not see one bomber come to grief.

I wondered what the pilot thinks of the infantryman. Several bomber pilots have told me subsequently that their most interesting missions were in direct support of land fighting and usually on those occasions they came away with light losses. One pilot has told me that from the sky the explosion of bombs looks the least terrible part of a battle.

'Your artillery,' he said, 'looks as if it is creating great havoc. It gives a continuous line of flashes and it looks to us as if nothing could live down below.'

That afternoon as our attack progressed I moved up two sections but had great difficulty in finding a suitable position for them. We were on a long forward slope and the flash or smoke of any firing from there would be liable to be seen by the enemy. Eventually I found an area where I could hide them and from where we could reach the most distant target we were likely to be given. Quickly we dug slit trenches for our own protection and three mortar pits. The fourth mortar we sited in a large shell hole.

We were preparing to fire from here when I heard a tremendous explosion behind us. I turned and, near the shell hole, saw a cloud of black cordite dust where a few seconds before Sergeant Johnson had been standing. Agonizingly slowly the dust disappeared, and I saw Johnson again, evidently unhurt, perfectly calm, walking in the open towards the slit trenches where his section was sheltering and signalling to them to remain steady and to start firing. I was astonished at his unconcern. More shells landed nearby and he continued to spread calm where others could have magnified fear and spread terror.

With an ample supply of ammunition we answered every call from the leading companies. Soon the commanding officer told me to establish an observation post among the forward elements and, leaving Johnson to prepare the cable and telephone, I went forward to look for a place with a commanding view. I made an uncomfortable trip up to the line. After passing battalion and support company head-quarters I saw no sign of life for a few hundred yards till I spotted Red Reed, our anti-tank platoon commander, who was trying to find a suitable route for his anti-tank guns. When he went off to reconnoitre a route on the left flank we parted company and after that I saw a few stragglers and then part of a rifle platoon, but I found nobody who could tell me exactly where our leading positions were. The fog of war had come down with a vengeance.

At last I spotted a hedge on a small rise and thought I might find a good observation post there. I had to pick my way carefully through bushes to get to the hedge without being seen, and a colleague, pointing to the hedge and the rise, said to me: 'It's hell up there.' But it looked quiet enough to me, so I cautiously went through the bushes and reached the rise. It made quite a respectable observation post. Our forward troops were in the valley in front, but I knew I would have no visibility from there. I decided that the rise, lonely as it then was, would be my post and made my way back. The enemy began to shell our area, and as one or two shells whistled and crumped near me I remembered the chap who had said: 'It's hell up there.' Here I was, alone and being shelled. How I hated it! If only I had company! The shelling did not last long and I continued on my way. It was dark when I reached my platoon area, so there was no point in manning the observation post before next morning. I sent a message to the sergeant in command of my rear section to look after his own local protection that night, and I crawled into a trench obligingly dug for me by Ben, my hard-working driver, and went to sleep.

As usual we were shelled that night. Infantry always had to fight an unremitting battle against enemy artillery, and the way we fought it was twofold. Firstly and most important of all, we had to get well dug in, with a roof of sods and brushwood over our heads, as quickly as possible. That made us safe against anything but a direct hit or a near-direct hit. When you have to dig in two or even three times a day it gets very laborious. Yet I never found a single man on a single potentially dangerous occasion who was too lazy to dig or who preferred not to. You would not have lived long in Normandy without a handy trench to jump into. Our second defence was to call on our own artillery to shell the enemy guns whenever the latter opened fire. In this our gunners always performed splendidly.

Early next morning I went out with an NCO to establish the observation post I had reconnoitred the previous evening. I spent some time liaising with our forward companies, one of whose officers pointed out some buildings about 1,000 yards away where the Germans were thought to be, but the countryside was quiet and we saw no movement at all. There was an anti-tank gun near our observation post so I felt well protected. I wanted to range on three important targets which the commanding officer would want to be bombed immediately if any counter-attack were launched against us. But hills and woods created a certain amount of dead ground in that area. I could range on two of the targets easily. The third I could not see. So I had to range on a prominent nearby feature and from the map calculate the correction from there.

After I had spent some hours at the observation post Sergeant Johnson came forward to relieve me. On returning to the mortar position I learned that our battalion had received congratulations from the brigade, divisional and corps commanders for our having made more progress than any of the other sixteen battalions who had been engaged in

124

this important thrust. The senior general also let it be known that he considered there must have been a number of acts of high individual bravery and that appropriate recommendations for decorations should be made.

Bravery wears many faces and I decided that that included remaining cool and calm under fearsome shelling, spreading that attitude to those around you and supervising the continuing and efficient firing of your mortars. Accordingly I wrote a recommendation that Sergeant Johnson should be awarded the Military Medal. I had in mind not only his conduct the previous day but also that that had been typical of his behaviour during the weeks in which he had been under heavy fire.

I heard nothing more and thought little more about it. But eighteen months later when the war had ended I met Johnson at a regimental occasion of some sort in England. He approached me and, pointing to the ribbon of the MM which he was wearing, asked demandingly: 'What's all this about, sir?' I did not think I should be drawn on the subject, so I merely said, not truthfully: 'Nothing to do with me, sergeant, but congratulations!'

Sergeants Johnson and Wetherick were great pals and leg-pullers. Johnson had missed part of the early campaign because of malaria, probably contracted in Sicily.

'He could have stayed in England because of his malaria,' Wetherick told me, 'but he came out here because he wanted to be with me. He is lost without me.'

But Johnson's version was that he came out to Normandy to look after Wetherick. 'He'd be lost without me,' said Johnson.

We learned that our thrust towards Villers was likely to ease the path of the Americans, who seemed now to have achieved a complete breakthrough. If we continued to threaten strategic points the Germans would not be able to spare troops to contain General Patton's advance. So our efforts must continue. There was hardly time to pause for breath.

Colonel Turner received preliminary orders for another attack and he took Ken Edwards, the carrier platoon commander, and me with him to reconnoitre some of the ground of the proposed advance. He did not want me to have any fire controllers with the attacking companies as he was satisfied that the observation post I was now using would provide a better view than anybody would get by accompanying the foot-slogging riflemen. Final orders were not given out till it was dark. The whole orders group of about a dozen officers squeezed into the colonel's tent and by the light of a hurricane lamp he showed us the plan and gave us his orders. Just as he had finished heavy shelling started, so we dispersed rapidly.

I wondered whether it was really necessary always to hold orders groups late at night and to start attacks soon after dawn! I returned to my platoon area about 11 p.m. Only the sentries were awake. So instead of calling the sergeants and giving them orders then, I merely told the sentries that reveille had to be at 5.45 in the morning. Zero hour was 7 a.m. I suppose attacks were often started so early in order to give us time to make a substantial advance before dark. But I think the psychological side should have been taken into consideration also. A man who rises at 5.30 or 5.45, who does not pause to wash, who quickly eats a cold and unappetizing breakfast, is not going to be at his fighting best at seven o'clock. Would not midday have been a better time to begin an attack?

After our reveille I gave out orders to the section commanders while the rest of the men prepared breakfast. I had to get to the observation post by seven o'clock with Monty my signaller and Ben my driver, and breakfast was not ready by the time we had to go. This was the first time for many weeks that I had had an observation post from which

I would be able to see an attack and I meant to make the most of the occasion. How much easier my job would now be!

Alas! Dense fog limited my visibility to twenty or thirty yards. I felt hard done by. It was as if I had been starved, then shown a banquet, only for it to be whisked away as I was sitting down to eat it. Once more all our firing had to be done from a map. This we did most assiduously. It was nearly nine o'clock when breakfast was brought to us. It consisted that morning of bread and butter, bacon and beans, biscuits and marmalade, and tea. It was most appetizing and welcome.

The attack made good progress in the face of light opposition, and after two or three hours the riflemen were on their objective, another significant and brilliant performance. I moved up with all three mortar sections and, leaving two of them tucked safely away in a valley, took the third to within 400 yards of the most forward area. From there we could fire at any distant positions we might be required to engage and I felt one section would not present too large a target if the enemy suspected our presence. We found several large trenches dug very thoroughly by the enemy and recently vacated by him in a hurry. They contained an abundance of junk including lists of soldiers in one particular unit, which I gave to our intelligence officer. There was also a pair of trousers. Was this a spare pair, or did someone flee without his pants?

Near this forward position was a high feature giving the best observation post we had found so far. From it I could see the countryside for eight or ten miles ahead. Main roads were clearly visible, little villages were to be seen amidst wooded surroundings, and, most interesting of all, Villers Bocage stood out so bright and clear that no one could mistake it. The artillery observation posts were manned in strength, each officer wanting to fire at various inviting targets and the most inviting of them all was Villers. But the efforts of the RAF had made that unnecessary, for the town was in ruins. It had been an original D-Day objective and it was now D + 56.

I took several of my platoon to this post so that they could see the land ahead and, incidentally, admire the view. We were there in that impregnable and commanding position for only a few hours. Just after darkness fell the battalion hurriedly moved off in convoy over that high feature and took up positions near the village of Actonville, which lies in a valley. That night move had one particular hazard: we did not know whether we would run into any mines. Had we done so, dealing with them in darkness would have been a very delicate and tricky proposition. But luck was with us and all went well. (How gingerly I felt my way forward over hedges!)

We did not dig in at once as there had been no enemy activity for eighteen hours and we were not in contact with the foe. We set up our mortars, then lay down to sleep behind our carriers. I put on an overcoat, wrapped a blanket around me and laid my head in the inside of my steel helmet. I was not cold and I was tired, and had no difficulty in sleeping.

Next morning I looked for a better position and found one in an orchard that was in front of a ruined farmhouse, which the medical officer was using as a regimental aid post. A brook trickled peacefully along nearby.

I ordered the chaps to dig in here as it was always possible the enemy would make a counter-attack or that he would shell our area with long-range guns. I established an observation post on a nearby hill, then sat down and awaited developments. For a couple of days we could hear artillery fire, though the noise of it got fainter and finally we heard it no more.

In a few days we had snapped through the German

defence line. A total of twenty-seven of our men had been killed in these operations, none in my platoon, and this was sixteen fewer than in the savage second battle of Hottot. Our four days' rest before the start of this battle had done everybody good. Our fading spirits had been restored. This must have been the battalion's best feat of arms since the landing on 6 June.

Attacks by battalions on our flanks now pinched us out of the battle. Villers Bocage was surrounded and taken. The huge American encircling move swept on.

At home the newspapers gave exciting news. 'Normandy front is "exploding" in new attack, says Berlin,' reported the *Daily Mirror* on 28 July. It quoted this report from the German overseas news agency's war correspondent in Normandy:

> The Allies have launched a major new offensive on the whole British front, including the most southerly points at Caumont, and over the invasion front generally.
>
> The Normandy battle is on the threshold of a new and decisive phase. Grim fighting is raging everywhere.
>
> Strong British groupings launching new thrusts under cover of a deep gorge north of Verrières have managed to gain ground but the Germans are counter-attacking.
>
> Big British concentrations of tanks and motorized forces south of Caen are at present being shelled.
>
> It may be assumed that Montgomery can now put 50 divisions in the field, including very strong new tank groupings. The British Second Army alone is estimated to possess 1,500 to 2,000 heavy tanks and the US First Army probably has the same.
>
> The Allied strip of land on the Normandy coast now resembles a blazing boiler whose safety valves are inadequate to prevent a great explosion.

On 3 August the *Daily Mail* headline was: 'German Front Collapses. Allies Win Greatest Victory Since Invasion Day.' 'British troops,' it was reported, 'have broken through the German positions fifteen miles south of Caumont, and an official spokesman described the British attack as a major success.'

Alexander Clifford, their renowned war correspondent, sent the following dispatch from Le Bény Bocage (ten miles south of Villers):

The spirit of advance was as clearly in the air today as the yellow dust itself. The whole second army seemed to be on the move forward. You could feel the excitement in its veins. You could feel it as plainly as we used to feel it in those mad desert advances.

The situation geographically is still so untidy as to be indescribable. But we are on beyond Le Bény Bocage, through a whole cluster of villages to the south east. We are on beyond Jurques. We are going ahead everywhere. Just here and there the Germans are holding and resisting.

The line of advance runs like a great hook around the west and south of the area between St Martin-des-Besaces and Le Bény Bocage, and there are Germans still in it. In woods here and there and along the bushy banks of streams little enemy battle groups are fighting, but it is no longer an organized front.

I could list you the name of a hundred villages but they are only confusing. The important thing is this instinct of movement and success which has seized the army. There is a feeling that a chance is being afforded to us and we are taking it.

Our mileage is admittedly not spectacular. We have made twelve or thirteen miles in four days which is not impressive beside those whirlwind advances in Africa.

But this is not a country where you can overrun empty square miles.

Where each field and each lane and each farm may be an enemy strongpoint you cannot expect a dizzy speed. You must measure our mileage against the quality of this close-grained country. Then you will see why these thirteen miles have bred this mood of success . . .

You could leave the main arteries of traffic and drive sideways into a quiet manless country. Unmilked cows grazed in the vegetable plots and chickens hopped in and out of parlour windows. The inhabitants had fled or been driven out by the Germans. The main tentacles of war had passed it by. Along the wayside you saw all the signs of a recent rapid advance. French peasants – men, women and children – gathered jubilantly to watch German prisoners being searched. Rommel had swept through this district a week before with an SS bodyguard, who had left bitter memories behind.

In the next place the people were trying to shave the heads of three women who had been too friendly with the enemy. The women hid in a shop but village tempers were roused and the crowd hunted them down. In the end they simply had their hair clipped off, not shaved. They sneaked off home in a disgrace that will never be forgotten.

THE NEW GENERAL
5–8 August

Our positions became non-tactical, so we were effectively at rest. Officers and sergeants were called to battalion headquarters where, with others from the Dorsets and Devons, we were to meet Lieutenant-General Brian Horrocks, newly

131

appointed commander of the corps we were in. General Montgomery was commanding British and American land forces and thus headed 21st Army Group. The British component, Second Army, was commanded by Lieutenant-General Miles Dempsey, and this was divided into a number of corps, one of which was now to be commanded by Horrocks. Red Reed, who seemed to know these things, said Horrocks was supposed to be one of the country's top generals.

We dressed as smartly as we could for the occasion, wearing our best battle-dress (if available), web belts with pistols on the right side and ammunition pouches on the left. The battalions paraded in three sides of a square and as General Horrocks arrived we were called to attention. It looked like being a formal parade, and out of the corner of my eye I took careful note of the general's manner.

He simply said: 'Gather around me, sit down on the grass and smoke if you want to.' He proceeded to give an informal talk, almost all of which showed he had a pleasant sense of humour and what seemed like extremely shrewd judgement. First he got us in a sympathetic mood by praising our division. The reputation of the 50th, he said, stood very high in England on account chiefly of three things: its good patrolling, its doggedness in battle and what he called its healthy contempt for enemy tanks.

He said the division, having been in action for nearly two months, deserved a rest and needed a rest. He promised us four days out of battle at least; and hoped it might prove possible for us to be out for longer. But the door of the German defences was beginning to open and if we put every shoulder to the door and pushed hard it would be flung wide open. Then would start a new type of warfare – the pursuit. 'Pursuit,' he said, 'just means motoring along roads. I am a better general at motoring than fighting.'

The Germans were showing the same signs of cracking

as they showed just before they collapsed in North Africa. Their wireless communication was lacking security and they were organized into battle groups which had weak co-ordination. He instanced the case of a battalion which sent out a wireless message in clear: 'We are surrounded in village X ... Can the 21st Panzer Division immediately counter-attack please?' The reply the battalion received was that the panzers could not counter-attack. Knowing this, we put down a heavy all-night artillery barrage on the village of X, and nothing more had been heard of that enemy battalion since.

General Horrocks told us there had been cases of Germans fighting in our prisoner-of-war cages and the guards had had to stop them. 'You may say, "Why stop them fighting one another?" but the point is they are beginning to fall out among themselves.'

He explained to us the large encircling movement planned to trap the enemy between Falaise and Argentan and said in order to molest and worry them inside the trap four strong thrusts were being put in. One was to Caumont; another to Villers Bocage, which had just been pinched out; the third was to Thury Harcourt; and the fourth (which interested us) was to Condé-sur-Noireau. To get Condé it was necessary first to take Mont Pinçon, a high strategic feature which dominated the whole of the northern French plain. A brigade of the 43rd Division was going to try and take Mont Pinçon and if it failed he would put in the whole of that division with the support of all his artillery and all the heavy bombers he could lay his hands on. After that it would be our turn to push the attack on to Condé. (It was always a mystery to me why the whole of the 43rd Division was not used in the first place without seeing whether a brigade could take Mont Pinçon by itself.)

After trapping the Germans in the Falaise and Argentan gap Montgomery planned then to roll them up against the

Seine and give them the choice of fighting on either the nearside or farside banks. It was Hobson's choice for them, because if they fought on the nearside bank they would eventually be pushed into the river, and if they fought on the farside they would have to fight without their heavy equipment since the RAF had destroyed most of the Seine bridges. (As it turned out, the Germans did not fight on either bank.)

General Horrocks added that this was not the time for a soldier to be in England. The battle had reached a decisive point; once we crossed the Seine the way was open. The rocket bombing of London was distinctly unpleasant and we must finish the war as soon as possible.

As we walked away from the talk one of my friends said to me: 'God, we're going in again in four days' time! I don't think any general can possibly imagine the effect his words have on a soldier when he says, "I'm putting you into battle again in a few days' time."' Half of me agreed with him; the other half was happy to be out of danger for four days. The soldier thinks of all the battles he has fought in the past, of all the narrow escapes he has had from death, of his pals who one by one have fallen; and he wonders how much longer his luck can last. The average infantryman does not fight many battles before he becomes a casualty. If he has fought in six major attacks without being hit he knows he won't last another six. There is a feeling that sooner or later death catches up with you. That is the feeling, but it is not what actually happens. True, a rifleman kept in the line without relief for a long time is almost certain to become a casualty, but casualty and death are not synonymous. Three, four or five people are wounded and survive without permanent injury for every one who is killed. All the same, it is not nice to think that the best that can happen to you is to be wounded.

On the whole the general's talk was well received. His

homely and humorous manner was appreciated and clearly he spoke as one who was the master of his job. What was soon to impress us enormously was that his forecast of German moves proved to be substantially correct. They were on the verge of cracking. We took Thury Harcourt, Condé and Caumont, the Falaise pocket was tied up, and we moved forward, hardly molested, to the Seine. The enemy had nothing behind the Seine and, as Horrocks had said, the way was open. Then the motoring really started and we reached Holland before we met major opposition.

Horrocks incidentally had fought under Montgomery at Alamein and in the subsequent pursuit of Rommel. In 1943 he was wounded during an air raid in North Africa. He was in hospital for a long time after that and it was not until 31 July 1944 that he was finally passed by army doctors as fit. Three days later he was again in battle under Montgomery's command, one of three generals who hastily replaced three who Montgomery thought not good enough. (After the war Horrocks went into business and he later became a popular television personality.)

The British public had been kept informed of the decisive events that were upon us. On 7 August the *Daily Mail* published the following report:

A senior staff officer at General Montgomery's head-quarters said last night: 'My view is that the next two or three weeks may be the most critical of the war. It does look as if Germany is going to be faced with tremendous disasters in many places and a terrible time ahead.'

The officer disclosed that the Allied campaign in Normandy is going almost exactly to the schedule planned in London several months ago . . .

The officer backed up General Montgomery's policy of building up large reserves before cracking through the German defences. 'While it meant that the earlier stages of the campaign had to be slower, one hopes that the later stages of the campaign may be quicker than we expected,' he said . . .

The officer said that two things – the security of the beaches and the need to accumulate forces and supplies – had so far influenced the course of events, and went on: 'It was a very trying period for General Montgomery at first. You and I probably felt things were going very slow during that time and wondered if it was not possible to quicken things up and change the original plan. But the Commander-in-Chief kept his plan and I think he was very wise that he did not try altering it to any marked degree . . .

'Unquestionably the enemy has decided to fight this battle out here and any reserves he can produce are endeavouring to get along here on push-bikes and on foot and on railways as far as they are allowed. It is frightfully difficult to see how these reinforcements can be sufficient to enable him to retrieve the situation – a situation where he has a very big open flank. It is very difficult to see how he could set up and fight it out with any success.'

In Normandy we settled down to four days' rest in delightful warm weather, spending most of the time washing our clothes and ourselves. We found wash-bowls from ruined and deserted houses, filled them with water from the stream nearby and bathed ourselves. Many of the chaps in my platoon sunbathed, practically naked, and got quite tanned. Sergeant Wetherick brought up the kit-bags for us to have a change of clothing. I erected my camp bed and slept in the open. Life for a while was pleasant and lovely.

We did some training during the afternoons because I wanted to improve the standard of wireless communication within my platoon. For this I enlisted the help of Junior, the signals officer, who had recently joined the battalion. He had been training to be a schoolmaster before he was called up. He had a ready wit and a lively sense of humour and I found him good company and a helpful friend during the rest of our service together. He let me have another signaller, Ginger, who was a Salvationist who spoke in a high-pitched squeaky voice. Ginger never drank, not even a rum ration on a cold night, and nobody could make him swear, though some of the chaps often tried to. When he joined the platoon he told me he knew more about wireless than his mate Monty who had been with us for six weeks. But very soon he settled down to be good friends with us all, and the four who made up the complement of my carrier, driver Ben, signallers Monty and Ginger and me, always got on well together.

Our wireless training was not very successful. I sent three senior NCOs out in different directions to see what range they could get out of their sets. Two of them were receiving well when 800 yards away from the control set; the third when 600 yards away. Nobody was in communication when 1,000 yards away. Yet the range of the sets was supposed to be at least 1,000 yards in the worst conditions. We rarely got these sets to work well and none of us considered them satisfactory for communication between attacking troops and the mortar position. The sets were small enough to be carried by one man in battle, but not powerful enough for battle use.

HITLER'S WORST DAY

9–18 August

The general was as good as his word; our rest was four days exactly. On the hot and dusty afternoon of 9 August we got into our vehicles again and travelled forward to catch up with the fighting. Compared with the early times in Normandy the battle was moving fast. Once it had seemed that the front line would never move; now in four days it had moved fifteen or sixteen miles. We travelled through Villers Bocage and Aunay and all of us were stunned at the extent of the destruction there. Both those towns were wiped out except for a few isolated buildings which included the tall church at Aunay. There were wide open spaces in both places and sometimes it was hardly possible to know where the roads had been. Where buildings still stood they were usually so severely damaged that the only practicable thing to do was to pull them down. The official name of the British forces at that time was the British Liberation Army (BLA), and as we gazed at the destruction and desolation of Villers Bocage Monty, my signaller, observed: 'Blimey, we've been doing some liberating here, right enough!' The sight of such complete ruination was later to become familiar in Germany.

There was a vast amount of traffic on the roads, with supplies of all kinds being brought up. After travelling what seemed many miles we passed the administrative and rear areas of other battalions. Their fighting elements were farther ahead. We had never expected that in four days the battle would move ahead so fast.

We harboured up for the night on a hillside within sight of Mont Pinçon. The situation was obscure. The commanding officer knew we would have to make an attack soon, but he knew neither the start line nor the objective. Other battalions were in action at the time, and we were to be committed when their attack was completed. I wondered whether it was necessary to dig in that evening. Nothing was known about the enemy so I thought he must be some distance away. Everything was quiet. But as I wondered my mind was made up for me by the sound of shells whistling towards me and overhead. They landed in the valley beyond our harbour area. A little while later a battery of our 25-pounder guns opened up from the valley, and I knew then where the enemy shells had been aimed. Our guns did a lot more firing but there was no more enemy activity. Colonel Turner ordered the battalion to dig in, in case the enemy resumed his artillery fire, but most of the chaps had already started digging before the order came around.

Late at night we received orders to move forward. We left our harbour area at 3 a.m. and in the dark drove over the steep Mont Pinçon, passed through a village and reached our assembly area, where we waited for several hours. We had been warned that the village at the foot of Mont Pinçon was often the target for German artillery, but there was no shelling as we went through it.

When our attack began on 11 August we had two objectives: the village of St Pierre-la-Vieille and some high ground on the right and slightly behind it known as point 229. I sited the mortars in a farmyard and, as the riflemen began their advance, gave supporting fire. Then I decided to move the weapons forward to a hedgerow near Colonel Turner's command post. Soon shells were falling all around us. After firing from there for some time I was called to the command post where I found a collection of unhappy officers sheltering behind a Sherman tank. Turner, smoking his pipe as ever, muttered an annoyed oath every now and then when a shell landed near. He had attacked initially with one company of about 100 men because there were supposed to be only thirty enemy soldiers in the village. But there were many more than thirty and the company was held up. So Turner sent a second company to help them. Good progress was made and now he desperately wanted to reinforce them with the carrier-borne weapons of anti-tank guns and mortars. He had sent an officer to reconnoitre a route and it had taken this officer twenty minutes to go 100 yards because artillery fire made him spend most of the time in a ditch. He reported that a wide and deep stream barred the way to carriers. There was a bridge over the stream, but it was being so heavily shelled that he reckoned that if carriers used the bridge fewer than half of them would get through.

The colonel ordered that one of the anti-tank guns should be put in position near the bridge in case the enemy counter-attacked with tanks. Red Reed had the job of siting this gun and he later told me it had been impossible for the crew to remain at their gun positions. They spent all their time under cover a dozen or so yards away. Had a tank alarm been given they would have had to leave their cover and man the gun, but they would then have been greatly exposed to shell fire.

On the mortar position we had some hectic moments. The shelling was heavy and several times it was so close that I thought some of us must be hit, yet always we escaped. There were several bursts very near Sergeant Johnson's section but whenever I went to see how this section was getting on I always found Johnson was keeping them calm, and they were probably wondering why I visited them so often.

In the middle of this battle, when we were firing a lot and digging in when we weren't firing, the orderly room sergeant from battalion rear headquarters arrived to tell me that Private Lorty (as I shall call him) had to go on leave immediately. And so Private Lorty put aside his mortar bombs, picked up his personal military equipment, and with a 'So long, chaps' joyously marched away. Lorty had first asked me for compassionate leave while we were at Hottot in July. I sent his application to the adjutant (the battalion's administrative officer) and no more had been heard of it. Every week he worried me, and every week I worried the adjutant. Now, about six weeks after he had put in his application, the leave was granted, and with such urgency that he had to be taken out of a battle still in progress.

Lorty's story was a tale of woe. He had been in the Malta garrison when they had fifty rounds of ammunition a man and orders to fight to the last round. He told me (jokingly?) that if Malta had been invaded it would not have taken him long to bury forty-nine of his rounds. His brother was a prisoner of war, and at the end of June 1944 his own home in London was bombed. It was to get his family fixed up in a new home that he had sought compassionate leave. Now he was on his way.

But while he was in London his family was bombed out once more, so he had more trouble to put up with. After many extensions of leave he eventually came back to us in November, when he was even more nervous than he had been previously. He refused to go into action, was examined by a doctor and found unfit.

To return to the battle, during the afternoon Colonel Turner pointed out to me a hill in front of us and told me, as I thought, to go there, establish an observation post and mortar any Germans I could see. I asked where our nearest troops were and was told they were about 300 yards from the hill, so I took a dim view of being sent on my own to an isolated point which might be infested with enemy. As I was preparing to go I noticed shells falling on the hill and I said to an artillery observation officer: 'That looks an unhealthy spot for me to be going to.'

'Are you going there?' he asked in astonishment. 'We're shelling it now!'

So I returned to the colonel and told him I would have to wait until the artillery had finished their shooting. He did not seem to understand the necessity for me to wait at all, and his attitude puzzled me and alarmed me. Then it dawned on him that there had been a misunderstanding. 'I don't want you to go there,' he said. 'I want you to mortar the hill-top from an observation post somewhere around here. That hill is probably an enemy observation post.' And so, if I had not casually spoken to the artillery officer I might gaily have wandered up to a hill I was supposed to mortar! We shot at the crest for quite a long time and we could see our bombs falling in the target area. We saw no enemy movement near there, however, so I think the assumption that it was an observation post must have been wrong.

The village of St Pierre was surrounded by a belt of woods and for some hours there was severe fighting in these woods and the streets. One of my friends told me afterwards that he had once walked around a corner to check the position of troops next to him and saw a tank in the road. He was overjoyed to think that we had got our supporting tanks up – until he recognized it was a German tank. He got around the corner again very quickly.

One remarkable humane act was performed in this battle. After a brief encounter both sides withdrew slightly, leaving their casualties in no man's land. A German came forward slowly with a Red Cross flag; so one of our stretcher bearers, with a Red Cross armlet, went out to meet him. They met in no man's land. The stretcher bearer looked at a British casualty and saw the man was dead. The German looked at his wounded and prepared to carry him back to his lines. When the German saw our stretcher bearer had nobody to carry away he made signs to him, requesting him to help carry the wounded German back. This the stretcher bearer agreed to do, and as he carried the enemy back to his medical station he passed through all the German defences. Then he walked back to our positions. At first he was walking directly in front of the line of fire of a Spandau machine-gun. Then in deference to the extreme annoyance shown by the man behind the Spandau he moved to a track to the side of his line of fire. During all this time an unofficial local truce was strictly observed.

Late in the day, when three of our rifle companies were still fighting in the area of the village, the commanding officer sent in his fourth and last company to attack point 229. This was led by Horace Wright, at that stage the only officer commanding a company who had been continuously in the campaign since D-Day. From our observation post the artillery officer and I watched the attack. We saw Horace's team round up a dozen or so prisoners, and they reached their objective without heavy fighting.

On our taking point 229 the first phase of the battle ended for us, though we still had three companies in contact with the enemy holding St Pierre. While it had been a bad day for us, running up against such stiff resistance and suffering severe casualties (fourteen dead and nearly fifty wounded), it had been a good day for our neighbouring battalions. On our left the Devons had made considerable headway and then the Dorsets had been pushed through them beyond St Pierre. In order to reinforce success our battalion was withdrawn from St Pierre and directed to move up along this left flank. Thus a very deep thrust was made towards Condé and the disorganization of the enemy was nearly completed.

The feeling among our officers was that Colonel Turner had fought this battle cleverly. The rumour was that he had never much liked the idea of a frontal attack on the village in the first place, and he had told his superiors this, and the battalion's experience seemed to have borne out his judgement. Any colonel determined to take the village at all costs could have lost most of his battalion without gaining a worthwhile prize.

The Germans were left at St Pierre but the push on the left flank cut them off from the rest of their army, and they were visited at night by a severe concentration of fire from massed medium-calibre guns. After that those who were still alive surrendered. We learned afterwards that instead of there being thirty men in the village, as we had been told, it was defended by nearly 600. When we later walked over the woods and houses that they had fortified we were astonished at the strength of their position. It seemed almost impossible for it to be taken by direct infantry assault.

The entire German defensive situation was now nearly cracked. The battle of Normandy was moving rapidly towards triumph. The huge American encircling movement from the south was fast approaching Argentan. From the north the Canadians were moving towards Falaise, only twelve miles from Argentan. And the four British thrusts at the northern perimeter of this encirclement – through Caumont, through Villers Bocage, to Thury Harcourt and towards Condé – were prospering.

But these thrusts were on a very narrow front. In our case we may have driven a corridor ten miles deep into the enemy defences but it was only about a mile wide. The enemy in front of us was demoralized, disorganized, defeated; but the enemy on our flanks was still there, firing strongly but knowing little of what was happening. Thus when we pulled away from St Pierre and drove along the road to the left to take over leading positions several miles forward we had a most uncomfortable journey, being under shellfire from the flank most of the way. I was travelling on a carrier with other officers of the orders group. As I was the last to get on it I had to sit on the top, and whereas the others could take shelter by ducking down below the sides of the vehicle all I could do was to lie flat on it and hope for the best.

That road was jammed with traffic. Squadron after squadron of tanks was moving up, and each tank made such a din that it must have been heard miles away, and kicked up a cloud of dust so high that it must have been seen miles away. No wonder German artillery was firing continuously at the road. Owing to the noise of the tanks and the carriers I could not hear the shells whistling over. Now and again I saw an explosion ahead of us, and sometimes behind us. An angry patch of thick black smoke would appear, the hedge would be torn apart, and I would lie helplessly on the carrier, cursing it for its noise and its lack of size. We were being shelled from the left, and I thought sometimes from the right too. On the left a fierce battle was raging, for I could hear the sharp report of tanks firing.

When we reached the troops who were to be relieved I found their mortar officer, looking dirty, wet and miserable, sheltering in a hole that had been dug in the hillside. Most of his platoon was scattered about so securely under cover that one had to look hard to find out where they were.

'This is the mortar position, old man,' he said cheerlessly. 'I am afraid I can tell you little about it, and everything I can say is bad news. We have only been here a few hours ourselves and most of the time I have spent in this trench. The enemy shelled us continuously when we arrived and it was murder to get out in the open. I have only got two mortars. There they are' (pointing to very good positions in a valley). 'I lost two carriers in the battle the other day, and another two got hit this morning as we were coming along the road. The enemy is in front of us, but we don't know exactly where and probably in substantial strength.

'Most of the shelling has come from the left flank, and it is big stuff that is coming over. There was a sniper in the woods on the right this morning, but after he had fired at us a couple of times a party of us went over and sorted him out. We fired Bren gun bursts at the tree tops, mortared the woods, and then we fired an anti-tank Piat at where we thought he was. He has not worried us since so I don't know whether we got him or not. Even if we didn't hit him we probably scared him so much that he has gone away. And that's about all I can tell you. Sorry it's not a cheerful tale, old man.'

We had some time to wait before the main part of our battalion arrived, so we chatted. I knew this man had landed on D-Day and of the nine battalion mortar officers in the 50th Division who had done so he was the only one who had not yet been wounded or killed. I who landed on D + 2 was the second oldest battle survivor. So I asked him: 'To what do you owe your longevity?'

'I owe it to the fact that I know everything the training manual advises and I always do the exact opposite,' he replied. 'To what do you owe yours?' he asked.

'I know what the training manual says, but I always use my own judgement,' I answered.

Conditions were very uncomfortable when the rest of our battalion marched up, about an hour before dark, for the enemy artillery on our left flank began shelling us again and I could hear explosions all around me. In addition our own medium-calibre guns began to shell St Pierre, which was 800 yards away, and some shots landed sufficiently near to us to make us wonder whether they were ours or not.

I am sure the morale of my platoon went down when they arrived to find they were under artillery fire because they had already been shelled a lot while moving along the road. None the less their morale went down still further when they asked me: 'Which way is the front, sir?' and received my reply: 'All ways. The main enemy positions are straight in front of us. Artillery fire is coming from our left flank. On the right there was a sniper in the woods this morning and he may still be there. Behind us is St Pierre, and after the artillery bombardment it is going to get this evening we have got to be ready for any stragglers who might come in from there and give themselves up.'

We were shelled before we had time to dig in and most of us took shelter behind or under the carriers. I noticed one private soldier who was usually very nervous take some writing paper out of his pack, calmly lie down on the ground and write a long letter. Presumably he found it helpful to have something positive to concentrate on. A sentry reported that he had noticed some movement in the wood where the sniper was supposed to be, so I posted an extra Bren gunner to cover that direction, but I think the report must have been false because no more movement was seen. When the enemy artillery was quiet we dug ourselves in as fast as we could. We could hear our medium-calibre guns still pounding away at St Pierre, and we realized that our artillery barrages were far mightier than the Germans'. To be at the receiving end of one of theirs was bad enough. I can scarcely imagine what it must have been like to have been at the receiving end of one of ours. It is a wonder to me that the Germans did not crack sooner than they did.

Our experience was a case of the darkest hour preceding the dawn, for by next morning we could tell that the battle had moved away from us. I reconnoitred an observation post that was actually to my rear. It was on a high point near the road along which we had previously advanced. Twenty-four hours earlier I would not have stayed there a moment longer than was necessary even if it had given me a view of all the riches in the world. Now everything was quiet. The commanding officer sent out protective patrols in three different directions and from my viewing post I watched them go out. They met no enemy and it was not necessary for me to fire in their support. The only enemy we saw from my post was a group of stragglers walking slowly and aimlessly away from St Pierre. They were going away from us and we let them alone. The artillery officer thought they were not a worthwhile target for him, so he allowed them to walk into someone else's hands.

We waited apprehensively for a bout of shelling to begin, as we always did, but no sounds of war came to our ears. We still did not wander far away from our slit trenches because one dare not take unnecessary chances. Although I refused to be over-optimistic I thought it was, to put it mildly, a good sign when I saw artillery officers wandering across the mortar positions as if they were out for a Sunday afternoon stroll. They told me they were reconnoitring gun positions for their next move, and that seemed to me to indicate that the enemy was getting farther away.

During the evening Jimmy James, our company commander, invited the officers to a bottle party at his slit trench and we all duly arrived with our spirit ration. But almost before we had opened our bottles we were disturbed by the whine of a shell which sent us all helter-skelter into the nearest trench. The shell frightened us all and destroyed most of the rations of company headquarters. Jimmy decided that the party should be broken up as he did not want all his officers annihilated by one shell. So, sheepishly tucking our bottles under our arms, we returned to our various platoons and, taking shelter in our own trenches, settled down for the night. No trouble came to us during the darkness.

But just in front of us the Dorsets were having a frightening time. In the area of their battalion headquarters shots were fired. The alarm was raised and the Dorsets started to shoot back. My opposite number, Jackie, a Canadian, jumped into his battle trench and found a German there. The German surrendered. For some moments there was frantic and confused firing, until someone realized that no more bullets were coming from enemy Spandaus or Schmeissers. All the raiders were captured and they quickly told the whole story. The Germans were pulling out and to cover their withdrawal had sent this party in to counter-attack us. But these sixty men were in no mood to counter-attack anyone, and they seemed to have no special interest in the success of the withdrawal. So they crept forward silently towards our positions and without knowing it had penetrated as far as battalion headquarters. To attract attention they loosed off a few shots and then surrendered as soon as they could to those who began to return their fire. In the confusion of the night it was some minutes before they could surrender in safety.

On hearing of this event Colonel Turner warned our rifle companies to be particularly alert at night-time in case the enemy repeated these tactics at a later date. He also emphasized that General Horrocks's estimate of the enemy was correct: some were beginning to lose their will to fight.

The battle was now won, or very nearly won. At home the newspapers reported on 14 August that General Eisenhower, supreme commander, had issued the following order of the day:

Allied soldiers, sailors and airmen – Through your combined skill, valour and fortitude you have created in France a fleeting, but definite, opportunity for a major Allied victory, one whose realization will mean notable progress towards the final downfall of our enemy.

In the past I have in moments of unusual significance made special appeals to the Allied forces it has been my honour to command. Without exception the response has been unstinted and the results beyond my expectations. Because the victory we can now achieve is infinitely greater than any it has so far been possible to accomplish in the west, and because this opportunity may be grasped only through the utmost in zeal, determination and speedy action, I make my present appeal to you more urgent than ever before.

I request every airman to make it his direct responsibility that the enemy is blasted unceasingly by day and by night, and is denied safety either in fight or in flight.

I request every sailor to make sure that no part of the hostile forces can either escape or be reinforced by sea, and that our comrades on the land want nothing that guns and ships and ships' companies can bring to them.

I request every soldier to go forward to his assigned objective with the determination that the enemy can survive only through surrender. Let no foot of ground once gained be relinquished, nor a single German escape through a line once established.

With all of us resolutely performing our special tasks we can make this week a momentous one in the history of this war – a brilliant and fruitful week for us, a fateful one for the ambitions of the Nazi tyrants.

I never found out who actually received such orders of the day. I have not met anybody who read one out or had one read to him. The cynic may think they were issued mainly to be published in the papers.

After a couple of days we returned to the village of St Pierre and the high ground near it, from where we were to protect the flank of an advance the 43rd Division was making. We travelled back in convoy and all our vehicles were left in a thick orchard while we specialist platoon commanders were given quick orders and ran off to do hurried reconnaissances. Colonel Turner wanted the mortars in the east of the village because he thought that was the safest part of it, so I went off to choose a position there. But I had not been following the way on a map when we entered the village, and while I was selecting landmarks by which to orient myself the colonel saw me walking westwards. His remarks to me were so plain that it was unnecessary for me to orient myself further. I simply walked in the opposite direction and knew that must be right.

I located a good mortar position on the reverse slope of a

wooded hill. The distance between the trees was just enough to allow a clear field of fire in any direction. Most of the chaps did not dig in here as we seemed a long way from the battle and were merely in a protective role in case the flanks were threatened. However, I noticed a warrant officer making somebody dig a deep slit trench for him. 'I'm taking no chances, sir,' he explained. 'Do you remember on that hill behind Mont Pinçon that I was digging in when nobody else was, when all of a sudden the enemy sent a few shells over? You couldn't see the fellows for dust after that, they were digging so fast.'

My insistence on always establishing an observation post led my platoon to regard me as a nuisance. With the enemy out of sight they were quite willing to relax and go to sleep, but I said we had been put there to protect a flank and we could not protect it unless we observed. I set out with two sergeants to reconnoitre a suitable post and, having settled on a satisfactory one, noticed Colonel Turner walking with another officer across some fields. The colonel stopped and looked studiously at a map, and it was evident when he approached me that he was uncertain of his exact position, so with some pride and attempted diffidence I read out the map reference of where he was standing. He looked at the ground around him and said: 'Yes, that's right,' and as he continued on his reconnaissance I hoped I had atoned for my map-reading shortcomings earlier in the day.

Our observation post gave a view of quite interesting and pleasant country. One could see two ranges of low hills, with a valley between them, and there was also a wooded valley between our post and the first range. Although the observer had a view of miles of countryside a lot was hidden by woods and hills. The NCOs took it in turn to man the post for two hours. They were not lonely because there was a section of Bren gun carriers nearby and a company of riflemen a few hundred yards away. I visited the post once or twice every day and I used to check regularly that our wireless communication was working satisfactorily.

It was while we were in that restful position, on 15 August to be exact, that Hitler learnt the full details of his army's defeat. He was absolutely shattered. 'This is the worst day of my life,' he moaned to his staff.

Though neither I nor my friends knew it at the time, the Allied forces under the command of General Montgomery had inflicted on the German army the biggest single military catastrophe that Hitler suffered throughout the entire war; bigger than the surrender of one of his armies at Stalingrad, bigger than the destruction of his tanks by the Russians in the great battle around Kursk.

We knew our victory was huge, but we did not know how huge. Soon the whole of Britain knew a lot. 'German armies in rout. Victory is complete,' ran the *Daily Express* headline on 19 August. 'We have won a decisive victory in Normandy,' wrote Alexander Clifford in the *Daily Mail*. Clifford's article went on:

> The German Seventh Army is now in full retreat. You can state this tremendous news as simply as that today. Overnight the situation has suddenly become sharp, clear and overwhelmingly important. The Germans here are defeated. That is what has, in fact, happened.
>
> Most of those German divisions are, after all, still trapped in the pocket. Only yesterday did the Germans themselves recognize the extent of their plight. The gap is now down to three or four doubtful miles. The panzer divisions are trying to fight their way through it in a tremendous running battle. You can call the victory decisive without hesitation. It does not mean that the Germans will immediately cease fighting. It does not mean that this particular battle will not drag

on for a few days yet. It does not even guarantee a big bag of prisoners in the end.

But it does mean the best German divisions are irretrievably mauled and disorganized. It means they can never again bring a really serious force against us in western Europe. It means they will probably never again be able to organize any sort of a front in France. All our thrust is north-east now. The British and Canadians on the left and the Americans on the right are heading straight for the Seine. Between our stretching arms the Germans who fight their way out of the little pocket find themselves being still embraced and funnelled towards the bridgeless river.

The clue to today's situation is that the Germans never really knew they were trapped. They thought they could counter-attack against the Americans and shoulder off that whole southern flank. They thought they could break the trap instead of merely escaping from it. But something happened at midday yesterday. Someone suddenly got the true facts. A fantastic scramble to leave the pocket began. The German defeat was abruptly and glaringly revealed.

All yesterday afternoon German vehicles began to appear in the lanes and fields between Falaise and Argentan. They were all wildly striving to get east, every man for himself. The Seine ferries started to operate in daylight for the first time.

The tanks began to shoot their way east. The news spread from unit to unit. Right in the middle of the pocket they began to hand out white flags and table-cloths to the air forces. They could not really surrender because the units all around them were not surrendering. So the air force told them to keep right on waving or they would be bombed . . .

To get the full flavour of this victory, to realize why

153

the crisis had crystallized so suddenly, you must add up the three big blunders the Germans have made since D-Day. And you must keep in mind all the time their fatal blind spot – their lack of information.

Their first blunder was that they did not bring down enough strength at the beginning. They knew their best chance was to seal us up in Normandy. But they were terrified of another landing somewhere else. So they did not have enough troops here, and we broke out at the western end.

Their second blunder was when the pocket was forming. They sought to put matters right by a wild spectacular drive back to the sea at Avranches. That failed, and the pocket became a serious fact.

Their third blunder was the idea that they could break this trap instead of simply escaping from it. They thought the whole solution was to counter-attack at Argentan and swing back the whole American advance.

Back of it all – the crucial factor – is their lack of information. They cannot send up reconnaissance planes, their patrolling has never been good, they get nothing from prisoners. They simply cannot find out what is happening . . .

On 22 August the newspapers were reporting that General Montgomery had told his troops: 'The end of the war is in sight. Let us finish off the business in record time.'

In fact the German army had been executed in the Falaise gap. Coming up from the south the Americans had pushed a light screen as far as Argentan but did not have the strength to go further. From the north the Canadians had slowly battled their way to Falaise. Along the perimeter that had once been the Normandy beachhead the British had hammered the enemy. Now the Germans had to escape through a twelve-mile Falaise–Argentan gap before the Allies could close it. All the time they were very heavily bombed by the RAF and they were exposed to continuous observed artillery fire. For a long time our gunners simply loaded and fired, switching their aim from one target to another as they detected the various signs of frenzied activity. The killing was horrendous.

Among the impedimenta captured was a letter from a German soldier to his family. 'Lucky are they who become prisoners of war. It is a slaughterhouse here. The big pots always manage to clear out and the ordinary soldier bites the dust. Everything is topsy-turvy. We are retreating.'

Our battalion spent four relaxed sunny days in our reserve position; then we became non-operational and busied ourselves with preparations for our next move. Major Drewitt, second in command, called a conference of Support Company platoon commanders to consider how best we could lighten the load on our carriers, for he told us to prepare for a long journey. In the course of two months' fighting a lot of spoils of war and private souvenirs had been collected and were being carried on the vehicles. In addition many of us were starting to value our comfort and several extra blankets as well as a large amount of crockery had found their way on to most carriers. Plates were very popular because they made a meal a thousand times more appetizing than mess-tins did. All this overloaded the carriers and they looked now more like removal vans than fighting vehicles, so we had to cut down a lot.

I secured permission for an extra 15-hundredweight truck to come in my column and then had all the vehicles stripped of everything they contained. Then we gradually loaded them: weapons, ammunition, wireless sets, telephones, rations, small packs (containing toilet requisites, writing paper, etc.), personal web equipment, petrol cans and men. At Hottot some members of the platoon had seen an anti-tank gun carrier hit and as it had petrol cans in the seating compartments it caught alight; so we strapped the petrol cans on to the backs of the vehicles, the drivers refusing to have them anywhere else.

We also fitted several stays at the rear of each vehicle, and to these we secured mortar barrels in such a manner that we could unload them quickly and thus come into action without delay in an emergency. Eventually we had everything we needed on the vehicles and not much more, and we had it all where we could get to it easily. It may not have been wholly orthodox but it was what, in the light of experience, we wanted.

6

The Race to Brussels

NEW TYPE OF WARFARE

We were about to enter a new phase of the campaign, but I do not think any of the troops guessed how great was going to be the difference between the new type of warfare and the old. For two months we had fought for every yard of land. As we advanced we had looked with suspicion and fear at every hedge, house and hillock. We had come to regard every crest and every wood as inevitably inhabited by the enemy and we had learned that tremendous artillery support and endless automatic fire were necessary to dislodge him.

We had contested possession of an orchard with the German army for a fortnight or three weeks. We had fought a major battle for a tiny village and we had failed to take another village even though three companies attacked it. With all this as our past experience, how could we be expected to understand that there would be no opposition to our crossing of important river bridges and to our entering large towns and cities?

True, the fighting had yielded more results lately. In the battle for St Pierre the Dorsets and Devons had gained several thousand yards and held it; whereas in the bad old days of Hottot the Hampshires, Dorsets and Devons had gained several hundred yards between us in an energetic attack and had then given up most of the ground we had won.

True, the St Lô breakthrough had unhinged the German

army and given us room to manoeuvre, so that although we might still have to make a few frontal attacks there would always be somebody getting round to the rear of the enemy.

True, the news of General Patton's gigantic sweep had set us all agog; and the massacre in the Falaise gap had crippled the German army.

We understood all that and we hoped and expected that progress in the future would be easier. But we did not dream that our victory in the Normandy battle was going to pay such a rich dividend that not only towns, or even provinces, but whole countries were about to fall into our hands, and that in a few weeks we would be rejoicing in Brussels. The nature of the advance astonished us. Our wonder grew with every kilometre we travelled, every town we entered, every frontier we crossed.

While we were still at St Pierre Colonel Turner explained to us the form future operations were likely to take. He said generally the battalion would travel behind an armoured force, and whereas the armour might have to keep going continuously, we would move by bounds, waiting till the tanks had a lead of ten or twenty miles and then travelling that distance in one spell. We would then harbour up and wait possibly a few hours or a few days till the armour had gone twenty miles ahead again, then bound forward to catch them up. The tactical role of the armour was to get moving and keep moving; our tactical duty was to mop up everything they left behind and form a firm base behind them wherever they went.

Our battalion column contained something like 130 vehicles; thus if lorries were forty yards apart we would take up three miles of road. We had to watch the spacing, because if vehicles bunched too closely together they would present a tempting target for the German air force. On the other hand, if they were spread out too much we would occupy a lot of road space and that would make progress slow, as we were just a small part of a great column.

On a typical move an armoured division, with 200 tanks, three battalions of lorry-borne infantry and a vast assortment of other vehicles, would lead, followed by an infantry division of which we were but a ninth part. With ambulances, supply vehicles, repair trucks and lorried equipment for supporting weapons added in, the two divisions would contain thousands of vehicles, so if the infantry were to be anywhere near the armour, and supplies anywhere near either of them, each vehicle would have to keep reasonably close to the one in front of it.

We were frequently warned to expect opposition from the German air force, for as we drove eastwards we would be approaching their bases, but not once did they trouble us. Their absence surprised me in Normandy. I saw them attacking the beach just after D-Day and only on one other occasion did I see any number of planes. That was towards the end of June when I saw about twenty aircraft flying quite high behind our lines and being vigorously shot at by our gunners. Apart from that, I saw only three German aircraft, all lone reconnaissance planes cloud-hopping on misty days. I concluded from this that the German air force had been wiped out (three cheers for the RAF!), and as we sped eastward I never really took seriously any warning about them. As it happened, they did not trouble us. Major Drewitt, with his usual meticulous care for detail, ordered that Bren gunners should be positioned in various vehicles as air sentries.

On these long moves from Normandy to Brussels no infantryman footslogged. Speed was essential in pursuing this defeated enemy, so riflemen were bundled into lorries, Bren gun carriers, jeeps, vehicles of all descriptions – but mainly 3-ton TCVs (troop-carrying vehicles) – and driven forward. When fighting was likely to develop they jumped out of their vehicles and ran into battle formation. The scare over, or the battle over, whichever it proved to be, they returned to their lorries and resumed the journey on wheels.

Our battalion always moved in the same order of march: Ken Edwards, his caution never relaxed, leading with a section of Bren gun carriers, behind him the vanguard rifle company, then battalion headquarters, followed by the other three rifle companies. The supporting arms were divided among the rifle companies and placed under their command so that they would be close at hand if any section of the column was attacked on the road. That arrangement made life easy for some of the specialist platoon commanders, and for a long time I travelled in a carrier in the middle of the column playing a very inconspicuous part.

Edwards had strict orders to travel at 12 m.p.h., and Colonel Turner used to worry him so much about this that in the end he used to sit in his carrier and never let his eyes wander from the speedometer. Such a speed may seem modest but in some unaccountable way the lorries at the end of the column were always having to travel at 30 or 40 m.p.h. to keep their place. Now and again vehicles broke down and if they could not be repaired immediately the soldiers had to be transferred to another lorry or carrier. These long moves were a great strain on tracked vehicles like carriers and every time one broke down a greater load was placed on the others. There was very little time for the drivers to carry out their maintenance tasks and it was really a wonder so many of the vehicles kept going. I very rarely had more than one off the road and more often than not all my seven carriers and three trucks were roadworthy.

We were sometimes in a harbour area for three or four days, but all the time we were at a few hours' notice to move and it was thus impossible for the drivers to strip and clean their engines. On a typical day we would be told at reveille that no move was likely before 1100 hours. Just at eleven o'clock we would be told: 'No move before 1400 hours.' This would later be amended to: 'Prepare to move at 1600 hours', which in turn would be cancelled by a notice saying: 'No move until tomorrow.' That was always dangerous information, because on receipt of that message the chances were ten to one that in a few hours' time we would be ordered: 'Move immediately.' This may sound as if the army muddled through, but there was a perfectly reasonable explanation for these conflicting warning orders. We had to be ready to get on the road immediately the armour made substantial progress. Sometimes the tanks went on steadily; sometimes they were held up; then they might find an easy way forward. Each change in the battle echoed back to us. And in those times of confusion and bewilderment in the German army our spearhead situation was ever-changing.

The result was we ate many a meal in haste to find the haste unnecessary. We erected many a watertight bivouac (bivvy) which we never rested in, and prepared many a comfortable bed which we did not sleep in. Sometimes, when the hours of waiting grew into days and still we did not move from our harbour area, we wished we had made ourselves more comfortable when first we arrived. Only one shortcoming would have been inexcusable – not moving at the right time when finally ordered on to the road, however short the notice or whatever the previous order.

EVIL PICTURES
19–25 August

The distance of our first move was about twelve miles. All vehicles were marshalled in a large field near St Pierre half an hour before we were due to move. The battalion's motor transport officer rode round and round on his motor-bike satisfying himself that everything was correct; and then we formed up in our order of march, with Ken Edwards leading the way in his carrier. It was a sunny afternoon, 19 August, and as we motored along the roads the countryside seemed strangely quiet and peaceful. It might have been a part of England. There was a certain amount of abandoned equipment on the road to Condé, and it seemed unreal for us to be allowed to drive over these battlefields without let or hindrance. It was almost as if we had been lifted into a post-war period and were now touring the scene of past battles. Almost like that, but not quite.

Our caution did not relax. We still looked suspiciously at every hedgerow and every farm building. As we travelled over a ravine near the entrance to Condé I was thankful we did not have to fight our way across that obstacle because it was a natural defensive position, formidable and imposing. We rumbled through this old-world town which was badly battered about and looked deserted. The Noireau was so narrow that it hardly seemed worthy to be called a river. Some days earlier an engineers' party had reconnoitred Condé while the enemy was still in the vicinity, and when they came back they told us that they could hear sounds of drunken German soldiers making merry with women, who were presumably French. The bulk of the German forces had pulled out by then and it seemed probable that those who stayed behind were stragglers waiting to surrender who were having one last taste of the joys of wine and women before their inevitable entry into prisoner-of-war cages.

We harboured finally near the town of Flers. The route we had been given took us as far as the dispersal point in the centre of Flers, and at this point Red Reed, the anti-tank platoon officer, was stationed, directing the companies into their various areas. The mortar area was simply a field, but I did not complain at that because it was a large field, large enough for us to space ourselves out comfortably, and it was clean. In those days we expected no more than that. The time would come, towards the end of the campaign in

Germany, when troops would expect to find several large and comfortable houses in a harbour area.

Having got all my platoon safely in this field and allotted each section a different area of it, I now had to find Jimmy James, my company commander, to learn what he knew about the situation. Where was the enemy? Was it necessary for us to dig in? Would we be here long? How many guards were needed? Where was battalion headquarters? Did we have a battle task? Jimmy knew little. All he had been able to discover was that 'we would probably be here long enough for the troops to have a meal'. Later we learnt that the armour was some miles in front of us and still going forward. Although there was no opposition from enemy soldiers their progress was slow because of the many obstacles that had been placed in the road. The German soldier was always a hard worker. He dug deeper and more often than our chaps did, and his defence works always bore evidence of much industry. If he made up his mind to block our way by obstructions we could depend on finding those obstructions numerous and substantial. So for a long time the tanks could only move slowly and their crews spent a great deal of time removing huge trees that had been felled across the road and blowing up earthen road blocks.

As far as we were concerned the Germans had disappeared completely into the blue, so there was no need for us to dig protective slit trenches and we needed only a minimum of sentries. A deep latrine had to be dug in each platoon area, and once this was done the chaps concentrated on cooking their supper. Those sections that had serviceable petrol cookers used them; those sections whose cookers were unserviceable had to use open fires. We carried water cans with us, and when these were empty we filled them up from the battalion water cart, if it came around, and from the local water supply if it did not. We had many times been warned not to use the local water supply, but on occasions we were allowed to use it, if the water was boiled.

Drivers that evening were busy checking their engines and filling up with petrol from the motor transport department. Once the meal was over we prepared our beds. Each carrier carried a tarpaulin that was large enough to cover the vehicle and crew. So we laid our groundsheets on the grass, stretched out the tarpaulin to act as a roof over our heads, rolled our blankets and overcoats around us and, if we were lucky, slept.

If the weather was warm, the night dry, and the earth soft, one's bed would be comfortable. The tarpaulin was always fixed low over our heads in order to make a cosy bivvy, while in platoon headquarters we had an additional degree of comfort because Monty was usually able to get the BBC programme on his wireless set. At news time the fellows would always crowd around to hear the latest developments and they were always welcome whenever they came. Officially I suppose that wireless should have been used for military purposes only, but news keeps up a fellow's morale and I chose to regard that as a military purpose, as I think everybody else did. After the news there was liable to be soft lilting music, which aided sleep.

Flers was the first bit of France I had seen that had not been the site of a battle. Its citizens were the first I had met who had not witnessed the details of warfare with their own eyes. For us to see instead of the accustomed ruins, a town; instead of signs of death, life, was a refreshing experience. In Normandy we saw nothing but destruction: wrecked farmsteads, damaged villages, obliterated towns. I was familiar with the dismal face of the French peasant, the look of gloom, the look of despair, the look that might have meant anything. Lord knows those Normans suffered! It was a strange kind of liberation we brought them. For many, caught inescapably in a battle, it was the liberation of death.

But in Flers everything was different. The sun was shining, the houses were standing, the roads were clear, men and women were smiling and walking about in civilian clothes. It was Sunday, and whole families were going to church, as whole families used to in England a generation or two ago. There was father, with a rough complexion and a rather ill-fitting dark suit; mother, holding her hat on in the breeze, and wearing a dress that somehow or other looked as if it was worn only on Sundays; their daughter, teen-age, dressed in black, looking a little prim, and not daring to cast a glance at the strange soldiers on the right or on the left, but very conscious of their presence; and the young boy, on his best behaviour, his knees conspicuously clean, and walking quietly by his father's side. Where else could they be going but to church?

Seeing all these people walking in the streets gave me the impression that we were no longer in a battle area. I gazed at the folk, for I had lived with and looked at only fighting men for eight weeks and here were civilians, girls! It must be like that in England, I thought. Men and women going about their daily tasks, or their weekly devotions, dressed in ordinary clothes, leading ordinary lives. And here were we, soldiers all, men everywhere, a whole desert of men and not a single oasis of women anywhere, every man dressed alike except for a few stripes or pips and all with thoughts of war in our minds.

I wondered what those citizens of Flers thought of the English soldiers who had so suddenly descended upon them and camped in their fields. The civilians were quiet and not very demonstrative. We received a little wave occasionally, and that was all. They seemed afraid to let themselves go. But I had always been told that was an English, not a French, characteristic. I think they must have been frightened by their narrow escape, for the Germans had retreated practically to their doorstep before they broke and fled.

Liberation was not then in vogue, and probably they thought that had their town been situated twelve miles nearer the coast they might have experienced the usual slaughter that war brings instead of witnessing the hasty departure of the German army.

We remained at Flers for a few days, all the time dreading that our enemy would reappear. We had the warning orders that were to become usual, and the cancellations, and when we did move, on 22 August, our route was to take us through Argentan. The land there is slightly rolling country and as we drove over a hill we could see the town four or five miles away. The corn in the fields was tall and it looked as if the reapers should have started work on it long ago. Everywhere was the wreckage of battle; burntout German motor transport, shattered Sherman tanks, Spandau machine-guns and all the other disfigurements which fouled Europe's countryside for so many years. Argentan was badly knocked about, though the damage was not as terrible as I had expected and its inhabitants were bravely trying to repair what buildings they could. It appears that the road the Germans used for their retreat was nearer to Falaise than here.

Colonel Turner travelled along that road and he reported to us that the sight and stench of all the casualties nearly made him sick. It seemed a dreadful thing for us to have done to the enemy, he said, until one remembered what kind of enemy the German was. He told us of a photograph that he had seen that was found on the body of an enemy soldier. The photograph showed a civilian being hanged from a lamp-post in a street. About twenty German troops were watching the hanging, and someone had taken a photograph of the scene showing the men laughing. One soldier, seeing himself in the photo, had drawn a circle around his face and marked it: 'That's me.' He carried the photo about with him, evidently proud to show it to his friends.

British soldiers who had to arrange for the burials of some of the Germans near Falaise told me that the destruction of men and materials was unbelievable. The stink was so strong that they wore respirators while handling the bodies.

Months later when I was in Germany I took the opportunity to look through the family album of some German people in whose house my platoon was resting. In the album were the usual photographs – mother and father, son (in uniform), his fiancée, a few friends, father's house; and mixed up with all these snaps were a few atrocious ones. One picture showed a dead man on the battlefield. Those who have fought know how ghastly a casualty can look if he has been severely hit by blast and shrapnel. On seeing a dead comrade the British Tommy would wince and look the other way. But the German had stopped, taken out his camera (which he must have carried for that purpose), and snapped the casualty so as to expose the most horrible wounds. He duly had the snap developed and placed in an honoured position in the family album. There were other photographs (all in this album) of dead men hanging from lamp-posts; and so many snaps of graveyards and material destruction that it seemed to me that death and devastation had a strange fascination for this family. Before we saw this photograph album some of my platoon had begun to regard this family as 'good Germans'!

Going through Argentan we noticed that a headquarters was being established there and the sight of a private in the Royal Corps of Signals laying a telephone line provoked a heated argument in my carrier. Monty remarked that a signaller in the Corps of Signals received extra pay for being a signaller and he thought therefore he should receive extra pay too as he was a signaller. Ben, my driver, asked what signallers did to warrant extra pay. Why didn't drivers receive extra? There developed a fierce argument as to whether signaller or driver was the more deserving. I kept quiet, but my own reaction was that I would consider myself lucky if I got extra pay for tying lengths of wire together to help rear headquarters communicate with forward fighting troops. The system of army pay was quaint. An army presumably exists to fight, yet those who fought (infantry, tank crews, gunners) got little pay, while those who serviced them (Corps of Signals, Royal Electrical and Mechanical Engineers, Pay Corps, etc.) got more.

Once through Argentan we were held in readiness to clear some woods where it was thought Germans might be hiding, but we were subsequently ordered to move on without going through the woods.

During this pursuit Ken Edwards often used to say to me: 'You know, there might easily be thousands of Germans behind our lines. All we do is to motor along the roads. It is possible for them to remain in hiding for weeks. We might wake up one morning and find them in our rear.' However, the German soldier was not superhuman, and with his supplies gone, his command gone, his friends gone, his communication gone, he invariably lost the will to fight and was ready to surrender.

Whenever we moved the route was well marked with our divisional sign, but these could not easily be seen in the dark and as we moved through l'Aigle in the pitch darkness of the night of 23 August I did not envy Ken his task of finding the way. It was a wonder to me he never failed. It was raining heavily, so some outhouses of a farm were chosen for our harbour area. The farmers told us that two Germans had been there a few hours earlier but, although we searched the area thoroughly, we did not find them. Owing to the bad roads and the blackness of the night one or two of our vehicles were ditched and others were held up to allow another convoy to come through. Fortunately all my platoon arrived early and we quickly took off our wet anti-gas capes, which were supposed to be waterproof but were not entirely so, erected our tarpaulins and settled down to sleep. Ken, who had some carriers held up, waited in the rain for several hours before the last of the battalion column arrived. He did not get many hours' sleep that night.

We waited a few days between l'Aigle and Verneuil to allow other troops to move along the roads. We heard that the Seine had been crossed at Mantes and Vernon and soon after that Paris had been liberated. This was astounding news and when we shouted 'Paree libérée' to Frenchmen they seemed to know already. Finally we moved through St André to Pacy-sur-Eure, a few miles from the Seine, and there we heard the ominous sound of guns once more. The battle was only a few miles away, and our joy at reaching the Seine so swiftly and safely was tempered by the belief that we would soon be committed again to battle.

We were losing our TCVs (large troop-carrying vehicles), so evidently the fighting was only marching distance away. I noticed one platoon commander holding an inspection of weapons. I waited anxiously for orders. The intelligence officer had no definite news to pass on but he was pessimistic. I tried to obtain some information from the intelligence sergeant but all he could say, with indignation, was that his officer no longer kept him fully informed, apparently not trusting him to keep secrets. But I think the officer was right. He told us all it was good for us to know and, as he said, if anyone was captured he would be glad he did not have any especially secret information that must be kept to himself at all costs.

With Jimmy James and Ken Edwards I weighed up the possibilities of the future; we did not like the situation. Jimmy said when he arrived at the dispersal point at Pacy he could tell the battle was very near. We had had an easy advance up to the Seine, and it came as a jolt to think in terms of battles once more. But to have reached the river line was remarkable. I remembered the days of Hottot when the beachhead was ever so small. On newspaper maps of Europe it was scarcely large enough to be seen. In those days the Seine seemed an incredible distance away, far beyond our reach. Now we were there.

When Colonel Turner called the officers together it was to pass on a rocket he had received from his superior. Whenever the troops moved along the road the brigadier commanding our formation stood somewhere near the start point and waited to be saluted by the driver's mate of every vehicle. If the vehicle was an open one the mate had to stand up and salute; if the vehicle was closed he could sit to attention and salute. The brigadier always returned all salutes. Now he had told the colonel that driver's mates were not saluting him and only about fifty per cent of the officers were. Dear, oh dear!

His second complaint was that the straps of webbing equipment were being worn over the shoulder epaulettes of the battle-dress jacket, whereas they should be worn under. (I used to wonder why carrier crews had to wear them at all!)

Thirdly, when wearing berets in future we would have to have a coloured backing behind our cap badges; the brigadier left it to the battalion to decide what colour we desired. Turner was unwilling to make this decision because he was not a formal member of the Hampshire Regiment and he regarded that as a question for regimental officers to decide. So, with the enemy half an hour's ride away, with our future operations unknown, we solemnly discussed for three quarters of an hour whether the backing on our badges should be red for infantry or black and amber for the Hampshire Regiment. I think I saw a faint smile creep across Turner's face. Perhaps like me he was unable to take any of the proceedings seriously. I cannot remember what colour we eventually chose but I know we could not get that colour and we lived for many more months, quite happily too, without any stiff backing to our cap badges.

Finally, when this momentous question was settled, Colonel Turner announced that we were now keeping our TCVs and I judged from that that we had some more motoring to do before we took to fighting, so I went to bed with an easy mind.

We remained at Pacy for a few days and one afternoon I took a jeep and drove into the town to see what it looked like. There was military traffic everywhere, and it was all moving in different directions so, not willing to be caught in the middle of a convoy, I left Pacy and drove towards Vernon. There was a lot of transport on that road and I noticed General Horrocks pass me, driving his own car at high speed. Apart from a couple of ambulances going back with casualties there was little sign of fighting. As there was no shelling and people were walking about as if they did not expect any, I drove right into Vernon. The town had suffered a lot of damage; damage so great that it could only have been done by heavy bombing. Possibly the bridge over the river had been attacked several times before D-Day.

A number of shops were open and in one I bought a bottle of perfume for my girlfriend in London. Before I returned I had a drink in an *estaminet* that was well patronized by British soldiers. The mademoiselle touched my pips, counting 'Un, deux, trois. What is that?' she asked. Someone told her a captain, so she said, apparently thrilled: 'Oh, monsieur le capitaine,' and beamed at me and stood ready for me to order another drink.

The river Seine is wide. It may not seem wide if you are going from bank to bank in a pleasure craft, but it definitely does if you are going across in an assault boat. Beyond the far bank were two high peaks, and at one time these must have given the enemy observation of Vernon and the surrounding country, making it very difficult for the Allies to cross. Fortunately we had got across very quickly, but I could not help thinking what a formidable undertaking the river assault must have been.

When I returned to our harbour area and spread the news that I had been to Vernon and found it quiet and that the hills on the other side of the river seemed deserted, the morale of the chaps went up. The farther the enemy was away, the higher was their morale.

A TUMULTUOUS RECEPTION

26 August–1 September

We soon got our orders for the next move. But first of all the commanding officer told us that although there were plenty more American reinforcements there were no more British reinforcements, and in order to keep the divisions up to full strength it was necessary to disband one division and post the men from this one to the others. So the 59th Division was disbanded. I accepted the fact then that there were no additional reinforcements in England. We had deployed our full strength and that was that. But I later found people who believed that there were many soldiers in England, in training establishments and reserve divisions, who had not been in action and were never to go into action. I would have thought it would have been possible to staff these places entirely with men who had been wounded or who had had long experience in battle. That would have shared the hardships more evenly.

V1s (pilotless bomb-carrying aircraft) were becoming a real menace at that time, Colonel Turner told us, and General Horrocks's corps was going to drive north and north-east to Antwerp and thus cut off the Pas de Calais. Every mile we gained would reduce the number of bombs falling on London. There were three main As on the route,

Amiens, Arras and Antwerp, and the advance was going to total 240 miles. It was thought the Germans might have at the most 200 tanks in our way, so a force of 500 tanks was going to engage them. (We subsequently read in the papers that British troops were driving forward with the words 'every mile gained is a bomb less on London' on their lips.)

Our move from the Seine to Amiens was very similar to that from Flers to the Seine, except that by now we were beginning to believe that great advances were possible. Turner, with typical perceptive judgement, told us that as the Germans had not stood on the Seine their next possible river line was the Somme, but he personally did not think they would fight again until they reached their homeland. Among the troops was a feeling of expectancy. We thought we had seen the last of the German army. I believed the war would be over in a few weeks and that the man who had prophesied a six-month campaign would prove to be a pessimist. One of our officers thought the war would last at least until November, but most of us thought that was practically impossible. We were very conscious of the fact that we were winning. Some of us thought we had won. The advance seemed too easy and Monty (my wireless operator) could not understand how it was all happening. I told him repeatedly that it was the fruits of the victory he had helped to win in Normandy. At first he thought I was pulling his leg; then, when I kept saying it, he thought I was simply trying to raise his morale.

We travelled again behind an armoured force and moved irrespective of daylight or darkness. If the starting time was dawn we had to breakfast in darkness and, as we were not allowed to show any lights, open fires were not permitted. So if a petrol cooker was not working we had to find a nearby building and light our fire there. If the move was a long one we ate what rations we could in the carriers, and when we reached our harbour area we hurried to get our supper ready before dark. If we had no orders to move on a certain day we liked to breakfast early in case there was a change of plan and we were wanted on the road immediately. It was always a toss-up whether to cook a midday dinner or not. If we decided to cook, the chances were that there would be a hurried move before we had time to eat; if we decided to have a cold meal midday it was ten to one we would move during the evening and arrive at our new area in darkness. Then we would have to prepare a warm supper under cover somewhere and erect our bivvies in the dark.

On days that we did not move, but waited to, we spent the time brewing tea. It was a marvel how our cooks got six pints out of the ration. But however far they made the tea ration go, I told them to make it go farther. On rainy days life could be dismal because several of our tarpaulins leaked and the chaps found it boring to sit under these bivvies, listening to the rain beating down and watching some of it come through. You could brew a cup of tea, you could write a letter, but what else could you do? Wait. Wait for orders, and then when they came it always meant moving in a rush.

Operationally we were very lucky and had very little fighting to do. We combed woods, sent out protective patrols, caught a few stragglers, and that was about all. But, of course, when one went out on patrol there was tension in the air, for one did not know the area would be clear until one had been there and investigated. One might have to fight and, with the war racing to its finish, this was not the time to become a casualty. Ken Edwards, who continued to lead our column, was very wary. Approaching any village he looked anxiously to see whether their flags were flying. If so, he knew they had been liberated and he led the column in with an easy mind; if not, he went very cautiously, observing all the while.

I shall never forget those tumultuous days at the end of

August when France warmed to its liberation. Apples and pears were thrown at us as we passed through the villages, bottles of local 'firewater' were placed in our hands, little delicacies of food that we knew people could ill spare were showered upon us whenever we stopped for a moment, and it was all given with moving eagerness.

The young and middle-aged waved flags, shook our hands, danced in the streets, kissed us and behaved with enthusiasm and excitement.

A woman walking on her own along a country road clapped her hands continuously and said 'Merci, merci' all the time our column of 130 vehicles rumbled past her.

Old men wept for joy; old men who had fought their war and won it a quarter of a century previously and had lived through the shame and horror that had come to them when the next generation did not win over again what was really the same war. Outside one house a bearded man in shabby clothes stood rigidly to attention and at the salute while we passed. At a street corner nearby an elderly gentleman stood and solemnly beat a drum as we rolled by. He beat a deadly monotonous tune, but so firmly were his feet set apart, so decided his beat and so fixed his expression that one could see he regarded this as a military duty and he was as conscientious about it as if the whole success of the campaign depended on whether he beat his drum in a dignified manner or not.

In some villages the population brought chairs out of doors and sat on these all day long as different troops drove through. It was indeed for them the occasion of a lifetime. On all faces were such expressions of thankfulness and joy as I had not seen anywhere before. I was confident that they would remember Britain with gratitude for the rest of their lives.

For us also it was unforgettable. All the troops were deeply moved. 'Gentlemen in England now abed, shall think themselves accursed they were not here' – those lines were in my mind often. I wished then that we had had in our army the annoying young printer's apprentice I knew in Jersey who used to ask: 'What would it matter if the Nazis rule us? Would the man in the street be any worse off?' And the hairdresser who said: 'All governments are out for their own ends. I don't see that one is different from the rest.' These people would have received eloquent replies if they had helped in the liberation and seen the people they were liberating. I do not suppose anyone who did not undergo a Nazi occupation can understand what it meant, nor what the ending of it meant.

We travelled on 30 August via Crèvecoeur-le-Grand to Amiens, and it took us about an hour to get through Amiens for the streets were chock-a-block with military transport. The townsfolk looked on with amazement. They were surprised at being liberated – it seemed they could hardly believe at last they were free, although they had been freed the previous day by our advanced elements – but they were far more surprised at the vast amount of military equipment we had. I am sure they could have seen no such exhibition of strength by the Nazis, even in their hour of triumph. Tanks, artillery and lorried infantry were all in the town, and vehicles were nose to tail. I do not know for how many hours before our entry military traffic had been passing through Amiens, nor for how many hours after it continued to do so, but I had the impression that the road leading north-east from the town contained one solid block of transport. The citizens looked all ways, and wherever they looked they saw the British army. I wonder how long it was before their astonishment died away.

We camped that day in the woods five miles out of Amiens. We just had time to cook and eat our suppers before nightfall. When I went to sleep there was no news of what might happen in the morning. At midnight a runner from company headquarters woke me up and said the battalion had to move just before dawn. I told him to tell the guard to arouse the platoon an hour before it was light. When I awoke drenching rain was falling and the night was as black as could be. Under our tarpaulin we tried to get a fire going and cook breakfast. We succeeded – but believe me, cooking in the dark and eating in the dark is not a luxury. Because of the rain we kept our bivvies erected until the last possible moment, and then, in our haste and the darkness, we accidentally left behind one tarpaulin and one box of rations. But we got on the road in time, and with the coming of the morning the rain stopped.

We travelled thirty-five miles to reach Arras about 1100 hours, and on arrival there the commanding officer hurriedly gave out orders. Our task was to hold the town against any possible counter-attack, so he deployed the rifle companies along the main approaches. He told me to site my platoon in a central position so that I would be able to bring down fire in any direction. I made a careful, and I confess a rather long, reconnaissance of Arras and in the end, with the aid of Sergeant Wetherick, found what I was looking for – a garden large enough for six mortars to be sited in, surrounded by substantial walls for our protection, and with a large factory adjoining where we could enjoy shelter and rest. We were not required to fire. I visited the companies to see exactly where they were in case of emergency.

We soon made ourselves comfortable in the factory, where we found enough beds for us to have one each. We were able to cook indoors, eat indoors, and, apart from the sentry, live indoors. When you have lived in the open for a few months a building, any building, even a few spare rooms in a factory, seems almost like home. The manager of the factory spoke English and told me he had business connections in our country. Two sergeants got into conversation with him, and I saw the three walking away together. When the two returned they told me they had been drinking 'very good stuff out of frightfully posh glasses'. They said the manager had a lot of drinks in his room and suggested that if I had a word with him we could all have a party together.

'Go on, sir, let yourself go,' urged one sergeant, while the other backed him up with: 'Let's all get drunk together, sir. Our last platoon commander used to go out drinking with the boys occasionally, but we've never seen you drunk.'

I declined their offer.

The rest of support company were even luckier than I was. Jimmy James fixed his headquarters in the back rooms of an *estaminet* and the other officers joined him there. The publican, well aware that liberation normally happens only once in a lifetime, gave an unlimited number of free drinks to our troops and produced some choice wines he had successfully hidden from the Germans and kept for this day.

After a couple of days a proportion of the troops were allowed to go out in the town during the afternoons, and when it was my turn to go I looked at the shop windows to see what they had in their display. No shop had a large quantity of goods, but I was able to buy another bottle of scent and a pipe. The pipe I lost after a few days. The scent finally arrived safely in England. I watched a parade of the underground forces through Arras, and the civilians lining the streets did not tire of singing the 'Marseillaise'. The French national anthem is an enthusiastic song; this was surely an occasion on which to be enthusiastic, and the French people sang it everywhere and all day long. As the parade disappeared into a church people were still singing 'Formez les bataillons!'

I noticed a patriot accusing a collaborator. Five years of pent-up passion came out of the accuser as he raved at his enemy. A crowd gathered, and as the accused shouted back counter-accusations it seemed to me that a lively incident was developing. I could not understand the language very well and did not want to be asked to arrest an alleged collaborator without being reasonably certain that he was a friend of the Nazis. As the crowd grew, so the tumult grew, and before long the original quarrellers were forgotten. I walked on. In the *estaminets* everybody was offering drinks to everybody else, people were singing gaily (nine times out of ten it was the 'Marseillaise') and handing out to one another congratulatory thumps on the back. Everywhere there was excitement.

In England the newspapers announced on 1 September that General Montgomery had been promoted to Field Marshal. But the American government did not promote General Eisenhower because they did not seem to have the rank of Field Marshal in their army. So Field Marshal Montgomery's boss, General Eisenhower, appeared to have the lower rank of the two.

The *News Chronicle* (later incorporated in the *Daily Mail*) reported that the master stroke of General Dempsey (commander of the British Second Army who came under Montgomery's overall command) appeared to make the German defeat in France as complete as it could be.

A report from their correspondent S.L. Solon ran:

The German plan to maintain an organized retreat to the Somme has been smashed. Tonight a high officer on General Montgomery's staff disclosed that a captured German document revealed the enemy's intentions to be:

1. The German army was ordered to withdraw in four stages to the Somme, where a strong defensive line was to be established and held.

2. German rearguard units were to delay the Allied forces until such a line could be organized.

3. The withdrawal was to take place between 29 August and 1 September.

That, in contrast to the impossible orders issued to the German army in the past 60 days, appeared to be a realistic and logical counter-measure to the situation in which an army obviously has not the forces to stand and fight. This was the Allied answer:

1. The Germans were given no opportunity to re-organize their forces north of the Seine and build their first stage defence line.

2. The Germans were outflanked, cut apart and still further disorganized.

3. In the past forty-eight hours the British and Canadian troops have made the swiftest gains since the landings.

The advances have been spectacular. British troops which yesterday advanced from the Vernon bridgehead through Mandeville have today taken Grandvilliers, Haut Mesnil, Catheux. They crowned this magnificent sixty-mile advance in two days by taking Amiens. Amiens is twenty-two miles south-east of Abbeville. That is the only gap in this rapidly formed lower Seine pocket now open to the Germans. All the enemy coast defences, all the islands of resistance still holding out – and the total may add into several divisions – are now in danger of being completely cut off. Another British column advancing through Beauvais has reached Brouinlieu – an advance of forty miles in twenty-four hours.

Enemy vehicles have been seen moving north of Amiens, but the German transport problem is extremely critical.

Canadian troops are in Rouen. In a number of towns we have seen French flags flying although we have not actually reached them and that may indicate that the French Forces of the Interior have taken them over.

EVEN MORE RAPTURE

2–4 September

On the evening of 2 September the commanding officer called an orders group for 2000 hours. At that time, however, he was still at brigade headquarters receiving his orders, but I could see that Major Drewitt had an inkling of what was afoot. 'I think we are very lucky to have come all this way peacefully,' he said to a friend and I overheard him add: 'We shall be lucky if we go half our distance tomorrow.

Half an hour later Colonel Turner arrived. Unhurriedly he lit his pipe, examined his map, read his notes, then asked: 'Are we all here? Right, we'll begin.' In slow, measured tones and without showing any concern at all he went on: 'Tomorrow we get on the road behind the Guards Armoured Division and we keep moving until we get to Brussels. The Guards will travel night and day until they get there. We may be able to harbour up at night.'

There was complete silence as he spoke. Turner was as casual and routine-like as it was possible to be; but our minds were racing. Brussels! That was 100 miles away. It was unbelievable.

I jotted down rough notes. 'To Brussels, behind Guards. They not to stop at night. If weather suitable three and a half airborne divisions to be dropped on our left, to contain enemy near coast. This not to be told to troops until they actually land. May have to do operation without airborne support. Different plan. Start line crossroads 123456 on outskirts of Arras. Time past start point 1030 hours or 1400 hours.'

Colonel Turner explained that if it was a clear morning

these airborne divisions would be dropped and we would start at 1400 hours. (I recollected General Montgomery had said: 'We have further surprises for the Germans.') But if the weather was cloudy and unsuitable for the dropping of airborne troops we would start as early as possible, and that meant 1030 hours.

I thought there were going to be two different plans, one to be used if airborne troops took part in the operation, the other if they did not. But as I examined the orders with Ken Edwards it appeared that the only difference between the two plans was the time factor. And we could not understand why we should start earlier if we were not going to have airborne support. The possible use of air troops had to be withheld from our men in case they were not dropped, firstly because of disappointment, and secondly so as not to risk a breach of security. If any of our chaps became prisoner the knowledge that three and a half airborne divisions were waiting in England was dangerous knowledge to have.

It is known that the unlucky 1st Airborne Division were briefed for many different operations before eventually being dropped at Arnhem. So often were their orders cancelled that they grew to think they would never be dropped. Arnhem was something like the sixteenth operation that was planned for them. All the others were cancelled as either unwise or unnecessary in view of a rapidly changing tactical situation.

The night of 2 September was dark and cloudy, and when I awoke next morning the first thing I did was to look at the sky. There were a lot of clouds about but they were not very low. When I received a message 'Prepare to move at 1030 hours' I knew that meant the 1st Airborne Division was grounded.

But there were other mighty forces on our side. They were the underground fighters of France and Belgium. At

Arras the local leader telephoned to Brussels and said: 'The British forces are on their way to you now.'

At Brussels they got ready to make our way as easy as possible. These patriot forces were highly organized. Our orders were to hand all prisoners over to them. We were told not to stop on any account.

From St Pierre-la-Vieille to Arras, half-way across northern France, Red Reed, of the anti-tank platoon, had travelled on a motorbike as start point and dispersal point officer. He had encountered so much dust that his eyes were now sore and in need of a rest, so I was detailed to take over his job. At 1025 hours I reached the start point. I watched Ken lead the column in his carrier at 1030 hours. Although the speed was steady and the spacing between vehicles correct at the front of the column, at the rear there were in some cases long gaps between the trucks and some drivers were having to press hard on the accelerator to catch up.

When all the column had passed I got on my motorbike and rode to the head of it. Before I reached Ken he was in Douai, the town from which the Guards had started that morning. For some time I rode behind Colonel Turner's jeep because he was expecting to need me to liaise with the brigadier who was travelling along another road. For all the assurance with which Turner gave out his orders the previous evening I do not believe for a moment that he expected to reach Brussels without fighting a battle. At one point the road was impassable owing to an obstruction, so we were led along a detour of narrow tracks, and even these were cratered. The local inhabitants were filling in the craters even as we rode over them, and they did what they could to level the road all the time it was being used.

The frontier between France and Belgium was very insignificant. I do not think anybody noticed it. Anyway, there was no essential difference between the two countries.

Both had fought in 1940, both needed to be liberated, and both had well organized underground forces. What I liked least about Belgium was the cobbled roads. They made riding on a motor-bike uncomfortable, while carrier drivers had to be careful their tracks did not go into a skid. As we poured into Belgium I recollected the descriptions I had read and heard of the British Expeditionary Force's entry into the country in May 1940. I remembered the emphasis commentators placed on the fact that not a man walked – everybody was on a vehicle. I remembered descriptive passages about children throwing flowers at the Tommies, and the picturesque scenes as the BEF advanced along the cobbled roads. Well, here we are again, I thought. It was history repeating itself, only the circumstances were now different. This was no untried army entering Belgium – this was an army that had just won a decisive victory and was still sucking the fruits of that victory.

In 1940 children politely threw flowers of welcome at the soldiers. In 1944 the country was absolutely delirious with joy. Four years had made a difference. One could quickly detect a dissimilarity between the French reaction and the Belgian reaction. The French sang the 'Marseillaise', the Belgians 'Tipperary'. The French shouted: 'We are free,' the Belgians 'Welcome to our liberators.' When we were in France we did not consider the French attitude to be lacking in gratitude or profuseness. We thought the people were as warm-hearted as they could be. We could not imagine a better reception. It was only when we reached Belgium and were actually accorded an even more rapturous welcome that we thought of the difference between the two countries.

I looked closely at the people who lined the route here, as I had in France, because I always wanted to see what men and women looked like after four years of German occupation. At this time my parents and my sister were in

German-occupied Jersey, and I was relieved to find that the man in the street did not look disastrously ill or underfed. A little thin, yes; and very eager for a square meal, but their hardships did not seem to have been so severe as to cause permanent harm.

Villages that had seen their first Allied soldiers a few hours previously produced huge posters with the initials RAF and V . . . (the V for Victory sign of the underground movement) and hung banners across the street saying: 'Welcome to the British and Americans.'

I do not know how many good Belgian women screamed 'Boche, Boche' as we passed and pointed to some woods, or maybe to an isolated cluster of houses. We took little notice. Our orders were to push on. We could not stop for the odd German who was cowering in hiding and, having lost his courage, would inevitably lose his freedom. We could not stop for small bands of enemy who might be wandering aimlessly in distant woods, or for those who were paying a last fond farewell to their mistresses. All such could be left to the tender care of the Belgian underground. We were after Brussels.

The citizen army was greatly in evidence. One saw small groups of them everywhere, with British Sten guns over their shoulders. I suppose this was the first time they had been able to show themselves in public and they seemed very eager to be in the forefront. They obtained many prisoners. Some they ferreted out themselves, others were given to them by British troops. And as every truckload of prisoners was driven through the villages the inhabitants turned out to hiss and boo those who had caused them so much grief. The Germans showed great reluctance to surrender to the patriot army because they knew what to expect from those they had ill-treated. They more easily gave themselves up to us, probably hoping for kinder treatment. But they could not save themselves like that because we promptly, in the space of half an hour or less, handed them over to the Belgians.

I saw one girl member of the patriot forces, with her rifle slung over her shoulder, marching six Germans off to captivity. I will not say the enemy looked proud; the girl looked very satisfied, though. Many old scores were paid off that day. We passed Germans lying in the roadside with their throats cut, and others with fatal bullet wounds. Each dead German attracted a crowd of local inhabitants who gazed with hatred at the corpse. Even the sight of bloody wounds did not deter the onlookers. Many human beings lose their finer feelings in war. When death and horror have been your companions for four years your stomach does not turn over at the sorry sight of a dead tyrant.

The third of September was a hot day and not once did we stop long enough for food. We fed on fruit that was thrust eagerly into our hands by an exultant people and we quenched our thirst with the beer they gave us. It was thrilling to be advancing so rapidly.

We had our scares. On one occasion I saw a group of German troops marching with their weapons 'at the trail' 200 yards to our left. An instant later I saw that at their head an officer was carrying a large white flag. A very large flag. He did not want any mistake to arise. Ken Edwards covered them with a Bren gun while I sped back to the commanding officer to report what was happening. He came up to the front in his jeep immediately. By then Ken had decided to push on again, leaving only one Bren gun carrier with a crew of four to deal with all the prisoners. When the Germans marched in they were paraded in threes with the officers in front of their men. All their weapons were taken away. In a few minutes they were all disarmed and under the control of the Belgian forces.

On another occasion Ken received a report that there was a fairly large body of enemy troops 500 yards from the road on our right. He did not want to leave too many troops holding out behind us so he hesitated for a moment but, remembering that the orders were not to stop for anything that did not interfere with our progress, he carried on, leaving the enemy where they were. I do not know what happened to them. Probably they gave up as soon as they could. If they waited till the patriots got to them they were probably sorry.

It was twilight before our night's harbour area near Enghien was named and by the time we reached it, having passed through Ath, it was completely dark save for the glow that came from wrecked vehicles that were still burning. As we covered the last few miles the roads appeared to contain even more traffic than they had during the day. Supply vehicles were going back, and rear units were closing up. The more we pressed on, the more signs of battle we saw. It was obvious the Guards had not had things all their own way. Far from it. Burning vehicles were to be seen everywhere and one did not have to look far from the vehicles to see dead bodies. One heard the occasional crack of exploding ammunition.

I pitched my bivvy with support company headquarters and then set off with Ken to find out where the rifle companies were and to visit my sections attached to them. One section had not unpacked anything from the carriers. The sergeant told me the company commander was expecting to have to go out on a patrol and had ordered the mortars to stand by. Later in the evening a patrol went out but found no enemy. Members of my second section were cooking supper, intent on getting their rest as quickly as possible. Soon they would be wrapping their blankets around them and lying down to sleep beside their vehicles. The third section were not bothering about supper. They were having a cup of tea and were eager for sleep.

Very little was known of the general situation, but we

had travelled much farther than we expected to and the advance had been easier than we had dared to hope. Meanwhile, unknown to us, the Guards Armoured Division was entering Brussels. It was the night of 3 September, exactly five years after the declaration of war.

When I awoke next morning my first thought was: what time are we moving? But we did not move. We hung about in little groups waiting for orders.

I heard some firing behind us. It sounded like either a tank or an anti-tank gun going into action. Then there were occasional bursts of automatic fire. We had thrust forward so far that we had to expect to find small enemy parties still behind us, but after our experience of the previous day I did not think the enemy would be in a fighting mood. However, if his communications were disrupted too completely he sometimes had no idea how hopeless his situation was and he would fight on. I could not make out what this firing was. Nobody seemed to be paying any attention to it. I asked Ken what he thought. 'Let's see Jimmy,' he suggested. But Jimmy was not at his headquarters. 'Where is he?' we asked his batman.

'I don't know, sir,' came the reply. 'He went to an orders group a long time ago. I don't know whether he is still there.'

Ken and I were usually called to orders groups so we hurriedly checked that no messages had come for us and then, just to make sure we were not missing a conference, went to battalion headquarters and looked discreetly to see whether a meeting was in progress. But there was no sign of conference or of activity. Soon Red Reed arrived to tell us what was happening.

'General Horrocks was driving through this morning,' he said. 'He stopped and told me that there were a couple of German tanks behind us, not far away. "I'm going on," he said, "but the tank force will have to be mopped up." So I had to try and get a couple of guns into position to engage these tanks. Can you imagine it? Trying to manoeuvre anti-tank guns so that they can knock out a tank! We fired a couple of shots at one tank and it retaliated; and then we found out that it was supported by another tank.'

'Did you have any luck?'

'I don't think so. I think the tanks have pushed off. They might be anywhere now. I lost two damn good NCOs. They were wounded.'

A little while later a full battalion orders group was called. One rifle company was sent to follow the main armoured force into Brussels, while everyone else went in search of these German tanks. We motored along some narrow roads and tracks for a few miles and then the colonel stopped the column and established a command post.

The enemy had apparently been sighted and a distinctly untidy battle ensued. All my mortars had been allocated to different rifle companies so at first there was little for me to do. Remaining near the command post I heard much machine-gun firing. Then armour-piercing shots began to thud into the ground. The crew of an enemy tank must have thought mistakenly that our tanks were nearby. If they had changed from armour-piercing (which was practically harmless unless it hit armour or scored a direct hit on a human body) to high explosive we would all have been in great danger.

After a while Colonel Turner went forward with Ken Edwards in a carrier and Ken told me afterwards that once they turned a bend and found themselves facing an enemy tank a few yards away. The driver quickly drove the carrier behind some cover.

'I don't know how we got away with it,' said Ken. 'Face to face with a tank and it didn't fire at us! I just do not know the answer to that one. I thought we had "bought it".'

Eventually the colonel called me and told me two mortar carriers had been knocked out in the village. I went to see what had happened and, hearing Spandau machine-guns firing, ran pretty quickly. Then I felt considerable dampness on my thigh and assumed it must be blood and I must have been wounded but I wondered why it did not hurt. I put my hand to my thigh to check the bleeding, looked at my hand and saw the 'blood' was colourless. It was water. I had not been hit, my water bottle carried on my hip had.

I got to my carriers and heard a confused story. They had been at the rear of a column going through the village when an enemy tank appeared behind them and opened fire. My men jumped out of their carrier, ran into a cellar and watched helplessly as the tank fired at, and damaged, several of our carriers and lorries. The tank crew then raided the vehicles and took away some petrol cans, although they obligingly left our rations. Once the crew had our petrol they quickly returned to their tank and made off.

We loaded our mortars on to the trucks used by the rifle company and arranged for our carriers to be repaired by army maintenance units. One of my men was missing. I asked the Belgian villagers in the best French I could if they had seen a British soldier on his own. They understood a few of the words I used and replied that they had seen a wounded man carried away. Some hours later my man turned up, unwounded, having found his way to another platoon in the confusion of battle.

The local population was scared. On seeing our troops drive through their village they had been about to bring out their flags when the German surprise attack caught us on the hop, scattered us and sent the civilians back to their houses. Then the Germans made off, and now the Belgians once more were getting ready to celebrate their liberation. The encounter had been inconclusive. All we knew then was that the enemy force had gone. Prisoners we took later told us that the force had decided to return to Brussels and reorganize there, apparently not knowing then that the Guards were in control of the Belgian capital.

The battalion reformed as quickly as possible and returned to the main route. Once more our journey became a victorious procession, people all along the way being beside themselves with joy.

And one thing we knew now about our tanks: outgunned in Normandy they may have been, but in the pursuit battle they were first-class: fast, reliable, manoeuvrable. It seems we did not have good infantry tanks; but we had good cavalry tanks.

Early in the evening I saw in the plain ahead of us a large city of white, gleaming buildings: Brussels.

'THE WAR IS OVER'

4–6 September

There was more traffic in Brussels that evening than I had ever seen before. Soldiers on lorries, soldiers in tanks, soldiers behind guns were all moving to their appointed place or trying to find it. Whenever a convoy stopped people rushed from the pavements to shake hands with the Tommies, give them gifts and kiss them. On my motor-bike I could only ride slowly and I soon learned that the last thing to do was to stop and ask the way. The instant one did so dozens of eager Belgians would crowd around, each claiming either to understand the French I spoke haltingly or else to know English, and each directing me along a different route. Eventually I found support company headquarters in the main station. We picked out the first-class compartment of a train and made that our sleeping quarters. Battalion headquarters was 300 yards down the line.

Brussels had been *en fête* since the previous evening. When tanks rumbled through their streets the people paid little attention at first. After four years of occupation they were fed up with German tanks. Then some of the citizens looked again, and again. These were different tanks. Then it dawned. They were British tanks. They were free! The city went wild with an uncontrollable delight. In the morning, even before the area had been properly cleared of all enemy, a ceremonial march of the liberation forces was held. This was the order of parade:

Major General A.H.S. Adair (in a tank) commander of
    the Guards Armoured Division,
A section of the Household Cavalry (armoured cars),
General Horrocks's headquarters,
Free Belgian forces,
Units of the Guards Armoured Division,
A company of the Hampshire Regiment.

Now it was early evening. Our battalion's job was to defend Brussels and my first duty was to contact the mortar sections within their rifle companies. One was at Duilbeck, a suburb two miles out. The local people there said there were large numbers of enemy in many nearby areas. Six times the rifle company commander sent out strong patrols with mortar support to seek the enemy, but they never found a trace of him, so after that most of the information the civilians gave was ignored. They probably had accurate knowledge about the German forces twenty-four or forty-eight hours ago, but in the last day or so those forces had moved rapidly. The two mortar carriers were parked temporarily near a church and the streets leading to it were crowded with people eager to look at the carriers and see the magic weapons that had caused the downfall of the German army. Everyone was keen to talk but language was a great barrier. One girl who spoke French simply enough and slowly enough for me to understand told me that the minister of the local church had been taken away by the Nazis nine months previously because of his opposition to them and had not been heard of since.

I left that mortar section with the people of Duilbeck, judging that they would not lack anything, and paid a brief visit to my second section who were settling down comfortably in a brewery and whose job was to support the reserve rifle company. I did not think they would lack anything either.

At the other end of Brussels I looked for my third section, but after riding around on my motor-bike for about half an hour I could find no trace. I rode through several suburbs where our troops had not been, rather nervously performing a one-man victory procession. Wherever I stopped I was joyfully received. One enormous woman with a motherly smile and a monumental girth said: 'Tommy, I will kiss you. You are the first Englishman I have seen.' She did as she threatened. Unable to find that section while it was still light, I returned to our headquarters in the railway station. To my astonishment I found the duties of sentry being performed, perhaps uncomplainingly, perhaps sheepishly, by two officers. All the troops had gone into the city to enjoy themselves. Discipline had vanished, perhaps understandably and certainly only temporarily, so these officers were doing the duty of private soldiers. In fact many of the men were only a few hundred yards away teaching hundreds of Belgians to dance the Okee Cokee. The civilians gave their thanks by singing again and again and again 'Tipperary', which they seemed to think was our national anthem.

I was lured away from my headquarters by a wizened old man who clutched my arm and with his other hand took hold of Claude, my batman. 'Champagne,' he said insistently, 'champagne, champagne.' He led us away.

'Do you think it's all right, sir?' asked Claude with a voice full of doubt.

'Yes,' I said, 'let's go with him.'

He led us through a few back streets to his home, where we found a party was already in progress. Four soldiers had got there before us, and they were sitting down to a meal. There were about ten civilians who came and went mysteriously. One young man claimed my attention most of the time, telling me stories of the German occupation. He had to shout to tell me these yarns, for a gramophone played 'La Ligne Siegfried' over and over again, and a young woman sang joyously all the time it was played, but as the only words she knew were the title words I got rather bored at hearing her voice. Her sister swayed from side to side in rhythm with the music and, pointing to two children in the room, told me they were her daughters. She added, if I understood her correctly: 'Je ne suis pas mariée.'

I was first given some meat to eat. I do not know what kind of meat it was, but it was certainly the least appetizing I have ever tasted. I realized that to those Belgians a dish like that represented a feast and I felt sorry for them. I had to eat all the meat I was given, for I think they would have felt insulted if I had left any. I waited for the champagne, but first I was given a glass of beer, next some wine, and when finally the champagne was produced the young man triumphantly showed the label on the bottle to the whole company. The label said the drink was specially 'pour le Wehrmacht'.

The youth was bent on telling me a story about a parachute, and although I understood his actions and his words perfectly well he kept on repeating himself, as though he believed the more often he said a sentence the more fully would I understand it.

First he made a humming noise and waved his arms, to give the impression of an aircraft in flight. Then he became like a child playing soldiers pointing pieces of cutlery into the air and shouting 'boom, boom' as these imaginary anti-aircraft guns went into action. The plane was hit (I could tell that because he waved it from the sky), and then the airman descended to earth. 'La parachute, la parachute,' he cried. He finally produced the parachute from a cupboard where he had hidden it, and I understood that an Allied flyer had been sheltered by him for a year until the liberation. For some time the narrator argued with his father as to whether they had hidden the airman for 'un an' or 'deux ans'. Finally they wrote down the figures 1 9 4 3. That presumably was when the plane was shot down.

The girl with the swaying hips told me a story about her brother, the Gestapo and some throat slitting, but I was never really certain who had cut whose throat, so I just said: 'C'est formidable,' which I understood to be the right thing to say on doubtful occasions.

When the Belgians were told that some of the soldiers present were officers and some were other ranks they were puzzled for a time, until the explanation for this mixing together burst upon one man in a flash of inspiration and he announced, as proudly as if he was revealing a new truth: 'Toujours nous sommes amis – tout le monde. L'Anglais, l'Américain, le Belge, le Français – nous sommes amis, tout le monde.' I nodded agreement, but did not really see the connection.

With much ado our hosts produced a map which they had kept safely hidden for several years. This map showed all north-west Europe, and the end of the Siegfried Line (Germany's great defensive positions) was clearly marked near the Dutch–Belgian border. They pointed and gesticulated with their hands to show that the easiest way into Germany was through Holland. They insisted that the map had been stolen from a German engineer.

Our hosts also produced for our inspection a crystal wireless set which they, like so many others in German-occupied Europe, had made themselves. 'BBC,' said one of the party, pointing to the set and putting his ear to it, to indicate that they had received BBC broadcasts on it. (They could have been executed if the Germans had found this out.)

One could see that this was the greatest day in the lives of these Belgians. They wanted nothing more than to celebrate it with us. When we said goodbye our hosts added encouragingly, 'à Berlin'. I think they expected us to get there in a few days. We were all living on the heights of optimism.

Next day I located the position of my third mortar section, neatly tucked behind a railway bank. They were also supremely happy. Nearby residents were so friendly that they had offered beds in their homes for everyone, but the sergeant had to refuse this as he wanted his men to sleep close to their weapons in case of emergency. So the comfortable civilian beds remained empty while the soldiers slept on the hard ground with a tarpaulin for their roof and the earth for their mattress. They were used to that.

That morning Ken Edwards and I went to a local café and we had not been sitting there five minutes before we had an invitation from two ladies, each of them as old as our combined ages, to sleep in their house. Ken had doubts about the exact character of the invitation, and in any case it was necessary for us to sleep at our headquarters.

We were at the railway station when an NCO approached and shouted out: 'Have you got your civvy suit, sir?' As I did not answer he repeated the question and added: 'It's all over.'

'What's over?' asked Ken.

'The war, sir.'

'Oh, yes,' we said together, not very interested and certainly not believing him.

'Honest, sir, no leg-pull, it's on the wireless. Germany's given up and Hitler's gone to Spain.'

'Are you sure?'

'It's been given out on the wireless, sir. Everybody knows about it in the town. They're all going mad. You can't get through the crowds.'

I used to wonder what I would do when the war ended, and where I would be when that occurred. But doubt seized me now, because I had expected the news to come first through military channels. If Eisenhower had received the surrender of the German armies that news would have come down through the chain of command, and the battalion intelligence officer would have passed it on to us. (This belief of mine was wrong. When eventually the war did end the troops first heard about it from the BBC.)

'They've got a wireless at battalion headquarters. Let's listen there,' I said to Ken.

The commanding officer was out, but Major Drewitt was listening intently to the wireless.

'Have you heard the news, sir?' we asked.

'Nothing on the wireless,' he said briefly.

'We'll know at twelve o'clock,' said Ken, 'there'll be a news bulletin then.'

As I listened to the programme of music that was being broadcast I felt in my heart the tidings we had heard were false, for the music that was being played sounded very unimpressive and ordinary. I imagined that if the Germans had given up the advertised programme would have been cancelled and patriotic, national and martial music played instead, probably all day long.

The twelve o'clock news was very unexciting. Our hearts sank.

'It can't be true,' said Drewitt, 'because if it were I am sure we would be racing for Berlin as fast as we could go before they changed their minds.'

Back at my platoon headquarters Monty was crouched over his wireless and although he had heard no announcement the crowd around him firmly believed that the war was won. When I tried to tell them that the news was not official they regarded me as very much behind the times. And the Belgians continued to give free beer to British troops 'pour la victoire'.

A motor cyclist rode in. 'It's true. The mayor has announced it in the main square. All the people are going mad. It's been on the wireless, too.'

'Did you hear it on the wireless?' I asked.

'Yes, sir.'

'You heard it yourself? What programme then, because it was not on the midday BBC news?'

'I didn't actually hear it myself, but my officer heard it.'

'Who told you your officer heard it on the wireless?'

'He did.'

'He spoke to you himself?' I asked.

'No, sir, he didn't speak to me, but he heard it on the wireless.'

'Did he actually tell you that?'

'No, sir, but they all know about it at the supply depot.'

And so the conversation went on until all the troops thought I wanted the war to go on or that I wanted to stop the Belgians giving them pints of beer 'pour la victoire'.

Major Drewitt, seeing the danger that might occur if the troops were led to believe the war was over when it was not, told all the officers to emphasize that the news was entirely unofficial, that the BBC had broadcast nothing about it, and that it was more likely to be false than true.

But with all Brussels celebrating the end of hostilities and an announcement having been made from the main square, most of the soldiers believed it was all over. 'It's on the wireless,' they said. I could not convince them it was not.

As the day wore on and the BBC made no mention of the subject the chaps slowly began to believe the story was

only a rumour. After a few hours nobody in the battalion
said: 'I heard it on the wireless.' Nobody even knew an
officer who had heard it. And as the local population
sobered down the men reflected that the only good result of
the rumour was that they had been treated to a record
number of pints of beer.

(It has subsequently been stated that the rumour was
based on a broadcast from a Spanish radio station.)

At home the *Daily Mirror* reported on 5 September that
Brussels was captured after 'one of the most terrific forward
drives of the war'. Its report also stated:

General Dempsey's thirty-eight-mile-a-day tanks,
racing 232 miles in six days, have smashed into Holland. Last night they were at least seven miles over the
border after sweeping right across Belgium in less than
forty-eight hours.

This lightning drive was announced by the Dutch
Premier in a broadcast to the people of Holland.
Dutch officials in London said we had reached Breda,
once Rommel's HQ, thirty miles from Rotterdam. By
liberating the great Belgian port of Antwerp in a
twenty-five mile advance from freed Brussels, Monty's
men have given Hitler a Dunkirk of his own.

But he has no gallant fleet of little ships to rescue
the 100,000 Huns thought to be trapped between the
rivers Somme and the Scheldt with their backs to the
sea.

Monty's successes mean also that 300 miles of the
Siegfried Line from Aachen to the Swiss frontier is
now directly threatened by Allied arms.

Next day the *News Chronicle* correspondent Ronald Walker
reported:

Although the Germans are still fighting furiously at localized points, there can be no doubt that the retreat of the German army has become a rout. I cannot quote the author of the following sentence, but I pass it on as a statement made with a detailed knowledge of what is happening in northern France and Belgium: The disintegration of the German army is complete.

The Germans, who for years have been schooled into collective thinking, are now thinking individually. Their single thought is how to get back to Germany. Their last hope is the safety of the Siegfried Line.

This is the immediate picture; but if you take the long view there is the spectacle of Germany faced with the final major disaster. At the eastern approaches of Germany are the armies of Russia. The armies of Britain, America and Canada, with contingents of Poles, Norwegians and French, have arrived at the western approaches.

Inside Germany the enemy may be able to assemble sufficient troops to defend either the east or the west; but not both. Which is it to be? That question will soon have to be answered . . .

German divisions, or what is left of them, retreating along the Channel coast have been ordered to hand over their arms and equipment to holding troops and to make their way back to Germany as best they can. The holding troops are ordered to fight rearguard actions to enable their comrades to escape.

And these retreats are at the other end of the scale of the former German triumphal progress. These soldiers are often ragged and hungry, with their boots in tatters. They live like the mercenaries of old, on the country through which they pass. They have no means of communication.

For the first time the German army is starved of

equipment. Its tanks, guns, lorries, carts and equipment are scattered wholesale along the roads and in the fields, burned out and wrecked. The trains of supplies from Germany have ceased. We are now realizing in full the fruits of our overwhelming air power . . .

TO ANTWERP

7–12 September

Around midnight on 6 September, when we had been in Brussels just over two days, a runner from battalion headquarters woke me up to say: 'Warning order, sir. Prepare to move at 0630 hours.' My heart sank. Another early rising, with breakfast in the dark; another rush to pack the carriers and be ready on time! Where were we going now? Why the rush? Did it mean more fighting? If only that peace rumour had been true!

Our move was postponed a few hours, so we ate our breakfast in comfort. At 9 a.m. we set off for Antwerp, thirty miles away. As I stood on the start line and watched the battalion vehicles go past I saw everything was in a jumbled order. Some troop-laden vehicles had made a rapid move through Brussels, while others had been held up by the traffic, and, as there was no time to sort them out into their correct positions, armour, infantry, guns and other supporting weapons were all in a meaningless order. It seemed the whole population knew our destination and as we drove through the streets people waved goodbye and extended invitations to 'come back and see us again some time'. They gazed with unending awe at our equipment.

After the last vehicle had passed I had one final drink of Brussels coffee, then set off on my motor-bike. Long before I caught up the head of the column I developed a wobble at the modest speed of 30 m.p.h. and noticed that one of my tyres was completely flat. Fortunately I was passing through the village of Willebroek at the time and twenty yards from where I stopped was a motor repair shop. I pushed the bike into the shop and immediately two willing mechanics began to remove the tyre and mend the puncture. Within twenty-five minutes I was on the road again, thankful that the puncture had occurred outside an ally's repair establishment.

Just outside Antwerp I reached the head of the column. All vehicles had stopped. A young Belgian, dressed rather like a boy scout, spoke to me in English.

'The battle is going well today. Yesterday things were difficult.' He told me the centre of Antwerp was liberated, but the Germans were still fighting in the outskirts. The docks were in our hands.

Colonel Turner led the battalion forward, with the orders group just behind him. I did not know whether we were going to an assembly area preparatory to making an attack, whether we were taking over defensive positions, or whether we were establishing entirely new positions. But as the citizens of Antwerp were walking about in the open I concluded that if the front was near conditions must be fairly peaceful.

Antwerp gave us a tremendous reception, with relief and gratitude prominent among the expressions on the faces of the people. They knew what was at stake. First they had been liberated by a lightning armoured thrust, then the battle had hovered uncertainly on the city outskirts, and now reinforcements were driving through their streets to make certain their safety.

We were all moved by their welcome, though we had experienced such scenes many times before. Whenever we drove through a town in these circumstances my thoughts turned to my own parents and sister, who were waiting for someone to drive through the narrow streets of St Helier and along the country roads of Jersey. Having seen the elation of Brussels and Antwerp I visualized the elation of St Helier when their liberation would come. I thought how much more pleasant the act of liberation would be when both military and civilians spoke the same language and when troops were relieving their own kith and kin.

We went round and round Antwerp like a Lord Mayor's show, and I thought perhaps Colonel Turner wanted to convince the Belgians that we were in terrific strength. A member of the local resistance movement explained to him the positions the enemy were thought to hold, and he allotted areas to the rifle companies to occupy and defend. Once more the three mortar sections were attached to companies, so all I had to do was to join Jimmy James at support company headquarters, call that my headquarters as well, and then later set off and visit my sections.

Our headquarters was set up in a school, and as soon as the Belgians realized troops were going to be quartered there they organized themselves into little parties and each party procured a wheelbarrow or pushcart with which they fetched straw from a distant place and laid it down in the schoolroom for us to use as our bedding. This was done with great dispatch and urgency, and very willingly. In every way the Belgians were kind to us, and they attended to our every need – I think they would have done our guard duties if we had asked them!

I noticed they looked curiously at our petrol cookers and at the food we prepared for supper. It was not long before our fellows were offering chocolate to the children. One man who spoke English fairly well told me he had been a member of the Belgian army in 1940, but of course they had no proper equipment.

'One thing I notice,' he remarked, 'your troops don't salute the officers; they are all friendly together.' I told him that troops certainly did salute all officers, but such courtesies were usually dropped in a combat area, particularly when the enemy might not be far away and everybody was hastening to establish their positions and liaise with units on their flanks.

I set about visiting the rifle companies to see my mortar-men. One section had sited their two mortars behind a concrete wall at a railway station and were using a railway carriage as sleeping quarters. They were supporting a company that was really in reserve because there was a battalion of the Shropshire Regiment in front of them. The enemy had been sniping from a block of buildings 500 yards away, so it did not pay to show oneself too much; moreover the German artillery sometimes opened fire when they detected movement in our lines. Later on the Shropshires were pulled out and that left us in the front.

My second section was also in a sound position. They had dug weapon pits in a garden, they had a hut to sleep in, and they had run a telephone cable to an observation post previously constructed by the Germans to overlook the neighbourhood. Their complaint was that at night sniping shots were fired from nearby buildings in their rear, and an hour or two on guard was a hazardous and nerve-racking experience. During the daytime they searched for the sniper but never found him, and the conclusion was drawn that the shots were being fired either by a Belgian traitor or by a German masquerading as a Belgian civilian.

My third section was the best off. They had good observation from a railway bridge, a stone wall provided protection to the mortars from any bullets that might be fired in their direction, they slept under cover, and they were already making friends with a family living a few houses away. I was always nervous when my chaps started making friends with civilians, for they were certain to be invited into people's houses and the weapons might then be inadequately manned in an emergency. However, the sergeant never allowed more than two men to be away from the mortars at any one time.

The amazing thing about our battle situation was that the Antwerp civilians were allowed to walk about near our positions without let or hindrance. They even walked into what was effectively no man's land as if there was no battle anywhere. The whine of a shell would send them scattering, but when a bout of shelling ceased they would reappear and calmly continue on their way. However, as the days wore on and the shelling continued, and the battle positions did not move, they became less adventurous.

Autograph hunting became a craze. On seeing a soldier children would crowd around him, present him with a pencil and a piece of paper, and would not go away until he had written a signature on the paper. And of course the children made the requests for cigarettes and chocolate that had been made all through France and Belgium.

People now went souvenir-hunting on a fairly big scale. They schemed, manoeuvred and almost fought for cap badges, regimental insignia, divisional signs and badges of rank from British soldiers, and after a few days it was no rare thing to see a girl walking along the street with sergeant's stripes sewn on her dress, the divisional sign on her hat and a regimental insignia on her arm. When I remonstrated with my chaps for letting these things be taken off their uniforms they protested that it was more than they could do to keep them on. A crowd would gather around them, and as they were preventing one girl from taking their cap badge another would take their regimental insignia. Make sure all signs are sewn on properly, I humbly suggested.

A large quantity of spirits and wine had been captured from a German welfare store in Brussels and was to be distributed among the battalion. The ration came to nearly one bottle of wine per man but the commanding officer, taking a rather serious view of the loss of badges and signs, ruled that the ration should be divided among only those who could produce their correct uniform complete with all emblems. One of my sections objected to this on principle, so refused to accept any drinks at all. That meant more for the rest.

There is a sad story about the drinks for the officers. We pooled ours within the company, leaving several bottles of champagne, liqueurs and wines in the care of the guard. Several hours later, however, the guard and three of his friends were found completely drunk and all our champagne was gone. After that I kept what was left of our drinks on my carrier, and whether any of my platoon headquarters pinched a bottle or two of indifferent wine on the sly or not I do not know, but we never found any of them drunk or noticed any quantity of bottles missing, so I used to tell Jimmy proudly that clearly my chaps were honest.

I have one ugly memory of Antwerp. I was returning with a driver in a fifteen-hundredweight truck from visiting one of the mortar sections, and was anxious to get back to support company headquarters as quickly as possible, when the enemy started to shell the town. People fled indoors and left the streets deserted. At one corner, however, there was a frantic crowd; they stopped us and asked us to take two casualties to hospital. A shell had struck their house and two people, one an old lady, the other a young lady, were badly wounded. A civilian jumped into the front of the truck and showed us the way to the nearest hospital.

I noticed then the difference between the behaviour of a man who is trained as a soldier and one who is not. The soldier expects casualties, and when one of his friends is hit he takes him to a regimental aid post without any fuss. But the Belgians did not expect to have shells fired at them. They flustered, shouted, argued, and although they did get the casualties quickly to hospital they did not have the calm, or semi-defeatist, philosophy of a soldier. As we drove to hospital I ruefully thought of the Brussels rumour – 'finie la guerre'. Of a truth it was not.

We had orders late in the afternoon of 9 September to move out of Antwerp and concentrate in an area to the east. Another battalion arrived to take over the defence of the town from us. The civilians were thrilled at the sight of so much military traffic moving about their town, but in the excitement of their cheering they crowded on to the streets so much that they impeded the movement of vehicles.

After a couple of days in our concentration area we moved over the Albert Canal at Beeringham and took over defensive positions several miles ahead of that. There were few signs of the enemy. I sited the mortars in a spacious garden, and we slept in the outhouses of a mansion. We were invited to sleep in some nearby homes but I declined the invitation. You cannot fire mortars from a bedroom, and I had to be ready for any emergency.

The troops were loath to dig in as they had not seen the enemy for more than 200 miles and they were beginning to think they had seen the last of him. But I warned them that we now had information that the Germans were digging slits along a railway bank not more than 2,000 yards from us, and that one of our company areas was often under shellfire. When some long-range shells whistled over our heads and were heard to land near the bridge at Beeringham the fellows showed more willingness to dig themselves in, though they still did not take the fighting as seriously as in the days of Normandy.

A church 800 yards from our mortar positions provided a very satisfactory observation post, for from its tower one could see for miles around. A parapet wall around the tower ensured that one could not be seen. To reach the top of this tower one had to climb 202 steps, so after establishing the post I visited it only once or twice a day. I was alarmed one day to discover that the wireless link between the post and the mortar position had not been functioning for some hours. The operator at the mortar end was content to do nothing about the failure, and the operator on the tower thought the failure was no particular concern of his. I was furious at this and ruled that the link must be tested every fifteen minutes and any failure reported at once to a trained signaller. In addition we should always keep two spare sets available for immediate use.

The organist at the church used to practise frequently and consequently men in the observation post found the time passed quickly. On Sunday, while we were using the post, the normal religious service was held.

While we were in these positions we were beginning to get indications that our walk-over had come to an end. The enemy bothered us more than he had done at any time since St Pierre-la-Vieille in Normandy. The Beeringham bridge was a target for his bombers. In front of us he was fortifying a railway embankment. Then we heard that troops on our left had established patrol contact with him.

While two of my mortar sections were with me in this area a third section was with a rifle company in a forward position around the village of Beverloo. Visiting them to check that everything was in order, I motor-cycled to the village, rested the machine against the kerb and looked for a sign that would lead me to the company headquarters. All was deserted. I caught sight of a solemn face at a window, then of another solemn face. What was the matter? Then I heard the sound of shells tearing through the air. I hugged the buildings for protection, and after the shells burst I raced across the road and ran into a large building, just getting inside before a second salvo exploded. I was surprised to find I was in the company headquarters, where everybody was very calm.

A number of Germans had been seen moving some

distance in front of the company positions, so a fighting patrol was sent out to engage them. But the patrol could not find the enemy and other patrols sent out in other directions also returned empty-handed. The company commander thought the enemy knew we were in Beverloo; hence this shelling. A few more shells landing nearby as he spoke reinforced his opinion. He took me to see the mortars, sited in a churchyard, with the adjoining church providing an observation post.

After a few days the Germans withdrew and our battalion moved forward to keep in contact. The mortars were next positioned behind a farmhouse on our left flank and I spent several wearying hours wandering through woods to try to find an observation post. But visibility was always limited. The position was popular with my platoon chiefly because of the proximity of the farmhouse. It was sometimes said that the first essential in siting mortars was to find a good building for the chaps to live in. If there was a house to occupy they could keep dry and probably warm. They could cook their meals in tolerable conditions and could sleep comfortably. In training in England one had learnt to be a he-man; to sleep in the rain, live in wet clothes and go without food. In battle one learnt to avoid being a he-man.

However, we were in this position for only ten hours, for during the evening the commanding officer called a meeting of the orders group and gave instructions for another limited and careful advance. Our next position was in an open field with only a shed and a couple of hayricks for comfort. We set up the mortars and aimed them so that we could fire instantly at a couple of likely targets in front of our forward companies. I sent a wireless message in code to the battalion control set, stating my position and that I was ready for action. Then, having seen that the sentries were posted correctly, I climbed into the back of our fifteen-hundred-weight truck and prepared to sleep on a row of petrol cans. My driver and batman were with me.

Traffic was still moving along the road behind us and one or two drivers were using sidelights until angry roars from fellows who could hear aircraft, presumably hostile, overhead made them put out their lights. It was a wonder to me the whole column of traffic was not attacked, possibly with disastrous consequence to my mortars, but the aircraft were apparently intent on their mission and were not deviated by the tempting sight of so much of our military traffic. We heard their bombs explode and judged the target to be Beeringham bridge.

After that the night was quiet. Next morning I set off to find company headquarters and the first thing Jimmy told me was that the commanding officer was asking for the map reference of my position and wanted to know why I had not reported it by wireless the previous night. I had actually taken particular care to do this and had even helped the signaller to transcribe the map reference into code. So before reporting to Colonel Turner I visited the signals office and the intelligence office to ask them why my wireless message was not passed on. The signals office told me every message they received was sent to the intelligence office and the latter said they had received no message from me. But my signaller assured me that the coded message he had sent had been correctly acknowledged.

I told the colonel emphatically that I had sent him a wireless message immediately I got into position and he did not say any more. I assume he accepted my story. Junior, the signals officer, used to say it was impossible to bluff the colonel. If, for example, there was no telephone communication between battalion headquarters and a forward company, Turner would ask the reason. Junior would give his answer, and, no matter how technically he spoke, Turner would always think the problem through for himself and if he was not satisfied he would, Junior suspected, visit a neighbouring battalion to find out whether they had the same difficulties. And Junior did not expect to remain signals officer for long if Turner ever found another battalion had better communications than we did.

[7]

The Arnhem Disaster

HOLD AT ALL COSTS

13–16 September

We were ordered forward to take over positions from the
Irish Guards. Apparently in a quick dash an Irish officer
and a couple of Bren gunners had captured a bridge over
the Escaut canal just a minute before the Germans were
due to blow it up. Now there was a considerable bridgehead
and it had to be held 'at all costs' but without any visible
show of strength; the enemy must not know that we considered it vital. We were told that in about four days' time a
big attack would be launched from the bridgehead by other
troops.

Our rifle company commanders went forward first to
reconnoitre their new areas and came back with widely
differing stories. One said he was going to a situation where
the officers had erected a large bell-tent for their mess and
had 'white tablecloths on the table'; it must be a dream
position. But the others came back with tales of companies
being counter-attacked several times daily and ground
sometimes being lost.

The battalion vehicles drove across the Escaut bridge on
13 September. I think we all noticed a damaged German
88mm anti-aircraft gun sited on the bridge itself. We
travelled along a muddy path near the bank of the canal
until we came to a particularly large wood. Here we found
the Guards' battalion headquarters, and I was shown around
the mortar positions by their mortar sergeant who was

commanding the platoon as their officer had become a casualty a few days previously.

Their weapon pits were in a clearing between the wood and the canal. The ground was very damp and one could not dig deeply before striking water. But the sergeant explained to me that there was the same amount of moisture everywhere along the canal bank and the area forward of the canal contained nothing but thick woods which were unsuitable for siting mortars. They had been given a number of special targets which they must be prepared to hit at a moment's notice. One of these was just on the edge of one of the leading platoon areas. The idea was that if the Germans attacked and that platoon was unable to hold its area the mortars would fire there to force the enemy back again. That was how the Guards interpreted 'the ground must be held at all costs'.

I was relieved to find our company commander, the cool-as-a-cucumber Major Waters, saw it rather differently.

'Make your target 150 yards in front of that platoon,' he said. 'I'm in favour of mortaring the enemy but not of mortaring our own troops even if they have been over-whelmed.'

The only operational maps we now had were German ones as our advance had outstripped our own map-makers. We had to make do with these until we reached Nijmegen when British versions again became available. The German maps gave much more detail than ours; too much detail, we all thought, with the result that the salient points were not easily recognizable.

Our first night was undisturbed, which was a pleasant surprise. One could hear heavy guns firing in the distance.

The next morning began with machine-gun firing from one of our company areas. Several Bren magazines were loosed off. Hearing this I thought a sentry had spotted some enemy movement. Such a thing was not uncommon

213

and did not usually cause alarm. But when the firing continued persistently and grew in volume I decided to get through to our observation post on the telephone. Just as I reached the phone the sergeant in the post was ordering us to fire at one of the pre-arranged targets.

Then things began to happen. As the sergeant was engaging one target the intelligence officer dashed up with an order from the commanding officer for us to engage another target, and behind us three regiments of artillery opened up. The Bren guns were still blazing away at the front. Evidently the Germans were putting in a major attack against us. I decided to join my sergeant in the observation post.

On my way there I noticed some riflemen, instead of adopting fire positions, were taking shelter at the bottom of their trenches. It may have been a very human tendency to retreat into the bowels of the earth and let the battle look after itself, but if everybody had done this there would have been nothing to stop the Germans advancing into our positions and slaughtering or capturing everyone they chose. The only way to defend not only one's position but also one's own skin was to stand up and fight, however much of an effort was required to do this. I saw a carrier sergeant and a platoon commander going around their sections putting heart into their men.

'You won't see any enemy at the bottom of your trench. Get where you can see them coming and be ready to fire.'

When I reached the observation post the battle had largely subsided, though our artillery was still firing at likely enemy forming-up places in case they were organizing another assault. I got the whole story from my sergeant who had kept alert and calm throughout.

'It was this chap here, sir, who first saw them,' he said, indicating a rifleman on his right. 'He roared, "Look, Jerries!" and I looked where he pointed and saw five or six of them get up and make a dash for it. They were only fifty yards away from us when I first saw them. But they bolted away and made for those woods over there. I fired two shots with my rifle and I think I hit a couple because they fell and I did not see them get up again. There may be several of them still lying in the folds of the earth and hidden from us.

'Unluckily, when we saw these Jerries this Bren gun, here, which could most probably have got the lot of them, was stripped for cleaning and so couldn't fire. All the other Brens opened up, though I don't suppose many of the firers saw the Jerries from where they are.'

After the quiet had continued for some time the company commander sent out a patrol to search for the enemy. They came back with five prisoners and the news that they had left behind them seven dead. The group of twelve had been sent out with bazookas (light anti-tank weapons that could be carried by infantry). They had got within range of one of our tanks when they were spotted and tried to run away.

And so it turned out that what most of us imagined was a big-scale attack was only a twelve-man patrol.

The Germans must have known we wanted the bridge-head; that could not be a secret. The Irish Guards had captured it, then repulsed a number of counter-attacks. Now we had repulsed one more. We could only hope that our furious defence had not given away the vital importance we attached to the bridgehead.

Colonel Turner told the officers that the encounter had demonstrated the value of good communications. When the enemy was spotted this was at once reported to battalion headquarters. All telephone lines were working and the colonel got through to the artillery to obtain their support. 'We have enough artillery behind us to break up any counter-attack,' he said. 'It is only a matter of having good communications and telling the gunners where the enemy are, in time. If we can let them know they can break up any attack. But if the lines were ever out of order and we had to fight alone, that would be another story.'

After this activity the German artillery began to worry us and several shells landed near our observation post. A number of tanks were in our area to support us and they made a thunderous noise whenever they moved. We infantrymen, although very fond of having tanks near us, were always afraid that their noise would draw fire. When this happened the tank crews got inside their tanks and I imagine they were safe. We infantry either dug our slit trenches a bit deeper and busied ourselves putting a roof on, or we took shelter behind a tank.

On the third day we extended our bridgehead. Reconnaissance patrols had established that the area in front of our battalion perimeter was now clear. So at daybreak, with a section of eight infantrymen in front for protection, Colonel Turner and Major Waters went forward to reconnoitre no man's land in detail, an artillery officer walking behind them to select his observation post. I walked behind the artillery officer. New positions for the rifle company and a new mortar viewing post were chosen.

A second company also advanced to new positions. In order to site his slit trenches as effectively as possible their commander, Major Harley, with typical and I thought extraordinary conscientiousness, had walked out into no man's land the previous night and from there had looked around to judge the strength of his proposed defences. Then he moved his troops forward while it was still dark.

During a previous chat with him I had learned Harley had an unusual way of coping with the moral burdens of command. We had been in a bleak situation at the time and he surprised and amused me by searching through his well-stocked literary mind for a series of gloriously apt quotations to take the mickey out of various aspects of our predicament. That having been done, everything seemed manageable.

Harley was marvellously complemented by his second-in-command, Bruce, who was a Canadian. Tall, dark, handsome, with strong-looking eyes, the extrovert Bruce appeared to be the answer to a maiden's prayer.

This morning Harley was a little apprehensive because one or two enemy soldiers had shown themselves 100 yards or less away. Bruce went out with a reconnaissance patrol to investigate and returned half an hour later to say he had seen a German outpost. He suspected it was a mortar observation post because as soon as he left cover he was mortared. So he went out again with a fighting patrol and came back this time to relate a skirmish.

'Goddammit,' he declared, 'a Jerry threw a grenade at me and it made such a small explosion that I don't suppose it would have hurt a fly. What Goddamn grenades they must use in that army!' He seemed most indignant, almost pained, at their ineffectiveness.

The artillery officer bombarded the hedgerows in front of that locality, and I ranged the mortars on likely forming-up places. One of my sergeants came out to relieve me and about midday I returned to my platoon headquarters, hoping to get a breakfast. But before I started that I was summoned to a battalion orders group.

DEFINITELY NOT A BRIDGE TOO FAR

16–22 September

'Tomorrow [17 September],' said Colonel Turner, 'the biggest land operation ever undertaken is due to start. Using a single road as the axis of advance, three divisions are going to drive into northern Holland. The Guards Armoured will lead, followed by the 43rd and the 50th [us].'

Three airborne divisions were going to be dropped along the route to capture about five bridges intact, but plans were laid to cope with the situation if they failed, and Royal Engineer bridging companies were placed well forward in the order of march. It was hoped the armour would get very near to the Zuyder Zee. We who were towards the end of the column could expect an easy advance, but, once the armour had reached its northern objective and we were established across all branches of the Rhine, we were going to have to form a hinge on which two divisions could swing right, in towards Germany, and cut off the Ruhr. We were warned this was going to be a hard task, and two battalions of our division were briefed to occupy strategic points across the Rhine so as to guard the right flank of the attack.

The operation was planned to knock Germany out of the war that autumn. Once the Ruhr was encircled it was forecast Germany could last only another two weeks. It was to be a campaign, we were told, that would go down in the history books.

There was tremendous enthusiasm over the plan. One artillery officer told my platoon that he would have his guns over the Rhine in two days' time. The words 'over the Rhine' were music in our ears. One fellow suffering from a slight wound was told by the medical officer that he would be away from the battalion for two weeks, and by everybody else that the war would be over by the time he came back. Newly arrived reinforcements were told by the troops that they could just as well return to England as it was all over bar the shouting now.

But one of my sergeants was not as optimistic as the rest. 'It's all very well to say the campaign will go down in the history books,' he commented, 'but I hope it turns out to be in our history books and not in the Germans.' For my part I anticipated that our journey into the heart of the Reich would be very similar to our advance through France and the Low Countries, only instead of liberation it would be conquest, and instead of underground forces helping us we would have to be on our guard continually against sabotage.

The foregoing paragraphs are exactly as I wrote them when I drafted my story, as explained in the first chapter, a few months after the war ended. I have therefore been critical of the title of book and film *A Bridge Too Far*, which implies that if the attack had been planned to stop at the Nijmegen bridge and not to go on to Arnhem everything would have been all right. This is wrong. Far from being a bridge too far the Arnhem bridge was merely a route to the strategically important high ground between the north of Arnhem (which is itself north of the bridge) and the Zuyder Zee. That would then have completed only the first part of a two-part operation, the second being the encirclement and conquest of the Ruhr, leading, it was assumed, to the end the war. It was worth taking serious risks to end of the war; it would not have been worth taking these risks to capture four bridges out of five.

The phrase 'a bridge too far' is said to have been used by Lieutenant-General Frederick Browning, deputy commander of the Allied airborne army, but I am among those who doubt that he used the phrase because it would imply that he did not understand the strategy of the operation, which is inherently unlikely.

Field Marshal Montgomery published in his memoirs the written orders he issued at the time. The real objective, these stated, was the Ruhr. The orders detail what the Canadians were to do, how the British were to make the main thrust, what support on the flanks there was to be, and how some American divisions would help in that support and how other of their divisions would advance around the south of the Ruhr. In particular the orders for the British ran:

'The first task . . . is to operate northwards and secure the crossings over the Rhine and Meuse in the general area Arnhem – Nijmegen – Grave . . .

'The army will then establish itself in strength on the general line Zwolle–Deventer–Arnhem facing east, with deep bridgeheads to the east side of the Ijssel river.

'From this position it will be prepared to advance eastwards to the general area Rheine–Osnabrück–Hamm–Munster. In this movement its weight will be on its right and directed towards Hamm, from which place a strong thrust will be made southwards along the eastern face of the Ruhr.'

From the Escaut canal to the high ground north of Arnhem was about sixty-five miles. The move from there to Rheine–Osnabrück–Hamm–Munster would have been another seventy to ninety miles and the drive along the east of the Ruhr another forty to sixty miles.

Whatever the operation was it was not a bridge too far.

On the eve of this great endeavour Montgomery was supremely confident. On the day the attack started he broadcast this message:

The Allies have removed the enemy from practically the whole of France and Belgium, except in a few places, and we stand at the door of Germany. By the terrific energy of your advance northwards from the Seine you brought quick relief to our families and loved ones in England by occupying the launching sites of the flying bombs.

We have advanced a great way in a short time and we have accomplished much. The total of prisoners captured is now nearly 400,000 and there are many more to be collected from those ports in Brittany and in the Pas de Calais that are still holding out.

The enemy has suffered immense losses in men and material. It is becoming problematical how much longer he can continue the struggle. Such an historic march of events can seldom have taken place in such a short space of time. You have every reason to be very proud of what you have done.

Let us say to each other 'This was the Lord's doing and it is marvellous in our eyes.'

And now the Allies are closing in on Nazi Germany from the east, and from the south, and from the west. Their satellite powers have thrown the towel into the ring and they now fight on our side. Our American Allies are fighting on German soil in many places. Very soon we shall all be there.

The Nazi leaders have ordered the German people to defend their country to the last and dispute every inch of ground. This is a very natural order and we would do the same ourselves in a similar situation. But the mere issuing of orders is quite useless. You require good men and true to carry them out.

The great mass of the German people know that their situation is already hopeless, and they will think more clearly on this subject as we advance deeper into their country. They have little wish to continue the struggle. But whatever orders are issued in Germany and whatever action is taken on them, no human endeavour can now prevent the complete and utter defeat of the armed forces in Germany.

Their fate is certain and their defeat will be absolute. Good luck to you all – and good hunting in Germany.

Just before two o'clock on the afternoon of 17 September General Horrocks climbed on to a factory roof near the Escaut canal and waited to see paratroopers falling behind the German positions. Only when he saw the first wave of parachutists did he give the order for the land attack to begin.

A drumfire barrage opened up, the initial rounds falling in a semi-circle ahead of the attacking tanks. As the tanks advanced the gunners increased their range and the shells continued to fall in the pattern of a semi-circle, thus giving our forces protection from all sides. It was the loudest barrage I ever heard. The noise was unceasing. The guns were firing from some way behind the canal bank and yet the noise on our side of the bank was terrific and, in one sense, terrible.

To support the attack I had to fire concentrations of mortar bombs on several suspected enemy positions. Against the deafening din of the heavy guns I could hardly hear the gentle poop of six mortars firing. It was as if the artillery was trying to swamp the enemy with oceans of shells while we were adding a few bucketfuls of mortar bombs. We fired for the best part of an hour and although we stayed in the same position we did not receive any German retaliatory fire. No doubt they had more pressing problems to attend to than the location of my mortar platoon.

In the distance I could see parachutes floating down to earth, and I could see men dangling at the end of them. Above them, on both flanks, and in fact everywhere, were Typhoon aircraft, and now and again I saw the planes dive to attack and heard the nerve-racking swish as they fired their rockets.

The main bridge over the canal was about 700 yards to my right, and during a couple of brief lulls in the barrage I heard the rumble of tanks storming along it. One of my sergeants brought me the news that armour and equipment were 'pouring over the bridge, three vehicles abreast'. The traffic had been continuous for an hour and was still moving.

Every aspect of this attack reflected something big. The plan was big; it aimed at ending the war. The barrage was the biggest ever. The use of airborne troops was on a big scale. Three divisions of land forces had been concentrated for the assault, and many other divisions were performing diversionary or supporting roles. There were more troops in

19. A three-inch-mortar crew well dug in and about to fire. A mortar platoon contained six such weapons, with a range of just under 3,000 yards. Firing would be controlled by an officer or sergeant in an observation post, communication being by wireless (which seldom worked) or telephone.

20. British infantry ready to open fire from one of Normandy's many sunken lanes. The corporal should not have allowed at least seven men to bunch so closely together – one shell could have killed them all.

21/22. Frank Waters, MC, fought with the 1st Hampshires in North Africa, Sicily, Italy and north-western Europe. *Right*, Frank Waters in 1992.

23/24. E. G. (Horace) Wright, MC and bar, in the 1940s and *right*, in 1992.

25. The village of Vernon, on the Seine, in ruins. The 7th Hampshires have just crossed the river (27 August). Now a bulldozer is preparing a roadway for a bailey bridge to be built. The 1st Hampshires crossed here four days later to start their dramatic dash to Brussels.

26. As the battle for Vernon is being won, only a few miles away the Seine presents a peaceful scene. Here a raft is taking troops and equipment across the river at one of its narrowest parts.

27. Burning German vehicles litter the road as an armoured car of the Guards Division hurries on, non-stop if possible, for Brussels. A Belgian civilian smiles happily.

28. The Hampshires and other units received an ecstatic welcome in Brussels. Women climbed on to moving vehicles wherever and however they could, and crowds surged so far forward that people risked having their toes squashed by trucks.

29. Soldiers of the Hampshire Regiment moving along the Escaut bridge to take over important positions from the Irish Guards, preparatory to the attack on Arnhem.

30. When the armoured thrust on Arnhem was checked, infantry groups were moved to the right flank to give protection. Here soldiers are passing through Asten, ten miles east of Eindhoven.

31. Soldiers of the 7th Hampshires getting out of their vehicles at the approach to the strongly defended town of Cloppenberg. In due course a plan would be drawn up for each attacking platoon.

32. VE + 1. The author and Francis Morgan, his company commander, are supervising the rounding up of prisoners near Bremerhaven.

33. German troops on Lüneburg Plain, now scarcely interested in anything that is happening, hear news of their surrender and passively await captivity, 5 May 1945.

34. The author with five members of his platoon at the Riverside Club, Winsen, June 1945. *Left to right*, Cpl Burton, L/Cpl Seaman, L/Sgt Enon, Lieut. Picot, Pte Stock, L/Cpl Kipp.

35. A memorial at Le Hamel 'to our glorious liberators'. The inscription, which is in English and French, recalls that the Devon, Hampshire and Dorset battalions 'were the first troops to land at Asnelles and Le Hamel on 07.30 hours on D-Day, 6 June 1944. From here they started on their victorious advance to free many towns and villages in France, Belgium and Holland, and were the first British infantry to enter Germany.'

36. Eight Hampshire veterans and two French officials at the Le Hamel memorial in 1984. Seven of the eight had been wounded, three of them twice, and two were wearing wooden legs; one had escaped from captivity. Between them the eight wore one DSO and four MCs. *Left to right*, Tony Mott, Cecil Thomas, two French officials, David Nelson-Smith, John Littlejohns, E. G. (Horace) Wright, Geoffrey Picot, Gordon Layton, Malcolm Bradley.

this attack than in any other I had known. It all looked like an advance in overwhelming strength on a very narrow front, for the chief effort was being made along one main road which led through Valkenswaard, Eindhoven and farther north to obscure towns with the then little known names of Nijmegen and Arnhem.

When the noise of battle receded we waited for news; not anxiously, but expectantly. The confidence we had felt when we heard of the daring plan had been increased by the glimpse we had caught of the huge forces we were employing.

'How far have they got now?' many of us asked the intelligence officer that afternoon.

'No definite news yet,' the cautious man always replied.

Later in the day the commanding officer sent for me and told me one of our rifle companies was being sent forward to secure protection for the flank of the attack. I had to arrange for a mortar section to accompany them. I returned to my platoon and nominated the section that usually worked with that company.

'Why is it always my section that is chosen for these sticky jobs, sir?' demanded the sergeant angrily. 'Why can't the other sections do a bit? It's always this section that has to go.'

'It's you who's going this time,' I replied, 'because you always work with that company. The other sections get their turn in the long run, I can assure you.'

He was dissatisfied, but he complied.

That night I travelled up the main road where the traffic was still moving three abreast and found the company headquarters in a roadside house. The harassed commander was trying to clear up several problems simultaneously. By the light of a torch he anxiously studied his map. Two men held a blanket over the window so that the light would not show outside.

'Where are the stretcher bearers?' the major was asking.

'Here, sir,' came a reply from the darkness.

'Does anybody know where the carrier commander is? Has the quarter master arrived with the meal yet? Is there any sign of the truck with the blankets?'

I moved on to see my sergeant and found him settling down for the night with his chaps in a shed. The mortars were mounted in a back garden. I saw no civilians anywhere.

'We had one engagement against a Spandau nest,' he reported pleasantly, the earlier dissatisfaction having disappeared. 'I think we got him because after a bit he stopped firing. We had a German mortar firing at us, too, but his bombs didn't land very near. The company lads tried to get that mortar, but he cleared out before they got to him.'

Next morning, back at the canal bank, stories were beginning to circulate about incidents that had happened during the attack. In the main it appeared that the battle had gone well, in spite of our losing nine tanks early on. One story said one anti-tank gun had knocked them all out. Another version was that Typhoon aircraft had hit them by mistake. Our armour had reached Eindhoven and, finding it strongly defended, the commander had left a force to deal with it while the majority of the tanks by-passed it and pushed on.

We heard of an example of amazing German courage. Faced by the severe drumfire barrage, they had not retreated; nor did they cling to the protection of their slit trenches. They got up and, as the barrage lifted and landed farther back, they walked forward through it, firing at our chaps as they came. However much we loathed the Germans we respected their courage. There was skill in the manoeuvre, too, and our men had difficulty in coping with it. 'E'en the ranks of Tuscany could scarce forbear to cheer.'

A complete ban was put on any transport moving back,

and at one stage casualties were evacuated forward – a most unusual thing and only possible if the advance is exceptionally rapid and comprehensive.

There had been a deception plan, though nobody was certain on that day to what extent it had worked. All during 16 September, the day before the attack, another of our armoured divisions had sent bogus wireless messages designed to give the enemy the impression that an assault was to be launched eastwards, whereas in fact it was made northwards.

One extraordinary story thrilled us. Before the start General Horrocks wanted to know the approximate strength of the enemy in Valkenswaard, a small town three miles behind the German front. Accordingly, two men of the Household Cavalry (a reconnaissance regiment) drove their little scout cars over the Escaut bridge at high speed and raced along the main road through our positions and into enemy-held territory as fast as they could. They took the startled Germans completely by surprise. They continued at break-neck speed until they had driven through the entire depth of the enemy positions. Then they got out, assured the local people that this was not their liberation (that would come tomorrow), had a quick look around to find out what they wanted and returned along the same road at a speed of something over 60 m.p.h. On the way back they were chased down the road by the fire of sundry Spandau machine-guns, but the bullets went behind their cars as the machine-gunners under-estimated the speed.

The Guards Armoured Division, we were told, had smashed their way through the German positions and were advancing with enthusiasm northwards. But they were operating on a very narrow front and the ground they had gained was really only a corridor, very long and still lengthening, but no wider than three or four miles. Troops had to be stationed all the way along this corridor to protect it from flank attacks.

It was to help protect the road that our battalion was taken out of the bridgehead and deployed in groups along the corridor, each group being on average 600 yards apart and sited anything from 200 to 1,000 yards east of the road. It was imperative that the road should remain open; if it was cut the impetus of the attack would inevitably slacken and that was the last thing we wanted. We had to strike a mortal blow before the enemy could recover.

I sited the mortars in a clearing of a wood that gave on to the road, somewhere near the centre of the battalion perimeter. We had crossed the border into Holland but that occasioned no interest. Our eyes were on the maps, looking eagerly at the places reached by the leading tanks, and far beyond. A tank crew repairing their tank near the mortar position warned us that there were still Germans roaming about the woods.

Before dark I set off with some colleagues to find an observation post. We wandered along tracks and through woods for twenty minutes before we saw any of our troops, and I was nervous lest the first soldiers we should meet should be German. Eventually I established the observation post on a hayrick, only to find the wireless set did not work. By the time my signaller had coaxed it back to life it was dark, so I could not register any possible emergency targets. On returning to my platoon area I immediately organized a defensive plan for ourselves in case an enemy patrol reached us. Our sentries were alert, and even belligerent. Then I settled down to sleep on a bed of long grass and soft moss. Convoys were still moving up the road. The noise they made did not cease, day nor night.

Next morning I ranged on the emergency targets that were to be engaged if our rifle companies wanted protection, and arranged for the observation post to be manned continuously. I did not expect any trouble, for by now any Germans as far back as we were were not likely to be in a fighting mood. But I believed in taking too many precautions rather than too few. War was played for high stakes. You could not afford to take one unnecessary chance.

I asked the intelligence officer what news there was of the attack. 'They're getting on well,' he replied. 'Eindhoven has been captured, though after we got it German aircraft came over and gave it a hell of a bombing. I believe they also bombed the bridge over the Escaut canal last night, too.'

'How far has the armour got?' I asked.

'I don't know exactly, but they're getting on towards Nijmegen.'

'Is that where we are supposed to end up finally?'

'No, we go on past that to stop just north of a place called Arnhem.'

Apart from protecting the road against a flank attack – and the danger of this was slight as we were so near the base from which the attack began – there was nothing for us to do except watch the convoys moving up and wait for our turn to get on the road. As far as I could judge the entire Guards Armoured Division of tanks and lorried infantry, and supplies for both, had gone through, possibly 2,000 vehicles. The 43rd Infantry Division had begun to move up and between their battalions a vast amount of bridging equipment was in convoy. Now and again we saw airborne troops taking supplies by land to the parachutists, some of whom by now had been relieved by ground troops.

It was an amazing and thrilling sight to sit on the grass bank and watch these enormous quantities of military equipment go by. The whole armoury of the fighting man was shown to us, and the display was most impressive. First we might see a squadron of tanks, noisy Shermans that seemed to have to make such an effort to go fast, yet always managed to maintain a good speed, some with a short gun, others armed with a long, wicked-looking 17-pounder gun.

Behind them 3-ton lorries with supplies, 15-hundredweight office trucks and a lot of repair impedimenta. Then a Royal Engineers bridging company whose lorries carried exceptionally heavy loads. A dozen or more of these would be followed by a convoy of medium-calibre field or heavy-calibre anti-aircraft guns, the latter mounted on a square platform carried by four huge wheels and pulled by a lorry; with trucks containing the gun crews either in front or behind. There were batteries of 25-pounder guns, each gun with its own ammunition trailer, the gun and trailer pulled by a powerful lorry which also housed the crew. There were Bofors light anti-aircraft guns pulled by a truck, with men sitting on the gun aimers' seats.

Behind all this might come an infantry battalion with all its varied equipment: jeeps, each packed tight with driver, company commander, batman, signaller, wireless set, large map case and a mountain of kit; carriers performing the job of pack-mules, carriers towing 6-pounder anti-tank guns; troop-carrying vehicles with men squashed uncomfortably on top of one another; trucks with rations and colour-sergeants sitting on top of the rations; DUWKs with troops riding in them, not sure whether they were in a boat or a car; staff cars with more officers than they usually contained; wireless trucks with complicated-looking equipment.

Then possibly behind the infantry battalion would come a convoy of airborne troops with supplies in three-ton trucks; more bridging equipment; support battalions with noisy carriers containing medium-calibre machine-guns and heavy mortars; Royal Electrical and Mechanical Engineer detachments with repair vehicles of all sizes, petrol lorries, water trucks; more guns. The procession was continuous.

The three-divisional attack probably needed something like 6,000 vehicles. Had these been spaced forty yards apart the convoy would have occupied nearly 140 miles. And if a steady speed of 15 m.p.h. had been maintained the column would have taken over nine hours to pass one spot. But movement could not be smooth and regular. For hours on end the convoy would be stationary as the battle was fought several miles ahead. Thus the vehicles clogged the road for days. We had been told that even if everything went well it would be four or five days at least before our turn came.

Whenever vehicles stopped there was much banter between their occupants and my soldiers.

'Look! There's my mate,' cried Monty my signaller, as he recognized a pal in a DUWK. 'Where've you come from?'

'We've just been moved up from Brussels,' answered his friend dismally.

'Cor, Brussels!' snorted Monty. 'You've been living with the base wallahs!'

'What about you,' retorted his mate, 'what are you doing here? You're having it pretty cushy, aren't you?'

'We've been in the bridgehead that you've just come through,' replied Monty proudly. 'It'll be a change for you to be in front of us.'

Troops in the convoy would often ask our chaps:

'What are you doing right back here?' or 'How much longer are you going to stay in this rest area?'

My lads would shout back: 'What were you doing when we liberated Brussels and Antwerp?' or 'Well, it's a change for somebody else to be doing the fighting this time.'

One day we received an issue of German rations instead of British food. First one complaint was raised, then another, and shortly the whole platoon was in uproar. The jam was like rubber, the margarine was rancid, the meat was bad. 'No wonder the Germans are on the run if this is what they are fed on' was a typical comment. So I brought the medical officer along to look at the food, and he confirmed at once that the meat was bad. He did not condemn the jam as inedible, though he told the chaps that he held the same opinion about it as they did. To get the meat condemned officially was easy. The doctor said he would willingly write the necessary certificate.

'When shall we get another issue?' asked a dozen eager voices.

'In about three weeks' time,' replied the doctor, 'when it won't be any use to you. I can condemn the meat now if you want me to, but the certificate I write has to go back a long way to various authorities before anyone will issue another meat ration for you, and by the time you get it probably three weeks will have gone by. You won't want it then, but you can claim it if you want to.'

On that the matter was dropped, but there was considerable prejudice against any future issue of German rations.

As we waited day after day for the various convoys to go past, and as their speed seemed to be slower and their halts longer, the suspicion was born in many of our minds that all was not well up at the front. For a time nobody mentioned his doubt.

Then one of my soldiers burst upon us to say: 'I've just heard that the road's been cut. A hundred Germans and two tanks are supposed to have got across the road, and cut off the Guards Armoured Division and part of the 43rd division.'

This story was later confirmed, and one result of the cutting of the road was that General Horrocks was separated from the majority of his troops. He later told us that a carrier platoon escorted him along a detour outflanking the main body of Germans and enabled him to get near the leading formations again. Eventually the enemy were dislodged, but we continued to hear reports of the road being under fire and of its being effectively cut at times. One column of service vehicles was said to have been attacked and to have suffered losses.

As our armour pushed northwards various enemy formations in the west of Holland were in danger of being cut off. These people were therefore keen to move eastwards to try to cross our narrow corridor and link up with the rest of the German army. The fact that this manoeuvre would bring them nearer to their homeland was probably an encouragement to them.

In spite of this many were on the verge of cracking. North of Antwerp, we were told, a large number gave up the fight and were deserting, when they were confronted by a strong-willed, monocled, one-legged Prussian officer who, standing at a main crossroads, imperiously ordered them back to their units. By this and other examples the German army regained its discipline and cohesion – and kept it for another seven months.

PROTECTING THE FLANK

23 September–2 October

At last our turn came to move forward and we left our positions at 5.45 a.m. just as it was getting light on the morning of the twenty-third. The marshalling was done in the dark, and a regimental policeman let through an artillery convoy in front of me, so that for most of the march my platoon was separated from our battalion. We overtook vehicles wherever we could and eventually reached our correct place.

We drove through Eindhoven, where considerable damage had been done by German bombers a few nights before, and then we left the main road and entered the village of Lieshout, where we had to protect the right flank of the corridor. We were relieved to find that this was our only task because the intelligence officer had previously told us of his fear that we might be rushed to a place where the enemy was giving trouble. He had expected us to have to relieve a tank battalion and contain the enemy while the armour manoeuvred for a flank attack.

Lieshout promised to be more peaceful than that, for there was neither sign nor report of the Germans. We watched staggeringly large numbers of supply aircraft flying in the direction of Arnhem and we assumed strong reinforcements were being flown in. The aircraft, however, might have been carrying supplies. With a great depth of feeling in my heart I wished those airborne troops well.

We stayed at Lieshout only long enough to have a hot supper and a night's sleep, and then moved on to the neighbouring village of Stiphout, and thence through Veghel to Boekel. At Veghel, which was on the main road to Nijmegen, we passed American paratroops who were being pulled out of the battle for a rest. There were signs of fighting everywhere: dead Germans in ditches, smashed guns on the roadside; and I reckoned we would be in action before long.

At Boekel the battalion had to be prepared to repel attack from any direction, so I sited all the mortar sections in gardens in the centre of the town and established an observation post in the steeple of a church, using a wireless set for communication.

Colonel Turner thought we were in a potentially dangerous area, several miles away from any other troops. The Dutch residents were told not to hang out their national flags in case they were seen by the enemy. That first night I was on duty at the battalion command post, which was in a school, from 3.30 a.m. to 6.30, and for most of that time we suffered intermittent shelling. The colonel thought the Germans had discovered his headquarters, so at dawn he moved everybody away and set up his command post in a field. Slit trenches were quickly dug, and all telephone cables relaid. My mortars were only 300 yards from the school, but I decided not to move.

When Sunday came the padre held a church service in the school and the colonel allowed up to twenty per cent of the men to attend, the rest remaining at their posts. I was on my way to the service when I was called to see Turner. 'Were you going to church?' he asked.

'Yes, sir, I was, but it doesn't matter,' I replied.

'I didn't mean to stop you going,' he said. 'You could have come to me afterwards.'

He told me the positions of other battalions had been altered and our rear was now exposed, so he wanted at least some of the mortars to be aimed in that direction. I returned to the mortar position, made the necessary adjustments, and then went to church, arriving in time for the singing of the last hymn and the national anthem.

By 26 September, when we moved to Mill, most of us realized that the great land-based attack had been held and, though we did not know the details of the Arnhem fighting, it was obvious now that the war would not end before the winter. We were at Mill only for a day and during that time my men congregated in a farmer's barn for a sing-song led by the farmer's two sons playing mouth organs. I went outside to check that no undue noise could be heard because I did not want our position to be given away.

We next moved to St Hubert, three miles away, where from a tall church you could see the lowlands of Germany. Again the mortars were sited centrally, and there was no evidence of enemy activity.

One of our rifle companies, accompanied by a section of mortars, by officers from nearby supporting units, and by me on a motor-bike, patrolled into the village of St Agatha, so near the German border that we were not sure where the sympathies of the people lay. The streets were deserted and we looked suspiciously at faces which remained at windows too long. From one point we saw in the distance two German soldiers walking about unconcernedly. A Reconnaissance

Regiment officer told us that had been no uncommon sight in recent days, and an artillery officer said the previous day he had seen a whole company of Germans lining up for their dinner so he had fired a heavy barrage at them and their cookhouse.

From St Agatha I rode to Oeffelt, where another of my sections had accompanied another rifle company on their investigative patrol. All was quiet and I returned to St Hubert. There I was astonished to be welcomed back as a long-lost brother. Everyone seemed delighted to see me. Soon I learnt the reason. That afternoon a motor cyclist had sustained a serious accident and had been taken to hospital. The hospital informed us of the registration number of the motor cycle, and this was the number of the machine I had been riding. Everybody concluded that I had had a serious accident. In fact the hospital made a mistake with the number.

We left St Hubert to go into a reserve position near Beek, south-east of Nijmegen. The commanding officer arranged for an advance party to look for billets for the men. I took one of my sergeants with me and the first likely-looking place we entered contained many large, almost magnificent, pictures of leading Nazis. We tore a picture of Hitler into two, and consigned photos of Ribbentrop and Goering to the waste paper basket. The Dutch inhabitants nervously apologized that they had been forced to display these photos and said they were as pleased as we were to see them destroyed. We had our doubts.

Later we chanced upon a large house, or possibly it was a private hotel, with five empty rooms, each large enough for about eight fellows to sleep on the floor. The occupiers of the other rooms were friendly and most co-operative. The room I chose for my headquarters had a bed in it and before anybody else could speak I said: 'That's mine!' It had only a wire mattress, but at that time to sleep on a springy wire surface, and not a hard floor or the damp earth, was the height of luxury. I could imagine no greater comfort, not even at the Ritz. The chaps were quite happy sleeping on the floor around me. True, they envied my bed; but after all they were sleeping on wood, which was more comfortable than stone and warmer than the earth, and they were inside a house, which was better than being in a slit trench, and the house was comfortable and undamaged.

Moreover the area was quiet. No Spandau machine-guns could be heard, no noise of artillery barrages disturbed us, not even the occasional odd shell came our way. It was understood we were to remain in the area for four or five days. The god of war was being kind to us, we thought.

At 9.30 p.m. we were all in bed. Monty tuned a spare wireless set into the BBC and before going to sleep we enjoyed some soft, sweet music. I turned over and closed my eyes. The telephone rang. Just testing the line from battalion headquarters, I thought. I heard Monty repeat the message he received. 'Warning order. Prepare to move at first light tomorrow. Further details later.' And so vanished our dreams of five comfortable, carefree days.

The sentries woke the platoon with this disagreeable news at 5 a.m. By now we were all fed up with breakfasting at this hour, so we cooked nothing and decided to eat later whenever we could. We marshalled without incident and journeyed about six miles to Nijmegen. A thick mist enshrouded us as we entered the town and the weather was the coldest it had been that autumn. I soon realized that both the mist and the chill were caused by a smoke screen which covered the bridge. We crossed the river Waal and harboured just north of it. There we cooked our breakfasts rapidly and ate them hungrily.

I noticed two generals and a number of senior artillery officers driving forward in staff cars. 'People like them don't go up to the front for nothing, I know,' remarked one of my veterans.

Around midday the commanding officer told us we were to relieve the East Yorks, who were in a difficult defensive position and were being severely and continually counter-attacked. We could expect quite heavy shelling, but not on the Normandy scale. On the way forward with the advance party I heard the loud and frightening crack of airbursts (shells exploding in the air, instead of on impact with the ground), and the thought of jagged shrapnel entering my body was not pleasant. I noticed with amazement a few Dutch civilians, women among them, completely uncon-cerned at the shelling. In fact they took fewer precautions than most soldiers.

My opposite number in the East Yorks was an old friend. He talked to me enthusiastically about the attack his battal-ion had made a few days previously to capture the ground they now occupied. One platoon had charged with fixed bayonets and cut the throats of a dozen Germans in their trenches. He confirmed that they had been counter-attacked but thought the position had stabilized now.

'Over there is Bemmel church,' he said, pointing to a very badly damaged church. 'Don't go near there unless you have to. The enemy can obviously see it and he shells or mortars it most of the time. It's had one direct hit already and it's a wonder it has not had more.'

The ground was very flat for miles around. Only a small cluster of houses here, a little group of trees there, provided any cover. The mortars were deeply dug in and there were a couple of houses 100 yards away where the men could rest and shelter. But the weapons were 2,000 yards behind the front, which was a long way considering their maximum range was only 3,000 yards. Moreover the platoon was not manning any forward observation posts, though a number of possible targets had been agreed with the commander of the most exposed rifle company. I thought my first job in the morning would be to look for an observation post and my second to see whether I could find a suitable position for the mortars nearer the front.

When my platoon arrived the change-over was performed quickly and efficiently. Soon after it was dark we prepared to sleep. With the rest of my platoon headquarters I was in a cellar. Monty tuned his wireless into the BBC and we heard for the first time the full horrifying story of the Arnhem disaster. Airborne troops ten days on their own with enemy completely surrounding them! Short of food and water. Scarcely any ammunition. Squeezed into an ever-decreasing area. Fighting against tanks and self-propelled guns with only infantry weapons. And only 2,000 of a division of perhaps 8,000 got back to Nijmegen.

It was a story the like of which none of us had heard before, almost the ultimate catastrophe. And the survivors seemed to be a different breed from the rest of us.

'It's hell to be pulled out before you've done your job,' one told the BBC. I could not imagine any of my men making that complaint. I think the airborne soldiers were different from the rest. Firstly, they had deliberately volunteered for what they knew was a difficult and dangerous job. Secondly they had been kept waiting and waiting and waiting in England for this one encounter, so that in the end their enthusiasm and battle-fury were of a very high order.

The ordinary infantry, on the other hand, had not volunteered for anything. And secondly, once they entered a campaign they probably had to stay in it, fighting for month after month, until they were wounded or killed, or the campaign was won.

Perhaps it is fair to say the airborne troops needed the wholly committed dash of the 100-metre sprinter while the infantry of the line needed the dour plodding of the marathon runner.

Although it was only on 2 October that we learned of the

Arnhem disaster the people of Britain had been told four days before. The *Daily Mail* reported on 28 September:

Two thousand troops of the First British Airborne Division were evacuated from the Arnhem bridge-head out of 7,000 to 8,000 dropped in the area, according to an American broadcast from Paris last night.

The speaker said the figure may be higher. About 1,200 wounded were left behind in the care of the Germans and British doctors who stayed with them. The Germans claimed that they held 6,150 prisoners including 1,700 wounded and that British killed numbered 1,500 . . .

A correspondent with the British Second Army has given his reasons for the failure of General Dempsey's spearhead to relieve the airborne forces. After the weather he blames the difficult canal-intersected countryside, where our tanks had to keep to elevated roads and were consequently good targets for hidden German 88mm guns.

And a dispatch from Alan Wood with the Arnhem airborne force ran:

This is the end. The most tragic and glorious battle of the war is over, and the survivors of this British airborne force can sleep soundly for the first time in eight days and nights.

Orders came to us yesterday to break out from our forest citadel west of Arnhem, cross the Rhine, and join up with the Second Army on the south bank.

Our commander decided against a concerted assault on the Germans around us. Instead the plan was to split up into little groups, ten to twenty strong, and set out along different routes at two-minute intervals, which would simply walk through the German lines in the dark.

Cheeky patrols went out earlier tying bits of white parachute tape to trees to mark the way. To hinder the Germans waking up to what was happening, Second Army guns laid down a battering box barrage all afternoon.

The first party was to set off at 10 p.m.; our group was to leave at 10.04 p.m. They went round distributing little packets of sulphanilamide and morphia. We tore up blankets and wrapped them round our boots to muffle the sound of our feet in the trees.

We were told the password – John Bull. If we became separated each man was to make his way by compass due south until he reached the river.

Our major is an old hand. He led the way and linked our party together by getting everyone to hold the tail of the parachutist's smock of the man in front of him, so our infiltrating column had an absurd resemblance to some children's game.

It was half-light, with the glow of fire from burning houses around, when we set out. We were lucky; we went through a reputed enemy pocket without hearing a shot except for a stray sniper's bullet.

Another group met a machine-gun with a fixed line of fire across their path. Another had to silence a bunch of Germans with a burst of Sten fire and hand grenades.

WHERE IT ALL WENT WRONG

Could the attack on Arnhem have been successful; could the second part of the plan, to cut off the Ruhr, have been accomplished; and was it possible to end the war in that year of 1944?

We know that by 3 September, when we reached Brussels, the enemy had been routed in the northern sector. There was no organized resistance to our armoured columns or to the motorized infantry following closely behind. If these forces had been strong enough, and if they had had sufficient petrol and ammunition, they could easily have surrounded the Ruhr. Whether that would have ended the war is something we cannot be certain about, but it would have been a development of huge importance, possibly decisive.

We also know that the attack on Arnhem, started on 17 September, was a failure. So the question is: could it have been started earlier, preferably much earlier, and could it have had greater strength, preferably much greater strength?

Consider these events and their dates:

August 15:	Hitler hears full details of the Germans' disaster in Normandy and wails: 'It's the worst day of my life.'
August 17:	Mongomery sees Bradley (American land forces commander) and puts forward a plan for the British to advance on Antwerp, the Americans on Cologne; then for the two, with forty divisions between them, to encircle the Ruhr and thus to open the way to Berlin; and meanwhile the entire Allied southern sector merely to be held defensively. Montgomery thought Bradley agreed with the outline plan. Bradley later said he had not agreed, he had only reckoned some features had merit.
August 20:	Eisenhower (supreme commander) decides that the British forces should be directed to Antwerp and the Ruhr and the Americans to Metz and the Saar. He was therefore

putting the main US strength 150 miles south of where Montgomery wanted it.

August 23: Eisenhower's headquarters issues a situation assessment. 'The enemy in the west has had it. Two and a half months of bitter fighting have brought the end of the war in Europe within sight, almost within reach.'

August 23: Eisenhower and Montgomery meet. Montgomery pleads for one knock-out blow to be delivered in the north, at the Ruhr. The British with seventeen divisions are not strong enough to do this alone, so he asks for twelve American divisions to help.

Eisenhower refuses, adheres to his broad-front strategy, but says the northern thrust (Ruhr) can be supported by what the Americans can spare from their Metz/Saar attack, which would be possibly six or eight divisions, and that in addition the northern thrust can have priority of supplies.

September 2: Montgomery and Dempsey (Britain) meet Bradley and Hodges (US). They split up with divergent views but it is learnt that Bradley, far from giving supply priority to the north, is giving it to Patton 150 miles to the south.

September 3: (The day we captured Brussels.) Montgomery, assured of support from three airborne divisions, considers starting his attack on Arnhem on 6 or 7 September.

September 4: (Day we captured Antwerp.) Montgomery again asks Eisenhower to support one full-blooded, end-the-war thrust to the Ruhr and thence Berlin.

September 5: Eisenhower insists on the two attacks but

repeats that the Ruhr effort can have supply priority.

September 7: Montgomery says that unless he has more supplies he will not be able to take the Ruhr.

September 10: Eisenhower and Montgomery meet. Montgomery speaks so angrily that Eisenhower taps him on the knee and says: 'Steady, you can't talk to me like that, I'm your boss.' Montgomery complains he is not getting supply priority. Eisenhower replies that by priority he did not mean absolute priority and he refuses to scale down the Metz/Saar attack.

September 11: Montgomery tells Eisenhower that since he is not getting supply priority he cannot attack the Rhine (i.e. Arnhem) until 23 or 26 September.

September 12: Eisenhower's chief of staff tells Montgomery that Eisenhower is stopping the Saar attack and that the transport of three US divisions will be diverted to increase Montgomery's supplies in the north and that the whole of the American maintenance will go to the US divisions near Montgomery's flank in order to support him. So Montgomery orders the Arnhem assault to begin on 17 September.

September 14: Eisenhower approves of Patton continuing his Metz/Saar attack. The US transport was *not* diverted to help Montgomery's supplies and the US divisions on Montgomery's flank did *not* get maintenance priority.

Thus perished the British 1st Airborne Division and all chance of ending the war in 1944.

The American Lieutenant-General James Gavin, who commanded a US airborne division in this attack, subsequently said that if Montgomery had been allotted three extra American divisions the entire thrust would have been successful and the war would have ended much sooner than it did.

What did the Germans think of it all? After the war the noted British military historian Bruce Liddell Hart interviewed all their leading survivors.

'All the German generals to whom I talked,' he reported, 'were of the opinion that the Allied supreme command [Eisenhower] had missed a great opportunity of ending the war in the autumn of 1944. They agreed with Montgomery's view that this could best have been achieved by concentrating all possible resources in a thrust in the north towards Berlin.'

8

First Battalion's Last Battle

A SUPERB OBSERVATION POST

2–3 October

To return to my story, not far from Bemmel with my companions I was about to doze off in the cellar of a house 100 yards away from our mortars, the weapons themselves being about 2,000 yards from the front line and there being no established observation post.

In one of the forward rifle company areas sentries heard movement in the woods in front of them. Platoons stood-to. In the moonlight the company commander saw the enemy forming up, 100 yards away, to attack him. He lost no time in calling for artillery and mortar support.

Down in my cellar the phone rang. 'Fire on target number two,' I was ordered.

I jumped up, pulled on my boots, gave the alarm and raced to the mortars. The chaps turned out briskly and were soon dropping bombs down the barrels. A few seconds later the artillery opened up behind us with a full roar. Fire control was a little primitive that night. The company commander stood by the telephone and said when to start and when to stop, and whether he wanted the fire to be rapid or normal. A man in the cellar shouted the order to another who stood outside the house; and he relayed it to me. From me the orders went to the men on the mortars. They fired.

Now and again the danger to the company would recede; but soon we would be told to stand-by again; later we would have to fire to help repel another expected attack. Then all would go quiet and we would return to bed, and to sleep, only to be awakened again with another urgent call to engage the same target. Four times we stood down, and every time we stood-to again.

We could only fire by the map as it was too dark and there were too many woods in the target area for anyone to see the burst of our bombs and correct our aim. None the less the commander appeared very satisfied. He said most of the bombs seemed to fall either where the enemy was forming up, or in front of his forming-up place, thus deterring him from attacking.

Now that the commander knew how close the Germans were to him he felt distinctly uncomfortable. In some places the front lines were less than fifty yards apart, so if the enemy was to be prevented from rushing across no man's land fire had to come down swiftly and accurately. The officer concluded that the enemy did not realize what positions his men were occupying, so he made sure everybody kept under cover. On one occasion one mortar bomb landed short, falling just in front of a platoon position. The officer was pleased. 'If the Germans see some of our bombs landing there they won't realize we are occupying that position.'

After dawn stand-to I looked at the map to see which was the best route to take to reconnoitre an observation post in that company area, and I decided on one particular road which my East Yorks pal had told me was safe as long as I used all available cover. Luckily, before I set out I was summoned to battalion headquarters, and I arrived there just in time to learn that our entire area was under attack and the Germans were giving their troops heavy covering artillery fire. Colonel Turner hastened to his command post and I slid smartly into a nearby slit trench. Turner called for artillery and heavy mortar fire to protect our forward troops. He looked thoughtful as he pondered on which of his companies needed most help; but also, I sensed, undisturbed.

Somebody raised the shout: 'Here are some Jerries coming!' Immediately there was consternation, bewilderment, fear. How had they come right through to battalion headquarters? Oh, God! Surely they hadn't broken through? The confident Major Drewitt, whose task it was to organize the defence of the headquarters, yelled out firmly: 'Carrier sergeant, take your men to the road and watch for any approach from there . . . Those men over there, watch the left flank . . . You two, guard the front.'

Then the enemy came in sight. Twelve of them were moving down the road – with an escort of three British soldiers. 'It's all right, they're prisoners,' shouted a man in the carrier section, and in a moment everyone became brave.

'You had better go up to that exposed company,' Colonel Turner told me, 'because it looks as if they need a mortar observation post. The major in command will tell you what targets to register, and he may be able to point out some enemy positions to you. If he does, mortar them hard. I don't know how you are going to get through, though, because an armoured car was shot up along this road earlier this morning' – he was pointing to the road I was intending to use. 'I don't think it is safe for you to go either on foot or in a carrier. There must be another way up.'

We looked again at the map. 'If you go across country,' the colonel said, 'I believe you have to go through these woods. Anywhere else you can be seen.'

I suggested the company should send a guide, and this was agreed. I could see the distance was going to be too great for the wireless to work, so I planned a relay system; one set at the observation post, a second at battalion headquarters and a third at the mortar position. The guide led me and my wireless operator along muddy ditches and through thick woods. He made us hug the hedges as much as possible. At one spot we had to jump up on to a road, dash swiftly across it, and fall quickly into a ditch at the far side.

When we reached the farmhouse that constituted the company headquarters the commander, Major Harley, took me to a window and showed me the woods and houses where he had observed the enemy.

'Don't go too near the window, old man, or they will see you. I don't think they know we are using this place. They fire an occasional shot in this direction, but I think it is just to see whether it draws any reply.'

Standing well back, I looked out of the window.

'You see that large white house at the corner of the wood on the left,' the major went on quietly, almost in a whisper, 'the enemy are there. All along that wood, straight in front, there's swarms of them there. You see this carrier abandoned in the dip, two fellows walked up to it as cool as anything this morning. That's what makes me think they don't know we're here. If they knew they would hardly walk out into the open like that. The majority of the Germans are in that wood. We could hear them forming up there last night. I could see them there this morning, too.'

The major took me upstairs and, looking to the right, he pointed out a crossroads, a couple of buildings and some more woods. 'There's Germans in all those places,' he said.

His company appeared to be in a salient of their own, with enemy from fifty to 200 yards away on three sides. I do not suppose the troops had slept that night. Now that it was daylight and there was a period of quiet, most were sleeping near their posts. The sentries remained alert. I took up my position in a ground floor room from where I could look through a window.

'No. 2 section stand by,' I wirelessed to my mortars, and

paused to give the chaps time to man their weapons. 'Ranging, one round, fire.' I waited while the order was relayed, heard the explosion as the bomb was fired and counted twenty seconds before I could expect to hear the whistle of the bomb falling 'over my left shoulder'. Swisssssh! Thud! I did not see the bomb burst but judged by the noise that it had exploded in the wood, which was very satisfactory for a first shot.

'Down 100 (yards), one round, fire.' Again a pause for the relaying of the order, then the explosion of the bomb being fired, twenty seconds' wait, the prolonged swissssh coming over my left shoulder (I wondered how near to me the bomb was going to fall), then the flash as the bomb landed, and the bang of the explosion. That one landed in front of the wood.

I had got a bracket now on the edge of the wood, so I increased the range by fifty yards, brought another section of mortars into action, and fired six rounds from four mortars into the woods. I raised the range another fifty yards and put down heavy fire towards the centre and back of the wood. I could not see the bombs bursting but I could hear them. There was no doubt they were falling in the wood.

'Left six degrees, four rounds mortar fire' – I was aiming now at the white house the major had pointed out to me. I heard these bombs fall but I could not tell exactly where they had landed as they were too far back in the woods, and I had a suspicion one or two were falling too far over to the left.

'Down 100, repeat,' I ordered. I saw one bomb fall to the left of the target, the next exploded on the grassland between our company and the enemy woods; then I saw a cluster fall around the house, including one directly in front of the main window. I thought the bombs were falling as accurately as I was likely to be able to get them to, so I put down several rounds of rapid fire on that target, and then said to Harley: 'I think it might be wise to pause for a bit now, or else they may suspect we are using this farmhouse for observation.'

I noticed that Bruce, his second in command, was sleeping on a bale of hay. Harley, who had been up all night, looked very tired and I expect he was longing for Bruce to wake up so that he could have a few hours' sleep. But he would not have deliberately wakened Bruce until his own eyes were so heavy that he could not keep them open.

I crept quietly up the staircase and took up a position from which I could see the enemy posts on our flank. I ranged a section of mortars on the crossroads, as that was the centre of the target area the major had indicated, but owing to tall trees and dead ground I saw neither of the first two bombs. I dropped the range, saw one bomb explode and felt confident, judging by the sound, that the other had landed nearby. For a few seconds I mortared that area strongly. I had by now ranged on all the nominated targets and I had also mortared various known and suspected enemy positions. If there was any further threat the company could simply call for fire on a specified target and we could be reasonably sure of landing our bombs where they were wanted.

I arranged for a sergeant to relieve me and when Johnson arrived he was quite happy to find the enemy so near. That did not worry him nearly as much as it did me. I explained to him the targets on which I had ranged, checked that the wireless was working satisfactorily, and then went back along that tiring and muddy ditch, over that risky road, through the thick woods to battalion headquarters, and from there to the mortar position.

I now had time to wash and shave and, it being now 2 p.m., ate my breakfast.

EXPENSIVE VICTORY
4–5 October

Our front line was an untidy zigzag. We were occupying the farthest positions the ground troops had been able to reach when striving for Arnhem. Some of these places were difficult to reach unseen and, having exposed flanks, were difficult to defend. It was now necessary for our battalion and others to reorganize ourselves into an efficient defensive line, and this was to be done by attacking to take good positions, not by relinquishing any we had.

We needed to capture the villages of Haalderen and Baal and the woods between them and flanking them. Then we would have established a large semi-circular line north of Nijmegen which would be easy to hold, for attackers would have to cross 500 yards of open ground.

The 1st Hampshires' part in this involved mainly an attack by one company commanded by Frank Waters. The commanding officer gave out his orders the night before. There was little to say for the plan was simple. Frank's company had to cross a certain start line at noon and make a limited advance to their objective. A second company had to move up to support them. The colonel wanted the mortars sited well forward at the beginning of the attack so that we would be able to support the troops all the way to their objective and could harass any immediate counter-attack. A fire programme was laid down, and in addition Colonel Turner wanted a mortar observer to go with the attacking company.

We feared that as soon as our advance started the enemy would reply with heavy artillery fire.

'I hope your counter-battery boys are on form tomorrow,' said Frank to the artillery officer, referring to those gunners whose job it was to engage and neutralize German batteries.

'We'll do our best,' replied the artillery man.

250

'Are you happy about this party?' Colonel Turner asked Frank. 'I mean as happy as one can ever be about any party.' (The word party had a strange meaning in the army.)

'Yes, sir,' replied Frank, 'as happy as one can ever be about a thing like this.'

The commander of the supporting company added his piece.

'I hope it all goes well tomorrow, Frank, old man.'

'Yes, I hope it goes well, too,' answered Frank, 'and I hope you get on OK.'

'Thanks, old man. Best of luck.'

Conversation at these times was brief; and definitely not scintillating.

When I got back to the mortar position I called the section commanders together to give them details of the forthcoming attack and gave out my orders for the part we had to play. None of them was very happy about it, and when I mentioned we had to have a fire observer with the attacking company I am sure they all quietly asked themselves: 'Will I be the one? Surely it's not my turn again.'

I delayed detailing who it would be, for I had decided in the morning to suggest to the commanding officer that I should undertake that task, leaving a senior sergeant in charge at the mortar position.

But Colonel Turner would not hear of it. 'I want you here near my command post,' he said, 'I may need you.' So I nominated the sergeant whose turn I reckoned it was.

This was our first set-piece attack since our battle at St Pierre-la-Vieille in Normandy. Were we going back to those days? With all that German artillery waiting for us! Even more dismal than the immediate prospect was the clear evidence that we would presumably need to fight one more Normandy-type slogging match before we could begin another, and we hoped, final, pursuit.

At 10.30 next morning I set off in a carrier to reconnoitre a mortar position immediately behind the locality occupied by Frank Waters's company. I could find nobody who could point out any area that was comparatively free of attention from German gunners. The rear elements of the company said they were regularly shelled, and they had suffered casualties the night before. The forward troops in the follow-up company said their positions were uncomfortable and advised me to keep clear of them as long as I could.

I knew from past experience that riflemen did not like to have their own mortars near them because they feared that they would receive a lot of fire aimed at the mortars in addition to what was aimed at them. So they invariably warned me that their area was subjected to particularly heavy shelling. If I believed that too readily and also avoided selecting dangerous areas like roads and valleys, I would have nowhere to go. I just had to disregard advice, choose the best site and stick to it.

I chose an area of fairly soft ground in a clearing between two woods, and I told the chaps to start digging in as it was a safe bet that the next few hours would bring more danger than we wanted. They dug in with a will and my sergeant went forward to join the attacking company. For communication he took the smallest wireless set we had as he never liked having a cumbersome set on his back when he went into action.

At noon the company began their attack. We fired at our pre-arranged targets on a time basis, for fifteen minutes at a wood, for the next ten at a crossroads, for the following ten at another likely enemy position. A tremendous artillery barrage supported the attack. As usual the Germans quickly retaliated with their artillery and I waited anxiously to see whether we would be in their target area. I could hear and see a heavy concentration falling on the edge of some woods about 400 yards in front of us, and when another concentration went over our heads I guessed our turn would come soon.

Meanwhile we continued firing on to our pre-arranged targets. Monty, manning his wireless, could not get through to our observer, but my other signaller, Ginger the Salvationist, was in constant communication with the battalion command post, from whom we received various instructions from time to time. I could tell Frank's company was making progress because the commanding officer was most anxious that none of our bombs should land south of a certain road which I knew was near their objective.

The enemy barrage began to fall on us. By this time the chaps had dug pits large enough and deep enough to hold a mortar and others to hold its crew, so we all dashed into these pits and took comfort from the thought that only a direct hit, or a very near miss, could harm us. But the comfort we took was only relative. It was hardly real. One could hear the shells approaching for a few seconds which seemed of interminable length. The swissh grew louder and more violent. One's heart panicked and one's knees shook. 'No, don't let it land near me,' one appealed to an Omnipotent Being. The first shell burst with a wicked, terrifying crack. Hot, jagged pieces of shrapnel were flung fifty to 100 yards through the air to injure or kill whoever they hit, if anyone. A reeking smell of cordite wafted over the trenches. A few seconds later the next shell landed, and then the next, and so on, possibly for five, ten or fifteen minutes. The human heart suffered palpitations over and over again.

When the fury of the attack was over, temporarily, we rose from our trenches, looked around at the angry, disturbed earth and the gaping shell holes, and shuddered at the thought of what would have happened if a shell had landed in one of our trenches. Then we continued to fire our weapons, as directed from the command post.

We soon jumped into our trenches again, and this time I found myself in company with one of the steadiest of men under fire, Corporal Danny, who in the days of Hottot had once cheerfully accompanied me on a curious and adventurous patrol after observing uncomplainingly: 'The commanding officer's barmy.' Now he swore indignantly and fiercely because the blast from a shell had blown over his brewcan when he was making tea for the lads.

When that concentration lifted I went around all the weapon pits and found the chaps were in a steady mood. We continued firing vigorously at the targets we were given. The shelling of us continued spasmodically throughout the afternoon and when we were not being shelled we were firing our bombs. Our experiences were repeated over and over again. By the end of the afternoon it was a wonder to all of us that so many shells could fall within such a small area without doing any damage to anybody or putting a single weapon out of action.

In an effort to establish contact with our observer sergeant I sent Monty forward with his wireless set to the start line, but he returned half an hour later to say he had not been able, even from that forward position, to contact our man. He had seen the Durham Light Infantry launch an attack and expressed unbounded admiration for the way they swept across a field under shellfire.

In due course Frank Waters's company reached their objective. In fact one platoon, not realizing they had gone too far, went on another 400 yards and had to be recalled. Our observer sergeant rejoined us.

'It's hell up there, sir, absolute hell,' he said. 'I honestly don't know how anyone can survive it. I dived into a ditch for cover once and must have damaged the wireless set because I could not get anything on it afterwards.'

We began to think about what would happen during the evening. The Germans might counter-attack at any moment, so I looked around for a safer area. Our present position was unhealthy. We moved the mortars some distance away to a site near a damaged farmhouse; the troops would feel more secure there than in open slit trenches.

I busied myself with the tasks that always confronted one at the end of a battle and on the occupation of new positions. Weapon pits had to be dug, mortars had to be provisionally aimed at likely targets, ammunition had to be replenished, the strength of the night guard and the positions of the sentries had to be decided, communications had to be established with forward companies and with battalion headquarters, observation posts had to be set up where and if necessary. At the first opportunity I travelled to the command post to obtain the latest news of our companies, to confirm that the map reference of my new locality had been received and to hear the latest information about the enemy. I found that during the battle the command post had received a direct hit from a heavy mortar bomb and several nasty casualties had been caused, including fatalities. My friend's overcoat was riddled with shrapnel; fortunately he had not been wearing it at the time.

Back at the mortar position conditions were fairly quiet. We thought we had chosen a good area after the hot spot we were in during the fight. One of my senior NCOs brought up supplies from a base depot. He went first to our original position where he was horrified to see the ground pock-marked with shell craters. Our movement signs led him to our new site.

'How many casualties, sir?' he asked anxiously.

'None,' I answered.

He flared up. 'Don't treat me like a child. I've seen our firing area. I know there must be casualties. Don't treat me like a child.'

He mustn't speak to me like that. But nor must I get on my high horse. We were battle pals of long standing. I looked at him. Our eyes met. We both paused.

'There were no casualties,' I affirmed quietly.

'Unbelievable,' he muttered. 'Unbelievable.' But he did believe me.

I had spoken too soon. There was sporadic shelling and an airburst wounded two fellows who were standing inside our farmhouse. But we continued to consider that our house was as safe a place as any.

The din of warfare was as loud that night as it always was after a daytime encounter. One or two shells landed uncomfortably near Sergeant Johnson's section and demolished the rooms next to their sleeping quarters. So tired were some of the chaps that they were not even awakened by this happening. Next morning they viewed the damage with more curiosity than alarm.

The attack had been successful all along the divisional front, so we now held satisfactory and firm positions. But our battalion had suffered heavily, chiefly from the enemy artillery and mortars, and as many as twenty-two men were killed, including Red Reed, our anti-tank platoon commander. This was a much shorter, narrower but clearly fiercer, fight than at St Pierre where the death toll was fourteen. In the fifty-four days between those two events we had not lost a single life. That must have been a minor miracle.

BACK TO ENGLAND

6 October–December

A few days later we were pulled back to Nijmegen. Then we moved forward again to Elst, midway between Nijmegen and Arnhem and on the left of the main road. The enemy were in the hills of Arnhem, glowering at us, but conditions were fairly quiet. We were moved back to Nijmegen, and then forward again to Bemmel, near Elst but on the right of the Arnhem road. Some of us seemed to be forever going over Nijmegen bridge, for the battalion's rear headquarters was in the town. The bridge was shelled frequently. Camouflage nets were erected along it and smoke was often used to screen it.

Along the road leading to the bridge notices warned drivers to increase the spacing between vehicles to eighty yards. One Royal Engineers' sign read 'Nij Brij', followed by urgent exhortations to drivers to travel as fast as they could. 'Don't dilly dally on the way.' Driving over the bridge was rather like going through flames. When approaching it you steadied yourself and made sure there was no obstruction to fast movement, then you drove at full speed, fearing all the time that the noise of your vehicle would drown the whistle of an approaching shell; and, having reached the far side safely, you could breathe a sigh of relief.

At Bemmel, where we stayed for a fortnight, I again alighted upon a dream observation post. It was a badly shattered two-storey cottage, now not much more than a ruin, about fifty yards in front of our most forward position and somewhat to the right. The company commander did not want his troops to occupy it because it could only have held a handful of men and there was a danger that the noise and commotion involved in handling and moving weapons would have given away the fact that we were occupying the cottage and would have alerted the enemy to the probability that we were strongly entrenched in copses and woods nearby. But he had no objection to the ruin being occupied by one observer, or at the most two, provided we made no noise and entered and left by slightly different routes so that our footsteps did not create a path which (surprisingly easily) could have been detected by enemy aerial reconnaissance.

So, taking great care how I approached the cottage, I entered through the back door, crept silently upstairs and sat down on the floor well away from the open space that had once been a window. There was an extensive view of a low-lying area and, 400 or 500 yards away, of copses and buildings where the enemy might be. Whispering instructions into my wireless set, I brought down mortar fire on all likely targets.

Thereafter I arranged for my senior NCOs to take turns at occupying this post for a day at a time with orders to bring down fire on any area where they detected movement and, if they saw nothing, to fire harassing shots from time to time. I visited the post once every day to check everything was in order and, though we would speak only in whispers, to give my NCOs about an hour's companionship during their lonely vigil. It took about forty-five minutes to walk, clamber and crawl from the cottage to the mortar position.

There was little enemy activity but we had to be careful about our every movement because the high ground north of Arnhem gave the Germans a general view over our area. It was mainly our fire from this cute observation post that enabled us to dominate no man's land, always an important task.

One night-time, when all was quiet, a sudden burst of Spandau machine-gun firing was heard. Then silence. By unimaginable bad luck my friend Harry Wise, who had joined the battalion with me in England, happened to be walking about on some duty and he was hit in the stomach. The chance against that must have been tens of thousands to one. I was myself about at the same time and I met him, walking with the assistance of two comrades, to the regimental aid post.

'It's not too bad,' he told me. After being seen by the medical officer he was taken to hospital and we all thought his wound was not serious. We were shocked when, eight days later Colonel Turner told us his condition had suddenly deteriorated, and next day that he had died. 'Don't go into the infantry, my son,' his father had always told him.

A useful assessment of how the campaign was going appeared in the *Daily Mail* of 14 October. Alexander Clifford wrote:

The fighting to tidy up the shapeless British front in Holland is growing stiffer. The newest development is the drive eastward which the Second Army has started from half-way up its great salient. The attack went in near the village of Overloon, and it is still going on in the soggy fields and damp woods of that flat, dreary countryside.

Both here and down on the Scheldt the Germans are resisting strongly and methodically. They are determined to prevent us from reshaping the front the way we want it. They know that when we do we shall be in a position to launch another full-scale offensive.

It is true that the great thrust up to Arnhem was eighty per cent successful and twenty per cent failure, but from the point of view of the next operation it is the twenty per cent of failure that must be considered. We could not follow through immediately and complete the drive as originally planned, so we must start afresh and plan things anew.

The Arnhem semi-success left us with this salient thrusting up like a great thumb into Holland. It was a promising position if it could be quickly exploited, for it threatened all the Germans in western Holland. But it could not be quickly exploited. Now it is an awkward shape that must be rationalized and simplified.

So we are engaged in a large-scale mopping-up operation with the emphasis for the moment on these two points – the mouth of the Scheldt and the area towards the Meuse east of Eindhoven. The Germans have had plenty of time to get their breath and regain their balance. Their resistance is now fully planned.

They have sorted out their jumbled divisions and have distributed new equipment and arms. They have got their supply routes organized to suit the new circumstances. They have fully got complete control of their own army again . . .

They are putting in strong counter-attacks . . . designed to throw the next phase of our operation off balance and do as much damage as possible. They are always on a local scale and their function is basically defensive. But they are now stronger and more co-ordinated than they have been for some time.

The Germans can now switch troops systematically from one part of the front to another. They have had time to lay minefields and map out their defence plans. They have recovered very cleverly from the mess they got themselves into at Falaise . . .

Early in November we were moved back to Nijmegen for a few days' rest and during that time the officers were required to report to a cinema at Bourg Leopold to hear a talk by Field Marshal Montgomery. As many officers as could be spared from all units in the 50th Division were there, many hundreds of us, with the result that the cinema was packed.

At one minute to eleven o'clock a staff officer walked on to the stage. 'The Field Marshal will address you in one minute,' he declared, 'so you have sixty seconds to clear your throats and generally get comfortable. After that there will be no coughing and no noise of any kind.'

So we coughed a bit, fidgeted a bit, then there was silence, and exactly at eleven o'clock the short, slight figure of Montgomery strode on to the stage. Everything was going well, he announced, he was in complete control of the campaign, making the enemy dance to our tune, and in any case the Lord mighty in battle was on our side. Throughout a thirty minute talk there was not the slightest noise apart from his voice. Afterwards some of my friends reminded me that when a battalion went into battle the orders clearly stated whether supporting arms like tanks and artillery were 'in support' or 'under command'. In the first case the battalion commander told them what support he wanted and they decided how to give it (if possible) and in the second case the battalion commander gave them orders which they had to obey whether they liked it or not.

'We're all right now,' my pal reckoned. 'The Lord's not just in support. Monty's got Him under command.'

I have since learned that Monty's speech technique seldom varied. In recent years a friend has told me that my description of the procedure and substance of his talk to the officers of the 50th Division in Belgium in 1944 could be almost exactly applied to his talk to the officers of the 78th Division in Tunisia in 1943 when he was welcoming them to 'his' Eighth Army. When Monty found a phrase, a style or a gesture that worked he repeated it wherever he went.

We had one more spell at Elst and another at Bemmel. Then we returned to Nijmegen to learn that we were now non-operational. Life became quiet, peaceful and almost comfortable. But what was afoot? There were comings and goings, an air of mystery and an abundance of rumours.

Then I was notified of my future by the commanding officer, but must tell only those immediately concerned. I was to go back to England on a refresher course. To England! 'Yes, sir.' But refresher course?

Well, actually, the 50th Division was being reorganized, to put it nicely. Broken up really, and its soldiers used to reinforce other divisions in order to bring them up to full strength. Montgomery never would fight with weak divisions; he always insisted on their being at full strength, although that meant fewer divisions.

And as the 50th had fought in North Africa, Sicily, Italy

and north-west Europe its most experienced people would return to England to take charge of the army's training, and its less experienced soldiers would reinforce other divisions in Europe. As far as the 1st Hampshires were concerned, twelve officers and 100 men would go to England as instructors. That of course wouldn't include me, but as I had been a mortar officer it was right that I should have a refresher course in the work of rifle companies, in England; and as everything was secret nobody must know. And I would be leaving with a dozen or so others at 7.30 a.m. tomorrow.

People were going hither and thither. I had no idea where the members of my platoon would end up. All I could tell them was that I was leaving tomorrow after an early breakfast, and the best of luck to them. One or two asked me to apply for them to join me wherever I went, but I did not think I was going to be able to do much about that, nor would they necessarily want to join me after I had finished my refresher course.

With a small party I travelled to Ypres, and thence to England. The prospect of England, of course, was good news, but the virtual winding up of 50th Division was bad news; as ultimately was my course, for it implied the end of my mortar command and the start of something more dangerous. But in war you always adopt a short-term view. The long term may never happen. And in any case I was out of the campaign for some time.

Why was the 50th Division chopped? Max Hastings in his book *Overlord*, a somewhat critical assessment of the Normandy campaign, published in 1984, writes:

> 7th Armoured, 50th and 51st Divisions had been brought home from the Mediterranean where they had gained great reputations specifically to provide the stiffening of experience for the British invasion force. (June 1944). From an early stage there were rumours

among the men of 50th Division that they were expendable, that they would be used on the battlefield for tasks in which the rate of attrition would be high. Curiously enough this did not seem greatly to dismay them, and 50th Division's record in Normandy was very good.

I personally never heard these rumours, but thanks for the compliment, Max.

Between 6 June and 17 November the 1st Hampshires, whose fighting strength was usually between 500 and 600, lost 231 killed, which was nearly twice what most battalions suffered, and about 1,050 wounded, the exact number not being known. Total casualties therefore were approximately 1,280. In other words, with each casualty being swiftly replaced by a reinforcement, the battalion was effectively twice wiped out.

And at the end of that it was still a superbly efficient fighting machine!

9

Across the Rhine

OUT OF THE BATTLE LINE
December 1944–March 1945

Almost the first thing I did in England was to marry Joan
Bradley. We had first met when I was in the Pay Corps at
Bournemouth and she, a London civil servant, had been
evacuated there. We had never become officially engaged
but early in 1944 I had proposed to her and she had
accepted.

Our wedding was rushed because I was able to give only
a few days' notice of my impending arrival, but we were
able to assemble fourteen members of our families to attend
the service at Herne Hill Methodist Church, London.

I was incidentally the third of my parents' sons to marry
in Britain during the war while they, in Jersey, had not met
any of these brides. It was possible for people in England to
communicate with friends in German-occupied Jersey by
means of twenty-five-word messages conveyed by the Red
Cross every three or four months. So while my parents
would have had knowledge of these events, they could have
had no idea what kind of daughters-in-law they were getting.
I am pleased to add that as I write this Joan and I are
celebrating our forty-fifth anniversary.

After two days' compassionate leave in London I had to
travel to the Isle of Man to start my course. Joan followed
a little later and we were able to live together in a small
hotel.

There were about 150 fellow officers on this course and a

handful of us were living out of billets with our wives. When we arrived for the morning parade it was not unknown for the others to sing the well-known hymn 'Art thou weary, art thou languid, art thou sore distressed?', though the third question scarcely applied.

I was astonished to find that this refresher course was simply a one-month condensed version of the two-month conversion course I had done at the same place twelve months before. There was no point in my reporting this to anybody because in such a huge hierarchical disciplined organization as the army I would simply have been advised to mind my own business and to do as I was told.

It was quite fun when we were all sent out on tactical exercises. We would be given orders by a commanding officer; then we would have to reconnoitre the ground and draw up a plan to show how, at the head of 100 soldiers, we would fight our way to the objective. Some of these exercises were exactly the same as those I had done a year earlier, so occasionally I gathered a few pals together and told them it was not necessary for them to race all over the countryside and work everything out; if they would spend fifteen minutes with me I could tell them everything they would find on the reconnaissance and what the instructing staff's ideal plan was; and of course if they would like to stand me a few beers or the odd gin and tonic that would be acceptable.

One day we were given a certain exercise. We had to imagine that from point A we had been ordered to attack and capture point B, but that attack had failed and we were now at point C in a rather disorganized state. We were again ordered to take point B. How were we to do it?

Late in the afternoon we assembled in the lecture hall for our various groups to report on the plans they had drawn up. One of the officer students delivered the assessment of his group. No, said a senior instructor, that was quite wrong. He should have taken such and such a course. On the contrary, persisted the student, he was sure his group's suggestion was right because this was what he had learnt from his experience in Normandy. No, that's absolutely wrong, fiercely insisted the instructor, the student must have been badly at fault in Normandy; this was the official solution to the exercise and that was that. But some other Normandy veterans supported the first student. I did. His assessment seemed to make sense.

Soon there was the father and mother of a row, the instructors reminding us of the width of their experience and of their standing, not to say their seniority, while we countered with what we had learnt in battle a few weeks previously. Neither side gave way. Things got heated and for a moment I thought events could get out of hand. But they didn't. We quietened down. However, we didn't agree to differ. We just differed.

Those students who had not yet been in action were horrified at the dispute. What on earth should they do if they met this tactical situation in a forthcoming battle? And later that evening, when the wives heard of the argument, some began to fear that their men would be exposed to unnecessary risk because the instruction they were receiving might be flawed. But the truth was that no two situations would ever be exactly alike. You needed to understand basic principles and you had to use your own judgement how you applied them in each case.

Just before Christmas we were stunned to learn that the Germans, who so recently had been so near total defeat, had smashed through the Americans' defensive structure in the Ardennes. '25-mile gap in Allied line' ran the *Daily Mail* headline on 21 December. According to one report German panzer divisions and paratroop infantry had broken clean through and after a thirty-mile advance in three days were threatening Liège, a significant Belgian town liberated in September. Alexander Clifford wrote:

In the suddenly quickened atmosphere of the western front ideas are having to be revised. An army that was supposed to be beaten has suddenly launched a blitz. And it needs explaining.

I am afraid it means handing some bouquets to the Germans. But we should not balk at that. This very counter-offensive of Rundstedt's has shown again the need for estimating your enemy correctly . . .

We did know – and it was all published three weeks ago – that the enemy had been swiftly creating new utility divisions. We knew he had strong new panzer formations up his sleeve waiting for an opportunity to use them. But few people expected anything quite like this.

After all, we had been winning all along the line from Normandy to the Rhine. We practically won the war in August and September. The Germans, through all that time, had barely been able to launch one serious counter-blow against us. Judging by previous form, it seemed hardly likely they would be able to launch one now . . .

The Germans made a supreme effort of improvisation at Arnhem – which must always remain a brilliant victory for them. They got sufficient control of the situation to hold the rest of the front along the great rivers and the prepared defences . . . And behind the scenes they prepared the great recuperative gesture they are making now. They scraped together everthing good they had.

Their modified Tiger tanks began trickling in from the factories. New and improved guns and mortars equipped the freshly trained panzer divisions. Husky youths fresh from school, with a background of tough Hitler-Jugend training, came into the line. A brand new and militarily magnificent spearhead was fitted into the old tired Wehrmacht . . .

At the Isle of Man there was much gloom. The war seemed to be continuing indefinitely.

JOINING THE 7TH HAMPSHIRES

Towards the end of January my refresher course ended and I was posted to a holding camp in the north of England. Officers were not allowed to have their wives with them there. Nothing happened at the camp. Everyone just waited to be moved somewhere else. It was a hard, cold winter. Around the middle of February I was sent to a reinforcement holding unit in France. I waited there till early March when I was ordered to join the 7th Hampshires, who, as part of the 43rd Division, were momentarily out of the line, not far from the Rhine opposite the German town of Rees. The 7th Battalion had taken their full part in the battle of the Reichwald forest, a severe four-week slog which brought the army up to the banks of the river along all that section of its length. It was an encounter I was glad to have missed.

There were immediate disappointments in store for me. First, I had to lose my rank of captain, which was a temporary rank, and revert to lieutenant, which was my war substantive rank. The rule was that after three months in a temporary rank an officer became war substantive in the rank below, meaning he could not go lower than that. This rule was not of much use to me.

As a lieutenant I was given command of a platoon in a rifle company, the most dangerous office in the army. We still had to cross the Rhine, the widest and most easily defended river in Europe, and after that we would have to fight a last major campaign. It was March. What was my chance of seeing summer? Would I ever play another game of cricket? Was my recent marriage just a step to nowhere, a few days bliss before oblivion? These thoughts were ended when the natural commonsense of a soldier reasserted itself. My billet was comfortable, the weather was mild and dry, the food was excellent, my new companions seemed good chaps, and today there was no danger. Tomorrow? Let's wait and see. It may never happen.

I soon learnt that one of my new colleagues who had led a rifle platoon with distinction was being sent away on a course to learn how to command a 3-inch mortar platoon. The army had taken the best part of three months to teach me how to do his job, in case I did not know, and now he was going to be taught how to do the job I had been in for six months of ferocious fighting and extraordinary success. From one point of view it was absurd. From another it was fair. That chap had occupied the army's most exposed role for some months. Now he was to be trained for a command where the risk was smaller. I had had the luck to be in a situation of less than maximum danger for six months. Now it was my turn to experience maximum risk. Though this was fair, I was not overjoyed.

I was also less than thrilled when Lieutenant-Colonel D.E.B. Talbot ordered every man in the battalion to parade with his correct equipment, weapon and ammunition in front of him. Naturally it was laid down in training manuals how many men in a platoon had to carry a Bren machine-gun, how many a Sten gun, how many a rifle, where all the ammunition had to be, how many hand grenades there were per man, where they had to be carried, and so on. But I knew that even after a short experience every soldier took into battle just what he wanted and nothing else. For instance one man, who might be a strong thrower, might like to stuff into his pockets all the grenades he could lay his hands on. Another might not like any; perhaps he could not throw very far, or maybe he thought they were dangerous things to have in your pockets if machine-gun bullets were flying around in your direction. Again, some soldiers liked to be well loaded, perhaps overloaded, with machine-gun and rifle ammunition, while others liked to carry only the minimum so that they could exercise the maximum athleticism if required.

So for every soldier to show his theoretically correct weaponry a great deal of unswapping had to be done of things that had been swapped. Jack had to hand one grenade back to Mike and two back to Bill and he had to try to collect one Bren magazine he had given to George. The parade was pointless because when it was over everything surreptitiously went back whence it had come. This wasn't the way we did things in the 1st Battalion, I thought, but kept the thought to myself.

Quite a number of ex-1st Battalion soldiers had reinforced the 7th Battalion around this time and they were quick to boast in loud voices what a wonderful division the 50th was. I shared that view but it was not tactful to shout it from the rooftops now we were in a 43rd Division battalion, and as I did not want to see any ill-feeling arise I quietened these people down as diplomatically as I could. We should inflict our fighting spirit upon the enemy, not upon ourselves.

A TEXTBOOK ATTACK
March–May 1945

Our first operational role was to move to the west bank of the Rhine and defend a long stretch of it. The land was very flat, so you could see for miles in most directions. My platoon occupied a very large mansion nearly 2,000 yards from the river. In daylight we could do our job easily, merely by posting three or four sentries at various windows and arranging for a few machine-gunners to be nearby; the remainder of the platoon could rest. But at night I had to move a section of about ten men down to the river bank where they had to spend the hours of darkness standing in slit trenches and peering out at the river.

In order not to give away our positions they were forbidden to move in daylight. At dusk therefore they had to hasten by a specific route to the river bank, which took them perhaps thirty minutes; they had to stay there in trenches for the night; and thirty minutes before dawn they had to start on their hurried journey back to the mansion. Nobody imagined that the Germans would or could launch a substantial attack across the Rhine. We were on our guard against reconnaissance and fighting patrols.

The river bank section usually returned at 5.30 a.m. All the platoon were then roused and we stood-to against the possibility of a dawn foray. Half an hour or so later we stood down.

One morning, awakened by the noise of the section's return, I was surprised to find it was only 4.30 a.m. 'It's only half past four, why have you come back?' I demanded.

There was no proper answer. So I immediately ordered them to return to the river bank and stay there till the correct time.

'But it takes half an hour to get there,' they complained, 'so by the time we reach the river bank we would have to turn around at once to get back here before first light.'

'And that's exactly what you are going to do,' I riposted, 'and what's more, I'm coming with you to see that you do it.'

So, as I helped them along with a few well-chosen words, that is just what we did. And, sure enough, no sooner had we got to the river bank than it was time to turn round and hurry back to our mansion. I think I made my point. They did not take any liberties with my orders after that.

Our own area was quiet, but a neighbouring company was attacked by a German patrol and lost two men, taken prisoner.

The main British attack across the Rhine was launched on 24 March. We were a follow-up division and I sailed across near Rees in a motor-driven, armoured boat the next day, which happened to be my twenty-fifth birthday. Nobody wished me many happy returns. We moved to the battle area and quickly joined the advance. My platoon had to complete the overrunning of a village. Most of the buildings were burning as a result of our bombardment and we hastened through, Bren guns, Sten guns and rifles blazing. There was little opposition.

Next day we had to devour a similar village, but because it was thought the enemy was entrenched there my platoon was given the support of three tanks. The idea was that tanks and infantry would advance abreast, the tanks shooting up any suspected machine-gun post that threatened us and the infantry shooting up any suspected anti-tank gun or bazooka post that threatened the tanks. That worked reasonably well except that, although I walked down the main road alongside the leading tank, I could not communicate with its driver. It was no good banging on the side of the vehicle; he would not have heard that. We had to communicate by wireless; his, fixed and large, no doubt worked well; mine, small and jolting on my back, did not. This was one more example of infantry-carried wireless sets not working; they were too weak and suffered from too much jarring. In this case they failed to transmit over a distance of five yards.

During the Normandy battle one of my friends, Horace Wright, unknown to me at the time had worked out his own method of communicating with supporting tanks. He would collect two or three apples from any nearby orchard and carry them in his pocket with other ammunition. Then when he wanted to talk to the tank commander he would lob an apple into the lid of the turret, which would normally be open. When an apple fell on the tank commander's head he would realize somebody outside wanted to talk to him!

Our army had crossed the Rhine in great strength. In addition to powerful armoured and infantry forces the 6th Airborne Division (who had landed in Normandy on D-Day) had been dropped behind the enemy lines. The Germans were short of numbers, and possibly of good equipment too.

Soon we were sensing that we were near the breakthrough. In Normandy it had taken us seven weeks to burst the enemy apart. Now, east of the Rhine, it looked as if we might break them in one week. We were making a series of fierce, continuous attacks on very narrow fronts. On one particular part of our sector the 7th Hampshires were attacking with one company at a time. When the leading company had advanced a certain distance and completed its stint the second company took over to thrust deeper and still narrowly into the enemy's defence; then the third company and finally the fourth. I was to lead the final advance. We had to move across about 1,000 yards of mainly open country and capture a large farmhouse on the bank of a canal. If we could do this the German defences could be judged to be sufficiently open for the tanks to take over the lead next morning. Now that was a marvellous prize to be dangled in front of us!

To help us on our way we are to have a rolling barrage of artillery fire, moving forward at a predetermined speed, about 100 yards every minute. The barrage will make the enemy cower at the bottom of their slit trenches or in the cellars of their buildings. If we arrive at these positions the instant the barrage lifts we can kill or capture them all. But if the enemy spring to their firing positions before we get there they will be able to mow us down mercilessly.

All depends on our keeping up with the shellfire. 'Lean on the barrage', we have been taught in training.

273

'It is better to risk casualties from the occasional shell from your own side falling short than to allow the enemy a few seconds to recover.'

I place a section of ten men in front, in line abreast. I follow immediately behind, with the other twenty-five members of my platoon strung out behind me. The barrage starts and we move with it. For ten minutes I do not stop shouting.

'Keep up the pace. Don't slacken. Keep up the pace. Keep up. Don't stop. Keep up.'

A soldier complains 'But there's a Spandau firing at us from over there on the right. I had better take it on.'

'No,' I yell. 'Don't stop for anything. Fire the Bren back at him from the hip if you like, but keep moving. Throw a smoke grenade if you like, but keep up, keep moving, keep up, don't stop.'

Another soldier reports: 'Two wounded enemy here, sir, we can't leave them.'

I reply: 'Yes, we can. Leave them. Leave everything. Just keep up with the barrage, that's all we've got to do. Keep up. Keep up. Don't lose the barrage.'

'It might be dangerous to leave them,' the soldier persists.

'Shut up,' I bellow. 'Don't stop. Keep up. Keep up!' There's plenty of shells landing everywhere. I'm not surprised there's some wounded.

One of my men reports: 'There's movement on our left, sir.'

'Fire as you go with anything you've got,' I reply. 'But don't stop. Keep up, keep up. Faster, faster, keep up.'

I see a salvo of shells fall around our objective. A few seconds later Corporal Daley, a regular soldier who is commanding my leading section, enters through the front door of the house and I go in through the side door. We have got there without being seriously impeded at any stage of our 1,000-yard advance.

Daley stands at the top of a flight of stairs leading to a cellar or basement. In his hand is a grenade. He is wondering whether to throw it into the cellar in case there are any Germans there. He decides not to. But in case there is anybody he orders in his best pigeon-German: 'Kommen-ze oop.'

There is a pause of a couple of seconds; then up comes a German soldier holding a machine-gun in front of him and surrendering. Daley passes him along to me. I take the gun from him and push him into a room.

Daley tries his luck again. 'Kommen-ze oop,' he shouts.

And up comes a second enemy soldier, also armed, also surrendering. He hands his weapon to me and moves into the room indicated.

'Kommen-ze oop,' orders Daley again.

A third German comes up, then a fourth, and a fifth, and a sixth . . . Until there are thirteen of them.

If we had not leaned on the barrage, if we had given them time to recover their nerve and man their posts, they could have decimated my platoon as we crossed the open ground. Instead we have thirteen prisoners and there are a number of enemy wounded and possibly dead in the surrounding fields; and we have suffered no casualties.

I have one more personal duty, to crawl forward about fifty yards to check that the bridge over the canal has not been blown up. It has not.

It was a textbook attack. I never did better; neither before nor after. A nearby tank commander was most impressed. 'It was a wonderful sight to see your lads rushing into battle, mainly at the double,' he told my company commander, Francis Morgan. But it wasn't courage so much as mathematical calculation that had led to our swiftness.

A number of sharp, narrow thrusts like this were being made elsewhere and the armoured columns now took the leading role. On 31 March the *News Chronicle*'s S.L. Solon under the headline 'Annihilation is now at hand' reported:

> More than twenty armoured columns, pouring forth from the Allied armies in the greatest flood of armour yet used in this war, are loose in Germany. The security silence regarding the decisive advances that are being made is still on – and so is the most remarkable co-ordinated operation yet known to military history.
>
> For the rolling armour is following a master plan from the north to the south designed to grip all of Germany and strangle what is left of the German military machine. What is happening now is not a matter of improvisation. It is a planned exploitation of the breakthrough that has taken place over the whole front.
>
> It is intended to bring the war to an end before the enemy will have any opportunity to regain balance and form some sort of a front.
>
> This much can be said: the plan is succeeding and the hour of the Wehrmacht's annihilation is near. Large German formations, behind which our armour has advanced to cut their communications, are surrendering.
>
> German commanders are out of touch with their forces, and soldiers are discarding their arms and

surrendering. Naturally this is not happening at the same tempo throughout the front – war is not fought in such neat patterns . . .

Annihilation may have been at hand but unfortunately our war was continuing. The 7th Hampshires were now in a column making for Bremen. And on 10 April the *Daily Mail* reported: 'Bremen fights to end'. Alexander Clifford's dispatch read:

The Germans are really going to try to defend Bremen. Its great submarine and shipbuilding yards are less than five miles from our guns . . . Something that can almost be called organized resistance is cropping up . . . In itself it is very small. But it does amount to an attempt to hold the city.

The German parachute divisions are still fighting down to the south-west . . . Their communications depend entirely on Bremen. Now we are all up their flank and threatening their rear. And they have sent for anything that can be scraped up to hold the flank and the rear. A dozen or so German self-propelled guns are roaming the flank, which is represented by the road from Bremen to Bassum.

Odd training battalions and replacement regiments have been collected to hold the approaches to Bremen itself. SS men of the Horst Wessel outfit and Flemish Nazis of the Langemarck Division are reported to be preparing for action. The Germans are quite resigned to losing Bremen in the end. They have already blown up three of the city's bridges.

They have left only one bridge for the retreat of their parachutists. Their great point is to keep a way open for the good divisions to get out . . .

BERLIN OR BUST

This fighting was somewhat different from our campaigning in Normandy and the advance to Arnhem. In both those episodes my comrades and I had always been conscious of the Americans. For most of the Normandy battle they had been at our right shoulder and we at their left. On the road to Arnhem their airborne troops had captured a number of important bridges. Their toughness and above all their immensity had made a deep impression. Whatever was wanted they had plenty of it or would soon get plenty. Clearly they were not a nation it would ever pay to under-estimate, neither in war nor in peace.

They now had two or three times the number of men in the field as we British had and Eisenhower's directive had sent us north-eastwards while General Bradley's troops, well to the south, attacked eastwards.

Soon Germans were surrendering to them in masses. The German commander of Army Group B, Field Marshal Model, discharged all youths and older men from his army, telling them to go home and wear civilian clothes. Then he said front-line troops could do the same if they wished. One American soldier at Wuppertal in the Ruhr was given a squad of 68 enemy who had surrendered and told to march them to the nearest prisoner-of-war cage, a few miles away. By the time he got there he found his squad of prisoners had grown to 1,200.

Field Marshal Model soon reckoned he had done all he could for Germany and then shot himself.

Elsewhere the Americans had reached the river Elbe and had sent patrols across. 'We are on our way to Berlin. It's only fifty-three miles and there is nothing to stop us,' proclaimed one regimental commander.

But there was something to stop them. The orders of General Eisenhower. And thereby hangs a sad tale of history.

The zones of Germany that each of the main Allies was

to occupy after the war had long been laid down, but it was not thought wise for either the Russians advancing from the east or the British and Americans from the west to halt their attacks when the boundary of those zones was reached. Each Allied army was required to continue advancing until victory was achieved and only then to move back where necessary to the zone boundaries.

But Russia was already disobeying the agreements made by Stalin, Roosevelt and Churchill at Yalta in February 1945, firstly by forcing a communist government upon Poland and secondly by denying the United States and Britain access to our prisoners of war whom the Russians had freed during their advance into Germany.

So Churchill wanted Eisenhower to advance as far into Germany as possible and certainly to aim to take Berlin, deep in what was to be the Russian zone. Then the western allies could have made Stalin keep his part of the agreement before they allowed him to occupy all his agreed zone. But Eisenhower would have none of it. He was fighting a war, not playing politics, and Roosevelt, who was within a few days of death, backed him up.

Thus a large area of Europe was needlessly handed to the Russians. In due course the iron curtain descended along the middle of the continent, and the communists viciously misgoverned hundreds of millions of people for forty-four years, until their regime collapsed in ignominy and poverty, if you take 1989 when the Berlin Wall was torn down as the date of collapse.

FIX BAYONETS!

Throughout April danger was still attending every stage of the 7th Hampshires' advance, though life was somewhat easier than it had been in the Escaut–Arnhem area and much easier than it had been in Normandy.

279

I led my platoon up to a wide stream we had to cross. Enemy were believed to be on our left flank but nobody knew for certain. The orthodox tactic would have been to send a few men across first; then, if all was clear, for the rest to follow. But, I thought, might not such a leading group alert the enemy to the possibility that another group would shortly follow? So should we all rush across together at the same time, all thirty of us, before the enemy knew of our presence? I discarded the idea because of the practical difficulties. Thirty men at ten-yard intervals would occupy 300 yards. The stream widened and narrowed over that distance and meandered a bit. And some ground was smooth, some rough. We could not all have crossed in a couple of seconds. So, instead, we dashed across in groups of ten, and, having done that, we realized that there was no enemy anywhere.

But there were plenty of enemy at Cloppenburg, thirty miles from Bremen. In the book *The 43rd Wessex Division at War 1944–45*, compiled by Major General Essame and published by William Clowes and Sons in 1952, it is recorded that: 'the 7th Hampshires encountered fanatical resistance . . . The battle raged in the streets from house to house . . . Soon many of the buildings were on fire. Enemy shells and mortar bombs rained down on the battalion. Two self-propelled guns firing down the streets at point blank range and bazookas fired at high angle compelled the battalion to fight every inch of the way forward.'

I had got my platoon into substantial buildings dominating the centre of the town and reckoned the Germans would soon find their positions untenable. Then two tanks (I insist they were tanks not self-propelled guns, though the difference is not very great) dramatically appeared in the street and began firing at these buildings. The structures began to crack and fall. Soon our cover would be gone. There was not much future here. I looked around for my man with the Piat (an infantry weapon that could destroy a tank, but had an effective range of only fifty yards; it was generally reckoned you dare not miss with your first shot) and wondered whether I had better take over the weapon. It was all we had to defend ourselves and it was absolutely essential that it should be properly sited and fired as soon as the tanks came within fifty yards.

I need not have worried. It was customary to see that the Piat was always carried by one of the staunchest men in the platoon, and my well-chosen lad had got himself into a sound firing position and was preparing to give a good account of himself and thereby to save the rest of us. Then the tanks retreated and they did not return.

My company commander, Francis Morgan, distinguished himself in the Cloppenburg encounter and was awarded the MC. He said later that this was meant to recognize the company's performance rather than his own, but he was being unnecessarily modest.

In further battles we had casualties, including fatal ones, and I had to return to the unwelcome duty of writing letters of condolence to the next of kin. I always seemed to do this in a shattered cellar, by candlelight and sitting on an upturned wooden box. The task never did one's own morale any good.

Nevertheless after a month of leading a rifle platoon in the fighting east of the Rhine I came firmly to the opinion that this was less dangerous than leading a mortar platoon in Normandy. Since in the same conditions a rifle platoon would be much the more dangerous command it follows that the Normandy battle was by far the more horrendous encounter of the two.

As April wore on German resistance weakened. Groups began to surrender. Once, when a senior officer of the battalion saw in the distance about 100 of them on parade and apparently docile, he ordered me to go forward with a handful of men and take their surrender. This I did, first making sure that I was well covered by a number of carefully sited Bren guns. I did not propose to take any chances.

On one occasion we had been held up by enemy firing from a hillock about 400 yards away across undulating ground. I was ordered to lead a bayonet charge against them. In training we had been taught in these circumstances to place ourselves in the centre of the platoon. Then, after ordering the advance, to check that half our men were with us on the right, half on the left and that none had stayed behind, or, worse still, that all had not stayed behind.

'If you find you are on your own,' we had been instructed at the first Isle of Man course, 'it shows you are no damn good as an officer and you are certainly not going to live much longer. But if all your platoon are with you you are a good officer and you may even stand a chance of surviving.'

I took up my position in the centre, and ordered everybody to make a line and keep well spaced out, about ten yards apart. At that moment how glad I was that a number of my men were really tough chaps! One or two were regular soldiers who knew they were in the army to fight and made no bones about it. Some conscripts, too, had plenty of battle fury. The majority would follow a strong lead, whether it came from me, from the NCOs or from their pals. A few would be weak sisters. The rest of us would have to carry them.

(This can be regarded as the normal make-up of most platoons. A few strong toughies influenced a lot of others. The formation of airborne forces and commandos took a great many toughies away from the infantry of the line, who were thereby seriously weakened. It must have been judged by the War Office that what a handful of all-tough soldiers could accomplish together outweighed the consequent weakening everywhere else.)

I grip my Sten gun and take up position. Three strong men have Bren guns which they will need to fire from the hip as they walk forward. The rest have rifles and bayonets.

'Fix bayonets!' I roar. Then: 'Follow me . . . Forward!'

We are on our way. Out of the corner of my right eye I see half the platoon are there: out of the corner of my left eye I see the other half. So that's all right. The Bren gunners fire a few bursts, the riflemen fire frequent single shots, but all of it is deliberately irregular so that a pattern is not revealed. This is to make the enemy keep their heads down as we move towards them.

The chaps are well spread out. It's a steady pace. It's meant to be a deliberate pace because that can break the defenders' nerve. We are getting nearer. We have covered most of the distance.

Nobody's firing at us. The fingers behind one Sten and three Brens are ready to fire frenzied bursts at the slightest sign of movement in front of us.

We are twenty yards away now. 'Charge!' We run over our objective as fast as we can. There's nobody there. The erstwhile occupiers had taken the hint in good time.

For several days we continued to advance and the enemy continued to delay us with these tactics. He would fire a burst of machine-gun fire at us. We would stop, organize a full-blooded attack or an outflanking movement or an armoured vehicle thrust; and carry this out, only to find the enemy was not there, and then, having wasted thirty, forty or sixty minutes we would resume our careful advance.

April came to an end. We were still attacking, frequently accepting the surrender of groups of Germans, sometimes half a dozen or so, sometimes several dozen. We had bypassed Bremen and were approaching Bremerhaven.

My platoon was leading. One section of ten men advanced over rough ground in line abreast, about ten yards between each man. I was immediately behind them; and behind me in line astern were my other two sections. This was absolutely orthodox. Then the leading section came under fire. They fell to the ground and sought what cover there was in order to engage the enemy.

I crawled up to them to find out what was going on. The choices facing me were very simple. While my leading section engaged the enemy I must order either one of my rear sections or both of them to move to one flank or the other, to encircle the German post and attack it from the rear. Everybody knew the tactic. We had been taught it like a drill.

'No. 2 section, left flanking,' I ordered.

'Felix [who carried the section's Bren gun] has gone, sir,' replied the NCO commanding the section, 'gone' meaning he had run away just when he was wanted.

'Anyone else can take the Bren,' I yelled. 'Get moving!'

'But he's taken the Bren with him.' That was horrifying. To be deserting in the face of the enemy, which is what Felix was evidently doing, was bad enough, but to have taken with him the major part of his section's fire power was even worse.

So: 'No. 3 section, left flanking,' I ordered.

And No. 3 section duly moved out to the left, outflanked the enemy post, advanced to take it from the rear and found, again, that the enemy had retreated from there and we could all continue our forward move.

Some time after we had reached our objective without serious opposition the sergeant-major came across Felix (as I have called him) and naturally reported the incident to the company commander. If Francis had insisted on going by the rule book Felix would have been court-martialled and could have been sentenced to three years' penal servitude. Francis and I talked over this doleful prospect. Francis was sure the end of the war could be only a few days away, so maintaining discipline was not going to be a problem; we did not have to make an example of Felix. 'And,' I said, 'he's only nineteen and throughout the time I have had the platoon he has been a really stalwart soldier. I am amazed that he of all men should have made himself scarce.'

There was a pause, a pregnant silence.

'Well, if you agree, let's forget it,' ventured Francis. I thought he was being extremely brave because he must have been laying himself open to devastating rebuke if any senior officer learned and disapproved. I concurred.

'In that case,' continued Francis, 'if we are not reporting Felix for a court-martial, then officially he has done nothing wrong. That means you cannot punish him by giving him extra duties or in any other way. You can't even kick his arse.'

I told Felix that when a man got into trouble he was entitled to ask his record to speak for him. 'Your previous stalwart behaviour has saved you,' I declared.

Our situation was quiet. No firing could be heard. There was no sign of any enemy. We had no orders to move. The burgomaster of Gnarrenburg kindly surrendered his village to us.

On 4 May at 8.45 p.m. a news flash on the BBC announced that the Germans had surrendered unconditionally as from 8 a.m. the next day. My friends and I still took no chances. I had read that in the last hour before the armistice in 1918 some terrible hate-filled barrages had been fired for no honourable purpose. So we kept ourselves under cover until 8 a.m., though the precaution was unnecessary.

And we had no celebration. On the way across Germany

we had carefully liberated some bottles of supposedly good wine from enemy stores, and these bottles had been placed in the care of the cooks at rear headquarters. When we sent a messenger to collect them he found all bottles except one were empty and that one contained singularly unappetizing plonk; meanwhile the cooks were suspiciously happy.

But in any case our rejoicing would have been restrained because in the back of our minds there hovered an awful worry about the Japanese war. It would not be long before most of us were fighting in the Far East, we thought. Perhaps, too, the ending of the German war revealed that most of us were emotionally punch-drunk. We had wanted this victory and our safety too much to be able to enjoy it.

Meanwhile a strange scene had been enacted at one of the headquarters behind us. During the evening of 4 May Major-General G.I. Thomas, commanding the 43rd Division, had visited one of his brigadiers to give him his orders for the morrow. With a large map in front of them General Thomas was instructing the brigadier to capture Bremerhaven. There was a knock on the door and a staff officer entered to exclaim: 'The BBC have just announced the unconditional surrender of the German forces opposing Field Marshal Montgomery in north-west Europe.'

General Thomas was not impressed. 'I take my orders from the corps commander [Lieutenant-General Horrocks],' he declared, 'not from the BBC.' And, continuing to pore over his map, he went on with his orders.

Soon the staff officer entered again. 'A personal message to you, sir, from the corps commander. "Germans surrendered unconditionally at 1820 hours. Hostilities on all army front will cease at 0800 hours tomorrow 5 May. No advance beyond present front line without further orders from me."'

General Thomas was satisfied. His flow of orders ceased. He picked up his map case, then walked towards his car.

Thomas, said by Max Hastings in his book *Overlord* to have been a ruthless commander who had earned the nickname Butcher (though this was not known to me when I served in his command), turned to the brigadier and proclaimed: 'The troops have done us damn well.'

EMOTION STIFLED MANY A VOICE

In Britain the end had been expected since 3 May. On 5 May the *Daily Mirror* reported:

> Triumph day for Monty's men – Another million in greatest surrender.
>
> At 8 a.m. today more than a million Germans in Holland, Denmark and north-west Germany are laying down their arms to Field Marshal Montgomery in the biggest mass surrender of German forces since the armistice of 1918 . . .
>
> It is triumph day for Field Marshal Montgomery and his men. They have beaten the Hun to his knees along the whole of their front, and have written 'finis' to the German Reich.
>
> And today they bring salvation to the starving millions of Holland, and freedom to the people of Denmark, crushed for five long years under the Nazi jackboot. Amsterdam, Rotterdam, The Hague and the other cities of Holland will all be free today.

And they had a pithy comment from the leading German General in our hands:

> Field Marshal Von Rundstedt, recently captured former German Supreme Commander, paid striking tribute to Monty in an interview yesterday. Monty, he said, proved himself Britain's greatest general in

Libya, Tunisia, Sicily, Italy and again since D-Day.
Germany planned and wanted to invade Britain, but
never really tried, because she was too weak at sea.
The British fleet would have destroyed the Germans,
said Rundstedt.

On 9 May the Prime Minister Mr Winston Churchill,
speaking from the balcony of Buckingham Palace with the
King and Queen beside him, declared: 'In all our history
we have never seen a greater day.'

Montgomery made this comment in a personal message
to all ranks under his command:

We have won the German war. Let us now win the
peace.

We all have a feeling of great joy and thankfulness
that we have been preserved to see this day. We must
remember to give the praise and thankfulness where it
is due. 'This is the Lord's doing, and it is marvellous
in our eyes.'

I had often wondered, as I had taken part in the liberation
of large areas of France, Belgium and Holland, what scenes
would occur when my homeland of Jersey was liberated.
L.P. Sinel, who worked for the *Jersey Evening Post* throughout the war, kept a diary subsequently published under
the title *The German Occupation of Jersey 1940–1945*.
This contains memorable descriptions, as these extracts
(published by permission of Mrs E. Sinel) show:

8 May. It appeared early this morning that nothing
was going to happen, and there was keen disappointment; our spirits rose, however, when it was learned
the schoolchildren had been sent home and that loud-
speakers were being erected in various parts of the

town. Then the '*EP*' (*Evening Post*) came out with a message from the Bailiff (Chief Magistrate), who stated, inter alia, that the conclusion of the Prime Minister's speech would be appropriate for the hoisting of flags. From that moment we never looked back: everyone was excited and busy getting bunting ready for the afternoon, and by three o'clock thousands had gathered to hear Mr Churchill make his historic statement. The greatest crowd, of course, was in the Royal Square, which, with the windows of surrounding houses, was packed with listeners. As the Town Church clock struck three a cheer went up at the announcement that Mr Churchill was to speak; his statement was punctuated by cheers, especially when he referred to 'our dear Channel Islands', and when, at the conclusion the Bailiff hoisted the Union Jack and Jersey flag over the Courthouse, enthusiasm knew no bounds, and many wept unashamedly . . .

After appealing for good behaviour and to remain calm and dignified, the Bailiff led the singing of the National Anthem, but emotion stifled many a voice. The Bailiff had a great reception when he went off in his car, on his way to visit the French camp. By then flags had been unfurled all over the Island and church bells were ringing out for joy. The whole atmosphere had changed – wireless sets had appeared from nowhere, their owners putting them in front windows to entertain passers-by; cameras were clicking all over the place, and one was soon dodging motor-cars or motor-cycles which had for five years been hidden away from the Germans.

The Electricity Company turned up trumps and the light was on till very late, this being appreciated by the owners of wireless sets and those who held parties or impromptu dances. It was funny to see young men coming out of jail carrying their beds, to hear people openly discussing the news, to let off fireworks (yes, there were some!), to ignore the curfew and forget the blackout, but on everyone's lips were the words: 'Is it true?' The discipline of the Germans was excellent; they had had their last newspaper, had been carrying out demolitions of a minor nature, and throughout the afternoon and evening released their stores of food-stuffs for immediate consumption . . .

9 May . . . A terrific cheer went up from the crowd which had assembled around the harbours when a British naval pinnace came through the pierheads and later two naval officers who landed entered a car; when they got to the barrier at the landward end of the Albert Pier the police could not prevent them being mobbed. On arrival at the Harbour Office our first 'liberators' went upstairs and hung a Union Jack out of one of the windows; there were deafening cheers, the National Anthem was sung, and the toughest wit-ness could not restrain his emotion. It was expected that some ceremony would take place in the Royal Square about two o'clock, but a delay in the proceed-ings at Guernsey prevented this. In the early afternoon some formations of the RAF came over the Island and some time afterwards the first troops landed as the advance party; elements of many regiments continued to arrive, and these received a wonderful welcome . . .

Many Jersey boys were among those who arrived, and each and every one received a great reception – cheers, cheers and more cheers. The first Jersey officer to land was Captain Hugh Le Brocq, who left the Island with the Militia in 1940, and to him fell the happy task of hoisting the Union Jack on Fort Regent . . .

It was a glorious sight to see the Germans flinging

their arms out of windows at the various depots, or just throwing them on to a pile in the roadway, but the civilians who watched all this going on were well behaved and orderly. The Tommies who have arrived all wear a special shoulder flash consisting of a shield with the three leopards, and it was learned that they had been preparing for this particular job since last September; even up to the last it was thought that they would have to fight for the Islands . . .

10 May. Since the hour of liberation there have been incidents involving females who had consorted with the German Forces and who had earned the name of 'Jerry-bag'; collaborators and black-marketeers have also received rough treatment, but regrettable scenes took place this evening when one or two of these women were severely handled, and possibly but for the intervention of the troops would have been murdered . . .

11 May . . . The Gestapo were rounded up this afternoon, the name of the chief being Wolff, and the crowd which saw them in a lorry surrounded by Tommies with fixed bayonets contained many who had suffered mental or physical strain through their activities.

The whole campaign had been a grievous trial for the islanders. Their wilting spirits had been lifted in February 1944 by an American airman, Joe Kreps of Milwaukee, who landed on the island by parachute when his plane was damaged. As he was led away to captivity he shouted to all the people nearby: 'Keep your pecker up, folks, the big show is about to start.'

In June of that year it started. When Normandy was invaded the islanders felt their liberation was at hand. But, alas, the battle went away from them. The road from

Arromanches to Falaise to Brussels to Bremen was the wrong way for them. So they joked about it. 'The war is over and everything is set for the great victory parade. Suddenly General Eisenhower gallops to the head of the procession and cries: "Stop! We have forgotten to relieve the Channel Islanders!"' (From *The German Occupation of Jersey*.)

Meanwhile in Germany the army held an official thanksgiving service. It started with the singing of the national anthem, and then the chaplain said:

Lord, at the close of this campaign, we meet together before Thee to pour out our hearts in fervent thanksgiving for all Thy loving kindness to us during the long days of battle, and to dedicate ourselves afresh to the service of Thy Kingdom. We desire to thank Thee for the deliverance from the hand of our enemies; for the devotion, even unto death, of our comrades who have fallen in the fight; and for all the willing sacrifices made in Thy Cause. Grant to us, Lord, who have been preserved amid so many dangers, a due sense of all Thy mercies, that we may be unfeignedly thankful, and serve Thee faithfully all the days of our life.

It was July before I was able to visit Jersey and see my parents and friends. By then they had had two months of good nutritious feeding since the liberation, but most of them were still on the thin side. The house next to my home had been bombed and its three occupants killed when the Germans attacked the island in June 1940, but members of my family were not hurt. The islanders had suffered considerable privations but in general they had not been personally ill-treated.

In smart officer's uniform and looking very healthy, I thought I would make a good impression on my parents, but when my mother saw me she wept. My father rebuked her. 'Silly woman,' he said, 'you've got four sons. They've all come back safe and you cry because one of them has started to lose some of his hair.' My father, who was himself quite bald, did not regard that as very important.

My aunt Lily told me of an illuminating incident: 'On one occasion I awoke in the middle of the night very hungry. So I went downstairs to see what there was to eat. In the larder was a slice of bread. But that was for my breakfast. I realized that if I ate it then, I would have no breakfast. I looked at the bread and looked at the bread – and then slowly went back to my bed, hungry.'

10

Thank God for the Bomb

Shortly after the end of the German war I was transferred to a battalion that was billeted in comfortable huts on Salisbury Plain. I found to my joy that I was back again on mortars, but to my consternation that I was now in an airborne division that was going to the Far East. I seemed to have come a long way from that day in 1942 when I had been told that I was too weak, slow and dreamy to be fit for the field artillery! How dozy can you be in an airborne division? Some of the soldiers I was now in charge of were old campaigners, others had not yet been in battle. Arrangements were made for us to go to a firing range near Lulworth early in August.

On the evening of 6 August we heard that a new type of bomb, of vast explosive power, had been dropped on Hiroshima, causing colossal damage. Hurrah! Japan would have to surrender now or the whole country would be wiped out. But no surrender came, so on 9 August another of these super bombs with its message of irresistible power was dropped on Nagasaki.

I left the officers' mess early that evening and retired to my quarters a few hundred yards away. I had to leave for Lulworth very early the next day, so I wanted a good night's sleep. Next morning I arrived at the mess for a 6.30 a.m. breakfast on my own. The moment I opened the door I knew Japan had surrendered. The stink of stale beer and spirits was tremendous. Every available bottle seemed to have been opened and much of it drunk. The furniture looked as if a hurricane had blown through the room. Tables were either upside down or on their sides. Chairs were scattered everywhere, none of them now on their legs, and some no longer in very good condition. None of the wall pictures was straight and no ornaments were in their usual place. Above all was the all-pervading stink of stale alcohol. There had obviously been a drink-up, let-your-hair-down party which, because of retiring early, I had missed. We had lived for six years with death as our shadow. Now we could live properly, indefinitely, without fear.

The words Thank God for the Bomb can be taken literally. The two atomic explosions killed something like 100,000 Japanese. Without them full-scale war would have raged on the mainland of Asia, in the Pacific and finally in Japan itself. The American chiefs of staff estimated that this would cost one million Allied lives (mainly American, some British) and probably two million Japanese lives. On simple arithmetic the case for using the bombs was over-whelming.

Some propagandists have sought to show that the atomic bombs need not have been dropped as 'Japan was about to surrender'. I cannot in a personal story of my war examine this in detail, but the salient facts are that Japan, far from being about to surrender, did not even do so after one bomb was dropped. It needed two to persuade them. You have to be a million miles from surrendering for that to be necessary. And their armed forces had such aggression left in them that many of their soldiers were reluctant to accept the surrender order.

The airborne division that I was going to be in was never formed. I did not go in a glider. I did not see a parachute. But I now wore the red beret. (Naturally I have never done so since leaving that unit, nor have I ever regarded myself as an ex-airborne soldier.) My next posting, in the autumn of 1945, took me to Berlin to join a battalion that was part of the British garrison. After a while I regained my rank of captain. In Berlin I saw what a nation looks like in defeat. It was horrible. More buildings were in rubble than were standing. The people were in abject distress. They were servile towards us, grovelling to be allowed to open the door or do any service. Many women, it was well known, would offer any sexual activity for a bar of chocolate.

It was a very cold winter. There was little for us to do. We occasionally patrolled our area but all was generally quiet. What trouble we encountered came not from the defeated Germans but from the Russians. One day a bunch of Germans urged me to check on what was going on in a nearby shop. I went to investigate.

The shop had a fair supply of goods and one saleswoman. In the centre was a Russian colonel, shouting at the top of his voice, very drunk, and demanding all the goods and the woman for nothing, emphasizing his demands by wildly waving his revolver.

He was not supposed to do that in the British sector. I must stop him. I realized that the one thing I must not do was to draw my revolver. I did not relish a shooting match, even with a drunk. I would have been disappointed to have been shot dead six months after the war had ended by one of our gallant allies.

So I shouted with him, or at him: 'Bravo, Rusky, Magnifique, Bravo, Bravo, Rusky, Rusky', all the time giving him heavy congratulatory thumps on the back, which gradually propelled him towards the door.

Out into the road we went. I kept shouting 'Bravo Rusky, Bravo Rusky' until he faded away, having forgotten what he went into the shop for. Phew!

In the evenings after dinner in the mess I would sometimes go with some of my friends to the Femina night club in the Kurfürstendamm. Here there were endless champagne-based or gin-based cocktails for what in our currency was a very small price indeed and an orchestra, which seemed always to be playing 'Hear my song, Violetta'. The clientele was entirely made up of uniformed males. By that time there was a huge variety of uniforms in Berlin. I assumed they were all on our side.

Among my companions in this battalion were a number of officers who had been prisoners-of-war for several years. On their release they had received all the pay that was due to them during their captivity, so they suddenly had about three years' pay in their pockets. Some of them, over-compensating for their hard time, developed a considerable thirst. One was Dennis.

The junior officers were invited one evening to a dance in the sergeants' mess. There were quite a number of women in the garrison then: ATS personnel, nurses and so on. Dennis soon began to drink too much, so my pal and I gently but firmly led him away, across the barrack square, to our sleeping quarters, where we plonked him on his bed and left it at that. Fine.

But next morning Dennis had an enormous black eye. He apologized to us. 'I must have given you a lot of trouble last night. Sorry,' he said. 'Thanks for bringing me back here before I disgraced myself.'

My pal and I were mystified. He had not given any trouble. He had done nothing to give himself a black eye, nor had we given him one.

It was only on the day of my demobilization, in July 1946, that another friend, Charlie, told me what had happened. 'I had returned to camp about three o'clock in the morning,' Charlie confided to me. 'I had been out on the tiles, so I've kept it quiet till now. Imagine my surprise when, walking across the square at that hour, I met Dennis standing by a pool of water which was then practically frozen. He took off his jacket, laid it on the iced surface, and, addressing the world in general, said: "I lay this cloak down for you, my liege lady, Elizabeth." Then he fell flat on his face on the ice. That's how he got his black eye.'

'And he doesn't know he did all this?' I asked in amazement.

'No. And I'm only telling you now because you're going on the demob train and won't be able to tell anybody else,' concluded Charlie.

After demob I received this letter (I suppose everybody got a similar one) from the war office:

Sir,

Now that the time has come for your release from active military duty, I am commanded by the Army Council to express to you their thanks for the valuable services which you have rendered in the service of your country at a time of grave national emergency.

At the end of the emergency you will relinquish your commission, and at that time a notification will appear in the London Gazette (Supplement), granting you also the honorary rank of Captain. Meanwhile, you have permission to use that rank with effect from the date of your release.

I am, Sir,

Your obedient Servant,
ERIC B.B. SPEED

[11]

Questions I Am Asked

What was my narrowest escape and greatest hardship?

I had several narrow escapes. During the Normandy battle a fragment of shell or a nearly spent bullet made a dent in my steel helmet. Later, the water bottle I wore on my hip was holed. Once, a comrade taking cover beside me was killed by shrapnel. Such escapes were par for the course.

I underwent no physical hardship. The worst was going without sleep. Training in Britain was much tougher.

Did I see and kill Germans face to face?
How many did I kill?
Am I sorry?
Have I had nightmares?
Did it do any good?

I saw very few live Germans face to face. Now and again in an observation post I would glimpse one or two. Similarly when advancing at the head of a rifle platoon. When they were surrendering, sometimes being formally paraded for that purpose, I saw hundreds. Nearly all fighting takes place between hidden enemies, everybody being under the best cover they can find.

In the battle of Normandy my mortar platoon fired several thousand bombs. I cannot guess how many enemy soldiers that killed or wounded but the number killed, in effect by all forty-five-odd members of my platoon, must have been at least hundreds. That is what we were there for. At the head of a rifle platoon I had a shorter experience, usually with the enemy running away, but I and those under my orders must have killed some, perhaps dozens.

I am certainly not sorry, except in the sense of regretting the necessity, and I have had no nightmares.

Did this killing do any good? Yes, it saved the world. Not just the killing I did, but the killing done by my millions of comrades; that saved the world. By the end of the war the Nazis had exterminated six million Jews. If we had not won, millions more Jews would have been exterminated and after that presumably any groups of Gentiles that the Nazis chose to dislike.

Only our victory – and the small part played in it by my hand in the killing of those people – enabled Germany to reconstruct itself into the honour and quality of what we know as the post-war world.

How frightened was I?
Was everybody frightened?
Did many run away?

On a few occasions I was absolutely terrified. Once, when rockets were exploding around me, I prayed for the ground to open up and swallow me for protection. That can be called category one terror. It was exceptional.

Category two fear or terror was produced by normal heavy shelling. If, after one explosion, you were safe you did not have to worry until the next shell whistled in; if you were safe after that, not until the next one; and so on. It could go on interminably. It was not a pleasant experience but it could be borne.

Category three fear occurred when I was required to walk into danger (leading a rifle platoon) or stand to my task in danger (operating a mortar observation post). Then I found I had to take a conscious grip of myself, to steel my mind to the job in hand.

A fourth category arose from the continuity of exposure

to danger. If casualties in battle tend to be around twenty per cent, if you have fought five battles and are still safe, if the army has advanced only thirty miles from the coast, and if it's still 600 miles to Berlin, what are your chances of surviving till the end? That is the fear that eats away at you. Every man has only a finite supply of courage. It can get used up. Then you must have a long rest for bravery to grow again.

But life did not consist of only these categories of fear. Most of the time you were not under any particular strain. Everyday duties were not dangerous. You could be attending an orders group, checking your weapons, seeing everything in your platoon was to your liking; you could be eating, chatting, thinking, resting, driving, sleeping: mostly these activities were conducted in safety. And above all you were with your pals. There was laughter and good fellowship. Let the morrow take care of itself.

Everybody was frightened. I used to think that one or two of my friends were not. But I have learnt that they were. It was just that they had masterly methods of concealing their fear. We all took part in this concealment game. Thus, pretending to be brave, a man gave bravery to his comrades; as they, through their pretence, likewise gave bravery to him.

Wartime propaganda suggested that everyone, or nearly everyone, was a hero. This propaganda was necessary in order to create and maintain morale. We would not have won the war without it. Some later biographies continue in this character. Occasionally one reads opposite comments. Men are said to have thrown away their weapons and equipment, or literally to have shot themselves in the foot, or to have refused to go into battle. Where between these extremes does the truth lie? I have given in this book an accurate account of what I saw. There were men who did not pull their weight, but the army was strong enough to carry them.

Here are some facts which I take from Max Hastings's

book *Overlord*. The number of casualties (killed, wounded, missing and prisoner) suffered by the British forces during the campaign was 143,721. And the number of soldiers court-martialled for absence or desertion was 7,022. Thus the number of those who ran away was one-twentieth of the number of those who were casualties. No doubt others thought about deserting, or tried to, or nearly did. There were certainly weak sisters, but fortunately there were also strong sisters.

The experience of the 1st Hampshires suggests that an army figure of 143,721 casualties means that something like 200,000 soldiers were engaged in close combat with the enemy on a continuing basis. Very many more were occupied on various forms of support and supply. My estimate indicates that three or four per cent of those in combat deserted, and that ninety-six or ninety-seven per cent somehow performed their grim and terrifying duty, no doubt with varying degrees of determination or reluctance.

In the First World War deserters were shot, yet some people tried to run away and a number must have succeeded. I do not think any Briton was shot for desertion in the Second World War, certainly not in Normandy. Perhaps the question really should be: why did so many do their duty? Remember General 'Butcher' Thomas's observation: 'The troops have done us damn well.'

Can I define courage?

It is certainly not the absence of fear. It is more the doing of duty when you are terrified.

Did fear cause men to lose control of their bowels?

No, I never heard of this happening to anyone.

Were there discussions at orders groups or did you merely receive orders?

Did you ever receive orders to which you could have objected?
Did your men ever dispute the orders you gave them?

Within a battalion, orders groups were for the giving out of orders, not for the holding of discussions. I do not think any battalion or company commander would normally ask his junior for an opinion, though he may discuss a narrow detail on which the junior had particular knowledge. At an orders group you could ask questions, but that would be for elaboration or to cover an aspect not mentioned. I never heard a question asked which suggested that the commander was wrong.

Whether this system of one man giving orders and the rest obeying them operated at a higher level I do not know. There may have been discussion among generals when they assembled to hear their orders, but from what I have read I cannot imagine Field Marshal Montgomery being interested in any opinion but his own.

Broadly speaking, I never had cause to object to the orders I was given. Once or twice I suggested a slightly different course to the battalion commander, and to that suggestion he said either yes or no.

Nobody in my platoon objected to my orders beyond the occasional querying of whether it was really their turn again to undertake a hazardous task.

Do I know anybody who purposely tried to win a medal for bravery?

No.

Most awards were made in recognition of how a soldier had behaved in a battlefield crisis. This would not be pre-calculated behaviour by the man. It would be his immediate or instinctive response to a dangerous and desperate situation.

Some awards were also made to commanders of platoons, companies and battalions in recognition of the outstanding performance of their unit and of the part their inspiring leadership had played in this.

How did I feel when men under my command were killed?

Sad, but I did not take it in any personal way. We were all in danger, roughly equal danger. I did not regard a death as my fault, it was the enemy's fault.

Did I hate the Germans and Japanese?

Yes, while the war was on, but within a few years of its end I no longer hated the Germans. I always remembered that only those who were adult when Hitler came to power could be blamed.

Most of the prisoners they took were fairly treated. A minority were not, some were executed, but this was usually when the Gestapo interfered.

But whereas torture of prisoners was the German exception, it was the Japanese custom. Though I never had to fight the Japanese, I do not think I have forgiven them for that behaviour yet.

How did you know when to stop fighting?

If you were defending you stopped when the enemy ceased attacking you. If you were attacking it depended on circumstances. Sometimes you stopped when you reached your objective and other troops took over the advance. If your objective was the final target for the time being, on reaching it you organized your formation into defensive positions and then stopped. If you failed to reach your objective (a situation that did not apply to me as mortar officer) you stopped when you found it was not practical to go on and your commanding officer concurred.

Did you carry on fighting in the rain?

Yes, that had nothing to do with it.

Who buried the dead?

The bodies would normally be taken to the medical officer's post. Then a working party under a sergeant-major at battalion rear headquarters would dig the graves and bury the dead. It could not have been a pleasant job for them. Much later the bodies would be transferred to one of the war cemeteries.

Was it difficult to command older and more experienced soldiers?

No. Rank in the army was of total importance. You immediately did what you were told by a superior, and those under you at once did what you ordered. Neither age nor experience mattered.

Did I like soldiering?
What did I think of German soldiers?
What makes a good soldier?

There was much I liked about soldiering: its clear-cut hierarchical order and discipline, the outdoor life, the comradeship. I was surprised to find how many ordinary military skills I could, with training, master.

The Germans were first-class soldiers, I think we all accepted that. They used their weapons skilfully, they were strictly disciplined, and they were brave.

Anybody can be a good soldier except those who instinctively object to being regimented, to having to obey orders that may be given without rhyme or reason.

How did I feel when the war was over?

Whether you take the day the German war ended, when I was outside Bremerhaven; or the day the Japanese war ended, when I missed the gigantic party at the officers' mess; or the day I was demobbed when I travelled on a slow train with strangely subdued companions from Berlin across the face of western Europe, I think the answer is the same. I was emotionally punch-drunk. Six years of fearful danger, limitless thrills, bleak disaster, unqualified triumph, of living life at the extremity, had drained from me the ability to savour the moments.

When I collected my demob suit it hardly seemed an ecstatic triumph after six years of unprecedented effort; rather it appeared that other events now had to be tackled. I had a wife, we could look forward to having a family; and I had a job, when commercial activity picked up I could look for a better one.

Not in my wildest enthusiasm could I imagine that, the soldiers having won the war, the politicians would win the peace; and that we would have not only a virtual half-century of peace (so far) but that it would be accompanied by extraordinary improvements in the whole quality of life: in education, health care, welfare, business opportunities, leisure availability; in a prosperity whose intensity and spread was beyond the guessing of the timid lad of 1939 or the swaggering victor of 1945.

Have I been back to the battlefields?

I first went back to Normandy thirty years after the landings and I have been several times since. Arromanches has taken *le débarquement* to its heart, almost as Stratford upon Avon has taken Shakespeare. You can still see the ruins of the artificial harbour; you can see the pillbox into whose embrasure that tank gunner fired a vital shot from 300 yards; there is a magnificent museum showing among other things a sandtable model of the battle on the beach which took years to create.

A few miles to the east stands a statue of the Holy Mother looking down on the beach with compassion. There is no inscription; you supply your own thoughts. At Bayeux there is a large cemetery, a terribly large cemetery, where many soldiers of the Hampshire Regiment are among those buried. You can drive along the route of the 1st Battalion: La Belle Épine, Bernières Bocage, La Senaudière, Hottot. The area had not changed much when I visited it. There were still those little fields, thirty or forty yards square, bounded by thick, tall hedges; still those winding half-sunken roads; still the claustrophobic atmosphere, for nowhere did you get any length or breadth of view.

Hottot, where so many people were killed, was just a collection of buildings stretching 400 or 500 yards along the Caen–Caumont road; there was only one pub and only one garage. When you reached the eastern end of the village and looked south you saw why the Germans held on to it so ferociously, for it is a commanding feature; everything for ten miles south belongs to the holder of Hottot.

A memorial at the western end of the street names the battalions of the Devon, Hampshire and Dorset Regiments which fought there. Nearby is Hottot War Cemetery where many soldiers of these battalions are buried. As you walk through it, here and there you come across a name you know, and you remember him and how he died. Elsewhere you see a name you think you ought to know and you frown in puzzlement at your failure to recall the man.

The Bayeux and Hottot cemeteries are frequently visited by British people, on their own, or in twos and threes, or in larger parties. Some look for the graves of their friends. Others examine the register of graves for names they will recognize. Such is the sense of nearness, or if you like of intimacy, that when you find a tombstone you have been looking for you can almost find yourself saying Hallo, as if to a long-lost friend.

It is a shock to realize that the great majority of people walking about Bayeux and Hottot were not born when these events took place.

Would I rather have been in another branch of the army or in another service?

From the point of view of safety, yes. But having survived, no. The infantryman is the king of warriors. He lives closer to the enemy than anyone else and can be in almost continuous crisis. Lacking the psychological comfort of a large gun, vehicle, ship or similar equipment, he can cling only to his pals, and they to him.

Fortunately they will be part of the greatest team known to man: the infantry battalion. This is headed by the colonel, who shoots fewer big explosions at the enemy than other commanders and fights more through the deployment of the men he has trained and now leads. He operates through an intimate team of middle-ranking and junior officers who, receiving leadership from him, then exercise their own leadership on the teams they captain.

The comradeship that arises is very special. It is the brotherhood of those who have mastered themselves and served their team.

Was it worth it?

Yes.

In 1940 Churchill had warned that the world 'might sink into the abyss of a new dark age made more sinister and perhaps more protracted by the lights of perverted science'.

To avoid that we had to defeat 'a maniac of ferocious genius, the repository and expression of the most virulent hatreds that ever corroded the human breast – Corporal Hitler'.

To have played a proper part in that task is the greatest service anybody of my age can have rendered to our fellow men.

Index

Other than in the entry under his name
the author is referred to as GP

Abbeville, France, 180
Actonville, Normandy, 128
Adair, Major-General A.H.S., 192
air raids on Britain, 18, 19, 134,
    172–3
airborne forces, 182, 237
    American, 48
    D-Day landings, 39–40
    1st Airborne Division at
        Arnhem, 182, 238–9
    German, 16
    6th Airborne Division on D-
        Day, 46, 273
    (*see also* Arnhem operation)
Alanbrooke, Field Marshal,
        Viscount Alan Francis, 43
Albert Canal, Belgium, 207
Alençon, Normandy, 111
Alexander, General Harold (later
        Field Marshal, Earl
        Alexander of Tunis), 116
American forces:
    arrive in Britain, 28
    collaboration with, 58, 98, 278
    D-Day landing, 41, 46–7
    drive towards Germany, 158,
        200, 288–9
    encircling enemy, 144
    First Army, 129
    Flying Fortress raids, 36, 44
    killed by own bombing, 110
    St Lô, attack and breakthrough,

43, 108–11, 117, 120, 129–
    31, 157
    (*see also* airborne forces)
Amiens, France, 173, 176, 180
Antwerp, Belgium, 172–3, 199,
    201–6
Ardennes, France, 266–7
Argentan, Normandy, 111, 133,
    144, 153–5, 166–8
Arnhem operation, 212–43
    airborne troops land, 221–2
    attack outline, 217–18
    casualties, 237
    German courage, 224
    Royal Hampshires' role, 226–7,
        231–9
Arras, France, 173, 177, 183
Arromanches, Normandy, 45, 51,
    102
Asnelles, Normandy, 44
Ath, Belgium, 187
atomic bomb, 294–5
ATS (Auxiliary Territorial
    Service), 19, 297
Aunay, Normandy, 138
Avranches, Normandy, 111

Baal, Holland, 250
Bassum, Germany, 277
Battle of Britain, 17–18
Bayeux, Normandy, 41, 45, 54,
    306

BBC news reports, 79, 88, 114,
164, 195–6, 235
Beauvais, France, 180
Beek, Holland, 234–5
Beeringham, Belgium, 207–9
Belgium, 182–5
Bemmel, Holland, 236, 244, 256–
8, 261
Ben (GP's driver), 87, 123, 126,
137, 167
Berlin:
advance to stopped by
Eisenhower, 278–9
GP posted to, 296
occupation by allies, 296–7
thrust for, Montgomery's plan,
241, 243
Bernières Bocage, Normandy,
159–62
Beverloo, Belgium, 208–9
bocage country, 72, 108, 111
Boekel, Holland, 232
Bourg Leopold, Holland, 260
Bournemouth, 15, 17, 21, 37
Bradley, General Omar, 47, 109–
10, 240, 278
Bradley, Joan, *see* Picot, Joan
Bradley, Malcolm, 31–2, 80
Breda, Holland, 199
Bremen, Germany, 277, 280, 284
Bremerhaven, Germany, 286, 305
Bridge Too Far, A, 219
Brooke, Field Marshal Alan
Francis (later Viscount
Alanbrooke), 43
Brouinlieu, France, 180
Browning, Lt-General Sir
Frederick, 219
Brussels:
advance towards, 158–9, 161–
71, 181–2, 185
GP in, 191–201

liberation, 188, 191, 192

Caen, Normandy:
D-Day ojective, 40, 41–2, 46,
48
feint attack on, 85, 107–8
Canadian forces, 46, 108, 111–12,
144, 153, 154, 180, 200,
219
casualties:
Arnhem, 237
burying dead, 304–5
D-Day, 42
fatal and non-fatal, 134
German, 110–11
GP on, 301
letters of condolence, 101, 281
local truce for removing, 142
morale, effect on, 8, 75–6, 99–
100, 103
Royal Hampshire Regiment, 45,
75–6, 80, 95–6, 98–9, 129,
143, 256, 263
(*see also* Royal Hampshire
Regiment)
total, 302
Catheux, France, 180
Caumont, Normandy, 129–30, 133,
135, 144
censorship, 53–4
Chamberlain, Neville, 14
Channel Islands:
collaborators, 291
communication with, during
war, 264
early days of war, 14
GP's pre-war life, 9–10
GP's return to, 292–3
liberation, 202–3, 288–92
occupation, 15–16, 184–5
Churchill, Winston:
determination to win war, 16, 20

Montgomery's strategy
    questioned, 9, 43
on advance to Berlin, 279
on D-Day landing, 42
speeches, 17, 18
VE Day, 288
Claude (GP's batman), 103, 193
Clifford, Alexander, 130–31, 152,
    259, 266–7, 277
Cloppenburg, Germany, 280–81
collaborators, 178–9
Condé-sur-Noireau, Normandy,
    133, 143–4, 162
conscription, 14–15
Crèvecoeur-le-Grand, France, 176
Culin, Sergeant Curtis C., 109

D-Day landing:
  German defences, 42, 48–9
  Omaha beach, 49
  plan, 41–2
  preliminary reports, 38–40
  Royal Hampshire Regiment's
    role, 43–5
  (*see also* Normandy bridgehead)
Daily Express, 116–17, 152
Daily Mail, 86, 108, 130, 135–6,
    238, 259–60, 266–7, 277
Daily Mirror, 49, 129, 199, 287
Daley, Corporal, 274–5
Danny, Corporal, 78, 254
decorations, 98, 125, 303
Dempsey, General Sir Miles, 132,
    199, 238, 241
Dennis (inebriated ex-POW),
    297–8
deserters, 100–101, 284–5
Deventer, Holland, 220
Devonshire Regiment (2nd
    Battalion), 35, 74–5, 88, 93,
    131, 143, 157, 307
digging entrenchments, 57

(*see also* mortar platoon)
Divisions:
  Guards Armoured Division,
    181, 187–8, 191–2, 217,
    225, 227
  1st Airborne Division, 182,
    238–9, (*see also* Arnhem
    operation)
  3rd Infantry Division, 46
  6th Airborne Division, 46, 273
  7th Armoured Division, 262
  15th Scottish Division, 120
  43rd Wessex Division, 133, 150,
    227, 268–9, 280, 286
  50th Infantry Division
    at Arnhem, 217
    chosen to lead Normandy
      landings, 35
    Montgomery addresses, 260–
      61
    Montgomery on, 45–6
    mortar platoon commander
      casualties, 146
    reorganized after Arnhem,
      261–3
    reputation, 132
    war record, 261–3
  51st Division, 262
  59th Division, 172
  78th Division, 261
Dorset Regiment (1st Battalion),
    35, 97, 131, 143, 148, 157,
    307
Douai, France, 183
Drewitt, Major Geoffrey, 77, 96,
    103–4, 105, 155, 181, 197–
    8, 246
Duilbeck, Brussels, 192–3
Duke of Wellington's Regiment
    (6th Battalion), 99–100
Durham Light Infantry, 84, 254
Dymchurch, 17

East Yorkshire Regiment, 115–16, 118, 236, 245
Ectot Woods, Normandy, 120
Edwards, Ken, 30–31, 63, 85, 126, 160, 161–2, 168–9, 174, 183, 186
Eighth Army, *see* North African campaign
Eindhoven, Holland, 223, 224, 227, 231, 259
Eisenhower, General Dwight D.:
  broadfront strategy, 240–43
  disagreements with Montgomery, 9, 42–3, 241–2
  final advance to Berlin stopped, 278–9
  orders of the day, 149–50
El Alamein, battle of, *see* North African campaign
Elst, Holland, 256, 261
Enghien, Belgium, 187–90
ENSA concerts, 112–14
Escaut canal, Belgium, 212–17, 220–21
Essame, Major-General, 280
Evening Standard, 49

Falaise, Normandy, 111–12, 117, 133, 135, 144, 153–5, 158
Falklands War, 45
Far East War, *see* Japan
Flers, Normandy, 164–6
43rd Wessex Division at War 1944–5, The (Essame), 280
Frank (GP's signaller), 92
Free French forces, 200

George VI King, 35, 40
German forces:
  air force destroyed, 159
  airborne troops, 16
  atrocities by, 166–7, 195
  bravery of soldiers, 224, 305
  casualties, 110–11, 166–7
  counter-offensive in Ardennes, 266–7
  D-Day defences, 42, 48–9
  defence works, 163, 277
  equipment, quality of, 71
  Langemarck Division, 277
  rations, 229–30
  retreat, 152, 166–7, 179–80, 199–200, 278–9
  SS, 277
  surrenders, 86, 148–9, 185–6, 278, 281–4
  unconditional surrender of Germany, 285–7
  transport problems, 180
  underground forces, treatment by, 185–7
German Occupation of Jersey 1940–45, The (Sinel), 288–92
Gillard, Frank, 79
Ginger (signaller), 137, 253
glider-borne troops, 46
  (*see also* airborne forces)
Gnarrenburg, Germany, 285
Goering, Hermann, 18
Grandvilliers, France, 180
Greenwood, Arthur, 39
Guards Armoured Division, *see* Divisions

Haalderen, Holland, 250
Hamm, Germany, 220
Hammond, David, 54, 63, 98
Hampshire Regiment, *see* Royal Hampshire Regiment
Hand, Bill, 74
Harding, Field Marshal John (later Baron), 35

Harley, Major, 216–17, 247, 249
Hastings, Max, 287, 301–2
Haut Mesnil, France, 180
Hilary, HMS, 50
Hiroshima, Japan, 294
Hitler, Adolf, 48–9, 152, 240
Hobart, Major-General Sir Percy, 36, 47
Hodges, General (US), 241
Horrocks, Lt-General Sir Brian, 131–5, 149, 171, 188, 221, 225, 286
Hottot, Normandy, 72–6, 79, 86, 88–97, 104, 109–10, 155–6, 157, 254, 307
Household Cavalry, 225
Howie, Lt-Colonel C.R.:
  leadership, 63, 68, 71, 77, 79, 81, 91
  appointed CO, 52
  assessment of, 98–9
  concern for men, 84–5
  DSO, 98
  orders groups, 54–5, 56, 62–3, 72, 90–91
  psychological warfare employed, 86–7
  death in action, 96, 98
Howie, Major Thomas D., 109

Irish Guards, 212, 215
Isle of Man, 29–30, 264–8
Italy, 16, 28, 33–4, 116

James, Captain Jimmy, 63–4, 66, 69, 73, 75, 148, 163, 178, 203
Japan, 19–20, 294–5
Jersey, *see* Channel Islands
Jersey Evening Post, 288
John (Intelligence Officer), 86, 95, 102

Johnson, Sergeant, 96, 122–3, 125, 140, 249, 256
Junior (signals officer), 137, 210–11

Kennedy, John Fitzgerald, 17
King's Shropshire Light Infantry, 204
Kluge, Field Marshal von, 110
Kreps, Joe, 291

La Belle Épine, Normandy, 56–9
La Senaudière, Normandy, 59, 62, 66–71
l'Aigle, Normandy, 168–9
Layton, Gordon, 31, 53
Le Bény Bocage, Normandy, 130
Le Brocq, Captain Hugh, 290
Le Hamel, Normandy, 44–5
Leigh-Mallory, Air Chief Marshal Sir Trafford, 110
Les Roquettes, Normandy, 44
liberation:
  Antwerp, 202–3
  Channel Islands, 202–3, 288–92
  Flers, 164–6
  northern France, 175–6
  Paris, 169
Liège, Belgium, 266
Lieshout, Holland, 231–2
Lingèvres, Normandy, 70
Littlejohns, Major John, 61–2, 90, 92
Llandrindod Wells, 23–6
Lloyd, John, 30
London, German raids on, 18, 19, 134, 172–3
Long Melford, Suffolk, 30, 35
Lorty, Private, 140–41
Lovat, Brigadier Simon Fraser, Baron, 46

Maginot Line, 14, 15
Malta, 31, 141
Mandeville, Normandy, 180
Mantes, Normandy, 169
Meuse, river, 219, 259
Mill, Holland, 233
Millin, Bill, 46
Model, Field Marshal, 278
Montgomery, General Bernard
    Law (later Field Marshal,
    Viscount):
  abstemious life, 35
  addresses officers of 50th
    division, 260–61
  Arnhem, 219–21, 240–43
  Churchill's meetings with, 43
  confidence in victory, 71, 182
  criticized for slowness, 43, 115–
    16
  D-Day plan, 9, 34, 41–2, 77,
    86, 88, 107–8, 117, 132–6
  Eisenhower, controversies with,
    42–3
  manner, 34–5
  career prior to D-Day, 31, 33
  taking command of Eighth
    Army, 33
  promoted Field Marshal, 179
  qualities as commander, 34–5
  Runstedt on, 287–8
  ruthlessness with officers, 35,
    100, 303
  21st Army Group Commander,
    132
  unconditional surrender of
    German forces accepted,
    285–8
Monty (GP's signaller), 87, 92,
    126, 137, 138, 164, 167,
    173, 229, 235, 253, 254
Moorehead, Alan, 116–17
morale, 172, 99–100, 301

casualties, effect of, 8, 75–6,
    99–100, 103
  on D-Day, 39
  under fire, 95, 97, 146
  Montgomery improves, 33–4
  RAF boosting, 121–2
Morgan, Francis, 276, 281, 284–5
mortar platoon:
  carriers hit by tanks, 189–90
  commander casualties in 50th
    Division, 146
  counter-mortaring, 81
  digging pits, 81, 115, 118–19
  engaging enemy, 67–70, 73–4,
    79, 92, 95, 188–90, 212–17,
    226–7, 244–56
  fire control, 66–7
  fire power, 52
  GP's appointment to, 32
  Hottot, assault on, 88–96
  observation posts, 66–7, 77–9,
    90, 113, 124, 151–2, 207–8,
    244–9, 257–8
  overloaded vehicles, 155–6
  reaction to enemy artillery, 10–
    11, 124, 216
  siting mortars, 55, 57, 73, 81,
    94, 119, 177, 204, 207, 252,
    255
  wireless communications, 92–3,
    121, 136–7, 152, 208
Mulberry Harbour, 45
Munster, Germany, 220

Nagasaki, Japan, 294
Needham, Chris, 30–31, 51–2, 75
New Forest, 37
News Chronicle, 179–80, 199–200,
    276–7
Nijmegen, Holland, 213, 219, 227,
    235, 256–7, 260, 261
Noireau, river, 162

Normandy bridgehead:
  breakthrough, 43, 108–11, 117,
    120, 129–31, 152–4
  D-Day landing, 38–40
  GP lands, 7, 50–52
  GP returns to, 306–7
  victory, 152–5
North African campaign, 19, 31,
    33–4, 116, 135, 261
Norway campaign, 50
Norwegian forces, 200

Oeffelt, Holland, 234
Oran, battle of (1940), 50
Osnabruck, Germany, 220
Overlord (Hastings), 287, 301–2

Pacy-sur-Eure, Normandy, 169,
    171
Palestine, 31
Paris 41, 169
Pas de Calais, France, 172
Path of the 50th, The (Clay), 45
Patton, General George Smith, 88,
    117, 125, 158, 245
Pearl Harbor, 20
Percival, Lt-Gen. A.E., 20
Piat anti-tank weapon, 71, 281
Picot, Bernard, 50
Picot, Geoffrey:
  army career
    enlisted in RAPC, 14–15
    commissioned in Royal
      Artillery, 23
    joins Royal Hampshire
      Regiment, *see* Royal
      Hampshire Regiment
    mortar platoon commander,
      see mortar platoon
    promoted Captain, 81
    refresher course in England,
      261, 264–8

  rifle platoon commander, *see*
    rifle platoon
  glider regiment, 295
  demobilization, 297–8, 306
  courtship and marriage, 8, 64,
    264
  defends soldier for desertion,
    100–101
  infantry training, 28–30
  lands in Normandy, 50–52
  opinions and experiences, 299–
    308
  returns to Jersey, 292–3
Picot, Joan (*née* Bradley), 64–5, 264
Picot family, 16, 264
Pinçon, Mont, 133, 138–9
point 229 (St Pierre-la-Vieille),
    Normandy, 139, 143
Polish forces, 200
Portsmouth, 26–7

Quineville, Normandy, 41

Reed, Red, 123, 132, 140, 183, 188,
    256
Rees, Germany, 268, 272
Reichwald forest, Germany, 268
Rhine, river, 218, 270–72
rifle platoon:
  GP's appointment, 268–9
  textbook attack, 273–6
  wireless communications, 272
rolling barrages, 273–4
Rommel, Field Marshal Erwin, 33,
    34, 76, 131, 135, 199
Roosevelt, Brigadier-General, 48
Roosevelt, Franklin D., 279
Rotterdam, Holland, 199
Rouen, France, 180
Royal Air Force:
  Battle of Britain, 17–18
  bombing Germany, 108

Royal Air Force—*contd*
dominating battle zones,71
ground support, 66, 86, 95,
121–2, 128
mistaking targets, 95
Typhoon aircraft, 8, 95, 222,
224
Royal Army Pay Corps, 15, 17,
18, 20
Royal Artillery:
anti-aircraft training, 24–5
battery at Portsmouth, 26–7
GP transfers to, 20–21
Officer Cadet Training Unit,
Llandrindod Wells, 23–6
Royal Electrical and Mechanical
Engineers, 228
Royal Engineers, 218, 228
Royal Hampshire Regiment, 1st
Battalion, 31, 100
casualties
Commanding Officers, 45, 96,
98
D-Day landing, 45
Holland, 256
memorials and war
cemeteries, 307
Normandy bridgehead, 45,
75–6, 80, 95–6, 98, 129,
143
total, 263, 302
George VI's visit, 35–6
GP joins, 30–31
instructors from, 262
mortar platoon, *see* mortar
platoon
Normandy bridgehead, 43–5,
77–8, 79–80, 105–7,
124–5
Bernières Bocage, 59–62
Hottot, 72–6, 86, 88–97, 109–
10, 157

La Senaudière, 66–70
point 229, 139, 143
St-Pierre-la-Vieille, 139, 141–
4
Villers Bocage, 120–29
race to Belgium and Holland
Antwerp, 201–2
Arnhem, 226–7, 231–9
Arras, 177–8
Bemmel, Haalderen and Baal,
244–56
Brussels, 191–201
Escaut canal, 212–17
tanks at Enghien, 188–90
life on the move, 161–4
movement plan, 158–61
Seine to Amiens, 173–6
Royal Hampshire Regiment, 7th
Battalion:
engagements with enemy, 271–
6, 272–6, 279–85
GP as rifle platoon commander,
see rifle platoon
GP joins as lieutenant, 268
on parade, 269–70
Royal Navy, 288
Ruhr, Germany, 218, 219, 239,
241
Rundstedt, Field Marshal Karl
Von, 267, 287
Russia:
German invasion, 16, 20
occupying Berlin, 296
repulses Germany, 28
war gains in Europe, 279

Saar, river, 242
St Agatha, Holland, 233–4
St André, Normandy, 169
St Hubert, Holland, 233–4
St Lô, Normandy, 41, 55, 108–10,
120, 157

St Martin-des-Besaces,
    Normandy, 130
St-Pierre-la-Vieille, 139, 141–4,
    147, 150, 157, 161, 208,
    251
Salisbury Plain, 294
Scheldt, river, 199, 259
Second Army (British), 129, 132,
    238
Second Front, call for, 28
Seine, river, 134–5, 153, 169,
    171–2
Sicily campaign, 28, 32, 33–4, 116
Siegfried Line, 14, 195, 199–200
Sinel, L.P., 288
Singapore, 19–20
Solon, S.L., 179–80, 276–7
Somme, river, 179, 199
    battle of (1916), 42
Southwold, Suffolk, 36
Speed, Eric B.B., 298
Stalin, Josef, 279
Stiphout, Holland, 232
Studland Bay, Bournemouth, 37

Talbot, Lt-Colonel D.E.B., 269
tanks:
    D-Day landing, 44
    driving through hedges, 109
    in pursuit battles, 191
    Shermans, 227
    specially equipped to clear
        obstacles, 36–7, 47
    Tiger (German), 267
Taylor, Colonel George, 47
Tedder, Air-Marshal Arthur
    William (later Air Marshal,
    Baron), 43
Thomas, Major-General G.I.,
    286–7, 302
Thury Harcourt, Normandy, 133,
    135, 144

Tilly, Normandy, 70, 76
Times, The, 108
training and leadership,
    importance of, 47–8, 282–3
Turner, Lt-Colonel Tony:
    appointed CO, 112
    battle commander, 245–6
    on good communications, 215
    liberating Antwerp, 202–3
    move towards Brussels, 160,
        170
    orders groups, 119, 139–41, 149,
        150, 181–2, 189–90, 217–
        18
    qualities as CO, 118
    tactical ability, 143
21st Army Group, 132

underground forces:
    Belgian, 182–3
    Germans surrendering to, 185–
        7
    occupying territory, 180–81
    parades, 178–9
United States of America, 20
    (see also American troops)

Valkenswaard, Holland, 223, 225
Veghel, Holland, 232
venereal diseases, 18
Verneuil, Normandy, 169
Vernon, Normandy, 169, 171–2,
    180
Verrières, Normandy, 129
Villers Bocage, Normandy, 41–2,
    66, 70–71, 120, 133, 138,
    144
V1s, 172

Waal, river, 235
Walker, Ronald, 199–200
War Office Selection Board, 21–3

Warren, Major David, 45
Waters, Major Frank, 32, 63, 213, 216, 250–51, 254
Wavell, General Archibald (later Field Marshal, Viscount), 31
Wetherick, Sergeant Ernie, 32, 56, 66, 91, 112, 121, 136, 177
Willebroek, Belgium, 202
wireless communications, poor standard, 272
(*see also* mortar platoon)
Wise, Harry, 30, 258
women:
ATS, 19, 297
RA officers, 26
young soldiers and, 18–19, 30

Wood, Alan, 238–9
World War II:
declaration of war, 14
1940 German offensive, 15
Japanese surrender, 294
rumours of German surrender, 196–8
unconditional surrender of Germany, 285–7
Wright, Horace, 54, 143, 272
Wuppertal, Germany, 278

Yalta conference (1945), 279
Ypres, France, 262

Zuyder Zee, 218
Zwolle, Holland, 220